# PRAISE FOR VIRGINIA LANIER
## and

### *A BRACE OF BLOODHOUNDS*

"Her dogs are in a class all their own."

—*Mystery Review*

"Every chapter pulls you further into the story and ends with the zinger that won't let you put the book down. The book ends too soon. It's too bad we can't sit with Jo Beth on her front porch, with a glass of her freshly brewed iced tea in hand, and listen to more of her adventures."

—*Times-Union* (Jacksonville, FL)

"Whether it is tracking for a lost child, or catching a wrong-doing judge, Jo Beth and her trusty bloodhounds get the job done with grit, determination, heart, and humor."

—*Tales From a Red Herring*

"Virginia Lanier's series about bloodhound breeder Jo Beth Sidden is one of the best examples of how unconventional characters can enhance the core of a mystery. . . . Crammed with tidbits about bloodhounds and 'mantracking.' Characters are sharply defined and intriguing."

—*Ft. Lauderdale Sun-Sentinel*

## THE HOUSE ON BLOODHOUND LANE

"An amiable Brett Butler-like narrator and a cliffhanger of an ending."

—*Kirkus Reviews*

## DEATH IN BLOODHOUND RED

"It is rare when a writer can truly transport the reader and this is just what Virginia Lanier has managed with *Death in Bloodhound Red*. Every time her sleuth, Jo Beth Sidden, a chainsmoking good old girl, took her beloved bloodhounds and me into the swamps of Georgia I smelled every drop of sweat, felt every mosquito bite. For a new adventure I heartily recommend reading *Death in Bloodhound Red*."

—Nevada Barr, Author of *Track of the Cat*

"Absolutely fascinating . . . Jo Beth is a terrific character: smart, impulsive, idealistic and vulnerable."

—*Orlando Sentinel*

"Delightfully entertaining . . . Lanier has created a heroine every bit as memorable as Sue Grafton's Kinsey Millhone and Sara Paretsky's V.I. Warshawski."

—*Times-Union* (Jacksonville, FL)

"Melding good old boy humor and action-packed adventure . . . Lanier gives readers a thorough insider's look at a unique occupation and a detailed view of Southern life near the swamp."

—*Publishers Weekly*

"Sue Grafton meets Michael Malone in a dead-on voice that doesn't back off."

"It doesn't happen very often, but once in a while you come across a new voice that does everything right. Virginia Lanier is one of those lights in the darkness that makes up so much of what's offered to booksellers and readers today. . . . Lanier has an ear for dialect and mannerism that rings true in her depiction of the Good Ol' Boy inhabitants of the Deep South. In Jo Beth she has created a character with biting wit, backbone, and enough faults to keep her likable. The bloodhound lore woven into the story is fascinating, as is Lanier's obvious familiarity with the region she has set her story in. There's danger, duplicity, humor, and yes, murder . . . enough to satisfy the most discerning mystery buff."

"Literate, well-modulated prose, satisfyingly detailed descriptions, elements of Southern decadence, and a leisurely pace punctuated by thrilling moments of action all characterize a very appealing first novel."

Books by Virginia Lanier

*Death in Bloodhound Red*
*The House on Bloodhound Lane*
*A Brace of Bloodhounds*
*Blind Bloodhound Justice*

Published by HarperCollins*Publishers*

HarperChoice

# A BRACE OF BLOODHOUNDS

# Virginia Lanier

HarperPaperbacks
*A Division of HarperCollinsPublishers*

![HarperPaperbacks logo] **HarperPaperbacks**
*A Division of* HarperCollins*Publishers*
10 East 53rd Street, New York, NY 10022-5299

This book contains an excerpt of *Blind Bloodhound Justice* by Virginia Lanier. This excerpt has been set for this edition only and may not reflect the final content of the hardcover edition.

This is a work of fiction. The characters, incidents, and dialogues are products of the author's imagination and are not to be construed as real. Any resemblance to actual events or persons, living or dead, is entirely coincidental.

ISBN 0-06-101087-1

HarperCollins®, ![logo] ®, HarperPaperbacks™, and HarperChoice™ are trademarks of HarperCollins Publishers, Inc.

Cover illustration © 1997 by Peggy Leonard

A hardcover edition of this book was published in 1997 by HarperCollins*Publishers*.

First paperback printing: July 1998

Printed in the United States of America

Visit HarperPaperbacks on the World Wide Web at
http://www.harpercollins.com

❖ 10 9 8 7 6 5 4 3 2 1

*For my grandchildren,*

*Belynda Michelle Lanier Campbell*
*Brandye Wine Lanier Munger*
*Bobbie Mae Lanier*
*Danielle Marisa Lanier*
*Rex Warren Lanier II*
*Travis Quinn Lanier*
*Brandon Lee Lanier*
*Weston Phillip Lanier*

*And my great-grandchildren,*

*Ashley Marie Munger*
*Chelsye Allen Wayne Munger*
*Breanna Michelle Munger*
*Joseph James Munger, Jr.*

# ACKNOWLEDGMENTS

I wish to thank all these wonderful people for sharing their knowledge, support, and good advice:

Mary Michener, managing editor, *American Bloodhound Club Bulletin,* Ellensburg, Washington; Jan Tweedie, chief of corrections, Kittitas County Sheriff's Department, Ellensburg, Washington; and veterinarian Marlene Zahner, Schweiz, Switzerland, who are all expert breeders and trainers of bloodhounds and are familiar with the show ring. God bless, ladies.

Raymond Carter, Carter's Outboard, Adel, Georgia, for his expertise on boats and outboard motors; attorney Jack W. Carter, Adel, Georgia, for research and advice on bloodhound court cases and Georgia law.

Margaret Maron, author of the Deborah Knott mystery series and the Sigrid Harald mystery series, for her excellent advice and for taking a rank amateur under her wing and guiding her on the rocky path of publishing. All budding authors should be so lucky.

Dr. Christine Cotton, Dr. Manuel Cachan, and Marcy Umberger, modern languages, Valdosta State University. *Gracias.*

Mary Nix, Mr. Employer, Valdosta, Georgia, for being my right arm, computer teacher, adviser, coordinator, and, best of all, my friend.

Lori L. Whitwam, librarian, Indianapolis, Indiana,

who brought to my attention the horror of "puppy mills," where too many dogs each year suffer and die because of greed. Wear your STAMP OUT PUPPY MILLS T-shirt with pride, Lori. Scratch Riley's ears for me.

Kay and Ray Schmitt, San Rafael, California, Marin County Search-and-Rescue Team, and their bloodhound coworkers, Deke, Crockett, and Wellesley, one of many teams who train and devote their energies to help save lives all across America. We all owe them a debt of gratitude.

Randy and Von Nix, true entrepreneurs, Mobile, Alabama, for their hard work on my behalf and for personal appearances and stylish cosseting. Grateful thanks.

All the above-mentioned people gave me the correct information. Any mistakes are mine and mine alone.

# A BRACE
## OF
# BLOODHOUNDS

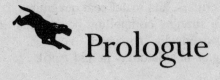# Prologue

On a perfect day in April that only south Georgia can produce in bunches, like bananas, I lost a friend—forever. Looking back, I cannot truthfully swear that I made the correct decision. It was a case of dammed if you do and dammed if you don't. No excuses. I did it, so I live with the aftermath.

My name is Jo Beth Sidden. I own a kennel where I breed bloodhounds and train them in search-and-rescue, drug searches, and suspected arsons. They are also trained to recover bodies.

I live on the edge of Okefenokee Swamp, or by another definition, the Land of the Trembling Earth, and the swamp is just as ambiguous as its name implies. It consists of more than five hundred thousand square miles of sand, muck, and water. It is populated with riotous primeval growth, many species of critters, and maleficent quagmires. It also possesses a strange, compelling beauty that draws you into its depths like a magnet.

It all began on a Saturday in mid-April. . . .

# Perfection, Thy Name Is April
## *April 13, Saturday, 8 A.M.*

Jonathan Webber and I were still lazily ensconced in the kitchen. He was feeding the last slice of bacon to Bobby Lee.

"You cooked too much bacon," I commented.

"You're just jealous because Bobby Lee is leaning on *my* leg instead of yours."

"Not true. Every time you give Bobby Lee something, I have to feed Rudy a bite. He's getting tired of biscuit balls."

"Your ornery cat would find fault with filet mignon," he retorted.

"Jonathan, love of my life, you and Rudy have to learn how to cohabit these premises during your visits. You two have me sandwiched in the middle of this feud. Can't you be friends?"

"He started it," Jonathan replied shortly, burying his nose in the paper.

I sighed. "He took exception to you picking him up by his neck scruff, dumping him into the hall, and slamming the bedroom door in his face."

"I couldn't make love to you with him pacing the floor and mewling objections. Besides, he assaulted me. I still have the scar."

I suppressed a smile. "He swatted you and connected with one claw. One tiny puncture that didn't even need a Band-Aid, and it happened four months ago. You two have been pouting and avoiding each other ever since. You have to make up."

Jonathan carefully folded the paper. He leaned his head under the table and in a falsetto voice began to croon, "Kitty, kitty, kitty, kitty!"

It was such a blatant failure I had to laugh. Rudy stared at him with contempt, twitching his tail in disgust.

"See? I tried." Jonathan sounded vindicated.

I snorted and stood to clear the table.

"Need any help?"

"You cooked, so I wash up. Go take a walk to help digest that enormous breakfast you consumed."

"Yes, ma'am. May I take Bobby Lee?"

"Only if you ask Rudy to go."

"Wanna take a walk, Bobby Lee?"

Bobby Lee lunged toward the office doorway, heading for the front porch where his leash hangs on a large nail. Jonathan knelt in front of Rudy, staring into his large green eyes.

"O Prince of Darkness, a.k.a. Rudy, would you care to go?"

Rudy began grooming himself. Jonathan grinned.

"The feeling's mutual, pal."

I stood at the sink and watched Rudy out of the corner of my eye. After Jonathan left, he stopped grooming himself, leisurely stretched, and then strolled to his water dish. I started a mental count: a thousand one, a thousand two. . . . Rudy disappeared from the kitchen before five seconds elapsed.

I stood on the back porch breathing in the morning coolness, the slight air currents barely moving the peach-fuzz growth at my hairline. Excellent mantrailing conditions. Low humidity, inconsequential breeze, and a thermometer that hadn't as yet reached 70 degrees. I could smell the newly mown grass in the field behind the kennel and hear the faint drone of the belly mower. Wayne cut the grass on Saturday morning in preparation for laying scent trails on Monday with the trainers. His theory was to give the air time to cleanse the field, making it easier for the novice puppies. Sounded good to me. All of us work six days a week, taking only Sunday off, but since it was Jonathan's turn to visit, I had absolutely no plans for today except to spend time with him.

I watched Jonathan approach from the south with the animals. Bobby Lee was tethered to Jonathan's belt on his short leash, keeping perfect rhythm with Jonathan's stride. With long ears flapping, tail held in a high arch, he was exhibiting a show ring's perfect form and his obvious delight at being alive. Rudy was alternating between a few steps behind and a few steps in front, as if he couldn't decide which position would give him the advantage.

I gave Jonathan an objective appraisal. At five feet nine inches tall, and weighing 165, he was two inches taller and forty pounds heavier than I. For almost five months, after rigidly dieting three days and pigging out for two, I'd managed to drop three pounds, from 128 to 125, and I'd maintained the status quo for a month. I was surprised that my insane diet had produced any weight loss; I was anticipating chronic heartburn.

Jonathan doesn't have a weight lifter's physique or classic good looks. His medium-brown hair and dark-brown eyes are the same as mine, but his hair lies neat and orderly around his ears and neck, while mine is a riotous, naturally curly disaster ninety-nine percent of my waking hours. But when he smiles, his face glows with intelligence and joy and love, and my heart beats romantic tunes on my ribs, and I wear a permanent silly grin.

We've been lovers since last November, but our emotions are still new and untested. Jonathan is the police chief for Eppley, Georgia, which is right on the Tennessee border in the northeastern part of the state, a little over three hundred miles away. Since we both have heavy work schedules, our arrangement is to take turns every other weekend to drive the long commute. I've had to cancel twice, and he's canceled once. We leave on Friday morning and have two nights and a day and a half together, starting for home Sunday noon. So far, we haven't achieved an easy familiarity, but we haven't experienced a single moment of boredom—at least as far as I know—so I guess it all evens out.

We walked together through the grooming room and into the kennel area. I automatically started pushing the utility cart, stopping at each caged run, opening the feeding panels, removing the large aluminum bowls from the stands, and stacking them in the cart. Jonathan started guiding the cart while I gathered the bowls.

"Whoever served breakfast this morning must be an excellent chef," Jonathan noted. "I see every bowl is licked clean."

"Donnie Ray Carver and Jasmine Jones had the honors," I said. "It's good there're no leftovers. If a crumb was left, I'd start yelling for the vet. Bloodhounds love food. If they don't eat, they're sick. It's also good for me that they eat every bite. The cost of feeding this mob has me teetering on the edge of bankruptcy every month when it's bill-paying time. I'd come unglued if they wasted any."

"I think you exaggerate," he asserted. "Just how much can—oh, let's say, ten fifty-pound sacks of good dog food cost? Surely that would feed all the dogs for a week."

"Ho, ho, ho." I chuckled with derision. "Surely you speak without proper knowledge. We've just picked up the adult males' and the spinsters' dishes. Do you know what they eat, every day, for seven days in this week you just mentioned?"

"No, but I sense you're going to enlighten me."

"You bet your sweet patootie," I intoned. "Listen and learn why your own three-year-old search-and-rescue bloodhound, affectionately known as Rhett Butler, currently under the care and feeding of your

Sergeant Mitchell Stone, was so expensive. Each
adult bloodhound, after turning one year old, eats
the following each day: six cups of top-grade com-
mercial dog meal; a pound of ground beef with less
than fifteen percent fat, which was selling for two
bucks a pound the last time I looked; a boiled egg—
they can't digest raw ones; a cup of cottage cheese;
a tablespoon of corn oil; a teaspoon of baking soda;
vitamin B-twelve; plus a good vitamin supplement
just like adult humans take. All this is combined and
moistened with skim milk. Two times a week we
mix in tomato juice. Three times a week we add
honey, and three times a week we add yogurt.
Carbohydrates, fat, vitamins, and minerals are carefully balanced."

"You're joking!"

"Don't I wish. Did I mention that they're fed
twice a day and the meals have to be mixed individually? Some bloodhounds have quirky digestive
systems. We keep a daily log on each dog from the
moment they're whelped until they leave the kennel."

"Sounds time-consuming."

"The understatement of the year," I said wryly,
"because I haven't yet enlightened you on the feeding schedule for the puppies. Even at three months
they're fed four times a day, and they consume
more food than the adults! The puppies gain four to
five pounds a week, so they need more food. I
won't bore you with any more details, but we boil
more eggs than the Easter bunny. I have to admit
that I've lusted after a couple of those lean Brahma

bulls that live down the road a ways, mentally planning a midnight rustle. I bet those suckers would lower my monthly meat bill."

Jonathan chuckled. "I guess that's why Sergeant Stone told me last Wednesday that if he didn't get a raise or a food allowance for Rhett Butler, he was going to apply for food stamps."

I looked at him and saw humor tugging at the corners of his mouth and a mischievous glint in his eyes.

"You devil, you," I said, smiling. "You've heard all this already from Mitchell. I hope you really praised him on his successful rescue last week."

"I was stingy with my compliments. Everyone in town, including the local paper, made a hero out of him, and everything they said was true. He did save the kid's life. The boy would've lain in that ravine forever if it hadn't been for Stone and Rhett Butler."

"So why not praise him?"

"Protecting my sanity. He talked about his bloodhound a lot before the rescue. Now he's impossible. I've learned more about that dog than I really need to know, especially his bowel movements."

"He doesn't!" I giggled.

"Oh, yes, he does," Jonathan said with mock weariness. "I'm apprised of color, consistency, and frequency."

"Well, I'll dispense no more bloodhound lore. Let's go pack for our picnic."

I saw Donnie Ray coming up behind Jonathan. "Hi, Donnie."

"Hi. How are you, Chief Webber?"

"Fine. Remember I told you to call me Jonathan?"

"Miz Jo Beth says to call you Chief Webber. She's the boss."

"You're cruisin' for a bruisin', Donnie Ray," I said, with part humor and part aggravation. "You know you call me Jo Beth, and he is Chief Webber. Mind your manners."

I put enough snap in the admonition that he was alerted. Donnie Ray is my videographer. In the past year he has become an excellent film technician, and, until just recently, he'd happily gone about the daily scut work that's also part of his job. Then his usual wry sense of humor subtly shifted and now sounds warning bells. He had a rotten childhood, and I'd taken over the task of teaching him southern manners. I'd have to find out what was bugging him. He is twenty years old, a slight, short, feisty, blond-haired, green-eyed boy who's moved in with Wayne Frazier since Wayne's mother, Rosie, moved out. Wayne manages the kennel and lives in an upstairs apartment in the compound.

"Yes, ma'am," he answered, sounding contrite.

I smiled at him and turned to Jonathan.

"The feeding pans are now in capable hands. Shall we scram?"

"You betcha."

We were crossing the courtyard when the harsh *bing-bong* of the first gate alarm sounded in the morning's silence.

Jonathan grimaced. "Which reminds me, what's the latest news on your ex these days?"

"Nothing more than the usual," I said, striving to remain calm. "Bubba Sidden Junior calls and hangs up without speaking, and he's been spotted parked by the front gate several times."

I had unconsciously lengthened my stride. Jonathan reached out, placing an arm around my shoulder and drawing me protectively to his side.

"Don't worry, honey bunch. I'll keep you safe."

Without knowing, Jonathan had just voiced my worst fear: him and Bubba, one on one. We reached the porch steps and turned together just as the second gate's strident buzzer heralded an immediate arrival. I mentally retraced the game plan I'd implement the second I knew it was Bubba: Run to the bedroom, grab the .357 Magnum—to hell with the .32 snub-nose—run back, and blow Bubba away before he could harm Jonathan. I drew a steadying breath and prepared for action.

As the vehicle turned left into the courtyard, I saw that it was a battered old clunker of indeterminate age with peeling paint and rusted side panels. I relaxed in relief, knowing that neither Bubba nor one of his cohorts would be caught dead driving such a pitiful excuse for transportation. The occupant was a blond female who pushed several times on the door before it reluctantly swung open with a teeth-jarring screech. I walked forward to greet her, wondering who she was. She didn't look familiar. In a town as small as mine, you don't meet many strangers. I decided she wasn't from out of state, because the car would've expired before crossing the state line.

She stood awkwardly beside the car, probably wondering if she should advance or stay where she was. I gave her a smile.

"Hello. May I help you?"

She was a little taller than I, wide in the shoulders, a plain face with red splotches. I couldn't tell if she was embarrassed or if it was her normal color. She could have been anywhere between eighteen and twenty-five; I'm not an expert on guessing ages accurately. She was wearing a plain homemade cotton-print dress that fit well enough, but the black, brown, and tan swirls were not her colors and did nothing for the beautiful true-blond sheen of her hair. Shoulder-length, it was parted in the middle and pinned back from her face with small childlike barrettes. She was wearing sturdy black shoes and white anklets and clutching a cheap plastic handbag to her chest.

I glanced up at Jasmine's window, raised my fist, and splayed my fingers wide. It was the all-clear signal. The gates are also wired to ring in her upstairs apartment to the right of the driveway. Her head disappeared from the window.

The girl's eyes followed my glance, raked briefly over Jonathan, and returned to me.

"I'm here to see Miz Jo Beth Sidden." Her back-woods twang was thick and fell softly on my ears. She was a homegrown Georgia peach.

"I'm Jo Beth Sidden. . . . What can I do for you?" I added politely.

"Can I talk to you for a little while?" Her eyes remained on mine, but her color deepened as she added, "Alone?"

"Of course," I said graciously. I turned to Jonathan. "Do you mind?"

"Not at all. I'll be in the common room." He gave her a reassuring smile as he passed her, but she didn't see it. Her eyes were cast downward.

"Come, let's sit on the porch. It's such a nice day. Would you like some iced tea?"

"Maybe some water, if it's not too much trouble," she replied.

"Not at all," I said cheerfully. "Make yourself at home. I'll be right back."

I hurried to the kitchen and hastily prepared a tray. I didn't want her to disappear before finding out who she was and what she wanted. I was curious. The ever-ready pitcher of tea went on the tray, with two glasses of ice, sugar bowl, spoons, and napkins. I also drew a glass of tap water, just in case it was what she really wanted. You're not supposed to ask strangers for any named beverage except the basic—water.

When I returned, she was sitting on the edge of the lounge with her back straight and feet together, still clutching her handbag.

"Would you rather have tea? It's freshly brewed." This was a fib, I'd poured it over two hours ago, but I was sticking to the familiar formula, trying to put her at ease. I poured a glass and handed it to her.

"Thank you," she said, taking two dainty sips before she put the glass down. Tension can make you feel like your mouth is full of cotton.

"Let's get the introductions out of the way." I was fussing with the tea tray, pouring my glass, spooning in sugar, and not looking at her.

"I'm Clara Ainsley's daughter," she stated.

"And a true daughter of the South, to mention your mother first," I blathered. "What's your—" The name finally registered in my brain, and I looked up to see her staring at me. Unshed tears were making her eyes look larger. I was appalled. "I'm sorry," I blurted. "Please forgive me. I'm so sorry for your loss. Your mother—"

I shut my mouth and jumped for tissues. The tears were running down her cheeks, and I was only making it worse. I'd read about her mother's accidental death. I'd also read the obituary, word for word, searching to see if any of my close friends were related and if I needed to send out sympathy cards. I even remembered her mother's age, thirty-eight. The name had taken ten seconds to recognize, which was nine seconds too long. I felt like a jackass.

Clara Ainsley's daughter blew her nose and wiped away the tears. "I'm sorry I made such a spectacle of myself," she said, in a dead voice, "but you're my only hope, and when you didn't even recognize her name, I just couldn't cope." Standing and still clutching her purse, she started to take her leave. "I'm sorry I troubled you. Thank you for the tea."

"Sit," I said, harsher than I intended. "Please sit," I added in a softer tone. "I humbly apologize. The man you saw earlier is my lover. We see each other so seldom, my mind was focused only on him. Do forgive me, please. . . ."

I hesitated and put my hand over my eyes, pretending I was distressed. I peeked through a narrow slit in my fingers to see if she was buying my story. I didn't feel bad about conning this girl; I didn't know her mother from Adam, but she'd made a statement that troubled me. Something about me being her last hope. I needed to know what was going on. Her expression softened, and she perched again on the edge of the lounge. I shook my head, ran my hand through my hair in a distracted manner, and again caught her eye.

"I really didn't know your mother, but I'm sorry that she died." I waited. She glared at me.

"Then tell me why she left a letter to me saying you'd make sure her murderer would be brought to justice!"

# 2

# Transmitting on a Different Frequency
### *April 13, Saturday, 10 A.M.*

"Murderer?" I echoed inanely. "Your mother was murdered?"

"Yes."

She sat there staring at me, still clutching her purse, her hazel-colored eyes reddened from weeping. I began to wonder if she had a large butcher knife or a gun tucked inside her handbag. I might be conversing with a nut.

"The newspaper said it was an accident," I said reasonably. "I believe she fainted and fell down some stairs?"

"She was murdered. She trusted you to help me, and you didn't even go to her funeral!"

She was working herself up and sounding resentful. I casually straightened in my seat and redistributed my weight so I could move quickly, should the need arise.

"Place your purse on the table, and sit in a more relaxed manner," I said in a compelling voice. "You're not making sense. We'll straighten out this misunderstanding when you can tell me what you mean about your mother trusting me, et cetera. Christ! I don't even know what to call you!"

I was surprised as all get out when she complied. She placed her purse on the table and slid backward in the seat while tugging on her skirt. She put her sensible shoes together in perfect alignment. With folded hands resting in her lap, she seemed to be waiting for further instructions. I now knew a little more about her. Either she was simpleminded or she was under so much stress she couldn't function without direction. I'd have to ask the questions.

"What's your name?"

"Gillian Ann Ainsley. My mama calls . . . called me Gilly." Stumbling over tenses made her grimace.

"Gilly, I'm going to tell you my story first. I'm Jo Beth Sidden, and I've lived in this town all my life. I have no relatives. I'm not married. I breed and train bloodhounds. I didn't know your mother, just as I've never met you before. That's the truth. Now I want you to tell me *your* story, giving me the same details about yourself and your mother. Do you think you can?"

I had slowed my speech, pronouncing each word distinctly and clearly. I had pointed at her and myself during my speech and maintained eye contact. My words sounded kind and considerate. I leaned forward a little to signal that I was all ears and awaiting her answer.

She surprised me again. I saw her lips twitch and she burst out laughing.

"I'm not tetched in the head, Miz Jo Beth," she squeaked, striving to contain her amusement. I sat quietly until she had her giggles under control.

"I don't know about you, but *I'm* having fun." I couldn't help being sarcastic.

"Sorry, Miz Jo Beth. It's the first time I've laughed since Mama died, God rest her soul." She snickered softly. "If you could've seen your face! If I had yelled *boo!* you would've jumped sky high!"

"Don't rub it in." I felt waspish and out of sorts. I hate it when I make a fool of myself.

"I'm doing this badly," she admitted. "You threw me for a loop when you said you didn't know my mama. She was a good Christian woman and raised me right. She never lied to me. She knew you and talked to you."

"What did she say about me?"

"Maybe if I showed you her letter?"

"Please do."

I kept my exasperation reined in and didn't roll my eyes. She hesitated, then reached for her purse and handed over a small envelope with *Gilly* written on the front in a childish scrawl. I pulled out a single folded note page, lined, and written in pencil.

*darlin gilly,*
    *when you find this I will be dead dont you believe that I commit suecide I believe in the*

*savior I dont run a way or drive in river or
slip in the bathtub he kill me and you go see
mrs jo beth siddens she help you be safe and
make him pay for him killing me he forced me
to help him in them woods of his the first time
I dont know what he do but last nite I find out
what he do and tell him quit or I tell mrs siddens he yell and then promise to quit but I see
his eyes and know he plan to do away with me
I sined to birth you but I thank god for ever
day I hold you pray for me your mother*

I read it twice, then carefully folded it and placed
it in the envelope. I was shaken by the contents.

"Mama quit school in the sixth grade to take care
of her mother. She didn't read and write too good. I
don't neither," she admitted, "but she made me go
to the tenth grade before she'd let me quit to help
her."

"Do you know who 'he' is in the letter?"

"Yes, the judge."

"What judge?" I asked, shocked.

"Judge McAlbee."

"Judge Sanford J. McAlbee?" I wasn't tracking
worth a damn. We only have one McAlbee who's a
judge around these parts.

"My mama kept house for him for twenty years."

The light bulb glowed above my head and I
remembered. I did know Clara Ainsley. I also knew
why she'd sent Gilly to me.

"Gilly, the man who was here earlier? His name

is Jonathan Webber. I want him to hear your story.
Is that all right with you?"

She was shaking her head negatively before I finished my sentence.

"Listen, Gilly, he's a police chief and he lives
way up in north Georgia, on the Tennessee border.
He doesn't know Judge McAlbee, and he's just as
important in his town as McAlbee is here." Not
true. A police chief of a small town is way down on
the pecking order from a superior court judge, but I
had to reassure her.

"Judge McAlbee can't give him orders or intimidate him. I'm going to help you, I promise. I'll keep
you safe. Will you trust me?"

"You remember Mama." She sounded relieved.

"Yes, I do."

She slowly nodded her acceptance. I had to think
of something to keep her occupied while I went to
fetch Jonathan. I didn't want to give her time to
think. She might yet bolt in fright.

"Would you do me a favor? I'd like for us to talk in
the kitchen. Would you take the tray in and brew
some fresh tea? I'll be back soon."

"Yes, ma'am."

"You're not afraid of dogs, are you?"

"No, ma'am."

"A bloodhound and a cat are inside. They're both
gentle and can be petted."

I lit a cigarette and took off to the common room.
Jonathan wasn't in sight, so I peeked into Wayne's
office. Jonathan, Wayne, and Donnie Ray were
playing cribbage.

"I hate to break up the game, guys"—I spoke and signed simultaneously; Wayne is hearing impaired—"but I need the big guy." I indicated Jonathan.

The three grinned, and Jonathan pretended he was reluctant to leave. At least I assumed he was pretending.

"But I'm winning!"

"Sorry, I really do need you now." I forced a smile.

"Maybe later," he said to them.

When we were out of hearing, I turned to fill him in.

"Sorry, hon, but our picnic is canceled. My visitor needs help. I'll just tell you what I know so far; then we'll both listen to her story. I want your assessment of the situation, but don't voice any negative opinions in front of her. She's shy and uncertain. We'll hold a conference later and exchange views, okay?"

"You didn't even recognize her." His tone was mild, but I knew he was disappointed.

"I knew her mother. She died a few days ago, went down a flight of stairs. She also left a note for her daughter. I want you to hear the whole story. Will you come?"

"Of course."

I squeezed his arm in gratitude, and we walked back across the courtyard. Gilly had put on the teakettle. The glasses were washed and polished. Napkins, teaspoons, and the sugar bowl were on the table. At least she wasn't shy in someone else's kitchen. Her mother had trained her well. She could be a housekeeper or flip burgers. Few choices for her in this town. I added ice and Gilly poured tea. I hurried through the introductions.

"I have to give you background so you'll know how I met Gilly's mother, Miz Clara. Over ten years ago, while I was still married to Bubba, we were out at his father's horse ranch, by special request. I wasn't a guest. I was filling in for Buford Senior's housekeeper, who was ill. I cooked and baked all day for twenty male guests: buffet style, with lots of southern finger food. On these Thursday-night get-togethers, the movers and shakers of Dunston County divvied up the spoils. Here they decided who could or couldn't run for political office, who could or couldn't climb aboard the gravy train. I'm sure you get my drift. They either played poker, watched porno films, or gathered in groups to broker their not-quite-aboveboard deals.

"By midnight I was exhausted, and the party was in high gear. Buford Senior rang the damn service bell, so I slipped on my four-inch spike heels (which Buford Junior insisted I wear when I served the men) and went to see what was needed. Judge Sanford J. McAlbee was an honored guest and a member in good standing of the good ol' boy network, but he surely couldn't hold his liquor. He had upchucked on the buffet, the floor, and a couple of cohorts who were standing within range. The baked meats now smelled like pig swill.

"Buford Senior ordered me to clean it up. I politely told him to go fuck himself and turned to leave the room. Judge McAlbee staggered over and gave me a clumsy open-handed slap across my chops. I turned to Buford Junior to see what he was going to do about it. My husband of three years contributed to the evening's entertainment by staring at his shoe tops, the murals on the walls, and anywhere else he wouldn't have to meet my gaze. I had on a tight-skirted dress. I reached down, hiked it up my thighs, and kicked the be-jesus out of the judge. He went down like he had been pole-axed. I'd aimed for his crotch with my pointy-toed shoes, but my skirt wasn't hiked high enough, and I connected solidly with his honorable kneecap.

"I changed clothes, mixed a full pitcher of margaritas, called a cab, and drank for courage. I knew the marriage was over, which didn't worry me. I also knew I'd made two omnipotent enemies with one misplaced kick, and that scared the hell out of me. When the kitchen doorbell rang, I expected the cabdriver, but it was your mother, Gilly. Someone had called her to come and collect her boss.

"Knowing those suckers wouldn't lift a hand to help her, with the judge smelling so ripe, I helped get him into the car and went with her to his house to help her unload him. False courage from booze and fear made me babble to Miz Clara about my kick and act fearless about any retaliation. I remember now how she was amazed at my audacity. At the foot of his long staircase we were almost defeated. We finally rolled the comatose lump up in a throw rug, tied a wet bed sheet around the bundle, and dragged him upstairs. We hit every riser on the way

up. Miz Clara seemed to enjoy hearing the thumps;
I know I did. That was the first and only time I saw
or talked to your mother. When she needed to send
you to someone for help, she must've remembered
me as a fighter. That's where she was found, wasn't
it, Gilly? At the foot of the staircase?"

"Yes, ma'am." She blinked and produced a smile.
"I want to thank you, Miz Jo Beth, for helping my
mama. It was right nice of you."

I ignored the lump in my throat and smiled back.

"You're welcome. Did you and your mother live
with the judge?"

"We had two bedrooms and a sitting room off
from the kitchen. I've lived my entire nineteen
years in that house."

"Gilly, what time was your mother found?"

"Just after I left for work on Tuesday. I work for
Miz Clampton over on the lake. I no sooner got
there before a deputy sheriff came to the door asking for me. They said it happened around eight-
thirty or so."

"Who found her, the judge?"

"Yes, ma'am. He said he was coming down for
breakfast and she was lying there." She sniffed,
fighting back tears.

"I know this is hard. It's okay to cry." I reached
over and patted her hand. She gave me a grateful
smile.

"Was your mother widowed or divorced?"
Jonathan asked.

Gilly squared her shoulders but stared down at
the tablecloth as her face flooded with color.

"My mama was never married. I was born out of wedlock."

I glared at Jonathan, and he raised his eyebrows to the ceiling. I patted Gilly's hand some more.

"Tell me exactly what happened all day on Monday, right until you got up Tuesday. Don't leave anything out, even if it seemed inconsequential at the time."

She stared at me with a quizzical expression.

"Even if it didn't amount to a hill of beans," I translated.

"We got up at six. Mama fixed our breakfast while I vacuumed our rooms. After we ate, I scrubbed the back hall's rubber runner and oiled it. I tried to help her all I could. She had so much to do, what with the cooking and cleaning and the laundry. Judge McAlbee was having a dinner party on Tuesday night. I washed the back door with sudsy ammonia, and then I had to leave for work. Mama was making pie dough. She liked to mix her dough a day ahead of time and store it in the refrigerator. She said it made the crust more flaky. I got home at eight, and the judge was just finishing his dinner. I helped Mama clear the table, and then I vacuumed and dusted the dining room while she did the dishes and mopped the kitchen floor. I waxed it while she had her bath, and then I took mine. She sewed on some buttons and repaired a rip on Judge McAlbee's walking-in-the-woods jacket. I read some from the Bible to her. Then we went to bed."

My God, and I thought *I* worked hard. They weren't servants, they were indentured slaves.

"Did you have any time off?" I was curious.

"When Judge McAlbee was out of town, we went to church on Sunday mornings and had lunch at the diner on Filmore Street. Mama always called it our treat."

"How much time did your mother receive for her vacation?" Jonathan wanted to be fair and get all the facts before believing McAlbee to be the bastard I already knew he was.

"Mama could take one week a year. But she told me it wasn't worth giving up the week's pay just to sit around and watch someone else wait on Judge McAlbee. It might make him mad at us. We didn't even own a car at the time. I'd been saving money from my salary and just recently bought one."

"Jesus Christ!" Jonathan had uttered the muffled curse before he could get his emotions under control.

Gilly looked confused.

"Chief Webber is upset because you and your mother had to work so hard," I explained.

"We just did her job."

"Indeed you did," I agreed. "When and where did she leave the note?"

"I almost didn't find it. Mama bought me a Bible like hers for my sixteenth birthday present. After I had mine, she told me she wanted to have her Bible with her when she died. I carried it to the funeral with me. I was gonna put it beside her just before they closed the lid on the casket. I was sitting there during the service and started feeling the pages, just remembering. I turned some pages and there it was."

"McAlbee didn't see you find it, did he?" I asked sharply.

"No, ma'am. He didn't go to the funeral service."

I looked at Jonathan, but he was staring at Gilly, appalled.

"Gilly, would you let Chief Webber read the letter?"

"Yes, ma'am." She handed it to Jonathan. While he was studying the letter, I decided I'd move Gilly into one of the visiting trainers' rooms. Whatever Miz Clara had discovered had been during the early morning hours after they went to bed on Monday evening. She was killed Tuesday morning. This was Saturday. Gilly wasn't safe in that house. McAlbee couldn't have two accidents happen close together, but he couldn't be sure that Miz Clara hadn't passed on what she'd learned to Gilly. I knew I had to get her out of there immediately.

"Gilly," I began, taking her hand in mine, "how'd you like to move in here with me? I have plenty of room, and you shouldn't be alone right now."

"That's mighty nice of you, Miz Jo Beth, but I have my own place now. I sure thank you for the invite."

"You've moved out of McAlbee's house?" My voice was shrill.

Jonathan reached over and pressed my arm. I struggled to control my emotions and took a deep breath.

"When did you move?" I asked quietly.

"Judge McAlbee told me I had to move right

away so his new housekeeper would have a place to stay. He told me Thursday morning before the funeral. I looked all Thursday afternoon but couldn't find anything I could afford, the rent was so high. I explained it to the judge Thursday night. He called me at work yesterday and told me about the Balsa Arms. I packed my things and moved after work last night."

I shuddered. The Balsa Arms was an old hotel downtown where winos and the almost homeless shared tiny rooms with large cockroaches and much larger rats. I'd worked a drug raid in the building last year and couldn't believe the squalor and filth. I knew Gilly couldn't have conversed with the judge without showing her feelings, thinking he killed her mother. I then remembered the one question I hadn't asked.

"When did you read the letter from your mother?"

"I thought it was a good-bye letter. I wanted to read it when I was really, really sad so it would cheer me up. I was just numb Thursday and yesterday. I woke up this morning, and it hit me how much I missed her. That's when I opened it."

I breathed a sigh of relief. Her innocence had kept her safe so far. Jonathan handed back her letter without comment.

"You're not staying another night in that pigsty. I'm not taking no for an answer. We're going to move you, right now, okay?"

"Well . . . I'll pay you what I'm paying them, if it's enough?"

"We'll discuss finances later," I answered. I had to protect her independence. I'd offer her some chores in exchange for room and board. She wouldn't accept a free ride. We Southerners have our pride.

"Jonathan, if you'll get your car, I'll make a phone call and we'll be on our way."

I pointed out the bathroom to Gilly, closed my bedroom door, and dialed Jasmine's number.

I said hello when she answered.

"I'm bringing home a nineteen-year-old lass whose possessions have been in the Balsa Arms overnight. Will you call our pesticide sprayer and tell him we need him in about an hour? I want to fumigate everything before we move them inside. One pregnant roach, and we'll have to breathe that low-impact junk for a month."

"You bet. Can I help?"

"Yes, you can. Would you open cottage number one to air it? Turn on the fan. Spray a little room freshener. Lay out some linens."

"I'll even make the bed."

"Thanks, Jasmine."

"You're welcome."

When Jonathan pulled up to the porch, I told him I'd drive. Gilly climbed in back and we were off. It was three miles to town. I was thinking of the white sand cove about three more miles out into the swamp. The gentle breeze blowing today would've kept the insects away. Jonathan and I should be there on a quilt, drinking cold beer and debating about when to open the picnic basket.

A large red fire truck almost drove up my backside before I heard the repetitive hee-haws that were supposed to signal its approach. I quickly pulled to the curb, thinking that some poor soul's insurance premium had just been readjusted upwardly.

"I wonder if it's close." Jonathan sounded wistful. All small boys want to race after fire trucks, even when they get old enough to be called men.

"Sorry, son. Dad's busy right now and can't drive you by the fire."

"Very funny," Jonathan remarked. "Please, Dad?"

I laughed. "Just look at what it's attracted already."

I had to wait until a long string of pickups raced by before I could pull into traffic. At the next red light a police car came from my right, made a wide turn in the intersection, lights flashing, siren wailing, and proceeded to gather speed. It was going in the same direction we were. I could hear the distant whine of another emergency vehicle drawing near.

When the light turned, I clicked on the left blinker and pulled to the left, cutting off the guy in the left turn lane. He wasn't very gracious. I'm sure the arm he waved out the window had a rigid extended finger attached. I sped down the block and hung another left.

"What are you doing?" Jonathan asked. I had burnt some rubber with the last turn.

"I just remembered I left the iron on."

"You never iron," he said flatly.

"I'll give you a riddle to solve on the way home

to unplug the iron. What's the question the speed patrols always ask when you're pulled over? I'll give you three guesses, and the first two don't count."

His eyes widened when he caught my meaning.

The officer usually asks, "Where's the fire?" Both of us could answer that one.

# 3

## Here Come de Judge
### *April 13, Saturday, noon*

Huddled in misery and slouched down so her blond hair wouldn't be a beacon to passersby, Gilly was mostly silent during the trip home. Jonathan had explained to her our belief that her temporary residence was aflame. As we turned into my driveway, the local radio station confirmed our suspicion with an excited description of the Balsa Arms as "completely engulfed in flames with no possibility of saving the wooden building."

With stoical good grace, she accepted the news that she now owned nothing but the clothes on her back. Her only wistful comment was a wish that she could have saved a couple of her mama's pictures. I decided then and there that if the opportunity presented itself, I'd make sure my next kick would be right on target. Somehow I'd find a way to produce a picture of her mother. Homeless, her mother murdered, no relatives, and a powerful man trying to destroy her; her wish was too modest to go unfulfilled.

I dropped Jonathan at the first gate so he could lock it. Security for Gilly was foremost. Even with Bubba playing his cat-and-mouse game of stalking me, I could take chances and leave it open in the daytime, locking it only at night, but not with Gilly here.

Jasmine walked over as I parked near the back porch. She's one beautiful black lady. We're the same height and weight, but on her everything is in the right places. She has casual soft curls and my hair is a kinky mop. Her complexion is one shade lighter than milk chocolate and glows with beauty. She looks elegant in jeans and T-shirt. In the same outfit I'd be mistaken for a car wash attendant. She handles and trains mantrailers and goes on drug searches several times a week. She's taking classes at the local college. How does she find time for sleep? She lives in the apartment to the right of the courtyard gate and across from my house. She's worked for me for a year now, and I don't know how I ever managed without her.

I introduced Gilly and invited Jasmine to lunch.

"I just made a huge salad. Shall I bring it over?"

"Great, it'll go well with picnic fixings."

Jasmine smiled ruefully, signaling her sympathy at my loss of time alone with Jonathan.

"You two go inside and start putting lunch on the table. I have something to tell Wayne."

I found him and Donnie in the grooming room.

Wayne was working on a harness, and Donnie was filling in the daily logs on the puppies. He had Sally's nine out to weigh. They were four weeks old and trying to climb out of the cart. I motioned Wayne over so I could fill them both in on Gilly and the need to keep the gates locked.

Wayne will turn twenty-one next month. He's six feet of muscle with brown hair and eyes, has a large open face, and is deaf. We are all excellent signers, with the exception of Jonathan. He's learning, but it is going slowly with only his brief weekend visits for practice.

I signed and spoke, explaining Gilly and the gates. "Remember, we don't know the enemy. I doubt that Judge McAlbee does his own dirty work. Make sure you know the person before admitting anyone."

They agreed. I asked Wayne to phone the exterminator and cancel.

I picked up a puppy. "Who's this?" I crooned in baby talk. He was adorable and appeared to be excellently configured. He sniffed my fingers and arm. I turned his narrow elongated head toward me and studied his patrician-looking nose.

"Let's name him Shakespeare."

I was guessing that he would have a good nose and could work drugs. We name our drug sniffers after famous writers and poets. At four weeks no one can predict with accuracy if a bloodhound will win at shows.

"You said we weren't gonna repeat names." Donnie Ray sounded indignant at my suggestion.

"I know, but look at his face and his coloring. He looks exactly like Shakespeare."

For the past five months, Shakespeare the First has been up in Monrose happily sniffing drugs for the Georgia State Patrol.

"I think this little fellow deserves the name," I added.

"They all look alike at four weeks," he muttered.

Donnie Ray's expression was sullen, but he added the name in the puppy's log. I glanced at Wayne, who was standing behind Donnie Ray, and raised an eyebrow in question. He signed he was worried. Donnie had been acting this way for a couple of weeks. Wayne can also read lips, so I mouthed, "Be patient, we'll talk later."

I walked over to the wall phone and dialed Susan's parents' ranch. She usually spends the weekends there. I was lucky to catch her, sans horse and answering the phone.

"Hi. How's the riding?"

"On the most glorious day I've ever seen? It's fabulous! I just came in to eat. Why aren't you out there in the swamp with your male hunk making out?"

"Something came up. I have a woman here whose only clothes are on her back. She's about your size. I was hoping you could come back in, make an emergency raid on your closet, and provide her with a few things. There's a good reason we can't go shopping. I wish I could explain, but it's another case I can't tell you about. Maybe later when it's all over."

"Saint Jo Beth to the rescue, and I work in the dark." She gave a theatrical sigh into the receiver, but I knew she was dying to participate.

"Exactly my size?"

"Maybe a little wider in the shoulders and hips."

"Age, coloring, and style," she demanded.

"Nineteen, blond and fair, and lousy."

"Will my shoes fit her?"

"I don't know. Bring some. Between you and me and Jasmine, we should be able to shoe her. I might as well tell you—you'll kill me if I don't—her hair's beautiful but needs styling. Bring your beauty tools. And, Susan, she works as a housekeeper. Don't outfit her for an evening at Sardi's. Also, don't go overboard. Just a few things, okay?" Susan's closet contains more clothes than most boutiques.

"Up yours, Sidden. See you soon." She hung up.

Susan Comstock has been my best friend from the very first day of first grade. Our marriages and divorces occurred near the same time, and we both have remained single. She owns and runs a bookstore downtown. I'd trust her with my life, but not with important secrets. She has trouble remembering what is tellable and what isn't, and she loves to gossip. I let her help me with some of my not-quite-legal dealings, but I'm careful to keep her out of controversy and danger. I love her and will not put her in jeopardy.

I went back to the house to have lunch. Jonathan was waiting for me on the back porch.

"Let's go eat," I said. "I'm starved, aren't you?"

"We have to talk. When are you going to call the sheriff and turn this mess over to him?"

"Well, Gilly isn't a fashion plate, but I wouldn't call her a mess. She has a lousy sense of style—like me, for instance."

"You know what I mean," he snapped, "the alleged murder and alleged arson. Sheriff Cribbs can protect Gilly. It's his place to investigate, not yours."

"I'm not calling Hank," I explained. "Our friendship isn't on solid ground yet. We talk and smile a lot, but he hasn't totally forgiven me."

"You told me Cannon turned up before you had a chance to investigate!" His tone was sharp.

"Yes, I did. That's what I told you both. You believed me and Hank didn't."

I had lied to both of them about that case. Hank knew I was responsible but couldn't prove it. Now Jonathan seemed to be questioning my veracity.

"I have a feeling I shouldn't be asking this question," Jonathan said in measured tones, "but I'm going to ask it anyway. Which one of us was correct?"

"You were," I said firmly, looking straight into his eyes and lying through my teeth. That's the trouble with lying. You tell one whopper, and then you have to tell three more to shore up the first one. It wasn't entirely my fault that I had to lie to them. They are both in law enforcement, both so straight-arrow they squeak, and they don't bend the rules. I sometimes bend, even break, the law in trying to help someone. If I'd worked alone, I might have admitted my participation, but Jasmine had been with me, and I couldn't put her freedom on the line. Alone, I could've told Hank and Jonathan the truth and to hell with what they thought. I truly think they both secretly dreaded this idea. They were afraid I'd commit some outrageous act and tell them about it, thus making them accessories. Then what? They either lived with the knowledge that they didn't report a crime of which they were aware, or they turned me in. Neither solution was acceptable.

"Since I opened this can of worms," Jonathan said with a bland smile, but sounding dubious, "we might as well go fishing. When you also told me you had no clue about Cannon's three sons' mysterious disappearance, I believed you. Did Hank?"

"No."

"Should I have?"

Well, here it is, showdown time. I sensed it was a pivotal question and answered accordingly.

"No."

"Asked and answered." His smile was weak.

I seldom beg, it's not my style, but just maybe sweet reason would tip the scales in my favor.

"Jonathan, today is a very good example of what I face. I can't go to Hank with what I have. I have no proof. Miz Clara said *he* in her note. She doesn't tell what she found, just hints at where. The *where* is my bailiwick, not Hank's. Who better to search the woods? You know the law. Do I have enough to ask Hank to investigate a superior court judge? If I brought these facts to your attention, in your city, would you ask for a search warrant and open an investigation?"

Jasmine stuck her head out the screen door.

"Dinner's on the table."

"Coming," I answered, happy to escape the present conversation.

Susan arrived with the back of her Lumina van holding enough outfits to keep Gilly's body stylishly covered for the next year. Susan declared they needed privacy and whisked Gilly away to the first cottage.

Rosie, Wayne's mother, moved out of the upstairs apartment when she and our local fire chief were married five months ago. She still brings us care packages filled with food because she's afraid we'll starve. Today's contribution was a huge beef roast, surrounded by potatoes and carrots floating in rich thick gravy. She had enlisted Jasmine to go with her to the mall to help pick out wallpaper for her kitchen, but I knew she had a not-so-secret agenda on her mind. She'd pump Jasmine in order to find out whether the four of us were eating properly and getting enough rest and what had happened during the last two days since she'd seen us. She did, indeed, keep tabs on us all.

Jonathan was lying on the couch with his shoes off, flipping through a magazine. He hadn't gone back to our pre-lunch conversation, and I was happy to let sleeping dogs slumber. He had been noticeably quiet at lunch; at least Jasmine and I had seen his reticence. She'd glanced his way occasionally with a puzzled look.

I was on the phone just finishing a weird ritual including a code-of-the-day, my code name, and the name of my latest case. On hearing this nonsense, Jonathan was openly eavesdropping, looking fascinated. I looked at the ceiling and continued.

"Yes, sir, that is correct. The name of the operation is the Case of the Murdered Queen. . . . I agree, chief, we must save the princess from the evil wizard. . . . Yes, sir, I need the complete dossier: real estate holdings, all banking records, and known associates. Judge Sanford J. McAlbee, Superior Court, Tenth District. Thank you, sir." I gently replaced the receiver.

I gave Jonathan an evil smile, relishing his astonishment.

"You want to take a crack at it? Go ahead and guess."

Jonathan rubbed his chin thoughtfully. "Is this your source for the computer sheets you retrieved down a dirt road last fall from behind the third pine tree, across the road from the small white adhesive tapecross on another pine tree?"

"Very good. You're right on target. Still think I was lying when I assured you my source was not a law-enforcement buddy?"

"Not after hearing that drivel," he answered with a wry grimace. "Tell me, my dear, is this computer hacker in a local loony bin or did you direct-dial the state mental hospital?"

I snickered with delight. "Neither. Any more questions?"

"I'm going to curb my curiosity before you tell me the identity of this nut. This might save me from ending up in handcuffs and being charged—along with you—for God knows what. I'd like to go on record with the following facts: What you're doing is illegal, immoral, and against my principles." He stood and stepped into his shoes as he delivered his sermon.

"Hey, where're you going?" I asked, when he turned toward the back door. "You're not giving me a chance to rebut. Immoral? What's immoral about trying to help Gilly?" I didn't receive an answer, because at first I was talking to his back, then to empty space as he disappeared out the door.

"Shit," I said in disgust. So it was illegal and against his principles. He's a police chief and righteous, so what else is new? But immoral? No way.

I looked up hopefully when I heard footsteps cross the porch. It was Donnie Ray who entered.

"Can we talk?" he blurted, looking nervous.

"Sure. Have a seat. What's on your mind?"

He walked closer to my desk but didn't sit.

"Can I borrow your car for a date tonight?" Quick and curt. He looked as if he had to force the words through clenched teeth and a locked jaw.

"Of course," I said with a smile. "Let's go over the rules."

"I know them by heart," he said harshly. "No traffic tickets or I'm out of luck for three months. Any accident that's my fault, my borrowing days are over. Put five bucks in the insurance jar in the grooming room. Replace any gas I use, and clean out the car on arriving home, *before* two A.M. Did I forget anything?"

"Just your manners. Plant your butt in a chair, Donnie Ray," I replied calmly. "Explain to me why you're acting so angry. What's the beef?"

He wouldn't meet my eyes. He was staring at the top of the desk.

"The rules ain't fair and I want a raise." His voice had dropped to almost a whisper. He still hadn't moved.

"Sit down, dammit!" I waited until he complied. "We are now going to have a nice calm discussion, and I will sincerely try to remember my manners, and you damn well better remember yours. Now, first point: traffic tickets. The car is only five months old so everything works. The only ticket you could receive is a rolling violation: speeding, reckless driving, et cetera. If you got a ticket for speeding—just ten miles over the speed limit—do you have any idea how much my insurance premium would be raised?"

He continued to look down but nodded his head.

"A nod is not sufficient, Donnie Ray, I want a polite yes or no, ma'am."

"No, ma'am."

"Well, I'm not going to give you a figure because I didn't tell you or Wayne just how much my insurance jumped when I added a nineteen- and a twenty-year-old as casual drivers on my personal car insurance policy, which is not used for business. I felt sorry for both of you, but I own a business and can be sued up the ying-yang if either one of you, God forbid, has an accident. To try and bring home the importance of following the rules and putting the ridiculous five bucks in the insurance jar, I was giving both of you a break. I'll give you a clue. If you and Wayne took turns and used the car every other night of the year, what you both contribute wouldn't cover the extra I'm being charged for you to borrow the car. Am I being fair on this rule?"

"Yes, ma'am."

"Next point: replacing any gas you use and cleaning out any garbage you deposit in the car, such as pop cans, burger wrappers, et cetera. Is something wrong with this rule?"

"No, ma'am."

"About the two A.M. rule. Nothing is open around here after midnight for more than forty miles in any direction except two convenience stores that don't allow teenagers to gather on their parking lots. This only leaves Johnston's Landing, where everyone goes to see and be seen. An hour and a half is plenty of time to shoot the breeze with friends, hold hands with your girlfriend, or screw her on Zeke Pammington's father's houseboat in the master cabin for ten bucks, or in the aft bunk bed for five— a thirty-minute limit on both. These rules seem fair to me. How about you?"

Donnie Ray was openly staring at me in consternation and with flaming cheeks. I waited until he mumbled an embarrassed affirmation.

"These rules are to protect all of us, Donnie Ray. Any cars seen on the streets after two in the morning, both city and county take down license plate numbers

and a description of the driver. The lists are combined
and typed up each morning by the file clerk at county.
The second time you make the list, a check mark is
added. The third time, they start pulling you over and
searching you and the vehicle. You know I'm not
well liked by a lot of the deputies and city patrolmen.
Some of them aren't above planting drugs on you or
saying you failed a breathalyzer test in order to get to
me. Bubba has a lot of friends who wear badges.
They blame me for his repeated trips back to prison.
When I hired you, I promised you a nice raise after
one year. That will happen May fifth—if you're still
working here—and not one day sooner."

He sat picking at the armrest of the chair and
looking miserable. He seemed close to tears. He
rubbed under his nose with his fingers, and I silently
handed him the box of tissues.

"Want to tell me what's going on?" I offered.

"I've got a girl. We've been dating for three
weeks. She . . . she doesn't think I'm making
enough money."

"I see," I said, to encourage him to say more.
"Anyone I know?"

"You know Mr. Jerkins over on Powell Street?
He has three daughters. Angie's the youngest. Her
name is Angel, but she likes to be called Angie. She
lives with her oldest sister in a trailer out on
Brackton Road." Donnie gave me a dark look. "Her
old man started trying to mess with her, and she had
to move out. He better never touch her again. I'll
make him sorry!"

My heart sank. I was gonna kill Wayne for not

telling Donnie Ray the truth. Wayne had to know he
was seeing her. The big lug was too softhearted for
his own good. I was gonna kick ass tomorrow, but
right now I had to stomp on Donnie Ray's heart and
crush the little tramp's fingers she'd dug in so
deeply in only three weeks. The phone rang at the
same time Jonathan opened the sliding glass door
and entered the office. I was temporarily saved by
the bell.

A controlled voice I didn't recognize began
speaking the moment I answered. She was filled
with tension and was speaking as precisely and
carefully as if her life depended on pronouncing
each word distinctly. It did, but I didn't know that
until she'd finished delivering her message.

"Jo Beth. This is Glydia Powell. Josh and I and
our three kids are camping out on the sandbank on
the left side of the Suwannee, two miles east of
Johnston's Landing. I brought the bass boat to the
landing to call you. After I hang up, I'll call Hank.
Josh is back at the campsite keeping people away
from an empty tent. There are seventeen different
campsites out here and all have been searched,
including the immediate area around them that's
accessible on foot. A teenager *thinks* he saw a
stranger lifting our Peter into a pickup truck. He's
been missing for forty-five minutes. He has asthma
and I keep his inhaler on a chain pinned to his clothing, leaving enough slack so it can rest in his
pocket. The inhaler, and six inches of chain, was
found lying ten feet from the empty tent in the
walking path. I wouldn't let them pick it up. The

stranger's truck is missing. It's a black Ford with dark-tinted windows. It has a gray cab-height camper shell. You said if I ever needed you, to call. I need you! Have I left out anything?"

"You're doing great, Glydia. Hang on, I'm on my way. Call Hank, then go back to Josh. You both guard the path to that tent. You did good. Is Dr. Sellers your doctor?"

"Yes. And I also have a spare inhaler in our gear."

"Hang up, Glydia." I spoke loud and clear. I finally heard a dial tone when the connection was broken.

# 4

# The Grim Reaper Hovers
## April 13, Saturday, 5 P.M.

Jonathan and Donnie Ray were alerted by hearing my side of the conversation. They were exchanging concerned glances.

"Donnie Ray, we have a call-out. Search-and-rescue. A five-year-old asthmatic boy. Possibly an abduction. Tell Wayne to load Melanie and Ashley for me. If Jasmine hasn't returned, load everything but her dogs. We have only two hours before first dark. Load our night gear and enough water for twenty-four hours. Questions?"

"Can I take both cameras? I want to try the new strobe for night work."

"You're not going."

"Why?" He acted surprised. "We need a good night search!"

"Ask me next week when I have the time to waste for explanations," I snapped. "Haul ass!"

He turned and fled.

"Here!" I called to Jonathan, as I tossed him a scratch pad from my desk. "Come take notes while I dress." I hurried to the bedroom and stripped off my clothing as I dictated instructions. "My telephone book is on the desk or in the middle drawer. It's wine-colored leather. Call Dr. Sellers at home. If you can reach him, tell him I need two inhalers for Peter Powell. Tell the druggist to meet me at the curb in front of Big B Drugs in fifteen minutes. Stay on the line. After he calls the drugstore, get some instructions on using one if we find Peter unconscious. Ask if I do anything different on CPR, et cetera. Call Sam or Ray Conner. They're brothers and live next door to each other. Tell them I need both bass boats and to load the canoes—just in case. Tell them night gear and grapples. They're to be at Johnston's Landing in forty-five minutes. Get a confirmation before you hang up."

I was now stepping into the shower and closing the frosted glass.

"What if the doctor isn't home?" Jonathan yelled over the noise of the water.

"His wife can handle it, if she's there. If no one's home, call Big B yourself. Ask for the pharmacist and explain. Tell him twenty minutes at the curb. Start calling!" I yelled.

I grabbed the shampoo bottle—it would be quicker—squirted a glob in my palm, and started smearing it on the important spots: behind my ears, between my breasts, on my wrists, and behind both knees. I rubbed the areas vigorously and sloughed suds with the cascading water.

I was damp-dried, dressed, and pulling on thick socks and joggers when Jonathan returned.

"How'd you make out?"

"The doctor's wife said she'd call the pharmacy and for us to call her back for instructions. I reached one of the brothers, I don't know which one. He hung up on me after I delivered the message. He said to tell you they'd be there."

I breathed a relieved sigh. On such a glorious day, I was so afraid they were out on the river fishing, deliberately leaving their beepers at home. They were ornery cusses, independent and proud, but no one in three counties knew the Suwannee better.

"Great," I said, heading back to the bathroom for a dry towel. Water was trickling down the back of my neck. I made a towel turban.

In the kitchen I pulled Rosie's roast from the oven, speared a large portion, and placed it on the cutting board. Using only a fork, I crumbled the meat into manageable sizes for sandwiches.

"Get a loaf of rye bread from the freezer. Ketchup and horseradish sauce from the fridge. This next call I want you to make will be a little tricky," I told him. I dealt out twelve frozen slices on the counter's Formica surface.

"Aren't you going to defrost the bread?" Jonathan asked.

"It'll thaw out before we get a chance to eat it." I slid a forkful of meat into my mouth. It was warm and succulent on my tongue. I took one more bite and told myself, No more. I can't run well on a full stomach, carrying a thirty-two-pound backpack. Melanie and Ashley have only two forward speeds, fast and faster.

"Call Leroy Moore's number for me. If he doesn't answer and his wife, Jackie, or one of his three daughters answers instead, don't mention my name. Say you have to speak to Leroy, immediately. If he comes to the phone, say only these words, 'Jo Beth needs you at Johnston's Landing ASAP,' and hang up. Got it?"

"Another ex-lover?" Jonathan questioned with a raised brow, trying to sound humorous.

"No," I answered shortly. "Just a guy I've loved more than God, or anyone else, since the first grade, without a smidgen of lust or desire. A deeply abiding, friendly, brotherly love. I doubt if you can comprehend such a radical notion, being a moralistic, macho, stereotype redneck male, but I wish you'd try."

With suffused cheeks, Jonathan spun on his heel and left the room. I guessed he didn't trust himself to utter one word. I sighed. When I start gearing up for mantrailing, the adrenaline flows, turning me into a vicious accusatory bitch. It wasn't Jonathan's fault that he was of the same gender as the slug who'd abducted Peter. I'd been walking around, dispensing orders and trying to push the idea of a sick, twisted pederast and what he might do or had already done to Peter out of my mind. I wasn't having any success.

Suddenly, a breathless Donnie Ray was framed in the hall doorway.

"You're all loaded and ready to go, Jo Beth," he said, panting. "Jasmine just arrived. She's upstairs dressing. She said she wanted Ulysses and Gulliver. Wayne's loading them now."

"Good. Pack twelve Diet Cokes into a medium-size cooler."

Rosie entered and insisted on finishing the sandwiches. When she insists, we all bow to her commands. She's barely five feet tall, and plump. She favors loud colors and loose tops over pants that never match. Her coal-black hair is always elaborately coifed and couldn't be mussed by gale-force winds.

I went to the bedroom and took my snub-nose .32 caliber revolver from the nightstand, opened the cylinder, and checked the load. I slipped on the harness and fed six extra rounds into its canvas slots. I was tying a large red bandanna around my stomach, my T-shirt hiked up to my boobs, when I entered the living room.

Jonathan was on the couch when Donnie Ray, lugging the ice chest and sandwiches, started through the office. He stopped and stared at my towel turban like he'd just noticed I was wearing one.

"You took a shower?" he blurted.

It was said in surprise, but I couldn't let it go in front of Jonathan. He might have the same opinion. Why waste time on a shower? I removed the towel and ran my fingers through my damp, curly mop.

"Donnie Ray, your powers of observation and your sense of smell need work. I was wearing perfume. After a year here, you should know that perfume deadens the dogs' noses. Wayne has taught you never to wear hair spray, aftershave, or cologne when working with mantrailers. Remember?"

"Of course," he said, stung by the reprimand. "But you never wear perfume!"

"Only when I have a gentleman caller," I explained, catching Jonathan's eye. Jonathan's expression softened, and I saw the hint of a smile.

Rosie bustled in and grabbed me in a hug. "Take care of yourself," she demanded. "Call us. I'll stay here."

"Susan is in the first cottage with a new guest. Go meet the guest and explain the call-out to Susan; then go home to your hubby. Jonathan, Wayne, and Donnie Ray will be here." I looked at Donnie Ray. "Right?"

"Right," he echoed, resigned to missing his date tonight.

I blew Jonathan a kiss and hit the door. Wayne had the van in the drive and was waiting for me.

"Guard Gilly," I signed.

He returned with, "Good luck."

I heard Jonathan yell and looked up. He was running down the steps. "Your friend Leroy answered and said he was on his way. I also forgot to tell you what Mrs. Sellers said about the inhaler: 'Regular CPR, and don't use it unless he's laboring for breath.' Is she a doctor?"

"Registered nurse. She and Doc Sellers have worked together for about thirty years now. She probably knows as much as he does. I was gonna

wait until I was farther down the road before I
called back for the information. Am I forgiven for
being nasty?"

"Sure. Hurry back."

"You bet."

I glanced at my watch as I pulled out. It was 5:25
P.M. I detoured three miles to Big B Drugs and
found Jimmy Lathem waiting on the edge of the
sidewalk with a small white bag. Jasmine would
only be a few minutes behind me. Not much daylight would be left to search. We were fifteen miles
from Johnston's Landing.

I hated the light bar and siren on top of the van
and hardly ever used them. I had a contract with
three counties and two prisons for search-and-rescue, drug raids, and mantrailing. Dunston County
had them installed on all my vehicles and had their
name under mine on the van's door. It was part of
the contract: small-time bureaucrats who wanted to
impress and stress their importance.

I'd be forced to turn them on today. Traffic is
heavy on Saturday afternoon in a small county: people coming home from shopping, picnicking, and
visiting; early revelers gearing up for a rollicking
night in slicked-down hair, new jeans, and polished
boots, driving their freshly washed and waxed pickups. They'd grab a burger, some chicken, or barbe-
cue before lifting that first can of Budweiser. Most
made minimum wage and would spend a third of
their week's pay tonight and tomorrow. If they
couldn't go to their ma and pa's to eat when they
ran out of money, along about Wednesday, they'd

borrow from a relative or friend until next weekend. Who could save and plan ahead, working for miserable wages with no promise of better prospects in the future? They struggled Monday through Friday so they could kick up their heels on weekends. If they could keep up the truck payments and have enough left over for gas and Budweiser, they were content. Too soon, a little gal would come along, and then the kids, and they'd be just like their ma and pa.

I left the window open and let the wind blow through my hair. Bobby Lee and Rudy were out for a run when I left. When they returned, they'd eat, and Rudy would curl up on the bed for a nap. Bobby Lee would sit quietly on the front porch waiting for my return, whether it was an hour, tomorrow, or next week. Jasmine had told me she felt sorry for him on the weekends I visited Jonathan. He kept a constant vigil, awaiting my return.

I had the speed up to fifty and couldn't do much to increase it. It was a two-lane hardtop, and the cars ahead couldn't pull off the road. Along here, on the way to the swamp, the shoulders are soft. I turned off the siren, which was bugging me, and just left the lights on. I didn't want to make someone nervous, maybe cause them to swerve onto the soft shoulder and flip. I could occasionally pass a car or two, but with oncoming traffic I had to stay in line like everybody else.

Finally, I reached the swamp road and was able to make some time. There were fewer cars and it was a straight shot all the way to the landing.

I pulled up to the dock and saw that Hank had arrived. He and a deputy were watching as Ray Conner backed his boat trailer down the concrete ramp and into the river. When he was in position, his brother, Sam, waded into thigh-deep water to release the boat.

"Hi, Hank." He hadn't seen me arrive. He turned with a tired smile. God, he looked terrible. His face was drawn and gray, and there were dark smudges beneath his beautiful brown eyes. His hair, black as crow's wings, looked lackluster in the bright sunlight. He is the sheriff of Dunston County, usually full of piss and vinegar—and himself. He doesn't have to wear a uniform, but he knows how great the sand-colored fitted shirt and tan gabardine slacks with the black stripe down each leg flatter his tall lean body.

We've been friends for years, and for a few weeks last year we had a brief affair. Our friendship endured the breakup, but it, too, was seriously derailed last November over the Cannon kidnapping.

"Howdy. I'll come help you unload," he offered.

"Thanks. You look awful. Have you been ill?"

"The last two days have been humdingers. I bet I haven't slept a total of four hours. I was looking forward to an early supper and twelve hours of sack time. God, I hate this kind of case! I know you're going to be very unhappy when you hear I've called in the GBI."

"Oh, shit. Why?" I demanded.

"I'm beat and not up to snuff. P. C. hasn't passed

his lieutenant's exam, and we need all the help we can get. I just don't have anyone to turn the case over to if I crash. Josh and Glydia deserve everyone's best efforts. How old is Peter, six?"

"He's five, Anna Lee is seven, and little Josh is nine."

We reached the van. Hank opened the cages and I attached the short leads to Melanie and Ashley. They dropped to the ground on command and began an eager whining. I handed both leads to Hank.

"Hold them a sec," I told him. I climbed into the van and took out two cans of Diet Coke. I picked up my yellow Day-Glo rescue suit and unzipped a breast pocket. Removing a handkerchief, I untied one of its knotted corners, picked up a tablet of speed, and retied the knot. Backing out of the van, I handed Hank a Coke.

"Listen, you politic hunk of correctness, I'd like you to take this pill. I'm telling you it's an aspirin. It'll help you make it through the night."

"I'll be able to function?" His eyes met mine.

"Yes."

He had two choices. He could take the speed or arrest me. Either action wouldn't surprise me. He was hurting, or I would never have made the offer.

He held out his hand, popped the pill into his mouth without inspecting it, and swallowed some Coke.

"Thanks for the aspirin," he said with a straight face.

"You're welcome," I replied, grateful that he had

complied. I needed him to keep John Fray of the
Georgia Bureau of Investigation off my back.

We gathered my gear and walked back to the
landing.

"Where're your department boats?" I scanned the
dock area.

"Both of them are at Fargo Landing. They're
searching for a missing rental that wasn't returned
last night. Since you beat me to Sam and Ray, I'll
commandeer a boat here when Fray arrives."

"How much lead time do I have?"

"I don't think he can get here before dark. You've
got about an hour and a half, I'd guess."

Sam and Ray had launched both boats and were
waiting at the loading dock. Hank and I started
handing down my gear to Sam. I glanced over at
Ray. The brothers look alike, with their curly pre-
maturely salt-and-pepper hair, which they haven't
had cut in ten years. They both have braided pigtails
hanging halfway down their backs. They are forty-
two and thirty-seven. Their notable difference is
size. Ray, the younger, stands just five feet tall,
while Sam measures six feet four inches. Ray would
weigh 140 pounds dripping wet, and Sam stopped
keeping track when he reached 250.

"Ray, do you have any objections to working
with a black lady?" I knew better than to say
African American.

He squinted up at me, moving his cud of chewing
tobacco from one cheek to the other, then spit a
brown stream of tobacco juice into the Suwannee
River.

"She got a good ass on 'er?" The question was asked in a polite voice, not a leer in sight. Ray was known throughout the county for his colorful descriptions and eloquent essays on local derrieres. I'd give anything to be a bird in a tree and overhear his description of mine. Maybe not.

"To die for, and I mean both descriptively and literally. Admire from afar. Touch her and you're dead meat."

"Don't you fret none, Jo Beth. Imogene would wipe up the floor with me if I messed around any." Imogene's his wife, who appears to be over six feet tall and weighs in the neighborhood of three hundred pounds. She's a giant version of a cuddly doll. Sweet and gentle, I doubt if she's ever raised her voice at him.

Melanie and Ashley were staring at the water and whining with excitement. Hank gave me his hand for balance, and I stepped the two feet down into the boat and gave the command for them to load. Next time I'll be seated. I was standing and then almost toppled overboard by their enthusiastic leaps. Sam grabbed me. I plopped down hard on the metal seat but managed to remain dry and retain most of my dignity. I ignored Hank's laughter.

"Jasmine will be here shortly, and Leroy's on his way. Can you bring him? I want to get going."

"I'll take care of Jasmine and Leroy. Good luck."

My good-bye was lost when Sam gunned the boat and swung south into the main channel. I waved at Hank's receding image.

The dogs are seasoned boaters and good

mantrailers, but they've had other training I was trying not to think about. They are the two best body-recovery dogs currently in the kennel. They sat with their noses pointed into the wind generated by our speed. Their ears were blown backward, and their eyes were slitted so they wouldn't lose moisture.

The river was rising every day, but it wouldn't crest for another week or so. That's why Sam and Ray hadn't gone fishing today; the water was too high for good results. Not venturing from my tiny kingdom too often, I was unaware of just how much water had drained into the river from the previous rains.

Sam shut off the outboard. The deceleration left a sudden silence that was eerie. We were still moving through the water, but I could hear a crow cawing from a pine across the river. I turned on my narrow seat to see what Sam was doing. He pointed over my shoulder, upriver and to the left. I looked and saw a small fishing skiff moving lazily in a circle, caught in a small eddy near the shoreline. I couldn't make out if anyone was in it. Sam restarted the engine and moved very slowly toward it, not wanting to create a wake and rock the smaller boat. As we drew closer I could see a figure with blond hair. She was wearing jeans and a colorful shirt and was huddled in the rear of the boat.

It took several heartbeats before I recognized Glydia. I was used to seeing her starched and efficient-looking in her white uniform, performing nursing duties at the Dunston County Hospital.

"Glydia!" I called to her. "Are you all right?"

We were close enough that Sam and I could reach out and steady her boat as we glided alongside. She raised her head and stared at us. Her face was blotched with red creases, her eyes swollen from crying. She finally stopped the soft keening noise that Sam and I had heard from several yards away.

She opened her mouth to speak and hiccuped. Usually when someone hiccups loudly, people laugh. Today, Sam and I didn't laugh.

"I ran out of (hic) gas," she explained. "I was in a hurry and I didn't check the tank. Would you please give me (hic) a tow to the sandbank? It's only a mile or so upriver."

Glydia is a solidly built woman, heavy and about the same size from her shoulders to her knees. She's about my height and carries the extra weight well. She must've been cramped in the position she was in when we found her. Her hiccups were coming from involuntary contractions deep in her diaphragm as air entered her lungs. I wasn't worried about the hiccups, but her voice was devoid of emotion and her eyes didn't look right. She didn't seem to recognize us. She had to be in shock.

# 5

## Looking for the Yellow Brick Road
### *April 13, Saturday, 6:45 P.M.*

I reached over and touched Glydia's arm. Her skin felt cool and clammy. I held on to her and glanced at Sam.

"Let's move her to this boat. She's in shock. We have to take her back to the landing."

We moved her over and settled her beside me. She was docile and didn't question the transfer.

"You want to tie up the boat or tow it back?" Sam was holding Glydia's boat rope.

"Which is quicker?" I unzipped a side pocket of my rescue suit and pulled out the walkie-talkie.

"Tying it up," he answered.

"Do it," I said, keying the mike.

"Rescue One to Base. Do you read me?" I waited impatiently. I knew we'd just lost any chance of daylight for searching. By the time we took Glydia back to the landing and made it upriver to the sandbank, it would be first dark, too late for good visual observations. The dogs' noses don't need daylight, but human handlers do.

"Base to Rescue One, I read you five by five. Over."

"Hank, get an ambulance rolling. We found Glydia. She was in her boat, out of gas, about a mile upriver. She's in shock. We're returning to the landing."

"I have the message. Returning to the landing. Ambulance needed. Ray left with Jasmine and Leroy ten minutes ago. Over and out."

"Out."

My breath quickened. We should meet them soon. They could take Glydia back, and maybe I could still salvage some daylight. Sam shot down that theory with his next sentence.

"We're overloaded. Won't be able to make any speed."

Shit. I hadn't noticed. I glanced down and saw we didn't have enough freeboard to spit on. I mentally totaled up the weight. We had almost eight hundred pounds of dogs and humans, not counting the gear. The wind had freshened with the disappearing sun. We don't have whitecaps on the usually placid water, but I could see little laps forming here and there where the sun still shone through the trees.

We chugged along at a snail's pace; the slow-moving current wasn't much help. I juggled people, dogs, and boats in my mind as I pawed through my pack and pulled out a thin piece of thermal material used as an emergency blanket. I unfolded it and wrapped it around Glydia's shoulders and tucked the excess under her body. She was docile now, but her condition could worsen. Maybe I should send Jasmine back in Ray's boat to help her. First, she'd have to off-load her dogs and Leroy onto the river-bank. They could wait for Hank to grab a boat and pick them up. It then occurred to me that Ray's boat was now almost as overloaded as ours.

When we met up with Ray, I'd already decided who went where. We placed Glydia on a cushion in the bottom of Sam's boat between his knees where he assured me he could handle her. I transferred to Ray's boat after he'd motored over to the riverbank and off-loaded Jasmine and her dogs, Ulysses and Gulliver, and Leroy.

Sam took Glydia back to the landing, leaving Ray, Melanie, Ashley, and me to roar upstream. Ray and I waved to Jasmine and Leroy, still on the bank. Hank would have to handle the logistics of getting everyone upriver.

Ray was pouring on the speed. The bow of the boat was rising, and the dogs were enjoying the rush of wind. Lord, it was good to see Leroy again! I'd sorely missed his solid comforting presence this past year. He has a homely face, flaming red hair, freckles, and is six feet plus and 220 pounds of muscle. We'd been inseparable in school. My brain got us into a lot of foolish adventures, and his mus-cle got us out of them. Jackie, his wife, knew there was nothing sexual about our relationship. I'd vis-ited their home often and was godmother to the middle child, Jo Anne, who has half my name. Jackie resented our closeness but had grudgingly allowed me to be part of their lives. Last year, though, she'd yielded to peer pressure from the gossipy wives in their circle of friends and had banned me from visiting their home and asking Leroy for help in searches. I hadn't appealed her decision, knowing how much Leroy loved her. For a year I hadn't had any contact with him. But few people know the swamp as well as he, and I needed him badly on this search. It was a five-year-old child, for God's sake. She should understand, but I didn't want to cause him grief.

A crowd of perhaps twenty people watched us pull up and unload. I asked for Josh and was informed that he was guarding the path to the alleged abductor's tent and wouldn't budge. I let the dogs find their preferred spot to pee. The onlookers watched the dogs perform this perfectly normal function with intense interest. It wouldn't have surprised me to see some of them whip out their cameras to record the event. Some people are dedicated recorders for posterity.

I stepped into my rescue suit and strapped on my gun holster. Even with the perfect 70-degree temperature, I knew I'd immediately start sweating. The suit is waterproof and made from a lightweight version of Kevlar. It's almost, but not quite, bulletproof. I wear it and suffer the stifling heat in summer because a snake's strike can't penetrate the material. Ray knelt and attached my shoe covers. He held my backpack as I slipped on the shoulder straps and buckled the belt at the waistline. He ejected a shell from the .22 rifle, picked it up, brushed off the sand, and reloaded. I carry it in a scabbard sewn onto my backpack. The .22 is for snakes. The snub-nose .32 is for snakes-in-the-grass.

I asked Ray to stay by the boat so he could direct the others to me when they arrived. After asking the bystanders which direction I should go to meet up with Josh, I turned and walked fifteen yards before I stopped and confronted the twenty or so souls who were keeping up with my progress.

"Folks," I said, raising my voice so the stragglers could easily hear, "you can't follow along with me. You'll obliterate any scent trail the dogs might find. Please stay back near the boat area. I appreciate your cooperation."

I traveled a few more yards before I turned and confronted the four males still on my heels. They were either stone deaf or had decided to ignore my request and tag along.

"Gentlemen, I sincerely trust you have not decided to defy my request, because that will lead to some unpleasantness."

"Say, girlie," a thirty-something smartass drawled, "just who do you think you are, bossing us around like hired hands? If we want to take a walk behind you, there's no law says we can't. Just what would this here unpleasantness be?"

He had a sneering look that was duplicated on the other three faces.

"Well, for starters, I could make a citizen's arrest

and handcuff you to a pine tree until the sheriff arrives," I said cheerfully. I raised my right hand and slowly scratched my left breast directly over the grip of the .32.

This brought snickers and laughter, and one slapped his knee. I was pissed by their attitude. We were wasting the last few minutes of precious daylight.

"Listen, you idiots, I'm trying to find a sick five-year-old child! Hasn't that penetrated your thick redneck skulls? Now, back off! You're impeding an official search-and-rescue." Uh-oh. Bad choice of words, Jo Beth. You let them get to you.

The laughter and sneers turned to mean mouths and narrow eyes. I sighed. Nothing seemed to go right today. I took one step back, planted my feet slightly apart, and took a deep breath.

"Come on, guys, be reasonable," I said in a calm voice.

The speaker leaned over and reached for his boot. Now, he could have a mosquito bite that needed scratching, but I've always been a pessimist. The inside of a boot, inside a thin sheath, is the favored place to stash a pigsticker.

I pulled the .32, held it with both hands, arms locked and extended, and began yelling. "Down on your bellies! Do it now! Hands behind your heads! So help me God, I'll shoot some kneecaps if you don't do it now!"

I took another step backward. If all four decided to rush me, I couldn't get more than one leg, possibly two; then the others would have a ball. A .32

won't stop a charging male in his tracks and could possibly make him more dangerous. I've been beaten and cut within an inch of death. I didn't want to kill these fools, but I also was not going down under their fists if I could possibly prevent it.

Their frozen expressions turned to disgust as they slowly followed my orders. I'd started congratulating myself mentally on my effectiveness when I heard a soft voice behind me.

"Don't shoot me, Jo Beth. I'm on the path behind you. Do you need any help?"

I shuddered with relief. I recognized the deep bass voice. It was Josh.

"I sure do," I answered in a shaky voice. "I was wondering how I was going to get these suckers tethered to a pine tree. Help me take off my backpack."

I felt his arms come around my waistline from behind and unbuckle my belt. When he lifted the backpack, taking the strain from my shoulders, I slipped each arm out, switching the gun from one hand to the other. Not taking my eyes off the lumps on the ground, I told him about the restraints in my backpack.

"They're in a green canvas pouch, the newest weapon in fighting crime," I babbled. "They're made of Velcro. Don't need a key. Lighter than handcuffs and just as effective."

One by one, on my command, the men crawled to a pine tree and put their arms around it. Josh fastened the new restraints. This was the first time I'd had an opportunity to use them. Jonathan gave them to me on my last trip upstate to visit him.

"Is there anyone you know in the crowd over by the boats you can trust to keep an eye on my prisoners?" I asked Josh, as I rubbed my arms to ease the tension. I could feel the adrenaline fading from my system.

"Yeah, Grover Dixon and Stace Conner are down there. Be right back."

I lit a cigarette and drew in the much-needed nicotine. With the present breeze the smoke wouldn't be a problem for the dogs. Both had stood quietly when I dropped their leads, moving back with me as I'd twice retreated. A lot of people think because bloodhounds are used by law enforcement, and cover more ground than other hounds, they're trained to guard and attack. Not true. They are gentle animals.

I once heard a teenager tell his date to keep back; bloodhounds were vicious animals and would eat her alive. I smiled when I heard a man inform his wife that bloodhounds were trained to attack. These two prized specimens I had with me would've shivered and whined and backed away if all four prisoners had jumped me and beaten me to death. They are trained to use their noses, not their large jaws.

When Josh returned with Grover and Stace, I asked them to watch the guys and keep their friends from releasing them. I recognized two of them, but the other two must've been from out of town. I told Grover and Stace to turn them over to Hank when he arrived.

Josh and I went up the trail to his campsite. When we were out of earshot, I stopped walking and turned to him.

"Josh, we found Glydia drifting about a mile back. She ran out of gas. She didn't look like she could take much more. I had Sam take her back to the landing. I don't want you to worry. She'll be taken care of. I'm sure she'll be all right after a little rest." I was fudging a bit on the details, not wanting to give him another burden to worry about.

"You mean to tell me she did as you asked and went back without a knock-down-drag-out fight?" he asked in amazement. "I tried to get her to sit and rest and let someone else go call you. What you're saying doesn't sound like Glydia!"

I saw I couldn't shield him. It was his right to know.

"Sorry, Josh, I didn't want to add to your worries. I'm not a nurse, but she looked shocky. I had Hank call an ambulance."

"Thanks for your concern, Jo Beth, but next time level with me. It'll make it easier on both of us."

"I will," I promised. "Now let's go find Peter."

When we arrived at their campsite, I told him I needed two objects that Peter had worn or handled. He went into the tent and returned with a toy and a soiled T-shirt.

"He plays with this a lot. He sleeps with it. It's like a security blanket to him." Josh's voice was husky with emotion.

It was a very battered G.I. Joe doll with a missing arm. I held out a Ziploc bag and he dropped it inside. I sealed it and placed it in my pocket and did the same with the shirt.

"Point out the man's tent and the road the

teenager thinks the truck carrying him used," I told him. He pointed out the tent and the road that ran near it.

"He was heading east?" I asked.

"That's right."

"Give this to Jasmine when she arrives. She knows what to do." I handed him one of the inhalers and Peter's shirt.

"Is she that colored gal we've been hearing about?" His voice was sharp. "The one who used to . . . the whore?"

"Don't start, Josh. I know you're upset, but Jasmine is an excellent mantrailer and could easily be the one who finds your son. Her dogs are just as smart and well-trained as mine. Keep that in mind when you meet her—and act accordingly."

"Sorry," he said stiffly. "I don't care if she's green-striped and . . . and believes in ghosts," he finished lamely.

I gave him a warm smile. "That's the ticket."

I presented my back to him. "Dig my headlight and flashlight out of my backpack so I don't have to take it off again."

It was now almost first dark. We were both unconsciously waving our hands over our faces to keep most of the hovering mosquitoes from landing and feasting. All I had to worry about was my face. Josh was routinely brushing his arms.

"You want your can of Off!, don't you?"

"No way, that's for the trip back. The odor would deaden the dogs' ability to smell just as fast as chloroform."

He handed me the flashlight and I stashed it in a pocket. I put the six-volt battery for the headlamp in a pocket and straightened the wire running up to the headband that held the lamp. I clicked it on, but it was the time of day when lights don't help. Not quite dark enough yet. I switched it off.

"When did you get here?" I asked.

"About ten A.M."

"I imagine Peter ran all over the campsite with the other kids."

"Before lunch, but not after. He took a nap and seemed tired. He took a picture book over to that fallen tree and sat there reading. Glydia and I took a short nap." He seemed embarrassed that they'd slept while his son was being abducted. "When we woke up, Glydia walked down to the river and asked Little Josh and Anna Lee where Peter was. They thought he was taking a nap with us and hadn't been watching him. It's my fault he's missing."

"Nonsense," I said briskly. "Stop beating up on yourself. It was simply a misunderstanding and could happen to anyone. Did you ever see the man?"

"No. I was busy starting the grill for the hot dogs and burgers for lunch. Then I set up the tent. I didn't walk around much and talk to people."

"Right. Still, guard the path to that tent. Don't allow any more traffic over there. I'm off."

I pulled the dogs to me and fished out several pieces of deer jerky, divided the treat, and fed it to them. I took out the toy and put it under one nose and then the other while I told them to seek.

"Seek, Melanie! Seek, Ashley!" I repeated the litany several times. They lowered their noses and went to work. I expected to be led around in circles in all the places where the kids had run and played. They led me down to the water, past my prisoners—who yelled "Abuse!" and spit in our general direction, but missed. The dogs ignored them. They were working and had only one thought in mind: They wanted to find the particular human who smelled like the doll. Once they lock onto a scent, it takes a great deal to distract them. They stopped momentarily, sniffing little Josh and Anna Lee's clothing and arms, smelling for the human they were seeking. The children were entranced, while the two women who were taking care of them kept wanting to pull them away. I explained the dogs were harmless, but it made little difference.

The dogs quickly moved on when they saw the scent trail continued, and we made some more circles and backtracked more than a dozen times. The dogs' eyes looked like rubies in the glow from the bonfires that were lit when darkness descended. I kept losing my night vision because of being pulled by the dogs toward the fire's light and then abruptly plunging into the heavy dark shadows. Soon we were back at the tent where Josh was standing guard in the path. They went into the tent several times during our journey, and now they turned up the path toward the stranger's tent. My pulse quickened. They moved into the heavy brush several feet from the path.

"What are they doing over there?" Josh called,

sounding anxious. "Peter wouldn't enter that thick growth. He's allergic to poison oak and water oak. He wouldn't get near it!"

"There's a breeze blowing. The dogs follow the smell, not footprints," I yelled. "The breeze blew the scent into the bushes, so that's where they search."

Josh didn't answer. I think he was doubting the dogs' ability with each passing minute. They couldn't be told which scent to follow; they had to make the same journey Peter made. I always tell people who aren't familiar with bloodhounds that their ability to smell is twenty times more powerful than that of a human. This is a reasonable figure. People hear this and are impressed. The real truth sounds way out in left field. A bloodhound's ability to smell actually rates hundreds of thousands of times better than a human's. This is difficult for anyone to comprehend, much less believe, but it is the truth. Some experts even venture to say it's more than a million times greater. These figures cause me to wonder just what machine they use to arrive at that conclusion.

The dogs arrived at the stranger's tent, went inside, sniffed the canvas floor, and came back out again. I held my breath when they went through the brush a ways, then moved back onto the road. This time they went left, not right, which would have led back to Josh. They were breaking new ground for the first time.

I expected them to lose the scent fairly quickly once Peter was in the pickup. It would be almost impossible for them to follow the scent down the road with Peter up in the cab. They started whining and milling around, only once or twice raising their noses to the breeze. Just as I was ready to call them off and give all three of us a rest, they lifted their noses and started down the road. They were weaving left into the brush at times, which I figured was where the wind had blown the scent. My heart was beating from the exertion and the fact that they were mantrailing a small boy who'd been abducted and was inside a truck when the trail was more than five hours old. Three hours is stretching the optimum search time, and each additional hour lowers your expectations. I'm talking general ground rules here. Sure, a lot of dogs have found their target twenty, even a hundred and twenty hours later, but these are exceptions. Some would even call them miracles.

One superhero larger-than-life bloodhound named Nick Carter, a legend of all time in the early 1900s, holds an unbroken record. On a trail more than 128 hours old, he followed a horse and wagon for over 250 miles and led the posse up to the stolen wagon and the murderer's front door. When confronted with the bloodhound and told the dog had tracked him every inch of the way, the shaken man confessed to killing the owner of the horse and wagon and his wife.

The dogs continued mantrailing and I followed, full of hope. But after five hours, I felt, with a heavy heart, that Peter had already been sexually molested and abused. I just prayed he was still alive. Without an inhaler, terrified, he could still die from a severe asthma attack. If the molestation hadn't killed him, and the monster didn't think he could be identified, he just might leave Peter alive. I had to find him.

The road curved to the left and then to the left again. I didn't stop to look at my compass, but I sensed we were turning back toward the direction of the campsite. My headlamp was adjusted to shine on the area directly in front of the dogs, and I held my head in the position that would give them the most light. I raised the flashlight and moved my eyes upward to see if I could see anything. I caught the light's reflection off the water and realized the road curved back toward the Suwannee. I stopped and stared. The dogs pulled me forward. They were leading me to a pickup hidden behind thick brush.

I held both leads with my left hand, removed my right glove with my teeth, drew the .32, and eased off the safety catch. The driver was probably long gone. I shined my headlamp into the back of the truck. My flashlight was in my pocket. I couldn't handle it while holding the dogs' leads and the gun.

Nothing was in the bed of the truck but a small ragged tarp and a five-gallon gas can. I walked forward, straining to hear. Nothing. I ducked my head and took a quick glance into the cab and quickly pulled back. I let the glove drop from my teeth, took a quick breath, holstered my gun, tugged the door open, and jumped back. Nothing moved. Any lawman would've laughed himself sick at my antics, but sometimes you get away with doing everything wrong. I shined the flashlight into the cab. Both dogs were in my way and trying to jump inside. I

pulled them back and closed the door. The cab was
empty.

The dogs pulled me around to the other door,
then toward the back of the truck. I shined my light
on the plates. Kentucky. Probably stolen. Not my
worry. This time of year was early for tourists. Most
came after school was out in June. A single man,
camping alone, should stand out like a sore thumb.
Local campers are friendly, and someone should be
able to give a good description when everyone was
questioned.

The dogs raised and lowered their heads and
started pulling me toward the river. I let them lead
me to the edge. From where I stood it was a three-
foot drop to the water. It would be difficult to tie up
a boat here but not impossible. There were only two
explanations. Either the man had a boat waiting
here, or this was where he had disposed of Peter's
body.

# 6

## Way Down Upon the Suwannee River
*April 13, Saturday, 8:30 P.M.*

When I arrived back at the sandbank, everyone whom I was expecting had arrived. I ran up to a beaming Leroy and hugged him.

"You look great, you big lug!"

"You do too, honey. How are you doing?"

"Hanging in there. You won't get into trouble for this, will you?"

"Nah. Everything's fine." Leroy always was a rotten liar. I felt terrible. What if I didn't need him and had caused a rift in his marriage for nothing?

He helped me remove my pack and held the dogs while I struggled out of my rescue suit. My clothes were soaked in sweat, and the breeze felt marvelous on my skin. I pulled on a long-sleeved sweatshirt for the mosquitoes now and the river later.

"Will you take the dogs down to the water for a drink while I smoke a cigarette?"

"Sure. Who are these two?" he asked.

I rubbed Melanie's head and gave her a bite of jerky. "This is Melanie and this one's Ashley," I said, giving Ashley his portion and watching it disappear with a single gulp.

"*Gone With the Wind* Melanie and Ashley?" he guessed, grinning.

"Natch. Let them wade if they want to cool off. Give me ten minutes."

He led them off, asking them how Scarlett and Rhett were making out. Our mantrailers are named after novel characters, famous heroes, and mythical gods and goddesses. Fire dogs are named after famous or infamous pairs of lovers. These are working handles, not the names registered with the AKC.

Jasmine and Hank were standing near the boats. I lit a cigarette and joined them.

"Have you heard how Glydia's doing?" I asked Hank.

"She's okay. It was shock. She's also being treated for high blood pressure. They said rest and fluids would set her straight. Find anything?"

I nodded and included Jasmine in my rundown.

"I found an abandoned truck that fit the description given by the teenager. It has Kentucky plates. The dogs led me to the water, where they lost the scent. Either he had a boat or dumped the body there." I looked at both of them and shrugged.

"Did you work both dogs?" Jasmine asked with a frown.

"I know, I know," I answered, "but they both

work better together as a team, and you know how good they are at their second career. I'll discuss it with Josh."

Hank was dividing a scowl between us.

"What are you two talking about? What's going on?"

"Nothing," I answered quickly, warning Jasmine with my eyes. "We were just discussing whether to use them one on one or as a brace."

"And this is what you're going to discuss with Josh?" He sounded like he didn't believe a word I was saying. He sure knows when I'm stretching the truth.

"Hank," I said reasonably, "you know how we try to make the victim's family feel involved. We try to let them know what we're doing and the reason we're doing it that particular way."

"Sure," Hank retorted. "Did you take the keys out of the truck, in case the perp returns?"

I shrugged and gave him an embarrassed signal that he'd caught me in a boo-boo. I thought it highly unlikely the perp would return, but truthfully, it hadn't even occurred to me to remove the keys. He was right. I'd pulled a boner.

"I'll send one of my men. Tell me how to get there." He acted smug. I felt like kicking him in the shins. I hate it when my sins of omission are pointed out to me. I gave him directions.

"What's the charge on those yo-yos you put under citizen's arrest?" he asked with a smile.

"You can turn them loose. They were obnoxious and tried to follow me. I'm not sure, but I think one

was going for a knife in his boot. I didn't wait to
make sure. I hate knives."

"Which one?"

"The one in the light-blue sleeveless shirt."

"I'll check out his boot. If there's a knife in there,
they're all going in. Will you testify?"

"Sure."

"I'll see you later," he said and left.

"He's gonna skin you alive if things go wrong,"
Jasmine warned.

"I'll worry about that later." I just wish I'd called
my friend and attorney Wade Bennett, the minute
I'd read that magazine article on admissible evidence using one or two bloodhounds. "I'll tell Josh.
He has a right to know. I'm going to talk to him
now. You ride with Sam. With Leroy in the boat
with me, it'll be a better weight distribution. Those
bass boats are low in the water when they're overloaded."

"I noticed that coming out," she remarked in a
wry tone, "and I was with Ray."

"Uh-oh. Maybe I should leave Leroy here while
we work the river. Ray can return for him if the trail
goes back on shore. Where's Fray? Usually he's
hollering at me by now."

"He was taking a statement from Mr. Powell over
by that truck a few minutes ago," Jasmine said,
pointing to a lone truck sitting back from the sandbank on a narrow two-path road. Most locals used
their boats for this side of the Suwannee. The roads
run through timber tracts and are often washed out.
The truck I was approaching was splattered with

dried mud, just like the truck with the Kentucky plates. Some locals do a lot of "mudding." They want to prove they can drive their trucks through anything. I wondered if the abductor had asked directions for camping out and had been given bad advice out of mischief, or if he was a local and familiar with this area. After seeing the Kentucky plates, I hadn't thought to wonder how he found his way into this place.

John Fray, Georgia Bureau of Investigation agent, had his briefcase open on the hood of the truck, shining a flashlight on his papers. He's very big on paperwork. I don't think I've ever seen him without a pen in his hand. He was wearing a navy jumpsuit, with GBI in bright yellow letters a foot high on the back. He had the matching cap with the bill turned to the back, as if he were a member of a SWAT team. I suppressed a grin. We always fight. This time it wasn't going to be my fault. I'd be on my best behavior.

Both men turned at my approach.

"Hi, Josh, Fray. Can I borrow Josh a second?"

"The search is called off, Sidden. It's nonproductive at night. We'll reorganize at daybreak. I'm not finished with Mr. Powell. You can talk to him later."

Josh stared at Fray. "Come on, Jo Beth," he said, showing his anger with a scowl and stalking away. I hurried a few steps to catch up with him.

"What did you find out?" Josh asked with impatience when we were out of earshot of Fray. We were walking toward his camping area.

"I found the abandoned truck, and the dogs lost

the scent. I came back to get Jasmine and her dogs and Leroy. We'll go back by boat and try to pick up the trail again with her dogs. Going by boat will save time. I need to discuss something with you. Did you know that if my bloodhounds find a felon, their testimony is accepted as evidence in a court of law?"

"No, I didn't. How do they testify?" he asked, showing me a small smile he dredged up from somewhere.

"Basically, if a bloodhound tracks a person and links him to a crime, even if there are no eyewitnesses, the fact that the bloodhound found evidence, and pointed it out with his nose, makes the dog an expert. However, there are certain requirements. The bloodhound has to be purebred. AKC registration is good proof. The dog must trail from the scene of the crime. It must be experienced and have records to prove it. All my bloodhounds meet every requirement.

"Just a few days ago I read an article on bloodhounds in a magazine stating that some states have added another requirement. The mantrailing must be one-on-one, meaning one bloodhound for each handler. I've used a brace of bloodhounds, meaning two, for a lot of my searches for over two years now. I confess, I haven't gotten around to checking if Georgia has this new law. For that, I apologize. I have two bloodhounds that work together better as a team. They are the best in my kennel in what they do, and I wanted Peter to have the best. I want you to know this, because if my brace of bloodhounds finds Peter and/or this guy, their testimony might be thrown out in a trial. If the law can't find any other convincing evidence without using the search, he could walk, even though we know he's guilty. You decide. Do I continue with two dogs, or do you want me to work with just one?"

"Use a dozen if necessary. Just find Peter. We'll worry about convicting the son of a bitch later." He spoke emphatically, biting off every word.

I had very carefully not discussed their expertise in finding dead bodies underwater, as much as ninety feet deep. The Suwannee is shallow. If Peter was anywhere in the river, my two could find him.

"Good, I said, patting his arm. "I'm gonna take off now. You should take little Josh and Anna Lee home. Put them to bed, and get some sleep yourself."

"The kids can sleep here. I'm not leaving until we get Peter back. Are you going to work on tonight?"

"Of course. John Fray has no control over me. I don't suffer fools and assholes gladly, and he's both."

"Bring Peter back, Jo Beth."

"I'll do my damnedest," I vowed.

After I gave Jasmine the T-shirt that Peter had worn, we loaded the boats. Jasmine would ride with Sam, and I'd be with Ray. Leroy agreed to stay. If we picked up a scent on shore, I promised to send Ray back for him.

I saw Fray and Hank walking down to the boats. Fray gestured with his hands while conversing with Hank. I waited until they stopped in front of me.

"Hi, sheriff, something I can do for you?" I ignored Fray, but he butted in before Hank had a chance to speak.

"Your nighttime expedition has just been canceled," he said, being his usual pompous self. "If you continue without authorization, I'll place you under arrest."

"Lordy me! Whatever for?" I said, using my best peach-dripping accent.

"For impeding an official investigation," he said stiffly. "Also, as of now you're taken off the case. I've instructed Sheriff Cribbs not to pay you for this search."

"I wasn't called out by the Dunston County Sheriff's Department," I told him in a civil tone. "My clients are Glydia and Josh Powell; therefore it's immaterial just what asinine instructions you gave the sheriff. If I choose to ride up and down the Suwannee River all night and tramp through the brush with my dogs, that's my God-given right. Anything else?"

"You're forgetting one thing," he countered, sounding victorious, "you're in a state fish and wildlife preserve. My word is law."

"Wrong again, Mr. GBI," I said, giving him the horse laugh. "We are ten miles from any preserve's border, state or federal."

Fray jerked his head toward Hank.

"She's right," he agreed.

Fray glared at me and spun on his heel, picking his feet up and putting them down, up the sandbar and out of sight.

"Thanks, buddy," I said to Hank, gleeful over Fray's rout.

"He's obnoxious, which is the reason I agreed with your lie," Hank replied, his eyes flinty. "You know damn well where we're standing is more than two miles inside Okefenokee National Wildlife Refuge and Wilderness Area. I can empathize with Fray. I too have felt the urge to bust you across your chops. He just left before temptation overrode his common sense."

"Now just a minute here, Hank," said Leroy. I grabbed his arm and anchored it against my body, holding on for dear life.

"Hank's right, Leroy. I deserved his comment. I'm more bitch than sweetheart at times. This was one of them. Back off."

I held on until I felt Leroy's muscles lose their tenseness. When I looked up, I realized Hank had gone.

Before we left, I took the sandwiches out of my pack and gave Leroy three, with ketchup.

"You never forget," Leroy said with a grin. "Do you still eat horseradish on yours?"

"Yep, it clears the sinuses."

I gave Jasmine, Ray, and Sam two each. That left three. Two for me and one to share with Melanie and Ashley. I can never resist their imploring looks. The minute they smelled the meat they scooted back closer where they could lean on my legs. Jasmine is made of stronger stuff. She won't feed hers junk food. The dogs learn very quickly whom they can or cannot con, and I'm at the top of their sucker list.

Both boats were now headed to the place where
the dogs had followed Peter's scent to the water's
edge. I had taken the dirty white tarp from the
pickup and staked it to the bank. It would be easy to
spot.

Ray had hooked up a Q-Beam to the battery and
attached it to the bow of the boat. Sam followed us,
guided by our light. His light would have robbed us
of our night vision by shining directly behind. I'd
just finished my first sandwich when we arrived at
the marker. Sam turned his boat around and idled
beside us while he attached his light. I went over the
plan again with Jasmine.

"We'll go downriver, staying near the bank, to
Johnston's Landing, cross over, and come back
upriver to the sandbank. You and Sam go upriver
approximately two miles, cross, and come downriver and meet us. Go very slowly so the dogs will
have a chance to catch the scent. Any questions?"

Jasmine shook her head. "Take care."

"You too."

Sam and Ray pulled away slowly, and we
chugged along in opposite directions. I pulled the
tab on a Diet Coke and ate my second sandwich. I
would have loved a cigarette, but we were going too
slow for the wind to keep it away from the dogs. I
was sitting in the middle seat, Ray was in the rear
near the motor, and the dogs were in front of me. I
had to watch them closely. They kept changing
sides. When they were both on the same side, I had
to slide over to the opposite side to keep the boat
from tipping. Each dog weighs close to a hundred

and twenty pounds. About every ten minutes I reinforced their scent smell by letting them sniff the
doll.

The gentle back and forth sway of the boat had a
somnolent effect. I found myself yawning. I kept
blinking and widening my eyes, which yearned to
close. I came fully awake in a heartbeat when both
dogs stiffened instantaneously, emitted excited
whinings, and looked ready to jump over the side
into the ebony water below.

"Stop," I said quietly to Ray. "Turn around and
slowly creep back. Stay as close to the shoreline as
possible. I want to see which side of the boat they
choose."

Ray made a circle and, barely moving through
the water, pulled close to the bank. I turned on my
flashlight and aimed it up in the trees. A lot of them
had overhanging branches, and I had no desire for a
snake to drop into the boat or on me without a light.
If one did drop in, I didn't know about Ray, but I
was sure his passengers would bail out quickly.

Both dogs started going from side to side, straining to return to the scent they'd lost. When we were
about twenty-five yards from the spot where they'd
first shown animation, they both stuck their heads
over the left side of the boat, on the shore side, and
sniffed close to the water. Then they raised their
noses and sniffed at the air currents. My heart
started singing softly: It's the shore, it's the shore!

After several yards, both dogs started their
excited wiggling and whining routine. I pulled both
of them back close to me.

"Can you pull the boat in close to that small scoop of dirt?" I asked Ray.

His answer was a laconic "Yep." He probably saved his eloquence for describing female posteriors.

Erosion over the years had filled the tiny cove with sand, and the water lapped gently on a level with the shoreline. The whole strip wasn't much longer than our twelve-foot boat. Ray coasted alongside with the motor off and moved forward and tossed the anchor up on the soft sand. When he tugged on it, it held, and he drew in line and wrapped it around a cleat. The back anchor snagged a cypress knee, which was just as effective as the sand. He drew in the rope and parallel parked. We were snug against the sand, and I stepped out of the boat without getting my feet wet. I turned to compliment Ray, and was unprepared for the dogs' revolt. They sailed over the side without an invitation to unload and charged up the sandbank as if the hounds of hell were right behind them. I tried to dig in my heels. I was yelling commands like crazy, but they almost pulled my shoulder blades apart before I could gain control.

Their comprehension of the English language is very limited. They know commands. Endearments are conveyed by the tone of my voice, not by what each word means. They are well aware, however, of what "bad, bad dog" means, along with "tsk tsk." Before I could scold them, my annoyance vanished, and I felt only elation. Both of them lifted their noble heads in unison, let forth their

wonderful joyous bays, and sang their song to cele-
brate success.

I let them pull me forward. Bloodhound mantrailers run mute and don't bay until they're certain they
are close to their target. I knew now that Peter was
close by. I should have restrained them until Ray
went back for Leroy, who's familiar with every
aspect of this primeval swamp. He knows firm
ground from dangerous bogs, quicksand, and
islands that only float on root structure, where you
feel like you're walking on a waterbed, to large
prairies of waving frondlike growth that resemble
fields of wheat. I've lived here all my life and
worked this swamp extensively for six years, first
training in its depths, then combing it for almost
three years in search-and-rescue. My total knowledge could be written on one fingernail compared to
Leroy's boundless wisdom.

I didn't do what I should have done. The search
was in my blood, and I was on a high equal to
Melanie and Ashley's. I was in my joggers—without
snake covers—and a long-sleeved sweatshirt. My
costly fang-proof rescue suit was in the boat, where
it couldn't help me a bit. I should be committed for
acting so unprofessionally.

I let them pull me through knee-high foliage with
only the undefined glow from my headlamp to show
the way. I hadn't even picked up the flashlight. I
turned my head back and forth, looking for dangers,
hoping not to see something that would prove I'd
acted rashly. The dogs veered right and stopped,
still baying their mournful-sounding victory. After

transferring their leads to my left hand, I raised my right hand up under my sweatshirt and worked my gun free of its holster. The dogs were on their long leads and were nosing at a pile of foliage about six feet in front of me. I whipped my head around to shine the light in a circle. Nothing. We were in planted pines that appeared to be five to seven years old.

I reached around the closest pine and tied the two leads around it, using a slipknot. I might want to leave in a hurry, and I wouldn't leave without my dogs. I took a few steps, drew in a deep breath, and mentally prepared myself for what I might find. I looked down at the pile with distaste. I didn't even have my gloves with me. It was newly severed pine boughs. The needles were bright green and would remain the same color for weeks. The temperature couldn't be lower than 65 degrees, but I felt goose pimples on my arms as I began to shiver. I reached down and tugged away a limb. It was about three feet long, and it was as full as a pine bough ever got. I felt a spot of sap; it was tacky on my hand. I removed two more limbs and saw a white sock and a small Nike shoe. I grabbed limbs with both hands and frantically tossed them aside. Peter was lying on his side in a fetal position, hands bound behind his back with gray duct tape. His legs were bound with the same tape. His back was toward me. I touched a shoulder and felt him flinch. I rolled him over and stared into the most terrified expression I had ever seen on a face: man, woman, or child.

"Peter, it's Jo Beth, the lady with the bloodhounds. Remember? It's all right, baby, you're safe. Look at me, Peter!"

After one fearful glance he had squeezed his eyes tightly shut. His breathing was becoming labored. The precious inhaler was in the pocket of my rescue suit in the damn boat. Dumb! Dumb! Dumb! I ran my hands over his small body, searching for bleeding or broken bones while I repeated to him that he was safe.

"Peter, you know how to breathe. Relax and take a calming breath. Concentrate on breathing. Relax and breathe. Relax."

I couldn't see any blood or find any joints that didn't feel right. His being able to breathe more easily became more important than taking the chance of moving him. I slipped the dogs' leads from the tree, put both loops over my left wrist, and scooped up Peter. I pounded back through the brush in a loping, disjointed run. He was as light as feathers. I knew I'd penetrated no more than a hundred yards, but it seemed to take forever. The dogs ran in front of me, keeping pace with my movement. Good dogs. They'd have to wait for their praise.

When I sensed we were nearing the boat, I started yelling, "Ray, I found Peter! Flashlight! Ray, I found Peter! Get the flashlight!"

We finally broke from the woods, and Ray was standing by the boat with the flashlight pointed at our pathway down the sand. He was jumping for joy.

"Lordy, you did it, Jo Beth! God damn! Praise God! God-oh-mighty!" Tears were running down his cheeks. Ray was mixing cuss words with his heavenly praise, but I was sure God would understand and forgive him.

Christ, my tears began to flow. I needed to be efficient and quick, not blubbery. I cry when I'm mad, glad, or sad, and also when other people cry.

"Shine the light on his face!" I yelled, laying Peter on the sand. I jerked off my headlamp and bent close to the duct tape on Peter's mouth. Ray hovered, holding the light steady. The bastard had wrapped the tape at least twice around Peter's head. It would be quicker to find the end and unwrap it than try to cut it off. It was wrapped tightly and had bonded together. I found the end and lifted Peter's head and started unwrapping the tape, bunching it into a wad to complete the circuit. Tears were leaking from Peter's clinched eyes. I thought it was a good sign. I hadn't seen his eyes open except for one brief moment, and that look would remain in my mind and come back to haunt me.

"Breathe, Peter. Control. That's good. Steady, now. I almost have it off."

I knew that removing the last round of tape was going to hurt, slow or fast, so I braced his head and quickly stripped it off his lips. I hugged him to me and grabbed Ray's flashlight and shined it on the boat.

"Bring my rescue suit and backpack, quick!"

Ray ran back and deposited both at my feet. I gave him the flashlight and dug in my suit pocket for the inhaler.

"Here's your inhaler, Peter."

When he didn't open his eyes, I pushed it against

his hand, and his tiny fingers clutched it and brought it to his mouth. He pushed one time, taking a deep breath. I continued to hold him. His breathing seemed to ease in seconds. Lord, bless the men who found and manufactured the medication that allows this child to breathe freely.

I held the light for Ray as he stripped off the tape around the boy's legs. I opened my pack and pulled out the first-aid kit with one hand. Ray opened it for me, after freeing Peter's legs. He found the tube of Vaseline, and I gently covered Peter's lips, face, and neck where the tape had blistered. I pulled out a plastic quart bottle of water from the pack and held it close to his lips.

"Thirsty? Here's some water." When he still didn't open his eyes, I removed the inhaler from his clenched fist and nudged his hand. He clutched the bottle with both hands, and I held him upright and watched him take several swallows.

"The man can't get you, Peter, you're safe. Will you open your eyes for me?"

He didn't answer or open his eyes.

"Please? You haven't seen my doggies. You like doggies?"

I saw his lips move, and I bent close to hear his thin reedy whisper.

"Man gonna get me. Coming back to get me."

"No, he won't, Peter. We're going to go to your daddy. Do you hurt anywhere, Peter?"

"Lip hurts," he whispered.

"Does your throat hurt?" I dreaded an affirmative answer.

"Nope."

His answer was what I wanted to hear. It meant he probably hadn't been abused, orally or otherwise. He was sitting on my thigh, and I hadn't seen him flinch or felt him fidget. He needed his father right now more than a physical.

"Load up!" I was speaking to Ray. The dogs, who had been lying quietly in the sand after drinking their fill at the edge of the river, thought I meant them. They arose, sailed into the boat, and took their places, facing forward like seasoned travelers.

Peter was shivering. I propped him between my legs, holding him with my knees, while I stripped off my sweatshirt and slipped it over his head, not bothering with the sleeves.

"How fast will this boat go?" I asked, settling on the seat and cuddling Peter in my lap.

"I'll leave dust," Ray bragged.

"Prove it."

# 7

## "Step into My Parlor," Said the Spider
### *April 13, Saturday, 10 P.M.*

On our earlier slow trip chugging downriver, I'd pondered the evidence available on the abductor's getaway. The Kentucky tag was wrong for the convoluted road. This, to me, signaled local or previously local. The teenager couldn't describe the man he'd seen loading Peter into the pickup, he was too far away.

A local could have camped there, seen Peter, and made his move when no one was around. If he was as brave as he was bold, he could have driven Peter to where the truck was parked, then strolled back to the sandbank even before Peter was discovered missing.

After we'd followed the scent trail by water, I knew the man had a boat stashed. He could have had one he'd brought in earlier with the truck, or he could have had it in the back of the truck. This wouldn't be feasible for a stranger to the area. Where was it now? He could have sunk it, made his getaway in it, or, if he was a local, it could be tied up somewhere. He could have risked leaving the sandbank, picked up Peter, and hauled him for less than a mile, hiding him under a tarp while the search was on. I shook my head. Guesses.

Having knowledge of the area, he could have taken a shortcut and carried Peter to where the dogs found him. He planned to come back. Unless he was a mental case, he wouldn't kidnap a child and leave him without molesting him then and there. Maybe he was hurrying back to establish an alibi. This thought caused chill bumps. If he needed an alibi, he might know Glydia and Josh and knew they were planning to camp out.

Lord, I hoped it wasn't one of Josh's friends. That would hurt more than a stranger's random act. My thoughts were making me cautious about contacting Hank on the sandbank, telling Jasmine, or roaring up to shore with Peter in the boat. I wanted to set a trap and catch the bastard.

Ray had the boat on plane and was proving he could, indeed, leave dust. I knew it wasn't much farther to the sandbank. I leaned back and Ray moved forward in order to hear above the engine's roar.

"Let's stop and coast awhile," I yelled.

The bow dipped to the water and we slowed dramatically. There was silence with faint echoes of sound still lingering in the air. I glanced at Peter, who still had his eyes tightly closed. At his age you close your eyes, and all the bad things go away. I leaned over and found the radio. Ray wasn't filling the silence with chatter.

"Rescue One to Base." Hank could've left the area, but I didn't think so. I waited a full thirty seconds before I tried again. I didn't want to fill the airwaves with a lot of noise; too many people make a habit of tuning in.

"Rescue One to Base." Earlier, from the sandbank, I had watched Hank load his four prisoners into the small cabin cruiser he'd borrowed. As he passed near me, he held up a pigsticker, a wide-bladed knife five inches long, and shook his head as if to say, One of these days. I had smiled and waved. Eons passed before he answered.

"Base to Rescue One. Over."

"Hank, is Mr. Initials still vocal? Keep it to the minimum."

He knew what I meant. Spell nothing out, ask no questions. Mr. Initials was John Fray of the GBI.

"In town tucked in for the night. Over."

"Close the office loudly, load friends, Papa Bear, and both cubs softly, *for sure,* and head for home. I'll be around the corner."

I heard silence and sporadic static while he deciphered my message. I'd told him to let everyone know the show was over and they could go back to their tents. Nothing more was going to happen tonight. He was to load Leroy, Josh, little Josh, and Anna Lee for sure and not listen to Josh's objections. Then he was to come downriver toward the landing, where he would soon spot us. This should make the abductor think he could go back to Peter when everything quieted down. Hell, for all I knew, the abductor could be on Interstate 75 headed for Kentucky. You can only guess, plan, and pray.

"For sure? Over."

"Absolutely!"

"You giving up? Over."

"You bet!"

"Understood. Out."

I'd told him he had to be kidding. I'd just begun to fight. He knew this. He likes to get in a little dig now and then. He (and a zillion other males) hates to take orders from a female without first questioning every aspect. It galls his soul. So be it. Amen.

Peter had relaxed a bit and fallen asleep. I turned slowly toward Ray and whispered, "Peter's asleep. We're gonna stake out where the dogs found him, hoping the man will come back when he thinks the coast is clear. After we transfer to the sheriff's boat, you can call it a night. When everyone sees what I'm holding, there'll be an uproar, I'm sure. So while it's quiet, I'm taking this opportunity to thank you for your help. I'll mail your check. Oh, I sure hope you have some of your deer jerky left from last hunting season. I need twenty pounds."

"I'll have to check. If we do, we'll get it to you in a few days. We 'preciate your business. While we're conversing, I'd like to say that your gal's ass is spectacular. I'd say she's right up there at the top of my list."

"I'll be sure and tell her," I said, amused.

"Nah, don't breathe a word. If we ever work together again, it'll make her self-conscious 'round me."

"As you wish," I said. I couldn't wait to tell Jasmine and see how her religious side handled her indignation.

The fact that I had told Ray that I hoped he had jerky, and he had replied that he'd see, was a charade that everyone who bought their products played out faithfully every time we ordered. Everyone in the county knew they hunted and trapped year-round.

Sam and Ray Conner are among a handful of free men in the county not firmly enmeshed in the quagmire of bureaucracy. The two brothers live off the land. They swear they have never filed income taxes, applied for a social security card, or called anyone boss their entire lives.

They sell deer meat, gator meat, and deer hides. They trap possums and coons and sell the hides. They raise bees, make moonshine, and grow pot. They eat squirrel, venison, turkey, wild hog, quail, fish, gator, and turtle. They make good money selling rattlesnake steaks and curing the skins. They also work as guides for hunters and fishermen.

We all pretend that they accomplish all this in the short hunting and trapping season. They pay taxes on their land but don't register to vote. They register their vehicles and buy tags and driver's licenses. They also purchase local hunting and fishing licenses. They pay cash for their purchases and bury the excess in fruit jars. They buy money orders to pay for electricity, propane gas, and telephones.

None of us condone their illegal activities, we all just aid and abet by buying their products. When I have a taste for fish, I call and it's delivered. Rosie makes a quail potpie that melts in your mouth. The dogs love the deer jerky. Live and let live. That's life in south Georgia.

We sat quietly. The freshening breeze created cat's-paws of tiny ripples that traveled the dark water, causing the boat to sway gently. The constant cacophony of croaking frogs was so ingrained with the other night noises that we no longer heard it. An occasional caw of a crow, the hoot of an owl, branches creaking from some wild creature moving through the thick brush would cause us to listen.

I called Jasmine and asked that she and Sam return and rendezvous with us past their original destination. I said nothing else. They should make it there before Hank. Ray and I heard a tiny buzz, slowly gaining in volume, long before they came into view. Sam cut the speed, then idled until we were side by side. They were unaware of the bundle I was holding until they were closer. I waved my hand and covered my mouth, indicating silence. I saw the glitter of Jasmine's catlike eyes in the reflection from the boat's lights.

"Peter wasn't harmed physically, but he won't open his eyes. He's asleep now, and I want him to rest until his family arrives. He was bound and gagged and left under a pile of pine boughs. We're keeping the fact that he's been found quiet and off the airwaves. We're gonna try to trap the bastard.

I've a hunch that he's local and on the sandbank, but I could be wrong."

"You're going to let me go with you, aren't you?" Jasmine inquired anxiously.

"You'd have to testify to a packed house," I warned.

"I can do that." She sounded confident.

"You were already on the guest list."

"How about us?" Sam inquired, forgetting to whisper. Peter didn't stir.

"Sorry, guys, you're civilians. You might get hurt."

"Civilians, my ass," Ray challenged, sounding insulted. He reached under the seat and produced a nine-millimeter Glock. "I bet I'm a better shot than both you gals combined!"

I held out a hand and he passed it over for inspection. Its shape reminded me of a water pistol I'd had as a child. Mine shot water, but I suspected this one would shoot a jazzed-up version of a dumdum bullet.

"Hot loads?" My inquiry was casual.

"Yep," he answered with pride.

I handed it back. "Hide it, and don't wave it around when the sheriff arrives. He despises hot loads."

"I wouldn't use it on him," Ray replied with disdain.

"You didn't get the drift, Ray," I informed him with patience. "The sheriff despises hot loads, regardless of who's shooting whom. Have you ever seen the hole they make?"

"I thought a bullet was supposed to stop whoever you shoot," he retorted.

"Well, there's stopping, and then there's stopping."

We heard a loud buzz as Hank roared downriver toward our position. Someone was manning a side-mounted searchlight, and it blinded us with its brilliance. Whoever had the wheel cut the power a tad late. Larger waves rocked our boats.

"Turn off the damn light!" I yelled above the idling engine as they slowly pulled closer. The light went off. Multicolored dots appeared in my vision. I closed my eyes and waited for them to adjust. I was sure no one could see Peter in my lap with the large dogs sitting directly in front of me.

"Ahoy there," called Hank.

I'd forgotten that small exhausted children can sleep through almost anything. Peter still slumbered.

"Is Josh on board?" I called, but didn't stand.

"Right here," Josh replied.

Ray and Sam had been holding our boats together, but now Ray picked up a paddle and worked us up close to the cabin cruiser. The side of the bigger boat was about four feet higher than ours.

"Hold the boat steady," I whispered to Ray, and stood up carefully. "I have a special delivery for you, Josh, from Melanie and Ashley. Peter is not injured, just tired. He's asleep." I raised him up, and Josh grabbed him from my arms.

"Peter? Oh, Peter! My baby. My baby." Josh became silent.

Then I heard loud sobbing and even louder squeals of delight from little Josh and Anna Lee.

"Can I hold him, Daddy? Let me see him, Daddy! Why doesn't he open his eyes? Let me kiss him, Daddy! Why are you crying, Daddy, is he dead?" His siblings were happy. Being an only child, I felt a worm of envy slither into my heart. I've heard pros and cons about brothers and sisters, but I still feel I missed a great deal growing up alone.

Hank leaned over the railing. My eyes had adjusted, and I could see him well enough from the boat light's glow.

"I'm sure he wants to thank Melanie and Ashley. He's a little busy right now." Hank's voice sounded funny.

My eyes were blurry. I sat down before I lost my balance and tumbled overboard.

"You got a rope on board that tub?" I asked Hank.

"Why?" he replied.

"I want to load the dogs onto your boat, and I won't ask them to climb that ridiculous ladder you just swung over the side."

"Why?" he repeated.

"The bastard is coming back for Peter, and I want us to be there waiting."

"Oh, really?" He sounded pleased.

"Move your ass, buddy. Time's awastin'," I said impatiently.

Hank leaned so far over the side, I was sure his feet weren't touching the deck.

"Who the hell do you think you are? I'm the sheriff, and I give the orders!" he told me, keeping his voice low. I could tell he wasn't angry, just protecting his male reputation because several other males had heard my command.

"If you fall face down out of that boat into this one, I bet it'll hurt," I said, cocking my head and peering up at him.

He pulled back and disappeared. Leroy's large torso moved into view as he swung the winch arm over the side and lowered the rope.

"Hi, there, my pretty," he said. "Grab the rope and hook up a dog. Which one's coming up first?"

"Melanie," I answered, running the rope through her harness, weaving it in and out of the leather and making a separate circle under her shoulders. I tied a fancy knot, slipped it tight, and wove a double hitch above it. That was just in case her harness straps broke while she was being hauled upward.

"Hi there, Melanie," he crooned, as he lifted her over and out of sight. We transferred the other three, and only Ulysses gave a frightened whine as his paws encountered space. He made a swimming motion with his feet, treading nonexistent water all the way up.

"Hello, Ulysses," Leroy crooned. "Helped me out. Sure you did. Good boy!" He reappeared. "All safe and sound."

I handed him Jasmine's and my bags of jerky. "Divide it equally and they'll forget they ever levitated. Would you tell the sheriff I'd like to converse?"

"Be nice, you hear?" he cautioned.

Hank appeared with his arms folded across his chest.

"Do you have a deputy on board, sheriff, sir?"

"Deputy Rigdon."

"Can he handle this boat, sir?"

"Of course."

"I'd like to suggest a plan. Have Deputy Rigdon follow us until we get to a small cove, then watch us unload and mark the spot well, because he has to come back and pick us up. The deputy unloads the Powells at Mr. Settles's bait-shop dock, then runs Leroy to the landing, where he can unload the dogs and cage them. The deputy tells everyone waiting at the dock that the search is over for the night. He leaves the landing and returns to pick us up when we signal. Leroy takes one of the vans, drives to Mr. Settles's dock, picks up the Powells, and sneaks them into the hospital to see Glydia. They keep Peter's rescue hush-hush. This late, there won't be any visitors on the second floor. Then Leroy drives back to the landing to await our return. The deputy sits hidden in a nearby cove watching for our signal. How'm I doing so far?"

"What's my role in this production?" He sounded amused.

"'Step into my parlor,' said the spider." I indicated the boat. "Jasmine and I will be your backup."

"'No way,' said the fly," he retorted.

"Then Jasmine and I will go. 'Course, when you appear on the dock with Peter and his family, it'll cut our chance of catching the scumbag from slim to zip."

"I go with my deputy and Leroy. You girls go home."

"Where?" I queried with politeness.

"Ray knows," he said, sounding pissed.

"Sheriff, sir, I'm paying Ray. He knows which side of his bread is buttered. I bet you've never spent a dime on his products."

"I haven't," he replied. He leaned over closer and whispered, "Promise not to shoot me instead of the perp, if we get a nibble?"

"With your present attitude, I'm not sure," I said, and looked away.

"Don't climb up on your high horse. I'll be down in a sec."

Ray leaned over and whispered into my ear, "I would've told him the location if he'd asked. Can't afford to rile the law."

"You knew that, I knew that, and Hank knew that," I said grumpily. "He was shinin' me on."

Ray chuckled.

"It isn't funny," I snapped.

"Yes'm."

Hank came down the ladder, sat down beside me, and said to Ray, "Ready when you are."

Ray turned the boat, and we began the trip back to the place of rescue. I leaned closer to Hank's ear and raised my voice above the engine noise.

"Back at the sandbank, you didn't tell anyone, even in confidence, that Peter had been found, did you?"

"You're not the only one, Sidden, who can formulate theories based on guesswork. I think he's a local too." We didn't speak again until we reached the cove.

Hank, Jasmine, and I watched the three boats pull away.

"Turn your head, Hank. Jasmine and I have to pee."

We walked over behind a bush, checked the area with our flashlights, and squatted. I had palmed tissue and a can of Off! while we were unloading our gear.

"Spray your face and neck," I whispered, and handed her the can. "When we suit up we'll be hot as hell, but safe from mosquitoes and snakes."

"Are you sharing with Hank?" she whispered.

"He can suffer."

Jasmine and I climbed into our suits, and Hank helped with our packs.

"Listen up," Hank said, starting his lecture. "Sit behind a pine tree for cover. If he appears, don't train your lights on him until he starts to move the pine boughs. We want this to be an airtight case. The dogs didn't mantrail him here, so their evidence is only circumstantial. Hold your flashlight away from your body, and make sure you stay behind the tree until I'm sure he doesn't have a weapon. He could approach from the water or from different directions in the woods. I'll place you when we get to the scene. And for God's sake don't squirm or move around or sneak away to take a leak. I don't want anyone shot. I'll have to admit, I'm not too happy with two untrained women with weapons on a stakeout. Do exactly as I say, and maybe all three

of us will survive. But don't risk a shot, even if the
perp is getting away, unless you're positive of the
other two's exact locations. Understood?"

We murmured agreement and started up the path.
I led; I knew the spot. I missed it the first time and
we had to backtrack, but I finally stopped in front of
the cut pine limbs. I gathered them and placed them
as originally found. Hank led Jasmine to a tree, and
I carefully marked the spot in my mind. He came
back and placed me twenty yards to the left of
Jasmine. He took a position about twenty yards from
me, slightly to the left and across from where he
thought the man would enter if he came in from the
trees.

I marked his position too and quickly scanned the
area with the light before I sat down and switched it
off. The moon was on the wane, and it was as dark
as smut. I couldn't see my hand in front of my face.
Even when my night vision returned there wouldn't
be any great improvement. With my gloved hand I
gently brushed away any straw or leaves that might
make noise if I moved. I cleaned an area so I could
stretch my legs if they started cramping.

The three of us were roughly positioned at three
corners, with the pile of pine boughs making the
fourth. Hank had wanted us where we wouldn't get
caught in a crossfire. I was sitting sideways behind
my tree, and I kept glancing at the other two positions so I wouldn't forget where they were.

With my legs drawn up, I placed my left arm in
the hollow between my belly and my knees. I drew
off my right glove with my teeth and pushed up the

cuffs of my suit. My watch face glowed an eerie green in the darkness: 11:32. Several minutes passed before I could see the lighter color of my suit against the darker ground. I cocked my head upward and could distinguish the lighter sky from the tree line. This was as good as it was gonna get. I waited what seemed like hours and again checked my watch: 12:10. This was gonna be a long, long night.

My backpack was to my right and slightly behind me so I wouldn't trip over it. I opened the flap, removed my water bottle, took several sips, and replaced the cap. I removed the emergency rations and munched on a granola bar. These activities used up another five minutes. I was bored.

I slowly stretched out my legs and put my arms behind me, bracing my upper body with my hands on the ground to relax the tension in my back. I began to ponder Gilly's predicament. We should have called the police when we arrived back at the house with her. Unaccounted for, she might be listed as missing when the ashes cooled and the fire department and medics started checking to see if anyone had perished.

It hadn't occurred to me yesterday afternoon, but maybe Jonathan had thought of it. He could have her call and say she was out of town or wasn't in her room when the fire started. If Jonathan hadn't called, I must remember to do it first thing in the morning. I didn't want to call any attention to Gilly. It was enough that Judge McAlbee and possibly some of his cronies were searching for her.

I wondered what had transpired that required the judge to wake Gilly's mother in the middle of the night and take her into his woods. Whatever it was had repulsed her and made her tell the judge she was going to report him to the authorities. She had also mentioned my name when she was sure he was going to kill her or have her killed. When he found out Gilly hadn't perished in the fire, my place would be the first place he'd check for her.

I stopped my mental speculations and carefully took a look around. Quartering off sections, staring into the darkness, then moving to another square, I made the full circuit: nothing. I was sure he'd use a light. He'd think he was alone. It would take cat's eyes to maneuver through this ebony maze of trees and brush without falling and making lots of noise. If he came, we would see his light or hear him. I didn't think he'd be able to sneak up on us.

I doubted if he'd come before 3 or 4 A.M. It was my theory that he would come by boat. I imagined he'd creep on board and use oars to get a reasonable distance away before he started the outboard. If he had to explain his absence later, he could say he'd enjoyed an early morning run on the river. If he left at midnight, his absence would be more suspect.

I felt a drop of rain hit my nose and heard the patter of drops racing through the trees. Great. Just what we needed. I felt around inside my backpack and found a plastic rain cap and tied it under my chin. My curly mop frizzed enough from the higher humidity caused by the dew. If it got soaked, then dried from the heat of my scalp and a helpful breeze, I'd look like I'd been hit by lightning.

I was waterproof except for shoes and socks, and I had a dry pair of each in my pack. So did Jasmine. I didn't try to suppress my evil grin or soft chuckle when I remembered what Hank was wearing, his summer uniform and a lightweight windbreaker for the mosquitoes. Neither was waterproof. He was gonna get soaked.

I stretched my legs out, rested on my arms behind me, and turned my face up to catch the rain. I was too warm in the suit and the cold drops felt refreshing. Feeling a small pressure on my left shin, and an added heaviness that shouldn't be there, I took a shallow breath and hoped to Christ I hadn't moved anything. A millimeter at a time, I carefully began moving my head forward so I could see what was resting on my leg. My gut had already screamed its guess and was having hysterics.

I knew God was punishing me for relishing Hank's discomfort from a pounding rain, for being mean to Jonathan, for welshing on my bet with Jasmine, and for my many other sins of commission and omission, too numerous to think about.

It seemingly took a couple of hours to move my head. I strained my eyeballs in the darkness, trying to see what species of snake was resting its head and a small portion of its length on my leg. Yep, it was a snake. I had a 60 percent chance the snake was nonpoisonous. There are king snakes, black-snakes, garter snakes, chicken snakes, and many, many more that call this swamp their home and have those beautiful rounded heads. That left the 40 percent that have ugly triangular flat heads. Most of them are diamondback rattlers, coral snakes, timber rattlesnakes, and cottonmouth moccasins.

At an appropriate moment the horizon seemed to brighten and thunder shook the heavens, startling me and the snake. I don't know if I involuntarily flexed a muscle or if the snake was reacting to the loud noise. Two tics later lightning rent the sky, and in the bright light I saw the snake's triangular head. Its mouth stretched open, showing fangs and the obscene white coating. My luck had just deserted me. I had a deadly cottonmouth moccasin resting on my leg.

# 8

## All the World Is Sad and Dreary
### *April 14, Sunday, 2:15 A.M.*

Cottonmouths are both vicious and aggressive. My only previous encounter with one happened during my senior year in high school. Leroy, Susan, and I had wandered off from a school picnic at Azalea Park. We were on a nature trail when we spotted a cottonmouth at the bottom of a dry sump, six feet deep and ten feet across.

Looking around for something to throw, I snatched up a clump of dried dirt the size of a baseball and tossed it. It landed on the snake's head. With incredible speed the snake charged up the embankment toward us. We turned tail and ran like the wind. After we were over our fright, we ventured back and stepped off the distance the snake had charged after us: six feet up and sixteen feet on the dirt trail before it had slithered off into the weeds.

Every muscle cried for relief. I sat frozen and considered my options. I couldn't think of any. I was worried about ankles, face, and neck. Everything else was protected. The rain increased, falling in solid sheets, and the noise was thunderous. I couldn't have heard a brass band playing a dozen feet away. I sat very still and sweated.

Another crack of lightning and rumble of thunder. The snake slowly moved across my legs just below my knees and disappeared from sight, its body blending with the darkness. I sat very still and sweated. I counted slowly to a hundred before I took a deep breath, then stood on shaky legs and leaned against the tree. I was so pumped, I bet I could have flown. I wanted to go home. I wanted to howl and release the adrenaline flooding my system. I wanted a cigarette. . . . That I could do. No one could smell anything in this downpour.

I fumbled out a black sheet of plastic from my back. I carried two, a six-foot square and a twelve-foot square, but it didn't matter which one I pulled out. Removing a glove, I unfolded the sheet, placed it over my head, and was left with a three-foot overhang. I brought each side around my shoulders and tucked them into the slash pockets of my suit at the waistline.

I took the overhanging plastic and held it against the tree, forming a small canopy. I unzipped my suit and hauled out my cigarettes and lighter. No smoke had ever tasted so good. I peeked around the tree and couldn't see a damn thing. The abductor could have strolled past the three of us, found Peter missing, and taken a hike without us knowing.

I smoked three cigarettes before my nicotine desire was slaked and my good sense came out of hiding. I drank some water and stood with the plastic away from my head, but it was still around my shoulders. I might need the canopy again. The rain eased somewhat, and visibility was now about ten feet. I leaned my head against the tree and checked my watch. It was ten minutes after three. I straightened up and stretched, trying to loosen my stiff muscles. I felt tired, the adrenaline was fading, and I was getting sleepy, but I wouldn't sit down again even if I fell asleep leaning against the tree. I wanted my face at least five feet above a crawling snake. Standing, my suit covered my ankles.

The rain fell steadily, hanging an opaque curtain slightly lighter in color in the darkness. Visibility was zilch. We had a problem. The two hours or so when I thought the man might appear were ticking away. What if he came and we couldn't see him? We weren't supposed to move an inch from our positions. Hank hadn't discussed the possibility of rain and what the alternate instructions would be. I'd certainly bring this omission to his attention at the very first opportunity.

I began another routine scan of the terrain. Futile, but I didn't think tramping over to where I thought Hank was standing would be a good idea. I could hear myself yoo-hooing and saying, "How about this rain!" He'd probably wrestle me to the ground and have me handcuffed before I finished the sentence.

I was staring toward the extreme right sector, the approximate place where anyone arriving by boat would appear. I saw a fuzzy section of the rain curtain turn a faint yellow. It seemed to be moving up and down a little. Oh, my God. Jasmine should be farther to the right. Could she be moving around?

I hugged my tree and dithered about what to do. It could be her, or the abductor, or a figment of my vivid imagination. Hank was twenty yards farther away from the light—if it was a light—than I was. He might not be able to see what I was seeing. Oh, Christ! I took a deep breath. I had to do something, even if it was wrong. A voice spoke in the darkness.

"Don't panic, Sidden. I'm five feet behind you."

I was three feet up the pine tree before my brain recognized Hank's voice.

I whirled and snapped, "I didn't panic. I just had a fuckin' heart seizure!" I pushed the words out with force. My diaphragm didn't want to produce any sounds until it recovered.

"Looked like you were trying to climb the tree."

"I'd cuss you out, but I'm too weak from fright. What do we do? I hope you took note that he came from the direction I predicted. I was right about his timing too."

"I'll buy you roses. Can you find Jasmine without turning on your light? Then you can scare her."

"Yes," I answered.

"Find her and stay there. I'm going after the perp. You go first. I sure as hell don't want you behind me."

"Up yours."

I moved around the tree and started walking, holding my hands out, trying to remember how the pine tree rows were planted. Stumbling into a merkle, gallberry, or titi bush wouldn't hurt too much. Hitting a solid pine tree is a whole different ball game.

After leaving one tree and reaching for the next, about three feet apart, I picked up a rhythm and was able to move faster. The shrubbery was cumbersome, and I slipped down once, but I never turned to check if Hank was behind me. The line of trees I was using as guideposts was leading me directly to where I thought Jasmine was waiting. I was dividing my attentive stare between the weaving light and her location.

"Jo Beth, you startled me!"

"You scared the hell out of me!" I clutched my chest. "My heart's going to throw in the towel before dawn," I whispered. I was trying to take some deep breaths. "First Hank, and now you."

She moved closer. "Where's Hank?"

"He's gone after the perp, and I'm going after Hank. Stay here."

"You're kidding, right?" She grabbed for me, and my plastic sheet pulled away in her hands. "What's this?" she squeaked, slinging it back at me. Anything unexpected in the rainy darkness seemed sinister. Wait until she heard about the cottonmouth. Maybe not. She was doing so well in swamp rescues, I decided I wouldn't mention the snake. She might want to change her occupation.

"We're both antsy," I said, to steady her. "Hang

on to a belt loop, and we'll shuffle over to back up Hank."

I had left my pack behind. Groping in the darkness, I checked to see if she had hers on. She didn't, but an unexpected hand across her back made her jump and gasp. I just flinched. My nerves were becoming immune to surprises.

"I was checking to see if you had your pack on."

"Ask next time," she replied shakily. "I'm a nervous wreck!"

"I don't feel like the Lone Ranger myself. Shall we go?"

The light was barely visible through the rainy mist. The abductor must be having trouble finding the pile of pine limbs. I tried to go faster, but I ran into a tree and slipped in the mud. We both went down.

"Shit!" I said with disgust.

"My sentiments exactly!" Jasmine agreed.

I was amused at our pratfall and her answer. I'd never heard Jasmine use a cuss word. She had embraced the strict Baptist faith seven years ago when she retired from the streets.

I dropped my flashlight when I fell. We both scrabbled in the mud, which was mixed with leaves and pine needles, with our gloved hands. Jasmine found it and we rose from our knees holding on to each other.

As we started forward, I saw two lights in the dark mist and they were converging. "Oh, Lord," I groaned, trying to hurry.

I was trying to penetrate the murk when I heard Jasmine moan, "Oh, no!" I glanced up to see that the lights had separated, one higher than the other, and heard a muted yell. A few seconds later a shot rang out. It sounded like a small firecracker in the rain-sodden air.

"Turn on your light!" I yelled to Jasmine.

We both started running through the brush, straining to see in the puny glow of the flashlights. Visibility was about five feet. It was like shining a light on a gray brick wall. I was ignoring all Hank's instructions. I was running with the light held in front of my body and I hadn't removed my glove or drawn my gun.

I was yelling with every breath, "Police! Freeze! Down on the ground! Now! We're coming, sheriff! He's surrounded!" I was bellowing like crazy, trying to gain a few seconds. I didn't think Hank was in control because he wouldn't fire unless he was in trouble or the perp was fleeing.

I was stumbling in slow motion, one hand up to ward off obstacles, the other clutching the flashlight in a deathlike grip.

Jasmine had been yelling the same nonsense, only she was striving to keep her voice deep like a male.

We finally reached the lower light; the higher one had bobbed off to the right. My light picked out Hank's lanky frame sprawled on his back with his gun still in his right fist. The blood covering his chest looked black against the lighter fabric of his uniform.

I dropped to my knees beside him, placed my flashlight between his legs, drew off my gloves, and ripped his shirt open. Jasmine hovered over us, holding her light steady on his chest and trying to keep the rain off his face.

Using his shirt, I wiped the bloody area, trying to find where he'd been hit. The blood was bubbling from a hole about two inches above his right nipple. I sent up a silent prayer, it wasn't close to his heart. I placed my left hand over the hole and applied pressure, then leaned back, unzipped my suit, and ripped the bandanna from around my waist. I folded it and applied it firmly against his chest.

"Give me yours, Jasmine!"

She managed to hold the light steady, retrieve her bandanna, and hand it to me. I folded it and added the extra padding.

We both heard the faint drone of an outboard coughing to life and readying for speed. We didn't comment.

"Call the deputy's boat and tell him to get an ambulance rolling to the landing. Tell him Hank's been shot."

Jasmine stood to remove her radio from her pocket. I shined my light on Hank's face. His lips were moving. I put my ear close to his mouth.

"Say it again, babe, I can't hear you."

"He had a knife. I missed him." Hank's voice was weak, but I heard every word. I heard a murmuring above but couldn't make out Jasmine's words. If only this lousy rain would let up!

"Listen, sweet stuff, it missed your heart, and I'm controlling the bleeding. As for missing him, as soon as you're back on the job I'll take you out to the shooting range. Give you a few tips. Improve your aim." I leaned close to hear his reply.

"Sweet stuff?" I saw a weak smile.

"Save your breath, you egotist!" I told him and grinned. "You know that we of the weaker sex babble and wring our hands in an emergency. In your dreams!"

Jasmine crouched down. "They're on the way." She spoke just above a whisper. "How is he?"

"Stabbed, not shot. Hank shot at the perp. He thinks he missed. Who wouldn't in this rain. He's lost a lot of blood, but he's healthy. I think he'll be okay."

"Praise God." Jasmine choked and wiped more than rain from her face. Several years ago, Hank had talked her off the streets and had cosigned a note so she could buy a small eatery. She adored him.

"Do you think you can find your way back to your pack? We need the rescue sled."

"I'm on my way," she said, and disappeared into the rain.

I sat and watched Hank's face in the glow of the light. The raindrops fell in a monotonous refrain. I've always been able to hear music in the rain, even as a child, but I wanted this music to end. I'd heard enough.

With a light to guide her, it didn't take Jasmine long to return. I glanced at my watch as she approached: 4:20. It amazed me. It seemed like it should be time for the sun to rise, if this damn rain would just go away.

She unrolled the body sled next to Hank and handed me the first-aid kit. I pulled out the gauze four-by-four sterile pads and ripped open several packets. I removed the bandannas and pressed the pads down quickly. It seemed the flow had been stanched to a slow ooze. Jasmine held the compress tightly in place, and I secured it with several strips of adhesive tape. She held Hank's head and shoulders in her lap while I wound a three-inch Ace bandage around his upper torso to anchor the compress.

We each placed a foot on the rescue sled and half lifted, half slid Hank into the bag. Jasmine pulled the rings in order to inflate the small cushions, and I placed them around his body and worked the zipper upward. The sled was waterproof and made of the same lightweight material as our suits. It had a vulcanized bottom of smooth strong rubber so the dogs could pull it easily. Hank was soaked, but inside the bag he would soon be warm enough to help combat shock. I zipped the sled up to his neck and snapped the hood over his head. He was wet but out of the rain.

I picked up Hank's .38 police special, placed it inside my suit, and rezipped. Jasmine quickly put her stuff in her backpack.

"Leave it," I said. "We'll pick up both of them on the way back."

"The way back?" She was trying to read my expression without blinding me with her light.

"Yeah. We'll get Hank to an ambulance and then come back and find the bastard."

"How?"

She was in the dark because I was thinking of a method I'd never used before, and I didn't know if it would work. We could only try.

"I'll explain later," I told her. "Let's get Hank down to meet the boat. Grab a ring."

We donned our gloves and grasped the rings at the end of the sled's straps, which were normally attached to the dogs' harnesses. We traveled slowly, shining our lights on the ground and detouring around any protruding roots or obstructing foliage.

We arrived at the small spit of sand five minutes before we heard and saw Deputy Rigdon. He was plowing through the water, running full out like he was going to nose the boat up on the sand.

"Shit!" I yelled, waving him off frantically and yelling to Jasmine, "Haul Hank back! Get him back!"

I stood my ground, still trying to signal. At the last second he cut the engine, spun the wheel, and water from his reckless and too-close approach lapped around my knees. I glanced back and saw that Jasmine had hauled Hank up the small bank so he wasn't submerged in water.

"You idiot!" I screamed. "What the hell? Are you out of your mind?" I suddenly noticed that the water streaming back into the Suwannee was moving his boat out from shore.

"Throw me a line!" I yelled. Through the rain a rope snaked out and landed six feet from me. I grabbed the end and struggled to get it around a pine tree. Jasmine ran to help. I hurried back to the water's edge.

"Toss the aft line!" I bellowed. Then I amended my command. "At the rear of the boat!" It was obvious I wasn't dealing with a sailor here.

"Watch out that he doesn't throw the anchor at you," Jasmine called with sarcasm.

He wouldn't be that stupid, I thought, but I dodged behind a tree. His boat handling left a lot to be desired. The rope landed, and I had to wade out almost waist-deep to retrieve it. I was thankful it didn't have an anchor attached.

Jasmine and I hauled the rear of the boat as close to shore as possible and tied the rope. I saw the deputy sling a leg over the side.

"Stay aboard," I yelled. Jasmine and I dragged Hank into the water and floated him between us.

Last year, I'd rescued a man who weighed 230 pounds. He had fallen from a tree stand into four feet of swamp water. He'd landed on his feet and broken both legs, but still managed to tread water and pull himself onshore. When the dogs found him, I put him back in the water, in the rescue sled, and floated him across three hundred feet of stagnant black swamp water so he could be airlifted out. My thoughts were on alligators the entire voyage.

"Swing out the winch," I called to the deputy, then had second thoughts. "Do you know how to operate a winch? Don't you dare lie to me!"

"Yes, I can operate a winch," he called. "I just don't know much about boats!"

"Tell me something I don't know," I muttered. "Throw over the ladder," I hollered.

Jasmine and I clutched the small handrail and steadied Hank between us.

"Climb aboard, Jasmine, and help him," I said. "I can hook up the sled. Ask the deputy for his belt, but *you* pass it down to me. He's a klutz."

The arm of the winch swung out, and the rope was lowered. Using the deputy's belt, I wrapped it around the sled at Hank's waistline and fastened it as tightly as I could. I didn't want him to slump downward when he cleared the water. The sled rose slowly, and when it was over the deck, I hastily scampered up the ladder.

When I got on deck, Jasmine had unbuckled the belt. I stared at Deputy Rigdon. He was of average height and weight. I'd only known him from search-and-rescue scenes. He was wet to the skin from conning the boat from the outside; he hadn't used the protected controls located inside the small cabin. He was fumbling with his wet belt, trying to thread it through his wet belt loops. I remembered he'd transferred in from some other police agency, but not from where. I got in his face so I wouldn't have to shout.

"I'll drive," I said with disgust. "I want to get all our hides back in one piece. Come point out the controls."

I turned to Jasmine. "After you check Hank's bandage, come forward. We need to talk."

Rigdon indicated what I'd need to get us moving.

"The sheriff said you knew how to operate a boat," I said, giving him an accusing look.

"He assumed I knew, and I didn't want to tell

him different. I don't fish, and I don't like to be on the water. I can't swim," he admitted, with a pathetic hound-dog expression on his face.

"How did you manage to get to the landing?" I was curious.

"Mr. Moore took it in."

"Ah-hah!" I said, now understanding what had occurred. "Leroy assumed you knew how to handle it, and you didn't enlighten him either?"

"Yes'm," he agreed, sounding miserable.

"I'm surprised you managed to hide in the cove and find us in this pouring rain, even though you almost rammed us."

"Ah . . . I think I should tell you, I sorta hit a cypress knee on my way out."

I stared at him, appalled. "Above or below the waterline?" I scanned the wet deck, then ducked and peered inside the small cabin. I was praying it was only rainwater I was seeing.

"Above—I think."

"Which side?" My mouth was dry, and my pulse was racing.

He pointed to the left side. I think it's called port, but not being a nautical person, I kept that knowledge to myself. I hurried over and shined the light down as I hung over the side. The bad news was a nasty scar gouged into the wood about eight feet long. The paint was gone and fresh splinters were visible. The good news was that the damage was about two feet above the waterline. I drew a shaky breath. So far, so good.

"Go back and relieve Jasmine," I told him. "Hold the sled steady in case *I* hit something too."

Jasmine appeared next to me while I fiddled with the controls. She stood close so we could talk and be heard over the rain and, I hoped, the engine noise.

She saw my surprise and relief when the engine roared to life and then my hesitation to try anything else.

"You *can* run this boat, can't you?" she asked, sounding uncertain.

Oh, my God, I'd forgotten the lines! Without answering her, I ran back to Rigdon.

"Have you got a knife? Give it to me."

He stood and pulled out a pocket knife. I hoped he kept it sharp. I ran to the aft line and hacked at the rope. The knife was sharp and sliced through easily. I ran forward and cut the other line.

Back at the wheel, I moved the throttle forward and saw that the boat was moving. I made a slow gradual turn and gave it more juice. Everything was just fine.

"You *don't* know how to operate this boat," Jasmine stated.

"At least I know more than the admiral back there," I told her with pride.

The twin spotlights were trained on the water, the wiper blades were clearing the rain from the windshield, the motor was roaring, and we were making good time. Of course, I couldn't see a damn thing in front of me, but I made frequent glances to the darker shoreline to make sure I was staying in the middle of the river.

"I'd like to hear about your experience with boats," Jasmine yelled in my ear.

"Twelve years ago, during our first year of marriage, Bubba let me steer his fourteen-foot bass boat with a forty horsepower outboard. I did it many times."

"How many is many?" she asked.

"Well, after the first year I was afraid to trust him on the water. He drank constantly. We went out about once a month, so—"

"You steered twelve times, twelve years ago? Oh, sweet Jesus." She moaned. I pretended I didn't hear her.

I saw the faint glow of Mr. Settles's dock and knew I was about two hundred yards from the landing. I cut back on the power, judged the distance to the rubber bumpers, turned the wheel, and floated up to the dock like a seasoned pro. Eager hands reached for a rope, and I showed them the frayed end.

"Anyone own a boat hook?" I called.

I heard laughter. Several bodies loomed near the boat and more hands held it against the dock until they could bring some line. The EMTs, wearing rain slickers, loaded Hank onto a stretcher and, after a brief examination, carried him away. Before they left, I had a short chat with him and could tell he was in pain.

"You did good, Sidden. Tell Rigdon he better be able to swim at least a mile and navigate a boat before I return to duty. Tell him to take lessons from anyone but you."

"Take a flying leap at the closest wild bear's ass," I retorted.

A middle-aged man in overalls and a cheap rain-coat approached me and tipped his sodden hat.

"Ma'am, I had some extra rope. I replaced your lines."

"Thank you. You can bill the county."

"No need for that. Glad to help."

"I certainly thank you," I returned politely.

"You're welcome," he answered, and left.

God, how I love Southern rednecks! Unsophisti-cated, and they'll go out of their way to help you and won't accept any payment. Good people.

Leroy came hurrying up and grabbed me in a hug.

"I've been playing cribbage with a photographer and a reporter over at Mr. Settles's shop waiting on you. They heard about the sheriff and followed the ambulance. I waited until they left."

"Good. Jasmine, Rigdon, and I are going back. We need a good boatman. Will you go with us?"

"Does Billy Graham hold revivals?"

"I want to take Melanie, but not Ashley," I said wearily.

"How do I tell them apart?"

"Melanie's the female, Ashley's the male. You *can* tell the difference, can't you?" I kidded.

"Even on rainy nights," he said.

"Tell Jasmine to pick one of hers. Where's the closest rest room?" He pointed and I hiked.

When I came out, Jasmine was waiting to enter.

"See you at the boat," I called.

When I stepped on board, I noticed Leroy was wearing a bright orange rain slicker and a cap like the ones worn by the Georgia state patrol.

"Where did you get the rain gear?"

"Deputy Rigdon borrowed it for me," Leroy said.

I eyed Rigdon's soaked uniform and raised my brows. "No one around your size?"

"The rain seems to be slacking off. My uniform will dry quickly."

It was about 60 degrees now and would fall a couple more before morning. The wind would be stiff on the water. His uniform better dry quickly or he'd catch pneumonia.

"Thanks for thinking of Leroy," I told Rigdon. He beamed. I didn't have the heart to deliver Hank's message. I'd wait until we were finished. I'm a prime procrastinator.

I glanced upward. The rain, indeed, seemed to be easing. My watch read 5:10. Would this night ever end? I was exhausted, and I knew everyone else was also. I peeked inside the tiny cabin and saw Melanie and Gulliver curled in big balls so they could fit in the small aisle of the cabin. Two narrow bunks were on each side of them. Wise dogs. They had enough smarts to get in out of the rain. Jasmine climbed into the boat.

"Let's roll, Leroy." I was leaning against the cabin wall.

"It's over two hours until it'll be light enough to search. You ladies get out of those rescue suits." He pulled over a duffel bag and presented us with two long-sleeved sweatshirts. "These are to keep you from getting chilly while you're taking your nap. But before you sleep, I'll serve you breakfast."

"Breakfast?" we both chorused.

"If you're talking about a package of cheese crackers and a Diet Coke, I'll break your arm," I threatened.

"And I'll take care of the other one," Jasmine quipped.

"Ladies, you get so bloodthirsty when you're hungry." Leroy pulled out a large thermos and two ceramic mugs. "Coffee," he said solemnly and pulled out a paper sack. "Four homemade sausage-and-egg biscuits. All compliments of Miz Maybelle Settles. When she heard you were bringing the sheriff in, she started cooking."

"How did she hear?" I couldn't believe our good fortune.

"TV reception is lousy out here. They do like most old folks and listen to the police band radio. Got a real nice set. She said Fridays and Saturdays are the only nights worth listening to. They turn the volume up so loud you can hear it across the Suwannee. Lots of people are grateful for the work you and Jasmine do. Rescues and such."

"Give two of the sandwiches to Rigdon. Have you had anything?" I said, my mouth watering. I was famished.

"I'm full as a tick. I ate almost an hour ago, and Rigdon has his own bag and coffee, thank you."

"Gimme the bag," I said, laughing. "I was only being polite. I could eat the ass end of a rag doll through a screen door."

"I'll motor along real slow," Leroy explained. "Rigdon and I will stop and look for your back-packs and pick up the ropes you left tied to trees.

I'll anchor around the corner from the sandbank and wake you at first light."

"I love you, big guy," I said.

"I like you a lot too," Jasmine said. She's always proper.

"I have you in my clutches, my beauties," Leroy said in his best villainous voice, twirling an imaginary mustache. His imitations are much better than mine.

"I hope you thanked Miz Maybelle for us," I said.

"I did, indeed. Very nicely. She gave me a message for you, Jo Beth. She said if I got a chance to tell you to mention that she and Mr. Norman, that's her husband, really enjoyed listening to your mysterious call to the sheriff. She said it took them almost two minutes to figure out your transmission. You know, the one where you talked about Papa Bear, cubs, and for sure, and you bet, and the like? She apologized for taking so long but admitted they're both getting senile."

My face flamed. Leroy and Jasmine howled. Rigdon stared disapprovingly at their antics. His stock climbed in my book.

Jasmine and I ate, and drank most of the coffee, and I smoked. Jasmine was asleep before I finished my cigarette. I snuggled down in the bunk, wearing the big sweatshirt, and sleep surrounded me like a soft blanket. I sank into its warm darkness.

# 9

## Oh, Lordy, How My
## Heart Grows Weary
### *April 14, Sunday, 6:45 A.M.*

Leroy woke us up at first light, which was about
thirty minutes before dawn. Only a faint paleness in
the east. The rain was over, and it had left the air
cool and damp. We suited up and poured the last of
the coffee from the thermos. We stepped over
Melanie and Gulliver, who were still snoring.

"Ready to travel?" Leroy asked.

"After I give you Hank's gun," I said, handing it
to him.

"You think I need it?" he asked.

"Yes, if he's a local. Do you know what he faces
if we unmask him as a child snatcher?"

"I know he'll have to move if he wants to keep
on breathing oxygen," Leroy said, sounding serious.

"Leroy, I know we're about ten years behind the
more progressive states, but even here the vigilantes
rode off into the sunset years ago. Even if he

escapes jail time, he'll lose his hometown, wife
and/or children, lifelong friends, relatives, and his
business or job. All he'll have left is his breath.
Look what he did to Hank when he tried to arrest
him. You need the gun."

"I'll take it," he said, humoring me.

When we pulled into the sandbank, only one
bonfire was roaring. A lone man was standing near
it, drinking a cup of coffee. The rest of the campers
weren't in evidence.

"He must've had some dry wood stashed,"
Jasmine observed.

"Native know-how," Leroy stated.

"Maybe not," I replied. "Jonathan starts his char-
coal grill with a full can of lighter fluid. It whumps
when he throws in a match, and the benzene odor
overrides the smell of the meat cooking. I'm always
afraid he's going to blow himself up."

"Sounds like an outdoors man," Rigdon
remarked, in a wry tone.

I decided now was the time to deliver Hank's
message to the deputy. I can find fault with Jonathan,
but I resent anyone else taking a shot at him. But I
was kind enough to draw Rigdon aside and deliver
the message sotto voce: He had a week to learn to
swim and take power boat lessons. I doubted the stab
wound would keep Hank away from his desk any
longer.

Returning to Leroy and Jasmine with an unhappy
Rigdon tagging along behind me, I told them about
my plan. Jasmine and I had to return to the truck
and mantrail the abductor back to this camp.

"Deputy Rigdon, were you the one who removed the truck keys?"

"Yes'm. Got 'em right here."

He pulled them out of his pocket and I waved them away.

"I don't need the keys. When you opened the door to the truck, did you sit in the seat, open the glove compartment, feel under the seat, touch the steering wheel, or even check to see if the truck would run?"

"No, ma'am," he stated with pride. He thought he knew where I was headed. "I opened the door with my handkerchief, leaned inside, and removed the keys. Butch will be able to get clear prints."

"I wasn't worried about fingerprints," I commented wryly. "Bloodhounds can't do much with them. I was worried about you leaving your scent inside the truck and masking or mingling with the scent we're seeking. Since we need an uncontaminated object he wore, or frequently handled, and we don't have anything, I'll have to pick up his scent another way.

"When a person walks, his or her body constantly sheds thousands of minute pieces of skin, hairs, fibers, and lint from clothing. Your body sends forth a cloud of odors that linger in the air. No two people in the world smell the same. With light rain, heavy fog, and high humidity, the smells are easier to trail. The constant heavy downpour we received last night might have dispersed the abductor's scent, pounded it in the ground, or blown it into the next county for all we know. All we can do is try.

"Deputy Rigdon, I want you and Leroy to remain in camp. Don't let anyone leave by boat or vehicle. Keep them here until we return. Jasmine and I will start trailing."

"Is that legal?" Rigdon asked, sounding uncertain.

"Tell them the GBI wishes to question them and they are to stay until Fray arrives," I suggested.

"What happens then?" Rigdon sounded worried.

"He won't be here before nine. They keep banker's hours."

"What if he's early?"

"Shoot him," I said, sounding serious. "He's not a nice man."

We unloaded Melanie and Gulliver and attached them to their long leads. Then we donned our suits and Leroy helped with our packs.

I turned to the men. "Listen, guys, we might not find diddly-squat, but then it's possible we might get lucky. I want you alert and on your toes when we reappear. If the dogs are straining forward, practically dragging us, or starting their celebrative baying, draw your weapon. This man is not going to sit quietly when he hears the dogs approaching. He won't be docile, and Jasmine and I can't properly defend ourselves while trying to handle a hundred and twenty pounds of mantrailer approaching victory. Do you get my drift?"

They both nodded in unison. I pulled Leroy aside.

"Listen, sweet pea, keep G, B, and I off our backs if he should arrive early. I just know the creep will start harping about us blowing the stakeout. I'll end up kicking him in the nuts and have to spend a month hoeing new potatoes on the county farm."

"Farewell, Petunia," he said sadly, waving an imaginary hankie.

"Idiot."

Heading up the narrow muddy two-path road, I knew our socks and shoes would stay dry about two minutes. We had passed by some tents but didn't see any heads emerge. The paleness in the east was now a tiny sliver of pink. We could see well enough to track.

Jasmine yawned, shook her head, and looked at me. "Do we have to do this quietly?"

"Nah, he wouldn't go near the truck again. I know now it wasn't his tent he made a quick trip into, and out again, carrying Peter. The tent was completely empty. Someone must have left it up and decided to come back in a few days. That means he knew dogs would be used, which reinforces my theory that he's local."

"Aren't you concerned that Deputy Rigdon might take you literally and shoot Fray?"

"Don't I wish! Nah. First, he'd have to check with someone in authority to see if it was legal."

Jasmine giggled. "What did you whisper to Leroy as we were leaving?"

"To drown Fray before I lost my temper and had to help with the spring garden at the prison farm."

"We'd both be there," she replied, with a devilish grin.

"Listen, glamour puss, that's a no-no. If Fray and

I ever do come to blows, stand clear. I'd need you more on the home front helping Wayne keep my animals fed. I've got to go."

I tied Melanie's leash to a pine sapling. I stepped off the road a few feet till I found a bush with a clear spot to hide behind. I started the complicated process of disrobing. First, I removed the backpack, looking around for a relatively dry spot to drop it.

Unzipping the suit, I pulled it down below my waist, drew it, jeans, and panties down to my knees, and held all of it forward with my left hand. I kept my right hand free to sweep back and forth over my buttocks to keep the horde of mosquitoes from feasting on my buns.

Talking about getting caught with your pants down. I was staring at the ground, thinking about absolutely nothing, when a pair of wet steel-toed work boots laced with rawhide strips suddenly appeared in front of me. Jeans were tucked into the tops just below the knees.

I ran a gauntlet of emotions in about one second flat: embarrassment, fear, then anger. I decided on compassionate compromise. It sounded healthier.

"Listen, fella, I'm not looking up, and I'm not looking for pot patches or moonshine stills. I'm searching for a bastard who kidnapped a five-year-old boy yesterday and used a pigsticker on Sheriff Cribbs during a stakeout last night. My name is Jo Beth Sidden. If you're local, or been around awhile, you know about me. If I stumble on a still or marijuana during a search, I keep walking, and I also keep my mouth shut."

I decided to let him join the conversation, if he so desired. I didn't want him to think I was nervous and running my mouth. Silence. I didn't know if he was thinking it over or planning on how to dispose of my body.

He might not be able to read and was thinking the large white letters on the back of my rescue suit meant I was L-A-W. I saw a dark stream of tobacco juice land about two feet to my right in the wet weeds. My silly mind yelled it was a clue, he chawed tobacco! I told it to shut the hell up. I didn't want a clue, or a confrontation, or a shooting match.

"I would appreciate you keeping this meeting just between the two of us," I said, carefully adding the right amount of aggravation and anger in my speech. "Anyone would look ridiculous in this position, including you! I scared you, now you've scared me. We're even. Just walk away now, okay?"

Never let them see you sweat. They value having guts above intelligence and wealth. After a week or so, the boots and jeans moved out of my vision. I squatted there awhile. An eternity, which in reality was closer to thirty seconds. Then I rose, leaned weakly against a tree to adjust my clothes, donned my pack, and strolled back to the road.

Jasmine hadn't returned. I leaned against a tree and lit a cigarette twelve feet from Melanie's nose. I would have done the same if the distance had been twelve inches. I planned to smoke three in a row, lighting a new one from the butt of the old one. I deserved nicotine and a good cry. I would settle for the nicotine.

Jasmine stomped out of the woods, and we merged at the road, collected the dogs, and began walking. I was still recuperating from fright and hadn't noticed her silence.

"Gimme a cigarette," Jasmine said.

I stopped walking and stared at her. "You haven't smoked in years!" I said, surprised. "You haven't smoked since Reverend Euttis B. Johnson of the Pentecostal—"

"Holiness Fundamental Gospel Church baptized me," she finished, biting off each word. "Unfortunately, he wasn't around a little while ago when I needed him. And neither were you," she added bitterly. "Can I have a cigarette?"

While I was trying to lower my bile, blood pressure, and adrenaline, I had failed to pick up her agitation.

"A cigarette won't help. You've been off them too long. It'll make your stomach queasy and you'll upchuck."

"So I upchuck. Gimme," she demanded.

I reluctantly shook one out and held her wrist steady. She was trembling. She finally got it going.

"What happened?" I asked, while I lit up my second.

"While I was squatting, I had a visitor. I trotted out my little memorized speech you told me to deliver—if and when it should ever be needed. He didn't say a dammed word, not one word!" Her voice had risen, and I now realized she was absolutely furious. This was a Jasmine I had never seen. She wasn't scared, just very, very angry.

"What did he do then?" I said, encouraging her to continue.

"I—" Her voice broke, and she gathered her emotions for another try. "I was so scared, my leg cramped, and I fell forward on my hands and knees. The bastard patted my fanny and left!"

"That's the second compliment you've received on your derriere in the past ten hours. What kind of shoes was he wearing?"

"Compliment?" she yelled. "Shoes?" She took a deep breath. "All I saw were rubber waders. I didn't try for a face scan. You cautioned me not to stare, remember?"

"You did great, Jasmine," I soothed. "Mine wore steel-toed working boots. I was scared shitless."

"Did he also pat your fanny?" she accused.

"Not nary a pat," I said, trying to sound envious. "'Course my buns aren't nearly as nice as yours."

That did it. We looked at each other and started to howl. We clung to each other tightly, stumbling around on the road. We both had on our packs. It's hard to get up if you fall on your ass with thirty-two pounds resting on your shoulders.

"Are you okay?" I asked, knowing that she felt as drained and weary as I.

"I could use six cups of coffee, a hot bath, and twelve hours of sleep. Other than that, I'm fine," she stated. She was drying her eyes.

I pulled off my gloves and fished the handkerchief from my pocket that contained the last two caplets of speed.

"This should give us the energy to continue."

We swallowed the pills and drank from our canteens.

When we reached the truck, we let down the tailgate, removed our packs, and placed them on its surface.

"Think this will work?" Jasmine asked, as she opened two quart-size Ziploc plastic bags. I had taken out two packets of 4-by-4-inch sterile gauze pads. I used my small scissors to cut open each packet. I pulled out a thin rubber glove and worked my hand into it, trying not to touch the palm and fingertip areas.

"The method has been proven in the field; it's nothing new. I'm just worried about the heavy rain, earlier, and what it did to the scent trail."

I had the two packets of sterile pads in my left hand and a glove on my right. Jasmine opened the driver's side door to the truck. I leaned in and removed one pad with my gloved fingers. I wiped it lightly over the seat in the area where the driver sits, then over the back of the seat and the steering wheel. I straightened and deposited the gauze in the bag that Jasmine was holding open. She quickly sealed it. We duplicated the process. We now had two relatively uncontaminated scent objects to refresh the dogs' scent memories.

We sat on the tailgate and rested a few minutes. I smoked. Jasmine didn't ask to join me and I didn't offer. The speed was kicking in. I felt feisty and raring to go, but I sat until I finished my cigarette. Speed masks fatigue, and I knew we needed the respite.

"Let's get this show on the road," I said. We untied the dogs, led them up to the truck, and opened the door.

"Seek!" I commanded Melanie. "Seek!" She jumped into the truck and smelled the seat, the dash, and the floorboard. She hopped out and started nosing the ground.

"Seek!" Jasmine ordered Gulliver urgently. "Seek!" As Gulliver entered the truck, Melanie began to go forward to the river, where they had originally trailed the abductor. I let her lead me to the water and then turned her around.

"Seek!" I urged. She went back toward the truck. We passed Jasmine and Gulliver on the way to the river. I rolled my eyes and she smiled. Back at the truck, Melanie jumped inside again, circled around and around, and sniffed. Down on the ground, she headed back to the river. I gently hauled her back and turned her.

Melanie lowered her head and began the basic pattern of search, moving in a figure eight and casting back and forth. She was trying to find the elusive scent that was hidden among thousands of others. The bloodhound's ability to find one faint odor, distinguish it from so many, and follow it faithfully still amazes me.

I glanced back, saw Gulliver reenter the truck, and knew they would soon catch up to us. Melanie suddenly lifted her head and sniffed the breeze. My heart quickened, but she put her nose near the ground and continued the pattern. False alarm. She still hadn't found what she was seeking.

I was about ready to reinforce her scent memory
when she lifted her head. She was, again, testing the
wind currents. She hesitated slightly, and there was
a subtle change in her stance and demeanor. Her
muscles tightened. She stepped a little higher and
seemed to raise her shoulders with pride.

Oh, my God, I breathed silently, she's pulled her
target scent out of the air in spite of the heavy rain!
The man could have walked this path earlier,
scouting the location, but that would have been
days or weeks ago. He had driven this road with
Peter, over sixteen hours ago, and hadn't walked
back to the camp. The scent she had discovered
had drifted out of the open window as he had
passed along this road. It seemed unbelievable, but
she had nailed it!

She started trotting along briskly, and I was thankful for the speed's help. Without it, my hip pockets
would have been dipping in mud. She veered off the
road into the brush. I didn't have time to see if
Jasmine was behind me, I was too busy protecting
my face from hanging vines. Soon we returned to the
road. The scent had been moved with the heavy
downpour. Next, we were threading through heavy
brush again.

I was partially bent over, one gloved hand up for
protection from trailing vines, when I spotted the
reason we had been inspected earlier. It was a carefully protected marijuana seed bed; two-by-fours,
six feet long, formed a six-foot square. The light
green marijuana plants were about five inches tall
and so thick they looked like a patch of mustard

greens. I tried not to stare, just in case the growers were lurking behind a tree.

Thick camouflage netting was stretched across the top about three feet above the plants, anchored to four pine trees. The sides were wired together and stapled along the two-by-fours resting on the ground. The netting was to keep pine straw and pine cones from bending and damaging the plants. The camouflage color was to keep the "eyes in the sky" from spotting the bed. The thin covering also helped to keep deer, hogs, and smaller animals from walking over the plants and crushing or eating them.

It was time for the pot growers to plant. The ground was warming up, and on most nights the temperature wasn't lower than 60 degrees. The seedlings would be pulled up in handfuls and carefully transplanted directly into the ground or into four-gallon buckets. After the rain last night, the dirt would be damp and soft. Punch a hole with a finger, stick the white roots of one or two plants inside it, and push down all around them. Tend them to the first frost next winter and harvest. They would provide you with many thousands of dollars—or six to ten years in a federal prison.

Melanie and I worked our way around the man-made obstacle and continued our search. When she seemed uncertain or hesitant, I pulled out the ziploc bag to reinforce the scent. Was this necessary? Humans can't tell and canines can't speak. She might think I was mighty dumb to believe she would forget. There are times when Melanie looks as if she is rolling her eyes at me, and at other times she seems grateful. Who knows?

When we were back on the road and close to the sandbank, I called a halt. I wanted to wait for Jasmine. Two independent mantrailings would help in court, maybe. We wanted to nail this sucker if we caught him.

Jasmine and Gulliver arrived. Gulliver and Melanie greeted each other like friends who haven't seen each other in years. I let them have their moment because I believed we were on a viable scent, and they were energized and pumped up from the trailing.

They sniffed the contents of the Ziploc and went back to work. I knew that without their noses we would be up the creek without a paddle in identifying the man. There could be other evidence or a possible witness with some clue, but I felt this was our only chance in the here and now.

The dogs picked up the pace. Jasmine and I began a steady loping jog to keep up with them. Animals can stop on a dime and we can't. We overran them a couple of times when they stopped to sniff, but generally we pretty much handled our end.

As we neared the first tent, the dogs began their wonderful baying. Jasmine and I exchanged exultant grins, and I managed a triumphant "Yes!" We were now running, trying to keep up with the dogs and not hold them back. We burst onto the white sand, and every visible eye was staring at us.

I saw Leroy and Deputy Rigdon running toward us from near the boats. The dogs turned and ran back toward Josh's camping space and the deserted tent. It sat back a short way in the woods. They were following the scent, and it had been blown to the edge of the sandbank. I had temporally forgotten that they were duplicating the exact trip the abductor had made earlier, only in reverse. I should have remembered they would go in and out of the tent.

The man was getting plenty of warning. I was hoping he would try to flee at the last minute and that the bunch of us—handlers, dogs, Leroy, and the deputy—could run him to ground. Flight was also circumstantial evidence. A preponderance of circumstantial evidence could convict and could also raise a reasonable doubt. Even if we ran him down, it was up to the lab technicians to match fibers from Peter's clothing to the perp or find something else solid to connect them.

We popped in and out of the tent. Jasmine and I were fighting to keep the leads straight so we wouldn't trip or cause the dogs to trip. Even with gloves, my hands would be sore tomorrow. I hated to think about my shoulders. The pull of an excited dog as large as one of these makes you use muscles you didn't know existed.

We raced down to the sandbank, meeting Leroy, the deputy, and several others who were following the action.

"Stand back!" I yelled, as we approached. "Stand back! Don't get in the way!"

They parted reluctantly, making room as we flew past them.

"Keep the civilians back, deputy," I yelled over

my shoulder. Christ, if a bystander was injured, if
and when we had a confrontation, Hank would kill
me. Rigdon had never been on a mantrailing search
that I was aware of.

I couldn't take the time to look back. We were
pounding across the open sand. Jasmine and I had
our hands full, just keeping up with the dogs. Both
Melanie and Gulliver ran up to a man with his back
to us, standing by a bonfire. Both dogs were baying
as they lunged at him. When two huge dogs hit you,
you know it. He staggered under the onslaught and
sprawled on the sand. I saw a mug of coffee fly
through the air, and he put both hands up to protect
his face. He turned over and tried to sit up.

The dogs weren't attacking him. They just
wanted to touch their noses to their target and
receive the pats and praise they both deserved. They
were slobbering all over him and trying to lick his
face.

"Hey!" he yelled, grinning at the dogs and trying
to push them away. "Go easy now, easy!" He was
laughing. "What's going on?" He looked up at the
audience ringed around him, acting like the good ol'
boy I had thought he was.

The dogs stopped baying. He was petting them,
and in the sudden silence we all stared—at Stace.
Stacy Conner, one of Josh's closest friends, first
cousin to Ray and Sam, who had taken us up and
down the river . . . was it just last night? It seemed
we had been here a week.

I shook my head quickly to clear it and looked
around for Rigdon. He was staring like everyone

else. I heard a couple of nervous snickers, a release of tension. Very soon they'd be rolling with laughter in the sand.

I handed Melanie's lead to Jasmine, grabbed Rigdon, and pulled him aside. I turned him so his face wouldn't be visible to the others. I whispered in his face, barely moving my lips. They could see me.

"Arrest him right now. Put on the cuffs quickly. Tell him in a solemn voice, damn you, you are arresting him for the kidnapping of Peter and for attacking the sheriff. Do it now!"

"What if the dogs made a mistake?" he whispered.

I got closer and took an in-your-face stance.

"This minute, deputy. So help me God, if you blow this collar here and now, if the sheriff doesn't cut you off at the knees, I will. You can take it to the bank!"

Rigdon spun on his heel and marched back to Stace, who was now standing and brushing off sand. Jasmine had pulled both dogs back out of reach. Leroy had his hand over his pocket that held the gun and was watching Stace closely.

"I'm placing you under arrest, Stace. Put your hands behind your back. Do it now!" I was proud of Rigdon. He sounded sure and confident, something I knew he wasn't feeling right this minute. He was afraid he was stepping into a pile of doo-doo.

Stace took a backward step. "Are you out of your mind?" He sounded both shocked and hurt.

"Wait just a minute here," came from someone in the crowd. I turned and saw it was Grover. He and

Stace were the two men who had guarded the trussed-up four who had given me a hard time.

Rigdon had grabbed Stace's shoulder, turned him, and was putting on the cuffs. Rigdon's back was to the crowd. I stepped out and held up a hand.

"Grover, this goes for you and everyone else. Don't interfere with Deputy Rigdon. I know you're shocked. I'm just as shocked as you are, but Stace kidnapped Peter Powell and stabbed Sheriff Cribbs during a stakeout earlier this morning."

"That's a lie!" Stace yelled.

"I don't believe you, Jo Beth!" Grover delivered loudly. "I've known Stace all my life. He's babysat for Josh and Glydia, for God's sake! I can't just stand here and watch you handcuff him like a criminal!"

"Stace will be taken to jail and processed. His rights will be protected," I explained. "Deputy Rigdon is doing his duty. If you interfere with a lawful arrest, you can be arrested. And also, if you try, you'll have to go through me."

"And me," added Leroy, moving to my side.

"Me too," Jasmine vowed, moving beside us. She was holding Melanie and Gulliver on shortened leads, the excess wrapped around her hands. I think the dogs were the clinchers. Everyone present had seen the dogs launch themselves at Stace, baying their heads off. Most here still weren't aware that bloodhounds are gentle and aren't trained to attack. A fistfight or scuffle was one thing. Two huge bloodhounds were something else. The small crowd remained silent except for Grover.

"Hang in there, Stace. I'm leaving right now to go get Aimee. We'll be at the sheriff's office as soon as we can. We'll get this all straightened out. You can get these people for false arrest and trying to damage your reputation! I, for one, will be glad to testify for you. And I'm sure your other friends here will too!"

"Thanks, Grover," Stace called as Rigdon marched him away. "Get Aimee to bail me out! I can use a new bass boat. I'll sue them for this, just wait and see!"

We made it to the boat without incident. Jasmine and I loaded the dogs, and Leroy helped us remove our packs. When Leroy pulled away from shore, Rigdon was by my side.

"Why did we have to arrest him right now?" he choked out. "He isn't going anywhere. Why did you make me stick my neck out a country mile?"

I gave him a cool smile. "Use your noggin, deputy. How else were we gonna get the clothing he's wearing for the lab to run tests on? I bet he hasn't changed a stitch since yesterday. He's camping with the guys. They like to pretend they're roughing it. He has evidence all over him. Get on the horn and call for two deputies to meet you at the landing, ASAP. Make sure one of them knows how to run a cabin cruiser," I cautioned wryly. "They have to come back and search his belongings that are left on the sandbank. He may have been stupid enough to have kept the duct tape he used on Peter. Or, God forbid, he might have changed clothes. Another thing. You don't know my dogs and haven't been on any search-and-rescue with any dogs, I'll wager. You don't trust their noses, but I do. He's guilty."

"I sure to God hope you're right," he muttered.

"One other observation, deputy, if you still need convincing. Stace isn't hard of hearing. The dogs were baying loud enough to be heard in the next county. No innocent man will keep his back turned from the excitement with a cup of hot coffee in his hands and let two charging, baying bloodhounds come at him. He had decided to brazen it out and was conniving to look surprised. If I'd only been a bystander, this would've proved his guilt to me. Think on it."

We arrived at the landing with two deputies and several early fisherman watching our approach.

I walked over to Rigdon. "Don't let Agent Fray of the GBI intimidate you. He puts on his britches one leg at a time just like you do. Handle this right, and Hank will be as proud of you as I am. Take care."

We all crowded around the deputies to hear the latest on Hank's condition.

"He's doing fine. Doc says the knife went in at an angle. Just caught the fleshy part of his shoulder. Barring complications, he'll be back at his desk in a week." Deputy Tom Selph delivered the medical bulletin. He turned to me. "How's the blind pup?"

"Just attained doghood."

"I'll give you a thousand for him, and that's my last offer."

I giggled. "Throw in a Porsche and I'd still laugh. Read my lips, Tom. He's not for sale."

"No harm in offering," he said gruffly.

"No offense taken," I assured him.

Leroy helped Jasmine and me unload and pack the vans. He waved as Jasmine pulled out of the parking lot. We stood facing each other.

"Oh, God, how I miss you, you handsome devil!" I choked, and lost it. He pulled me close and I sobbed on his shoulder. He held me at arm's length and smoothed his imaginary mustache. He assumed that quirky smile that made Clark Gable so perfect for the role of Rhett Butler in *Gone With the Wind*.

"Now see here, Scarlett!"

His nonsense stopped my tears but not the pain. I gave him a shaky grin and got the hell out of there.

# 10

## The Best-Laid Plans of Mice and Men
*April 14, Sunday, 8:30 A.M.*

The alarm alerted everyone as Jasmine and I opened the first gate. Wayne and Donnie Ray had the second one unlocked when we arrived at the courtyard. Jonathan and Gilly stood on the steps.

Gilly looked sensational. Susan had cut her long hair and styled it differently, giving her thick bangs and adding soft curls. She was wearing a white blouse, a jade-colored skirt, expensive-looking low-heeled sling pumps, and jade earrings. She was also wearing one of my aprons.

I hugged Jonathan, told Gilly she looked great, and greeted Wayne and Donnie Ray. Rudy and Bobby Lee were waiting on the porch.

"Wait here a second, everyone, I have to say hello to my roommates." I ran up the steps and knelt in front of them. I hugged Bobby Lee, fondled his ears, and moved my knuckles up and down Rudy's chest. I gave him a few murmured endearments and then went back down to tell the news.

After I delivered a brief version of the rescue, stakeout, and capture, Wayne and Donnie Ray left to put up the dogs and clean out the vans. They also had to finish feeding rounds, which had been interrupted by our return.

"Why the apron, Gilly?" I asked.

"I was fixing y'all some breakfast. There's plenty for you and Miz Jasmine," she added shyly.

"Thanks, Gilly, but I'm jumping into a hot bath and"—she caught my eye, and I saw the silent plea—"and I've changed my mind. On second thought, breakfast sounds good!"

Jasmine and I left to wash our hands and comb our hair.

"What are you cooking up now?" Jasmine whispered, as she dried her face. "As if I didn't know. You want me to take Gilly, so you and Jonathan can have 'quality time' before he leaves?"

I was brushing my teeth and spoke with my mouth full of toothpaste. "Sounds good, but I'm too beat to boogie. I'll have to marshal my last remaining strength to try and talk Jonathan into taking Gilly home with him."

"Boy, do you have your work cut out for you! I bet you dinner at Chester's you can't accomplish that feat."

"You're on," I murmured. I handed her a new toothbrush and entered the kitchen.

Gilly was placing a platter of scrambled eggs on the already laden table: biscuits, bacon, little fresh pork sausages, grits, and the delicious smell of freshly brewed coffee. I sat opposite Jonathan, and Jasmine joined us. The table had only three place settings.

"Have you already eaten?" I asked Gilly. She was pouring coffee.

"No, ma'am. I'll have something later."

I pushed back my chair and went to get china and silverware.

"Sit, Gilly. You're a guest, not a cook." I smiled at her and finished setting her place. She eased into the chair.

"Since you're the guest, would you please say grace for us?" I asked, sliding into my chair.

We bowed our heads and she prayed, "Heavenly Father, bless this food and all who partake of it. Amen."

Gilly spoke in a soft voice. In Georgia, and most southern states, grace is spoken over food from the high chair to the grave, a southern ritual.

After breakfast was over and the dishes were done, Jasmine took Gilly upstairs to her apartment, saying she wanted to visit awhile before sleeping. It was time to tackle Jonathan.

"Babe," I began, while we were lingering over yet another cup of coffee and cigarettes, "I have a big favor to ask."

"Who do I have to kill?" Jonathan crinkled his eyes at me, giving me a look that could almost melt the fillings in my teeth. "I know you, hot stuff. You ask favors freely. When you add the word *big,* I start to sweat."

"Gilly is in danger here. I think you agree. Will you take her back home with you for the next month?"

"To Eppley?" He was shocked. "The home of the most avid and nosiest gossips in the universe? Why do you think I drove you around my hometown at midnight with a sack over your head?"

"Get serious, Jonathan. You know I have a seminar starting two weeks from tomorrow. I have to find out what's going on with the judge and prove he murdered Gilly's mother. During my spare time, I have to keep this kennel operating and out of bankruptcy court. Jasmine, Wayne, Donnie Ray, and I are in and out of here all day long.

"I need help. I want you to take her, but not to live with you. Didn't your sergeant's wife have twins recently? Gilly cooks, cleans house, and would be a live-in babysitter. Do they have other children?"

"A three-year-old girl. But it won't work."

"Why not?" I pleaded.

"He's moonlighting four hours a night at a gas station. They can't afford her. Twins threw their budget out the window."

"She's free. I'll give her walking-around money. All they have to do is feed her."

"Still won't work. They don't have room. They live in a new double-wide trailer with three bedrooms. The kids' rooms aren't big enough to cuss a cat in. The twins are in one, the little girl in the other."

"Gilly can bunk with the girl."

"How do you know she'd do this? Have you asked her?"

"I don't have to. She'll be willing, believe me. You heard her describe the servants' quarters in McAlbee's mansion. She lived there her whole life. She needs to keep busy, just as she was taught. I could keep her occupied, but she'd think it was charity. This way she'll feel useful, and she'd be out from under my feet. Please?"

"I'll call my sergeant and ask. That's all I promise."

"Let me call his wife," I suggested. "She'll convince him."

"No way," he said sternly. "You manipulate me down here, and I jump through hoops. You're not going to manipulate my sergeant on my turf. I'll make the call."

"Yes, sir, chief!" I gave him a salute and a bawdy wink. He went to phone.

I sat and thought about what I had to accomplish tomorrow and the errand I still had to run before noon. I prayed that my high from the speed wouldn't desert me. There were things that had to be done before I slept.

I played with Bobby Lee's ears. When the room had cleared earlier, he had moved to my right side and was leaning against my leg. Rudy was probably sprawled in the middle of my bed, just to spite Jonathan.

Jonathan returned smiling. "I guess I have a passenger going with me to Eppley," he said. "I'm surprised how quickly Dalton accepted the idea. He agreed without even saying he had to check with Sue Ann. Said he hadn't had any peace at home for the past month."

"Was he saying p-e-a-c-e or p-i-e-c-e?"

"You have a dirty mind," he said, as he came around the table and reached for me.

"That's because I'm thinking dirty thoughts," I said, snuggling in his embrace.

Jonathan stared into my eyes. "I hope you and Jasmine don't make a practice of popping amphetamines when you get tired on a long search. What did you take, Ritalin? Dexedrine? Spancap? Those are the favorites up in Eppley. They're dangerous and highly addictive."

I pushed him away and gathered my thoughts. It was taking a moment to switch from passion to a discussion about speed.

"What makes you think Jasmine and I take anything?" I asked, buying time.

"A few months ago, a clutch of dieting housewives hooked up with a local dealer when they sampled his wares. They could go without eating, exercise for hours, and still have the energy to go home and give hubby some thrills. A doctor alerted me. Three of his patients were addicted. After you know what to look for, it's easy to spot. Glittery eyes and exaggerated arm movements, thinking you're a well-oiled machine when actually you're jerking like someone with apoplexy."

"We only took one small orange pill," I said with disgust. "I really think you're blowing this out of proportion."

"Sorta lopsided, with a line down the center?"

"Yes."

"Dexedrine. By prescription only. They used to be prescribed for people who wanted to lose weight, but not anymore. Too many people abused them."

"I've had in my possession a total of four pills for over a year. I gave two away, and early this morning Jasmine and I took the last two. You don't have to worry about me overdosing. I'll also cut down on my intake of crack and heroin," I muttered.

"Why are you making a federal case out of my friendly concern?" he asked, fully in the dark.

"Because just maybe I was feeling randy, and we stopped to discuss my drug habit," I snapped. "I'll tell you one thing, big guy." I gave a crude bump and grind as I headed out the door. "You sure missed a hell of a good time!"

I could still hear his laughter as I walked across the porch.

Upstairs, with Jasmine's help, I got Gilly excited about her new temporary home in Eppley, Georgia. Jasmine had taken her bath and was wearing a white corduroy jumpsuit. I felt grimy, but I had miles to go before I bathed. The two of them went over to the cottage to pack Gilly's clothes. Before they left, I informed them that I had a short errand to run and would be back in about thirty minutes. I told them to get sufficient luggage out of my closet to hold all of Gilly's goodies.

I marched over to the grooming room and opened the small safe where we kept the controlled substances we used to train the dogs. I also kept an envelope with several hundred dollars inside. You never know when you might need cash in a hurry, and this was one of those times. I pulled out two hundred for Gilly. That should hold her for a month. She had beautiful clothes and a job that would take up much of her time. Maybe she could get her hair done each week, or something.

When I walked up the steps to the back porch, Rudy was stalking back and forth, tail at full mast, quivering with indignation. I picked him up, over his protests, and sat on the chaise. I turned him on his back and began to rub his stomach.

"You and Jonathan have a spat?" I cooed at him in felinese.

Jonathan opened the screen door and joined us.

"You should pay me the courtesy of listening to my side of the story first," he said defensively. "Rudy always exaggerates."

"What happened?" I'm sure I had an amused glint in my eyes.

"Rudy took offense when I put my valise on the bed. That's it."

"My guess is that Rudy was asleep and you dropped the bag from a height of three feet or more."

"You were peeking in the window!" Jonathan gasped, with laughter.

"You two are worse than two small boys on a playground fighting over a ball! You're not even *trying* to make friends with him. If he sneaks up behind you and sinks a claw into your ankle in retaliation, you'll have to grin and bear it. Okay?"

"You shouldn't plant ideas in that pea brain of his. You know he's listening."

I laughed and set Rudy on the floor. He made a wide circle around Jonathan's feet and went back inside.

"Want to go with me to the drop and pick up the data on my Case of the Murdered Queen?"

"Wouldn't miss it for the world. Shall we take my car?"

"Sure."

Jonathan followed my directions, turning off Highway 301 onto a two-lane county hardtop. After two miles, we took a narrow dirt road that was still pitted with puddles of water after the heavy rains of last night. Two more miles and I told him to slow down. We were looking for a small lane leading to the right.

"This is a different drop from the one we went to in November, isn't it? I don't recognize anything."

"Oh, my, yes. The last of the great spy masters never uses the same drop twice. I receive a new codebook and the numbered drops the first of each month, regular as clockwork."

"How many, did you say, use his services?"

"He never mentions his other clients. I think there are four of us, and I found out that much purely by accident. My *chief* bought five books exactly alike from Susan one month, just three days before the first. When my codebook arrived, it was the book Susan had described. If she hadn't thought that the man was odd and buying five paperbacks exactly alike odder still, I wouldn't have heard about it. I figure he keeps one for a reference. Ergo, there are four of us."

"You lead a weird life, lady," Jonathan commented.

"It has its moments," I admitted. "There. Take that lane. It's supposed to lead back to a deserted barn."

Jonathan slowly maneuvered his large sedan through a sharp turn and then between two fence posts that no longer held up wire. He stopped in the open space, and we looked at a ramshackle barn with most of its siding missing. The whole structure leaned precariously to the right. The roof was ten feet closer to the ground on one side than the other.

A large brick fireplace was mute evidence that a farmhouse had once been there. The tall pole that had once held the dinner bell was still standing, but the bell was missing. I visualized a woman hurrying out of the hot kitchen, wiping her hands on her apron, and tugging on the rope. The iron bell would tilt, the large clapper hitting the side, and the pealing notes would be heard by the hands working in the field.

"Jo Beth?" Jonathan asked. "What happened?"

"Fire, I guess. They didn't rebuild, just moved away. Maybe the fire happened at night and they all perished." I shivered.

"You sound ghoulish."

"Sorry, I just saw the woman ringing the dinner bell."

Jonathan began humming a ghostly theme.

"Only in my mind, silly, not in person."

I opened the car door and started toward the barn.

"In there?" Jonathan was incredulous. "The whole thing could collapse at any second!"

"I suspect it has been standing as long as both of us put together. It should hold up five more minutes. Don't be such a ninny!"

"Since when is being prudent considered ninny-ish!"

"Ninnyish?" I was snickering.

"Ninny-like?" he corrected.

"Beats me," I said.

"Where's the stash—excuse me—the drop supposed to be?"

"Third horse stall on the right in the back. Under the hay," I answered.

"Stand clear," he ordered in a deep voice. "This is a man's job." He trudged into the barn and disappeared.

I began a loud countdown. "A thousand one, a thousand two"—I didn't look up from my watch until he skidded to a halt in front of me, holding out the package—"a thousand eight. Wow! You may not be brave, but you sure are fast!"

"Doesn't take me long to inspect a barn," he said, breathing hard.

"Aren't you going to open it?" he asked on the way home.

"What happened to immoral, illegal, and against your principles?"

"You're right. Don't open it or tell me what's inside."

"You got it," I agreed.

"I don't need to know. It would just upset me," he added.

"I concur." We rode in silence for five minutes.

"Open the package," he yelped. "Please?"

"It's for your own good," I said righteously.

He began to growl. I laughed and hugged the package to my chest.

"No, no, no," I sang cheerfully. He finally hushed.

When it came time for Jonathan to return to Eppley, he loaded Gilly's cases, tossed in his valise, and locked the trunk.

"I left Brent and Sue Ann Dalton's address and telephone number on your desk. I'll call you Monday night, like always. Will you promise me you'll use some horse sense when you start investigating the judge? I do have a pretty cushy job, but I still need to get my eight hours every night. When I worry, I can't sleep."

"I promise," I vowed, and crossed my heart. "Take care." We hugged. I don't like mushy farewells, especially with an audience.

I walked over to Jasmine, who was handing a small shopping bag to Gilly.

"Some munches for the journey," she explained.

"My contribution is six Cokes in the cooler on the back seat. Jonathan's eyes glaze on a long trip. He'll drive for hours without stopping for the necessities. If you have to go, tell him to stop at a rest room. If he doesn't comply within ten miles, remind him again."

Gilly's eyes filled with tears. "Y'all have been so nice to me. I really appreciate y'all's kindness. I never had anyone who did for me before, except Mama."

"Hush now," I said. "I'll call you Monday night, see how you're getting on. If you get lonely, give me a call anytime. You have my number. I'll find out what happened with your mother, I promise."

I hugged her, and she turned to Jasmine. With only a brief hesitation, Jasmine gave her a warm embrace.

As we were standing in the courtyard, waving at the car pulling away, Jasmine gave a derisive chuckle.

"How times have changed. Imagine a born-and-bred true daughter of the South wanting a hug from me, a black ex-whore!"

"I don't ever want to hear you describe yourself that way again," I said in anger. "It's like me saying, I'm an ex-child, or ex-baby, and it makes even less sense. It happened, you survived it, and it's in the past. You are a successful woman, working hard to achieve a college education. You're a competent mantrailer and dog trainer, and you can muck the hell out of the dog cages!" I was trying to inject a little levity into my uplifting lecture.

Jasmine gave me a wintry smile. "I look in the mirror every morning, Jo Beth. I say, 'You are an ex-whore who worked the streets from twelve years of age until you were nineteen.' It's the only way I can ever survive and have any future. I wish you could understand that. I can never forget."

She patted my shoulder and went upstairs. I stared after her long after she'd gone inside. She's a gutsy lady and she was right: I couldn't understand. No one could who hadn't walked in her shoes.

I swam toward the surface, searching blindly for light and trying to understand the noise that was forcing me to concentrate. I was so far under, the depth was more like a coma than sleep. I tried to force my wits to coherence, but they were scattered like cobwebs in an attic. Jasmine was speaking and shaking my shoulder.

"Are you awake, Jo Beth? Lord, I hate to wake you, but I knew you'd kill me if I didn't. Please wake up! Can you hear me?"

I opened my eyes. "What time is it?" I groaned and sat up.

"Four in the afternoon. Are you with me?"

After a long hot soak in the tub, polishing off three cold beers, I had fallen in bed. The beers were to neutralize the lingering effects of the speed. They were also quite tasty. It had been a little after one when I had crawled into bed. This meant I'd had less than three hours' sleep after functioning for thirty hours straight. I wasn't counting the brief nap on the boat. It hadn't been long enough to matter.

My gut tightened with dread. Something bad had happened. Jasmine wouldn't be awake herself if it wasn't important. She wouldn't have awakened me if the kennel was on fire, if all the dogs were safe. A person shouldn't have to hear bad news when exhausted and severely sleep deprived. It just wasn't fair! Well, who said life was fair? Who and what? I suddenly knew that something had happened to someone I cared a great deal about. I raised my head and looked at Jasmine.

"I'm awake and tracking," I said quietly. "What happened?"

Jasmine eased onto the bed and held both my hands. "Sergeant P. C. Sirmans from Hank's department called earlier. It was just after you had gone to bed. Donnie Ray saw me on the stairs, knew I was still up, and transferred the call to me."

I knew she was trying to ease into it gradually, so I sat and waited without showing impatience. I wasn't in any hurry to hear her news. As long as I didn't know, they were still healthy, functioning, breathing, and alive.

"He wanted to know if Leroy was here with us."

I closed my eyes. Not Leroy. Please, God, not my dearest friend in all the world. I must have swayed because Jasmine grabbed my shoulders.

"He's alive, Jo Beth! Leroy is alive! Oh, God, I'm doing this all wrong!" she cried.

"You said the magic words. I'll be all right now. What happened?"

"Sergeant Sirmans knew when the search ended. He thought Leroy might still be here. Leroy's wife—her name is Jackie, is that correct?"

I nodded. I couldn't trust myself to speak.

"Jackie," Jasmine continued, "had called the

station wanting to know where Leroy was. She had driven to the landing, and his truck was still in the parking lot. She heard about the rescue and arrest on the radio. She was worried that he was hurt."

"She thought he was with me. She wouldn't call here if Leroy was missing for a month. Tell me the rest."

"Sergeant Sirmans went to the landing and started asking people on the dock if they'd seen Leroy leave." She took a deep breath and again clutched my hands.

"A kid there had seen someone. He didn't know Leroy, but he had seen someone leaning heavily against a man who helped him into a red truck."

Oh, my God, Bubba. Bubba had Leroy! Wait, don't panic, Jasmine had said he was alive. How could she be sure?

"Go on," I croaked.

"Upon hearing this, Sergeant Sirmans called Hank. He's doing fine and running the department from his hospital room. He instructed the sergeant to put out an APB and for everyone to start searching. They found him about thirty minutes ago. The sergeant called Hank, and Hank called here."

"How bad is he hurt?"

"They don't know the extent of his injuries yet. Hank talked to the EMT who brought him in. He told me to wake you and tell you to go to the hospital if you are up to it. He says it's pretty bad."

I jumped up, staggered, steadied myself, and began throwing on clothes.

"I'll drive you," Jasmine said, helping by finding a pair of socks and my joggers.

"I'll be fine. You've had less sleep than I."

I looked up from lacing a shoe when she got in my face. "Read my lips. I'm driving. A statement of fact, not a request. I'm going for the car. I'll be out front."

"All right," I agreed. I had been doing some arithmetic. The rule is: one beer, one hour. I'd had three beers, and it was barely three hours since my last one. I felt lightheaded. Exhaustion might have something to do with my feelings, but I didn't want to wander over the middle line on my way to the hospital and encounter a logging truck.

I tucked my wallet into the pocket of my jeans and grabbed a hairbrush. I'd tame my frizzy mop on the way.

Jasmine got us there in record time. She's a very good driver. She had never owned a car or driven one when I hired her last year. I had paid for her driving lessons. I would never attempt to teach a friend how to drive. It's a very easy way to lose a buddy.

We didn't stop in the lobby. I knew he would still be in surgery. We ran up the stairs to the surgical floor. Near the nurses' station, I was stopped in my tracks by a wild-eyed Jackie.

She was in the surgical unit's waiting room and saw my approach. She looked disheveled and appeared hysterical. Her mother was hovering behind her and both were staring daggers at me.

"Jackie, I'm so sorry about Leroy. Have they told you anything about his condition?"

"Get the hell out of my sight! If you think you're going to see Leroy, you have another think coming! You are never to call him or speak to him again. You almost got him killed, you bitch!"

"Jackie, I know you're upset—"

"Upset? You think I'm upset? Let me show you upset! I promise you on my children and my mother's life if you ever speak another word to Leroy, if he lives, I'll leave him and take the children away from him forever! If he dies, and you dare show up at the funeral, I'll kill you!"

I saw her mother's eyes widen, and she reached for her daughter's arm. Jackie shrugged her off and took a step closer.

"Do you believe me?" she screamed.

"Yes, Jackie, I believe you. Please don't take your anger at me out on Leroy. He loves you so much. I promise I'll never call him or speak to him again."

I saw her intention and had time to stroll down the hall and back before her hand connected with my face, but I stood there and didn't move an inch. Maybe it would make her day. It sure wasn't going to brighten mine, but I had it coming. She had warned me last year, and I had broken her rules. She put every frustration in her life into that blow. My face felt like a blowtorch had breathed on me. My lip was cut and I could feel the warm blood trickling down my chin.

"Good-bye, Jackie." I said, with numb lips that didn't want to form words. I turned blindly and Jasmine caught my arm and led me down the stairs.

It was good that she had come. Left on my own, I would've run into a wall.

In the lobby, Jasmine handed me a Kleenex to wipe the blood. She pulled open the heavy front door and was holding it for me when a hand grabbed me from behind and turned me around.

"Hello, Sidden! You look terrible. We need a few words before you go." It was Timothy Sizemore, special features reporter from Channel 3's news team. A Kewpie doll: five feet six inches, 145 pounds, blond hair, blue eyes. He was perfectly styled, from his blow-dried hair to his tasseled wing tips. His face was in focus, and his words were crystal clear.

Suddenly, the world was silent, and all movement became slow motion. I watched with interest as Jasmine slowly appeared in front of him and shook her finger. I knew she must be telling him something, but no sound penetrated my vacuum.

He turned and gestured wildly to his photographer, who was trying to feed change into the Coke machine. Jasmine looked very graceful in slow motion. She brought up her right leg, clad in white corduroy, to connect with the top of Timothy's inseam. He did a slow sprawl to the right, then finally curled into a ball.

Real time returned in the parking lot as Jasmine hustled me across the tarmac and into her Geo. We didn't speak until she was on Highway 301, near the turn into our driveway.

"I'm so sorry, Jo Beth. I lost it when he started yelling for his cameraman. All I wanted was to get you out of there, and he was going to tape you all the way to the car, the weasel!"

"I was privileged to be able to view it in slow motion," I answered her dreamily. "Beautiful. Just beautiful."

# 11

## Picking Up the Pieces
### *April 14, Sunday, midnight*

I opened my eyes. I was in my bedroom, in bed, wearing pajamas, and the light was dim. I turned my head to the left and saw why. There was a navy-blue towel draped over the bedside lamp. Rosie was sitting in a comfortable chair with her feet propped up, sound asleep, wearing slippers and a robe, so I deduced she was spending the night.

I felt movement and glanced to my right. Jasmine was on the other half of my queen-size bed with her back to me, obviously spending the night also. Jasmine was not, however, causing the bed to move. It was Rudy. Near the foot, he turned again to find the perfect spot to catch forty winks. This was normal. He woke often during the night, jumping down for a snack or to prowl the darkness.

I must have done something strange to make them worried enough to pull double duty. Maybe not. Jasmine could've been exhausted and afraid she wouldn't wake up if I needed her.

I tenderly touched my split lip. It was swollen and felt like a grape was resting between my teeth and gum. My face was sore from nose to chin.

I eased out of bed so I wouldn't disturb my minders and went to the bathroom. Back in the hall, I stretched to assess the damage. Some sore muscles but I felt fine. Other than the split lip and bruised face, everything else seemed to work. I walked into the office and turned on a light. The clock said midnight. It was about 4:30 P.M. when I'd crashed, so I'd slept for more than seven hours. I couldn't remember anything after coming home. I didn't even remember getting home. We were in the car when my memory stopped. I stretched my brain trying to remember, found nothing, and said to hell with it.

The hectic events of the day had probably closed in, and I'd blown a fuse from exhaustion. Leroy. The pain came flooding back and I pushed it away. I went to the desk and looked up Glydia's phone number. Midnight was too late to call anyone, but I dialed anyway.

"Hello." Sounded like Josh.

"Josh, this is Jo Beth. I apologize for calling so late, but I was worried about Glydia. How's she doing?"

"Just great, Jo Beth. She's sitting here beside me in the kitchen. In the hospital today, she took her pulse, monitored her IV, then removed it and checked herself out around eleven this morning. All she needed was to hold Peter safely in her arms. We have you to thank. I don't remember if I did that last night. We both owe you a huge debt of gratitude."

"Nonsense. Glydia has come through for me in the past, and I plan on using her services whenever I need them for many years in the future," I said cheerfully.

Josh laughed. "You can use my services anytime. Just ask. Glyd is trying to tear the phone away from me. Would you like to speak to her?"

"You bet."

"Sidden, you know we both love you, but Josh's services are out. Find your own guy."

"Aw, heck," I said, in mock disappointment.

"Listen, gal, you know what I'm trying to say. Anything I've got, with the exception of Josh, is yours." Her voice broke.

"Don't get mushy on me," I said sternly. "I called to ask a favor."

"Medical report coming right up." Her voice softened. "I heard about what happened up in surgical and down in the lobby. I'm so sorry Jackie was such a bitch. Mildred called before eight. We remembered that you and Leroy were joined at the hip all through our school years. She knew you'd want to know how he's doing and that we'd be in touch. She called the minute he came out of the cast room."

Friends. Some can break your heart, and others try to mend it. Now *I* was getting mushy. There was a lump in my throat as big as a bullfrog.

"Jackie had the right, Glydia. She's his wife, and

I've been a thorn in her side for years. I should've been strong enough to fade into oblivion years ago. She blames me for almost getting Leroy killed. Did I?"

"This is not your fault, Jo Beth. He's got a severe concussion, four broken ribs, two compound fractures in his legs, some missing teeth, a broken nose, and a face that looks like beef liver. On the good side, he's strong and healthy. He'll make it, I'm sure. I hope that animal you were married to gets hung by his nuts!"

"How is Leroy's condition listed?" I asked gingerly.

"Critical but stable," she admitted, with reluctance. "But that's the severe concussion. Nothing else is life-threatening. Honest!"

"Will he be able to walk?" I dreaded the answer to this one. I sensed she was holding something back.

Her brief silence before answering confirmed it. "His left leg is pretty bad, honey. They did the best they could. Only time will tell. But listen, chick, Leroy can handle it, whether it's a limp, a cane, or even a leg replacement. That's the worst, I swear. His right leg should heal nicely."

"Thank you," I whispered. "Will you be home for the next few days?"

"Only till Thursday. I'm due to rotate to the day shift in surgical. You'll be getting your daily bulletins from the horse's mouth."

"Thanks, Glydia. I'll call you each evening, if it's all right."

"That's fine. Don't worry."

"I'll try," I said, and disconnected.

Leroy was in critical condition because Bubba knew it was a way to make me suffer. He must have gone to the landing when he heard about the rescue. He was probably standing behind a tree watching us when Leroy and I said our good-byes. He knew if he attacked me again, even his father, with all his political pull and his friendship with Judge McAlbee, couldn't help him.

With my restraining order in place, plus two prior attacks on me, he knew he'd be facing some serious jail time. But one-on-one with a man—and no eyewitnesses? If Leroy survived and Bubba was convicted, he wouldn't serve more than six months. To him it was worth it, knowing he had touched me where I was so vulnerable—wounding my dearest friend.

I was hungry. I went to the kitchen and scrambled two eggs, made toast, and poured a glass of milk. I debated if I should wake Rosie. She always complains if she's disturbed at night, says it's hard for her to go back to sleep. She looked comfortable. I decided to let her rest.

My kitchen activities roused Bobby Lee, and he moved to my side. I scratched his ears and shared my eggs and toast with him. His ability to heel without a leash and never get in the way is uncanny. He's been totally blind since birth and has memorized every inch of the house, kennel, and grounds. His eyes look normal, and he turns toward you when you speak.

When a bloodhound trails with his nose close to the ground, his huge ears gather the scent and channel it to his nose. Bobby Lee also uses his long ears to measure sound. A slight footfall, and he knows which way to turn. He can hear a person approaching the house from over fifty feet away.

He's a gifted mantrailer and drug sniffer, and he has captured my heart. This is the dog that Deputy Selph made a renewed offer to purchase for one grand. He couldn't buy him for a million dollars. Bobby Lee and I are soulmates.

It was now twelve-twenty. Much too late to call Hank. He needed his rest. I also knew that if his dispatchers didn't keep in close touch, he'd be calling them every half hour or so. He lives, sleeps, and breathes his job. I dialed his room extension direct. The switchboard at the hospital closes at ten o'clock. Hank would have an operative phone, or he'd be sleeping in his own bed tonight.

"Sheriff Cribbs." He answered after the first ring.

"Did I wake you?"

"Nah. Who can sleep in here? It's against the rules. If you nod off, they come in to take a sample or give you a pill. Have you gotten the word on Leroy's condition?"

"Yes. Thanks for letting us know."

"The sad part—"

"I know, I know," I interrupted. "You put Bubba inside, and they let him out. I've learned the hard way. Nothing new. The last time I saw you, you looked like death warmed over. Feeling better?"

"The prick only pricked me. I'll heal faster than a cat's ass—overnight. Do you and the dogs have a

solid case? I want you to make sure the animal—
who used to be my friend—doesn't walk."

"Stacy Conner is nailed. Don't fret on that score.
As for healing overnight, I'm sure you will," I agreed.
"You also catch bullets with your teeth and leap tall
buildings in a single bound. What else is new?"

"Something strange. I remember a party yelling
sweet nothings in my ear while I lay on the cold wet
ground."

"You were having delusions. Never happened.
Nighty-night." I severed the connection.

I wandered around trying to find something to do
in order to put off a dreaded chore. I took the packet
of information on Judge McAlbee out of its waterproof wrapping, spread out the computer sheets, and
began reading. Little Bemis had worked his magic. I
had all the skinny on Judge McAlbee, from his cra-
dle to the present.

McAlbee's daddy had died while young Sanford
was attending college. He had left his son the family
mansion, a meager bank account, and a pile of
debts. Judge McAlbee had suffered through some
lean years after opening his law practice. Six
months after donning his superior court robes, his
bank balance began a healthy climb, and his real
estate holdings grew by leaps and bounds. This was
unusual, since local judges are paid a modest salary.
You could place these computer printouts under the
dumbest state attorney's nose, and he'd smell a
skunk. He might not know the why and wherefore,
but he'd know the judge was not making his money
the old-fashioned way—by earning it.

I mulled over the information. Fixing cases for cash? Probably, but the three small counties his judgeship covered weren't profitable enough to account for all his wealth.

Whatever was going on in the woods where he took Gilly's mother must be the source of his wealth. She was so sure she'd be killed, it had to be bad. However, Clara Ainsley's definition of bad could have been a shade different from mine. She was naive and a devout Christian. She might have gone down those stairs by accident. Coincidences do happen. Gilly's hotel room going up in smoke could have been a righteous fire, with no evidence of arson.

Nope, I didn't think so.

I checked his real estate holdings to see how many parcels of land—heavily wooded or planted—would have to be inspected. Jesus. Twelve of his land tracts fell into the correct category: fifty acres or more and almost inaccessible. Four tracts were over ten thousand acres, and one was over eighty thousand acres. It would take me a month of Sundays to spot-check all the places where he might be conducting his nefarious activities.

McAlbee's wife had died twenty years ago. According to Gilly, he'd never had a live-in, nor did he have many dates; at least he didn't bring anyone home. He entertained a lot. Dinner parties for twelve, larger party bashes, but no intimate candle-light suppers for two. I wondered why he was still taking chances, building up more and more wealth. As far as I knew, he had no heirs, and, at sixty-three, he better get hot if he wanted one. I understood that some people consider wealth a scorecard, amassing it only for the sake of winning. Was he playing a game? Maybe.

I put away the papers and wandered back to my office.

Sitting at my desk, I knew I couldn't put off writing the letter any longer. I took my stationery into the kitchen, poured a Diet Coke over ice, and began to write.

*My dearest Jonathan,*

*I hope I can find the words to explain to you just how much knowing you has meant to me. We both have known from the beginning that this wouldn't last, couldn't last, because of who we are and the miles that separate us. The reason we must break off this budding romance had already happened yesterday before you departed—but I was unaware. It's ironic that my fear has always been for my lover, not my closest friend.*

*After our search was finished yesterday, Bubba sandbagged Leroy as he was heading home. There's a very good chance he may never walk on his own two feet again. This is the fate that awaits any man who stands too close to yours truly. Please spare me any protestation of manhood and your ability to protect yourself.*

*I'll remember you always. When I'm on our*

*island, and the sun is slanting through the trees, and I've popped the last can of beer in the cooler, I'll see you and hear your lovely nonsense. Take care. Meet a nice local lady and have lots of babies. I wish you a happy life.*

*Your friend forever,*
*Jo Beth*

I slipped into the bedroom and put on shoes, eased open the nightstand, and strapped on my .32 pistol. I turned off the gate alarms and picked up a flashlight. It was a moonless night, a repeat of last night without the downpour. I walked down the drive and placed Jonathan's letter in the mailbox. The flashlight was just in case. The rest of my life would probably be spent doing just-in-case routines. Not a very soothing thought for the early morning hour.

Back in my room I changed shoes for slippers, washed my midnight meal dishes, and slipped into bed. Everyone was asleep but me. Even the animals hadn't stirred and kept me company on my early morning stroll. The clock said 3 A.M. when I closed my eyes. I dreamt of Leroy in pain and saw a sad and angry Jonathan, both pointing a finger at me. I would've been better off if I had remained upright and watched the sunrise.

# 12

# A Lost Love and a Friendship Ended
### *April 15, Monday, 6:30 A.M.*

I was drinking coffee and puffing on cigarette number one when I heard the shower running. I didn't feel too bad, considering. My swollen lip had receded from the size of a grape to a raisin. My chin had a blue bruise. I felt pulled together enough to face the morning. Rudy was on my left, and Bobby Lee was in his reserved space by my right side. Both had eaten.

Jasmine appeared, looking crisp and neat. "I smell coffee," she said sleepily, then poured a cup and took her first sip.

"Did I say anything foolish last night? Maybe confessed to burglaries or random acts of mayhem?" I asked.

"You were exhausted and very docile. Have no fear that you blabbed your childhood secrets. How do you feel?"

"I'll make it. Did you get any sleep?"

"About thirteen hours, I'd say. I doubt if I moved a muscle the entire time. When did you wake up?"

"Midnight. I made some phone calls. Learned of Leroy's condition. Wrote a Dear Jonathan letter. Piddled around and was back in bed by three."

"Were Leroy's injuries sufficient to warrant breaking up with Jonathan without giving it some thought?" she asked quickly.

"Outside of a major concussion, and a left leg so crushed there's a very good possibility that he'll never walk on it again, I imagine that in about six months he'll feel just peachy."

"Oh, dear Jesus!" she exclaimed quietly. "I'll pray for him."

"Good. He needs all the help he can get."

"Quit beating up on yourself. It's not your fault!" She sounded ticked.

"The hell it isn't!" I retorted.

"What isn't?" Rosie echoed, shuffling in with a mussed hairdo and still in her robe and slippers. A rare sight indeed.

Rosie's fire chief hubby wouldn't be pleased with her deserting her conjugal bed. The only accepted excuse is a deathbed watch. My exhaustion would be viewed as feminine and frivolous. Her husband's a middle-aged redneck, and their marriage is only four months old. I hoped for her sake that the honeymoon wasn't over. I didn't want to be the reason for anyone else's distress.

I softened my voice and explained Leroy's condition.

Wayne entered after a perfunctory knock. I signed and spoke simultaneously, bringing them up to date. I sent Rosie home to fix breakfast for her husband. Jasmine left to do her makeup. We were all attending a breakfast meeting in the common room at seven o'clock.

I conduct a week-long seminar once a month to train law enforcement personnel to handle their new charges. Six trainers came in every weekday. The kitchen would be open these next two weeks before the seminar, so we could have more time with the trainers and the dogs. Wayne lingered while his mother and Jasmine gathered their things. He leaned over and closely examined my facial damage.

"What does the other guy look like?" he signed.

"She's without blemish," I signed and smiled. I explained Jackie's wrath. Wayne laughed. He can make a few sounds, but his laughter, consternation, or joy come out much the same. You have to see his face to observe the difference. The sounds are a cross between a bullfrog's croak and a crow's caw. He has a wonderful sense of humor and would rather tease me than eat.

I told him to send Donnie Ray over to my office, we needed to talk. I still had a few minutes. I then remembered that I hadn't heard our cook arrive.

"Miz Jansee cooking?"

"I opened the gate for her at five. She and I are not like some who sleep away the morning."

"You looking for a worm, as in the early bird gets?" I grinned.

"Duck next time," he signed, and winked.

When Donnie arrived, he stopped short in the doorway. I was seated at my desk.

"Come in," I invited. "I don't bite. We need to talk about Angie."

I refused to call her Angel. She didn't have a single angelic trait. He advanced and perched on the edge of the seat in front of me, acting like a nervous patient awaiting a doctor's dreaded diagnosis.

"Donnie Ray, I'm playing the mother role here. I hate to see you hurt, and I don't enjoy tearing out your heart and stomping on it. Most young people your age hate to hear 'I'm doing this for your own good,' but it's true. Wayne didn't interfere in your personal life because he's inexperienced in these matters and doesn't see the consequences. Unfortunately, I do."

"Y'all don't know her!" he blurted. "People have been picking on her all her life! She's good and kind and I love her! Don't you think I've heard some nasty rumors and them snickering when I take her someplace?"

"She's a promiscuous little tramp. Under her older sister's tutelage, she's been turning tricks since the tender age of thirteen. Her father found out and tried to help her. He finally gave up when he came home unexpectedly and she was in her bedroom with two boys, one white and one black. She told her father she was the filling for a salt and pepper sandwich. She thought it was funny. Almost everyone in town knows what goes on in that trailer where she lives with her sister—except you. I'm sorry, but she's setting you up."

"She's pregnant, Jo Beth! She's gonna have my kid. I love her!"

His anguish was evident in his voice. The poor schmuck. My guess was that she had let the pregnancy go past a trimester from carelessness and couldn't find anyone to perform an abortion. Her sister wasn't prepared to support her during the pregnancy when she wouldn't be able to work, so she was trying to find someone to dump the kid on. I also thought Donnie Ray was proclaiming his love too loudly. In spite of his lousy home life, he's basically a good decent kid. He realized what she was, but she was laying a guilt trip about the baby in his lap.

"Before you take on a responsibility that isn't yours, I have a suggestion. You've only been dating her six weeks. The chance that you're the daddy is infinitesimal, but I'll spring for a DNA test to ease your mind. Glydia Powell will take the blood samples. We should have the results in about three weeks. How does that sound?"

"I really would like to know," he said anxiously. "I feel so damn guilty! I can't desert her."

I sighed. "Donnie Ray, no way in hell will she allow the test. She knows the results will show she's lying. She'll make all kinds of excuses to keep from taking it, hoping to talk you into marrying her anyway. Don't let her put you through the wringer. Okay?"

"Can I have the car tonight?"

"Sure," I said with a smile. "You know the rules."

This brought a weak grin to his face. He was halfway to the door when he turned.

"Thanks, Jo Beth."

"Get outta here."

I told Bobby Lee to fetch his short leash. He scampered off, quivering in anticipation. His short and long leashes hang on nails on the back porch. He would rear up on the correct post, remove the leash with his teeth, and wait for me near the steps. I knelt in front of Rudy and rubbed his chest.

"It's a no-no, big guy, you can't go. Go take a nap."

We had played this scene often, so he knew his lines. He gave me a furious meow, lifted his twitching tail high, and departed in a huff. He wasn't allowed in the common room when meals were served. He's a consummate beggar. I walked out and attached Bobby Lee's leash to my belt. Then I had to wash my hands because bloodhounds drool all over everything held in their mouths. When they shake their heads, they can also sling drool ten feet or more. This is their only irritating trait, but they give so much they are automatically forgiven by all who own them.

I was late. Everyone was eating. I greeted Miz Jansee Tatum as I filled my plate from the small steam table. She's a mother of six, wife of a lazy drunk, and needs the money she earns part-time. She's only forty-five but looks older.

"Mornin', Miz Jansee."

"Mornin' to you, Miz Jo Beth."

I was her boss. She couldn't make herself call me Jo Beth, although I had asked her to several times.

"Everything looks delicious," I commented, as I filled my plate. Jasmine poured coffee for everyone at the table: six trainers, Wayne, Donnie Ray, herself, and me. The entire crew was there except for Lena Mae, my maid, and the veterinarian, Harvey Gusman. He had taken the job after his predecessor, Ramon Fontaine, killed himself last November. He visited the animals every day and worked on their charts, but he wouldn't join us for meals when I had the common room open. I had explained that they were considered working meals, and we discussed business. I had stopped by the small animal clinic, located on the front five acres of my property, and visited him several times, but he still wouldn't socialize. He seemed happy and was always cheerful. I'd think he'd be lonely, uprooting from New York when he moved here, but he didn't spend any time with any of us.

Jasmine returned to her seat, and when she had my attention she nodded toward the door. I turned and saw Harvey standing just inside the room.

"Think of the devil and, lo, he appears," I murmured.

"Pardon?" Jasmine questioned.

"Later."

I gave him a big smile as I approached, but his lips didn't get any wider in response to my greeting. His wasn't a happy look, and my gut clenched.

"Like some breakfast? I just filled a plate."

"No, thank you," he said politely. "I need to speak to you after you finish. I'll be with the puppies." He turned to leave.

"You have my undivided attention," I said anxiously, as I followed along behind him. "What is it?"

"Perhaps I better show you," he answered, without turning.

Harvey stopped in front of the pen that held Judy's last litter. They had just turned six months, and we had started advanced obedience training. Every puppy ran to the wire, bumping into each other in their haste. Two of them were high in the rear. Sometimes you wonder if you are raising a kangaroo. We appraise their topline at four weeks. These two looked unbalanced and gawky. If their form is good at four weeks, usually their topline will turn out good after adolescence.

"It's just their uneven growth," I said, feeling relieved. "You know some puppies go through this stage."

"It's Alexander the Great and Small," he said. I heard the desolate chill in his voice.

Harvey was referring to Alexander the Great, whom we had decided earlier would make a great mantrailer. He was the largest of twelve. The smallest pup had his slightly older litter mate's markings, so we had dubbed him Alexander the Small.

My eyes flew back to the animals. Both Alexanders were at the wire, not lying down, not trying to vomit, not showing signs of a swollen stomach. It wasn't the dreaded bloat, which is the number-one killer of bloodhounds.

Number two is hip dysplasia. My heart chilled. I quickly looked back in the pen and searched out the two. Alexander the Great was now sitting with his head down. Alexander the Small was walking back toward his sleeping quarters with a wobbling and swaying gait.

Tears burned against my eyelids. "Judy has had five successful litters!" I said hotly. "It had to be that damn bloodhound I hired to breed with her!"

"Jo Beth, I'm sorry for your loss, but you know that besides gene interaction it can also be insufficient pelvic and thigh muscle mass."

"The environment here is perfect," I snapped. "You know these puppies were fed and treated right!"

"And you know even when two perfect and proven dogs are mated, approximately thirty percent of the progeny can be afflicted."

"Is this the last whelping for Judy?" I asked.

"Do you want to take the chance?"

"'Course not. We'll move her out of the nursery and into drug or arson training," I said.

I stood and gazed at the others. "How many more?" I asked in sorrow.

"We'll watch. I'll check them daily. We'll just have to wait and see."

I glanced inside the sleeping area. Both Alexanders were lying down on the mat. "Can we give them a couple of weeks?"

"I found it in their X rays two weeks ago. It's obviously accelerating. They are now exhibiting stiffness and pain in their joints."

"Then we'll do it now," I said, pronouncing their death sentence.

"Let Wayne help me. You shouldn't be there."

"Why? Because I cry, and I'm not as stoic as a male? Wayne would feel the pain just as deeply. Besides, it's my responsibility."

We loaded them and took them to the clinic. I leaned over the table with each of them, cuddling and rubbing their stomach and ears while Harvey administered the shots. In less than two minutes both of them were gone.

I was sitting in the office smoking and making a list of possible search areas in McAlbee's holdings when Jasmine found me some thirty minutes later. She was carrying a tray covered with a napkin.

"Miz Jansee fixed you a fresh plate. You didn't eat, and she's emptying the steam table."

"I'm not hungry. Thank her for me."

"What's wrong?"

"Both Alexanders had hip dysplasia. We had to put them to sleep."

"I'm so sorry. Of course you're not hungry. I'll take the tray back." She turned to leave and turned back. "The others?"

"We don't know, as yet."

She nodded and left.

At 3 P.M., Jasmine and I headed to the first grid search on McAlbee's land. We were going to try to make two parallel lines through about two thousand acres, a long slim tract of land, roughly twenty acres wide and a hundred acres long. We would walk approximately two hundred yards apart through the narrow width from opposite sides. When we reached the other side, I'd scout to the left and find her van, and she'd go to her right to reach mine. We would give the dogs no scent, just use the compass and try to go as straight as possible. Also, it had to be a quiet journey because we didn't know what was out there.

I tried not to think about the possibility of making this comparatively short jaunt through the woods a hundred times and still missing our target. I was very glad it wasn't hunting season. Also, in April the production of moonshine slows. In the winter, when the north Georgia trees are bare, our local 'shiners produce for their northern brothers-in-crime. In the spring, when the northerners have sufficient foliage to hide their stills, our 'shiners only sell locally.

Jasmine had Caesar and I took Mark Anthony. We didn't use backups when we were simply hunting anyone's scent. We just put them in the woods, kept them straight with the compass heading, and on a silent passage. If they picked up a human scent other than ours, they would signal by their eagerness to go another way.

When we stopped at Jasmine's position, I hopped out and went back to her van.

"What handles are we using today?"

"It's your turn to choose."

"Okay. I'll be Rather and you can be Jennings," I suggested.

"Can I be Brokaw instead?"

"Done," I said with a smile. "Rather and Brokaw. Let's keep it short. Thirty-minute intervals. I'll start,

so mine will be on the hour and yours on the half
hour. Avoid any human contact. If you're caught,
give the searching-for-a-lost-dog story: the catch on
the van came undone and he skedaddled. If this happens, open your mike without removing it from
your pocket. Key it several times. I'll hear the clicks
and try to find you. Any questions?"

"Nope. Good hunting."

"Happy trails to you," I replied.

We unzipped our suits, removed the bandannas
from around our waists, placed them in Ziploc bags,
and swapped. This was in case we had to start
searching for each other.

She removed her key from the van and pocketed
it, leaving it unlocked. We might have to leave in a
hurry. We had spare keys hidden in magnetic boxes
under the right door of each van. She stopped at the
edge of the woods and whispered in Caesar's ear.
He took off toward the brush, and they both disappeared.

I headed for the opposite connecting road, where
I'd enter and come toward her, hoping we'd pass
within a couple of hundred yards of each other. She
would drive around to her van, where I'd be waiting
for her. Easier said than done, but it should work.

I grabbed the keys, whispered "hush-hush" several times into Mark Anthony's ears, and we were
off.

The woods were old growth, not planted pines.
The brush was thick but had few vines, so moving
through the weeds was fairly easy. I had almost
curbed my reluctance to step into waist-high weeds

when I couldn't see where my feet were landing. In the past when I stepped on a smooth root—the size of a snake's girth—I'd be stunned and then panic. Last summer I stepped on a medium-sized rattlesnake, and from then on I knew what a root felt like, compared to a snake's body. Now when I hit an unyielding roundness, I know it's a root. If it's soft and yielding and squirms, it's time to panic; I'm standing on a snake.

I made good time for about two hundred yards and then ran into a cypress slough. The water would be only a foot or so deep, but it was home to water moccasins and gators. To wade, or go around? I dropped my pack and shinnied about three feet up a pine, as far as I cared to climb. I looked to see if the slough ended in a few yards or went on forever. I couldn't see enough to make an educated guess, so I decided to wade. This close to the road and the noise of passing traffic, I doubted a great big alligator would be in residence. The young gators would be scared of me. A huge one would be angry at being disturbed. They like peace and quiet.

I dug out the waders, stepped into them, pulled up the straps, and fastened on my backpack. I stepped gingerly into the water and walked slowly, dragging my feet. This way, I was making waves, not loud splashes that attract hungry predators.

The water turned into firm ground, and I stepped onto the bank. The slough wasn't wide, but it could have run for several hundred feet if I'd tried going around it. I had made the right choice this time. Mark Anthony had led the way, only having to swim once. Some of these sloughs have underwater caves where the large gators go when the ponds start drying up.

That's another plus, working with an animal that's twenty-eight inches to the shoulders. I know I'm almost two and a half times taller; therefore, I have a warning of deeper water and can usually avoid wading in over my head. I can swim with a thirty-two-pound pack on my shoulders for a few feet, but I sure as hell don't like it.

Bloodhounds run with their eyes almost covered by the thick folds of skin over their foreheads. It is possible, however, for an occasional vine to snap, get under this protection, and inflict some eye damage. We had entered a patch of thick vines. I gave Mark Anthony the silent signal to retreat. We backed out and circled the area. It cost me some additional yardage, but it was worth it in order to play it safe.

The sweat was trickling down my clothes inside the sealed suit. I stopped and drank water. Mark Anthony had filled his belly just before leaving the pond. The black turgid water might not hurt me, but I'd have to be mighty thirsty to try it. I always carried plenty of water.

It was time to call Jasmine. I keyed the mike.

"Rather to Brokaw. Over." I spoke softly. Sounds carry easily in these woods. It was quiet for a moment, but not for long. Crows were cawing, sending the message that someone was trespassing below. Small birds were singing a happy chirping melody in the low brush around us. I once found a

tiny nest, only the height of my waist, holding two
miniature eggs colored pale blue and cream. Last
spring I peered into a small hollowed-out nest in a
drift of fallen pine needles and saw two tiny
goslings. Their wings were still wet and they were
trying to flap them dry just after pecking their way
to freedom from their egg incubator. The third one
was still hard at work, with only his head poking
through the shell. I didn't touch them, just took a
delightful peek and moved on. I never spotted their
mother, but I knew she would be near. All mothers
in the wild are very protective. They have to be.
There is a wide food chain out here. Predators eat
victims. They in turn are eaten, up to and including
the black bear that makes his home in the swamp.

The bears' only enemies are humans. They are
shot because they can travel out of the swamp at
night, range for over a hundred miles searching for
honey, and return before the sun comes up.
Beekeepers hate them. They place hives in lonely
woods so the bees can feed on nearby abundant nec-
tar-bearing bushes. A bear can destroy fifty or more
hives in a honey raid, leaving behind thousands of
homeless and honeyless bees and a livid beekeeper.

No answer from Jasmine. I tried again.

"Rather to Brokaw. Over."

Radios can malfunction. It happens occasionally,
usually to me. Anything that receives electrical
impulses or takes batteries will inexplicably cease
working. I'm cursed with gremlins.

I'd wait until it was time for her transmission.
Maybe she could reach me. We allowed for this in

our plans. If the first transmission didn't come through, we would wait until the second one was late before we changed any plan.

I knew these woods could distort sounds. Hank had four new signal towers installed out of his first budget last year. One of them should be close enough to relay the signal. I knew it was too soon to worry, but I did. We had checked the radios before we parted, and they had worked properly.

I kept tramping through the bush while the pessimist in me played the what-if game. What if she fell, had a badly sprained ankle, or even a broken one? What if she leaned over to release a vine, and a snake bit her on the face or neck? That was the only area vulnerable to snake fangs. What if Caesar had gotten bit, and she was hauling him out by sled, maybe going for antivenin, and she couldn't reach me to let me know? What if she ran into some antisocial men, stumbled onto something illegal, and didn't have time to warn me before they had her?

Playing the what-if game can be dangerous. The more scenarios I invented, the more my blood pressure rose. I started hurrying and tripped and fell forward, trying to catch myself with my hands and knees. My left wrist was jammed by a tree root and felt like a screwdriver had been inserted on one side and was protruding out the other. I stood and whimpered softly from the pain. Shit! I tried to massage it gently, but I couldn't stand any pressure at the pulse point.

I'd been careless for just a few seconds, and I was gonna pay in waves of pain radiating from the sprain. I knelt in front of a large tree and, using only my right hand, unbuckled my waist belt and shrugged off my pack. The damn wrist was swelling right before my eyes. I dug into my pack and found the first-aid kit. Popping it open, I removed a three-inch Ace bandage and wrapped my wrist so the elastic was snug but not tight. Maybe it would help hold down the swelling.

I fished out three Excedrins and swallowed them with water. I was awkward and slow but managed to attach my backpack correctly. I reinforced the command for silence by repetition of signals to Mark Anthony. I started marching, and the pressure of my steps seemed to keep time with the throbbing in my wrist.

My time to call was 4 P.M. This was when I had been unable to reach Jasmine. Four-thirty was the time when Jasmine should call me. I waited till four-forty, ten minutes past the calling time. Something was wrong, and I had to change my search pattern. I no longer believed it was a malfunctioning radio. I gave Mark Anthony the command to rest. I had to decide on how to proceed.

From my many days spent tramping through these woods and swamps, I'd developed a sense of distance and could roughly estimate how far I'd traveled. I believed I had advanced more than half the distance from my starting point to the end of the trek, in order to reach Jasmine's van. She had additional time for a head start, with me having to drive around the connecting road. I'd encountered only two obstacles and had lost little time compared to some paths out here.

Now for the kicker. Was I ahead of her on our parallel walk, or had she been detained early on? I drew an imaginary line in my mind. When I moved over the approximate two hundred yards that should have separated us, would she be in the half ahead of me or behind me? Should I advance toward Jasmine's starting point or turn around and search the area leading back to my van?

I fondled Mark Anthony's ears and fed him two pieces of deer jerky. I checked the compass. I had been walking due south. I signaled to Mark Anthony to remain silent, turned, and took the direction due east. In a short time, I should be near where Jasmine would pass or had already passed.

When I arrived in the corridor I thought Jasmine should have used, I looked around me. My not-so-dead reckoning was just short of wild conjecture. Right or wrong? South or north? Jesus.

I turned due south in the direction of Jasmine's van. You make your choice and go with it. It was transmission time for me, Rather trying to reach Brokaw without success. It was 5 P.M. There was plenty of time to hike out of the woods in a straight line. I didn't like placing all my money on one feeble horse. I'd try to spread it around.

I began a zigzag pattern, the first leg to the southeast for fifty yards, the second leg to the southwest for fifty yards, always advancing forward. This would take longer, but it would increase the odds of finding her. Maybe.

I didn't want to put Mark Anthony on Jasmine's scent out here where I wasn't sure she had ever made steps. I needed that ace in the hole in order to track her from her van into the wood. It was my only hope of finding her if my present pursuit ended in failure.

I ran into a dense collection of briars, assorted vines, and tough thick brush. I detoured in a more easterly direction. This made my return leg even longer. Jasmine missed her 5:30 P.M. radio check. I no longer anticipated hearing the radio come to life.

I walked out of the woods ten minutes before my radio check was due at 6 P.M. If I hadn't moved from my original track, I would've hiked to my left a few hundred yards to find Jasmine's van. Coming out where I thought Jasmine had traveled, I found my special sense I felt in the woods had deserted me. I was dead wrong. To the right, at least three hundred feet away, Jasmine's van looked about the size of a matchbox. I had less than an hour of sunlight, a few minutes of dusk, and then first dark. Jasmine was out there somewhere depending on me, and I had failed her.

# 13

## At High Altitude with Little Oxygen
### April 15, Monday, 6:15 *P.M.*

I picked 'em up and put 'em down all the way to Jasmine's van. Daylight was precious, and I wasn't going to waste any of it. A false dusk had spread through the trees, and the sun was low behind a huge old growth of pines. Pencil-slim strips of golden sunlight fell across the road, making the surrounding foliage look dark against the rose-colored sunset.

After reaching the van, I forced myself to take a five-minute rest. I filled Mark Anthony's water bowl from the five-gallon jug in the van and topped off my canteen. I drank deeply, then added water to replace what I'd used. I fed Mark Anthony beef jerky and then rummaged in Jasmine's glove compartment for some goodies so I wouldn't have to remove my backpack.

I found a box of raisins, a granola bar, and a Golden Delicious apple. I bit into the apple. As long as I was active, I could keep the pain in my wrist out of my mind. As I rested in the open doorway of the truck, the throbbing escalated.

The wrist felt better when I held it vertically. I slipped my gloved hand under the left strap of my backpack. That eased the pain, and it would also help keep me from banging it against a tree.

I threw the apple core into the bush for a possum or a coon. I fed more jerky to Mark Anthony, gave him the command for silence, and used my teeth to open the Ziploc bag containing Jasmine's bandanna. I thrust the material under Mark Anthony's nose and whispered the refrain, "Hush, hush. Find your man. Hush, hush. Where's your man?" I repeated it several times. It's not the words so much as the tone of one's voice that excites the bloodhound.

Mark Anthony started dancing the wiggle-jiggle, quivering in anticipation of the chase. He was loaded with confidence and seemed to be gloating. This would be easy. He'd know that scent anywhere!

I knew he was locked onto the scent when he entered the woods in the exact spot where Jasmine had disappeared earlier. The dew was adding moisture to the air, and there was little or no wind. The insects were out in force. When I started panting, I'd have to keep my mouth closed and blow out each inhalation with force to keep my nose clear. This sounds like something one would have to concentrate on to achieve, but not Georgia residents who live below the gnat line. It's something you learn as a child that becomes so automatic you don't even think about it.

We made good time for the first few yards and then suddenly ran smack into a slough. It was filled with old cypress trees, dark stagnant water, and God knows what else. Wading through a pond in bright sunlight in early afternoon is one thing. Entering unknown water and peering through murky dusk with darkness closing in is another.

I guessed that Jasmine had skirted it. She had just begun her journey and wouldn't want to stop and put on waders. Mark Anthony hesitated, made one figure eight, and turned right. At least I'd made one correct assumption today.

Jasmine had been right in her decision. The slough petered out after one sharp turn, and then higher ground appeared. The dew was falling, the light was failing, and my socks would be squishy within the next five minutes. Blisters, here we come! It is, however, easier to know you're gonna have blisters later than to shuffle forward in awkward waders now.

The waterproof flashlight was in my right thigh pocket, easy to reach. It was the time of day when light would hinder more than help. When total darkness arrived, I'd have to stop and fish out my hunter's headlight and put it on. I looked down as I walked and placed my feet with care. It was difficult to see roots or vines that could trip you. I was three feet behind Mark Anthony's rump and couldn't miss seeing the gyrations of his hips as he danced the hokey-pokey. His windshield-wiper tail looked like machinery gone berserk.

My heart soared. Jasmine was near. These movements from Mark Anthony were his celebration of victory when he was forbidden to bay. We surged forward, roots and vines forgotten. I saw a lighter blob against a tree. Mark Anthony was in Jasmine's face, trying to lick her. He was slinging drool with every turn of his head.

She had her hands up, trying to fend off his advances. I saw a flash of her beautiful white teeth as she grinned at me. I pulled Mark Anthony to the next tree and tied him, whispering fast praise and reminding him to be silent. There was a chance he'd break training from sheer joy. I stepped back, clicked on my light, shined it on the ground, and knelt by Jasmine.

"Ready to get the hell out of Dodge?"

"Lord, it's good to see you," she said softly. "I thought I was destined to spend the night out here."

"Nope. Ol' silly Sidden finally got her act together and rode to the rescue. What happened?"

"I had my radio in my hand waiting for your call when I planted my left foot to step over that fallen oak over there." She pointed to a large tree rotting away to replenish the soil. "My foot pushed right through a termite's nest. I fell forward and smashed my radio against the trunk. My foot turned and my leg wouldn't. My ankle's sprained and the leg is broken."

"Maybe it's just twisted." I couldn't tell with the flashlight shining on the rescue suit. I'd have to peel her out of it.

"I heard the bone snap." She was still whispering.

"Oh. Well, you have my permission to cuss. Hold the flashlight. Are you in pain?"

I dropped my backpack behind me and unzipped her suit.

"Any pain?" she hadn't answered the first time I'd asked.

"A little," she admitted.

"Which means it's hurting like hell."

I dug in my pack and found the first-aid kit, a morphine vial, and a disposable needle. I left them resting on the lid of the kit.

"Let's get your suit off."

With her help we got her arms free. I saw this was going to be a bitch of a job.

"Jasmine, you know when you hurt with movement. Try to slide your butt away from the tree so I can get you stretched out."

She inched her way forward and I pulled her suit down before I eased her flat. The sweat on her forehead matted her hairline. I slipped my good hand beneath her belted jeans, pulled up to get her weight off her buns, and slid the suit down with my aching wrist, ignoring my own pain. I had to do it twice to get the Kevlar to release. A moan escaped her lips. I could empathize. I felt like howling at the moon, and my wrist was only sprained.

I braced my useless fingers, which were now swollen like pork sausages, on her stomach and worked the pants down her legs with my right hand. I thought I'd never get the laces on her shoes untied. After I had her free of the suit, I wanted to kick back and rest awhile. Maybe have a cigarette or two. Grab a nap. Instead, I told her silly anecdotes sprinkled with spicy descriptions to distract her. I didn't know if it was working. I was too busy to listen for her comments.

It was now totally dark. Mosquitoes were droning in concert, along with other assorted night fliers. I needed my headlamp and a can of Off!, but I wanted to get the morphine in her so it would have time to dull the pain before I started hauling her out in the sled.

I propped the flashlight on the first-aid kit and unbuckled her jeans. They were snug. I'd have more luck peeling a grape with one hand than shucking her out of those babies. I found my scissors and, after making a shallow slit, started snipping at the material on her right hip.

"I hope these weren't a favorite pair," I said into the silence. "I know my next bit of news will brighten your day. When Doc Sellers wrote prescriptions for the drugs we carry, his wife, Faye, gave me a lesson on how to administer the medication. She used a grapefruit for show-and-tell. Man, I bet I was the best grapefruit popper in Dunston County. However, I have to confess I've never popped a needle into flesh before. You have the right to sue me later if I miss on the first couple of tries. Okay?"

"Don't you dare miss," she murmured.

I chuckled as I knelt in front of the flashlight to fill the syringe. I rested my forearm on Jasmine's hip and held back the cut fabric. I stabbed the needle into the hip area just as I'd been instructed.

"Thanks, boss. I hardly felt a thing."

"Liar. I'm going to fetch Caesar."

I took the flashlight and hurried over to where he was. He had been a jewel by not baying in excitement when Mark Anthony and I had arrived. Jasmine had secured him to a sapling before she had started her crawl. I gave him a quick hug, whispered sweet nothings in his ear, and tied him beside Mark Anthony.

Unloading my pack, I pulled out the rescue sled, a can of insect repellent, my headlamp, and my snake probe. I lit a cigarette and took a deep drag. I went back to retrieve her pack.

"Close your eyes. I'm gonna spray you with Off!"

I rolled her bandanna, placed it over her eyes, and fogged the air over her entire body. I sprayed myself and then went over to the dogs and poured half the water from Jasmine's canteen down Mark Anthony's throat and the other half down Caesar's. I wasted some, but they lapped away and managed to wet their whistles. I divided the deer jerky and told them to enjoy.

I pulled her pack close enough so we could converse in normal tones, then opened it and pulled out her snake probe. It was about two feet long in three collapsible sections. It is used to give advance notice to reptiles that we are invading their space. Closed, its diameter is slightly larger than a car antenna. I was going to use hers and mine as splints in order to immobilize her broken leg. She had two three-inch Ace bandages, and with my remaining one I should have enough wrap.

I smoked and planned. I wanted to allow time for the drug to kick in before I started moving her leg around.

After ten more minutes, I leaned over to inspect her features, keeping the light from her face.

"How you feelin'?"

"Wha—?"

I decided to start. She must be experiencing some relief. I taped sections of the probe to her leg and began passing the bandage over and under. It was easier and faster than I thought it would be. She was lying on a straw and weed surface. I was able to force the roll under her without moving the leg.

Now for the rescue sled. This would be no problem if I had the use of two good hands, so I tried a method I'd seen a hospital nurse use when I was a patient. I turned her body sideways and crammed the pliable Kevlar under her as far as possible. Pushing her on her back, I moved to the opposite side, worked the sled under her, and straightened it out. I pulled her leather belt from her waist and fastened it around mine. I'd need it later. I pulled the rings on the inflatable pillows, packed her in tightly, and eased up the zipper until it was locked under her chin. Jasmine was taking a nap. I watched her inhale a couple of times to be sure her breath wasn't labored.

I gathered everything up and repacked both packs, leaving out a twelve-by-twelve-foot camouflaged plastic sheet. One at a time, I lugged the backpacks over behind a tree near thick brush. I covered them with the plastic, tucking the extra sheeting underneath. I broke off some limbs from merkle bushes and placed them on the plastic to blur the square edges. Wayne could fetch them tomorrow. I carved a jagged scar on the tree trunk, placing it as high as the average buck would reach to rub his antlers.

I made a final check of the area, making sure I'd left nothing to warn of our visit. I lit a cigarette and took a few puffs while I untied Mark Anthony and Caesar and slipped the sled pulls over my shoulders. I stripped the cigarette butt and scattered the remains.

The trip back wasn't too difficult. I hooked both leads to my backpack strap and held the flashlight with my right hand. Thank God, Jasmine was out and couldn't feel the two roots I bumped her over. We were only about two hundred yards from the road. Mentally, I practiced my moves in order to load an unconscious Jasmine into the van using my one good hand. I would manage. I had no choice.

When I reached the edge of the forest, I turned off the flashlight and listened to the evening noises. When my night vision started working, I scanned the tree line on both sides of the road. Nothing stirred. I sighed, turned on the flashlight, and pulled Jasmine to the back of the van. I loaded Caesar and Mark Anthony first. I did everything quickly, afraid that if I stopped and thought too long, I'd realize it couldn't be done. I wanted to get her in the van before my mind decided it was impossible.

I opened the double back doors and eyed the height from the ground to the aisle flooring. Two feet or less. I took out the collapsible stretcher that I had added to the vans after the rescue of Mary Ann Miles last July. I laid it beside the sled and engaged all the small bolts to make it rigid.

Standing on one edge of the sled, I tugged Jasmine onto the stretcher and straightened her out. I pulled the restraining straps tightly over her chest and thighs. I undid her belt from my waist and wound it twice around her ankles, securing her feet.

Without pausing, I braced my bad hand behind the left side of the stretcher's handle. Putting most of the strain on my right hand, I came up from my bent-knee stance and raised the stretcher the required two feet and braced it firmly against the rear flooring. I was panting from tension, exertion, and apprehension. I was only half done. Jasmine was now at an angle, tipped from the van's flooring to the ground. I moved without thought. I leaned down and physically willed the stretcher up straight and braced it against my bent knee until I could marshal enough strength to slide it into the van.

Black spots swam in my vision, but I had done it! I had the dogs to thank for having strength in my shoulders. Strong dogs, pulling impatiently to advance, had given me muscles I didn't know I possessed. Maybe I'd take up wrestling. Nah, not very ladylike. I leaned weakly against the van for a few seconds before closing the door, then cranked up and got us out of there.

When we were clear of McAlbee's property, I used the CB radio to call Dr. Sellers. His wife answered and said he would be at the hospital when I arrived.

After emergency personnel took possession of Jasmine, I removed my rescue suit and went to the lounge to clean up. Later, I sat in the waiting room, holding my aching wrist, nodding, and catching a few Zs.

Someone was shaking my shoulder.

"She's fine. The break is clean and she's up in casting. It'll be a walking cast. I'd like to keep her overnight if possible."

Dr. Sellers plopped down beside me and lit one of his small cigars. I really didn't see how he had the nerve to fuss at his patients for smoking, but he did, without blinking an eye. He trailed cigar smoke behind him as he made his rounds. This was a smoke-free hospital. They'd toss you out on your butt if they caught you puffing anything. Go figure. Dr. Sellers didn't see me into this world, but he'll probably usher me out of it. He's in his mid-sixties, broad shoulders, with a gray beard and a matching head of hair. He looked and acted like he was forty.

"You'll get no argument from me," I said, rubbing my face. "Can I see her?"

"Go home. It'll be a while before they finish. What happened to your hand?"

He reached for my left wrist and examined the puffy fingers.

"Just a sprain."

"Follow me."

It was a command. I followed his smoke trail into Emergency and sat where he requested. He rested his cigar on the edge of an instrument tray. The nurses must love that. He unwound the bandage and cleaned the area. He prodded the swollen tissue, causing me to flinch.

"It's just a sprain," he said and wrapped it with a fresh bandage. He winked at me. "Glydia sings your praises to all who'll listen. You did good, Jo Beth. What happened to Jasmine?"

"She stepped on rotten wood during a field exercise."

"Quit using that hand for a week. Give it time to heal properly."

"Yes, sir."

"I mean it. Want to see Leroy? Visiting hours are over, but I can sneak you in." I knew he had heard the entire story.

"Thanks, but I have promises I must keep."

"Quit being so damn noble! Cheat a little."

"I did, Doc," I said wearily. "That's what started it all."

He patted me on the shoulder and left. I took myself home.

It was after ten when I unlocked the first gate. Wayne was waiting for me in the courtyard with the second gate opened. I explained what had happened and asked him if Donnie Ray was home.

"He had a short date tonight," he signed. "Angie refused to be tested. He says it's over. He got home over an hour ago."

"I'm not sure, but I think the baby has to arrive before they can test for DNA anyway. I hope she doesn't find that out, if it's true. Can you and

Donnie Ray pick up my van? Go upstairs and get a sock or something from Jasmine's clothes hamper. The packs are only a short way in. You should be able to track easily."

"You'll be alone," he signed. That was a rare occurrence, especially at night, with the four of us in residence. Wayne was thinking about Bubba. He might be lurking somewhere near, ready to pounce. I had considered it but was too tired to care.

"Lock the gates behind you. I'm taking a bath. See you in the morning."

I turned on the tap, stripped, and started the washer. I fetched two beers and saw that Miz Jansee had saved supper for me. I didn't even lift the foil to check the contents. I was thirsty, not hungry. I picked up a church key and went back to the bathroom to soak and enjoy my bottles of brew. I had three more after my bath. They kept the throbbing in my wrist pushed back in a corner, and I was feeling no pain when I closed my eyes to sleep.

In the common room during breakfast, I told the six trainers about Jasmine's broken leg. Wayne stood and outlined the day.

After almost everyone had left, Lena Mae approached as I lingered over my third cup of coffee. Lena Mae is my part-time maid.

"Mornin'." She stood waiting for instructions.

"Good morning, Lena Mae. The first unit needs cleaning, but do Miz Jasmine's apartment first. I'll

be bringing her home about ten o'clock. If you have
time today, wash the curtains in my office."

"Yes'm." She left.

She's a thorough cleaner, and she doesn't gossip
around her folks about what happens here. She's
dependable. I should be happy, but she always
leaves me feeling inadequate because I can't change
her and neaten up her life. My failure. My ego. I
understood why I felt this way, but I still itched to
do it.

Donnie Ray was crossing the room from Wayne's
office to the grooming room. I beckoned him over.

"Donnie Ray, I'm not catching the phone today
so it'll be your duty. Take the name and number.
Don't say if I'm in or out."

"Your wish is my command," he snapped briskly,
beaming at me.

"Wayne filled me in on last night. Good rid-
dance." I wanted to relieve him of having to repeat
unhappy news.

"A load off my shoulders," he agreed.

I carried my plate and silverware over to the bus
cart, complimented Miz Jansee on a perfect breakfast, and returned to the office.

I was dodging a phone call from Jonathan. He
would have called last night and, not being able to
reach me, would probably try sometime during the
day. I was not going to talk to him, and I was praying
the letter I'd written Sunday night would get there
today, but I doubted it. Living in the sticks, I always
add a day or two to the post office's estimated time of
arrival.

I decided to call Gilly. I didn't call her last night, and if I called tonight, Jonathan might be visiting. I dialed the Daltons' number in Eppley.

"Hello?"

"My name is Jo Beth Sidden, and I'm calling from Balsa City. Is this Mrs. Dalton?"

"Please call me Sue Ann. May I call you Jo Beth?"

"Please do. How is Gilly doing?"

"She's an angel sent from heaven! She already has the house under control and is great with the babies. I actually was able to take a nap yesterday. Thank you so much for your generosity."

"I thank you for taking her. Would it be possible for me to speak to her? I won't make a habit of calling during the day, but I promised her I'd check to see if she was settled in."

"Please call anytime you wish. I'll get her. . . ."

"Miz Jo Beth?"

"Yes, Gilly, it's me. How are you?"

"Oh, Miz Jo Beth, you should see the children! They are beautiful! The Daltons are so nice. I really feel at home here."

"That's great, Gilly. It might take longer than I originally thought to solve your problem. If you need me for anything, will you promise to call?"

"I promise, Miz Jo Beth. Thanks for being so good to me."

"You're welcome. I'll call you in a few days. Bye-bye."

"Bye-bye."

One chore done. I dialed again.

"Surgical ward."

"This is Mrs. Johnson. May I speak to Nurse Powell?"

"Please hold."

"Mrs. Johnson? This is Glydia Powell. How may I help you?"

"It's Jo Beth, Glydia. I didn't want them saying my name in case Jackie might be passing by. How's Leroy?"

"In and out and making sounds. He's off the critical list and he's stable. He should continue to be awake for longer periods and start talking sense by tomorrow. The doctors are relieved."

"So am I. Thanks, Glydia."

"Any time."

I let my fingers do the walking.

"Sheriff Cribbs."

"It's me, Hank. How's the shoulder?"

"It's fine, but who's me? I have a lot of soft feminine voices calling all day long."

"I bet you do," I agreed. "When can you go back to work?"

"I was ready to leave, but Doc says one more day."

"Then how many days at home?"

"We're still negotiating. He says a week, and I say three days, tops."

"Prepare for a week. I'll call you at home tomorrow, if I have the time."

"Make the time," he pleaded. "I'll go nuts just sitting around all day."

"Have Charlene rub your back."

Now why did I say that? He'll think I'm jealous of her. I was irritated at myself for giving him an opening.

"Charlene doesn't live there anymore."

"Pity. Listen, I gotta go. See you later."

"Parting is such sweet sor—"

I hung up on him and called Susan.

"Browse and Bargain Books."

"It's me. Are you busy?"

"At this hour? I'm only on my second cup of coffee. I've been reading about your exploits. Tell me all."

I gave her a capsule version of Peter's rescue, the chase, the arrest, Leroy's misfortune, and Jasmine's broken leg. I said she did it in a field exercise. I didn't tell her anything about McAlbee and my suspicions.

"You're going to pick up Jasmine this morning?"

"In a few minutes. How was your weekend?" I asked.

"Nothing, compared to yours. Mom and Dad had a visitor. He's a horse buyer from Ocala, Florida. They were at their matchmaking best. He's forty, divorced, and has scads of money."

"I can tell by the lack of animation in your speech that there's something missing. What is it?"

"About a foot in height and a waistline. He's maybe five feet tall and weighs somewhere in the neighborhood of two hundred and fifty pounds. I bet he can take a shower without getting his knees wet."

We giggled like teenagers.

"But how's his personality?"

"Forget his personality. Can you imagine the two of us walking into a room full of people?"

I tried. Susan is five feet nine inches tall, with shoulder-length red hair subdued with dye to a titian glow. She never goes out wearing less than four-inch spike heels. She's strikingly beautiful.

"It wouldn't work," I asserted.

"You bet your ass," she agreed. "Everyone would think I was a floozy he had captured with his wallet. Besides, if I wanted a Pillsbury Doughboy, I could find a local one with no trouble at all."

"You deserve a Rhett Butler," I said loyally.

"You can have Rhett. I want George Clooney."

"Don't we all."

"Not you, Sidden, you have Jonathan."

"Not anymore. I wrote him a Dear John letter late Sunday night."

"You didn't!" she screeched. "Are you out of your mind?"

"Listen," I lied, "someone just drove up. I'll talk to you later. Ta-ta."

I hung up in a hurry. She'd make me pay later, but I couldn't face her recriminations this early in the morning. I went upstairs and put together an outfit for Jasmine to wear home, then hoofed it to the grooming room and found Donnie Ray mixing puppy meals.

"Need any help?" I asked. The puppies eat four times a day.

"Wayne's got one more field trial to judge, and then he's coming in. I can manage."

"Anything on the need list?" I walked over to the pad to check.

"We're out of disinfectant for scrubbing the pens."

"I'll go by Dewitt's on the way to pick up Jasmine. Don't forget the phone."

"Nothing so far," he called to my departing back.

I took the van. It would be easier for Jasmine, wearing a bulky cast, to get in and out.

After leaving Dewitt's, I went to the office at the hospital to sign insurance papers for Jasmine's release. I obtained her room number and entered the elevator. My timing was lousy. Already inside were a nurse, an orderly, and Jackie.

I mumbled a low "Good morning."

In return I received a smile, a nod, and silence. A feeling of cold hatred seeped into my bones. She was projecting her hatred of me in the small enclosed space that separated us. That's one of the drawbacks of living in a small town. When you make enemies, Murphy's law dictates that you keep bumping into them wherever you go. I fled the scene as soon as the elevator door opened. My hands were cold, and a dull ache returned to my wrist.

Jasmine was propped up in bed looking lonely. When she saw me, she gave me a wide smile.

"What took you so long?" She spotted my wrapped wrist. "What happened?"

"We both screwed up," I said with a smile. "You ready to go?"

"Did it happen before, during, or after my rescue?"

"Before."

"I thought I had a fleeting memory of you being clumsy," she teased.

"I have a vivid remembrance of how much you weigh," I retorted.

Her face turned sober. "You got me in the van with only one good hand?"

"I'm sorry you missed it. I keep telling you I'm Superwoman; you just don't pay attention. You were snoring."

"Well, many thanks," she said in a sweet voice. "Do you think you can get me out of here?"

"Doc Sellers says you can leave?"

"Yes, yes."

"I'll go hunt up a nurse and a wheelchair."

"I can walk on this cast. I don't need a wheel-chair," she declared.

I just shook my head and left. Everyone thinks the rules don't apply to them or their injuries. With an infected fingernail that's healed, you ride to the curb in a wheelchair, being pushed by a nurse or orderly. It's the r-u-l-e-s.

When we drove into the courtyard, Donnie Ray ran out to meet us.

"You're to call Sergeant Sirmans at County right away. It's a call-out! Can I film it?"

"It depends," I answered. "Help Jasmine inside." I turned to her. "Why don't you stay with me today? Save the stairs for tomorrow."

"I'd like to go home, if you don't mind. I can walk fine."

"So be it. Help her upstairs, Donnie Ray."

I hurried inside and dialed the sheriff's department. The dispatcher patched me through to P.C. Sirmans, Hank's second-in-command.

"What's up, P.C.? This is Jo Beth."

"You're not going to believe me when I tell you where I'm standing and what just went down about fifteen minutes ago. Hank is tearing his hair out and raising Cain!" P.C. laughed.

"Are you going to tell me, or do I have to guess?"

"It's a humdinger! I'm standing in the parking lot of the Balsa City First National Bank, which has just been hit. The first bank robbery in this town in forty years, and Hank's missing it!"

# 14

## Clowns Belong in a Circus
### *April 16, Tuesday, 11:30 A.M.*

I chuckled along with P.C. It was funny. I bet Hank was having kittens.

"How many?" I asked.

"Two. They were wearing Halloween masks and totin' double-barreled shotguns."

"Who identified the guns?"

"A female bank teller, but don't worry, she described the guns accurately. Her husband's a skeet shooter and fills his own loads. She helps him."

"Anybody see the car they used?"

"Not that we've found so far. We're holding all the cars that were on the parking lot."

"I'll be there in twenty minutes."

"Right."

"Listen, hold those cars till I get there, okay?"

"Will do."

As I hung up, Donnie came rushing in.

"What is it?" he asked eagerly.

"Balsa City Bank holdup. You're not going. You want to load for a full search? I'll take Circe."

"Yikes, Jo Beth! Why can't I go? This would make a good training film, I bet. Please?"

"There are three reasons you can't go. The first two are double-barreled shotguns. The third is I'm the boss and I say no."

He fought his disappointment and knew not to argue. He nodded and left. He was growing up.

I was dressed okay. I didn't even need a bandanna to tie around my waist. No need for a backup today. I put on my holster, fed six extra rounds into the loops, and checked to see if the gun was loaded. I packed six Diet Cokes on ice and called Bobby Lee.

"Wanna go, big guy?" He shuddered with joy. "The long and short leads. Go fetch." He took off and I followed with the Cokes.

Donnie had Circe loaded when we got to the van. I glanced in back. My suit, gloves, backpack, and snake protectors were there. I hooked Bobby Lee to his safety belt and looked around. Where was Donnie Ray? The jerky bag was on the seat. The map case was at my feet. Nothing was missing. Maybe he was pouting. Just as I started the van, he came running across the courtyard from the direction of the common room, carrying a package.

"I asked Miz Jansee to make three sandwiches. One for you, and two for beggars. Did I forget anything?" He was breathless from hurrying.

"You did great. Thanks for the sandwiches. That was thoughtful of you."

"You're welcome."

I pulled out. No way would I put Donnie Ray, Bobby Lee, Circe, or any other coworker or animal up against two double-barreled shotguns. I'd learned my lesson with my beloved dog, Bo.

Crime-scene tape encircled the parking lot, which was almost full. I figured half the passengers were rubberneckers. I was fuming that P.C. and the deputies hadn't keep them off the lot. He had plenty of help. I counted five county cars and two city ones.

I parked parallel with the yellow tape, blocking one exit. I hooked Bobby Lee to my belt, opened the jerky bag, laid a piece on my glove, and held it under his nose. It was his signal that this was business, not pleasure. It disappeared with one chomp. I went to find P.C.

A city policeman informed me that he was inside the bank. I found him talking to a henna-haired woman in her fifties, Mrs. Cruise. She usually took my deposits and cashed my checks. They were standing behind a low partition, and I entered through a small swinging door to join them. I stopped. From fifteen feet away I got a good whiff of lilacs. I walked back into the lobby. When P.C. noticed me, I motioned him over.

"She's sprinkled with more toilet water than a commode," I informed him. "I couldn't take Bobby Lee any closer. What's the scoop?"

"There's good news and bad news. Just promise

not to yell when you hear the bad news. Hank is furnishing enough hollering without you adding yours."

"So lay it on me."

P.C. removed his cap, combed his hair with his fingers, and replaced the cap just so. He shrugged.

"One of the gunmen dropped a sack of money in the lobby as they were fleeing. That's the good news. The bad news is that it was handled by a city man and one of ours. It was given back to the teller, and she returned the money to the till."

"There goes the ball game," I said, with sarcasm. "City, I can understand, but a deputy? Christ!"

"It was Bennie Tatum, Jo Beth. He's a dispatcher, for God's sake! He was on his way to the bank to cash his paycheck on his lunch break. He heard the alarm and came running. Sorry." He looked miserable.

"Don't sweat it. When you look bad, you make me look bad. Where's the bag now?"

P.C. indicated where Mrs. Cruise was standing. I unhooked Bobby Lee and tied him to a table leg. Crossing the carpeted space, I tried to keep a neutral expression on my face, but I must have failed.

"Don't glare at me, young lady! Even I know you can't take prints off a pillow slip. I've waited on you at least a thousand times, and not once did you tell me that you used your bloodhounds to capture bank robbers. How was I to know that my fingers would be contaminating?"

I produced a weak smile. "You're right, Miz Cruise. It's not your fault."

I whipped out a handkerchief, picked up the worn pillowcase, and beat it back to P.C.

"She'll never clear another check for me, I bet," I said with a grin.

"I'm glad I bank with the union," he replied.

I untied Bobby Lee, hooked him to my belt, knelt, and placed the material under his nose. "Seek! Seek!"

He sniffed, lowered his head, strained against the lead, and headed directly to the swinging door leading to the tellers' windows and Mrs. Cruise. I hauled him back and took him off the scent.

I glanced around the bank. Several people were waiting and acting impatient.

"Can I let them go?" P.C. asked.

"Not just yet. I want to check the parking lot first. These customers in here will walk outside and mingle and gossip with the people standing out there. It'll confuse any trail we might find."

"Try to hurry. The natives are getting restless."

"Who would you rather face, the natives or Hank?" I asked.

"Good point. Take your time."

I stood on the steps and studied the parking lot. There was one double row of cars, with a center drive, and one row on each side facing the street. Three ways to get on and off the asphalt surface. About half the cars had occupants. I decided to try the middle row first, stopping at each car and questioning the ones inside. I could see the officers speaking to different people, getting statements, I guessed.

I stopped at a blue car with a man and a woman and stood by the male driver's door.

"I'm conducting a search using a bloodhound. Did you see the bank robbers leave?"

"Didn't see a thing," the man replied. "We had walked over to the jewelry store across the street. Came back after they left."

I thanked him and moved two cars down to ask Mrs. Singleton, a middle-aged spinster, the same question.

"Hello, Jo Beth. Isn't this exciting! How many were there, and how much did they get?"

"You didn't see any of them?" I asked.

"Wouldn't you know, I missed the whole thing! I had just left the post office. I picked up a letter from my sister and waited till I parked here to open it. You remember Opal, my sister? She lives in Decatur now to be near her daughter and her grandchildren. I sat here and read her letter, or I would've walked right in on them! How many were there?"

I was finally able to move on. The next car had a young woman and a small energetic girl in the front seat. She looked like a Henderson, but I didn't want to start on family connections. I told her what I was doing.

"I was putting on my makeup and this jack-in-the-box next to me kept jumping up and down on the seat," she snapped. "How long do we have to sit here? I've got things to do. All I know is police cars came screeching up on the lot, and now they won't let us go in the bank. I have enough on my hands with her and him. I can't stay here all day!"

· I glanced in the back seat to locate the *him:* a small boy, who looked to be about seven years old, sitting so still I hadn't noticed him. His hands were folded in his lap, and he was looking straight ahead. At his age, he should have been hanging over the front seat, wide-eyed and excited, watching the action. I was curious about his behavior.

"Would it be all right to ask the boy if he saw anything?"

"He's blind," she said bluntly. "He couldn't have."

"The quicker I finish, the sooner you can leave," I coolly informed her. "It won't take long. What's his name?"

"You're wasting your time. His name is Farley. Just hurry, will you?" Her voice and manner were contemptuous. I got the feeling that this woman wasn't coping too well with the boy's blindness. I moved to the rear door and opened it.

"Hello, Farley. My name is Jo Beth, and I have a bloodhound with me. His name is Bobby Lee and he's blind too. Are you afraid of big dogs?"

"No, ma'am." His head didn't turn in my direction.

"He didn't *see* anything either!" the woman retorted.

I saw red. She had about as much tact as a picket fence. As I straightened to let her have my opinion, I spotted P.C. walking toward me. I went to meet him.

"Take the lady sitting behind me and her little girl over to the far side and show them a car. Ask

questions or something. I want to question her son.
Give me five minutes, okay?"

"Think he saw anything?"

"I won't know until I ask." I whispered.

As they left, the woman was protesting and P.C.
was making soothing remarks. I stood at the open
door and drew Bobby Lee up close.

"I'm back, and I want you to meet Bobby Lee.
He's been blind from birth. I'm gonna let him put
his paws on your seat, and you can feel his ears. He
has very long ears. Okay?"

"Yes'm."

I patted Bobby Lee on the neck and then patted
the seat. He placed his large paws on the upholstery.

"I'm going to reach for your hand, Farley, and
place it on Bobby Lee's head. He loves having his
ears rubbed."

The small hand and the large head connected. I
was rewarded for my efforts with a smile of wonder
on Farley's face.

"There're so soft!" he exclaimed. "How old
is he?"

"Nine days ago he celebrated his first birthday. If
your mom will bring you out, you can visit the kennel and hold some of the smaller dogs. Bobby Lee's
too big to sit in your lap."

"She won't bring me. She's afraid I'll get hurt,"
he said matter-of-factly. "Next year will be better.
Dr. Sellers has talked her into sending me to a special school where they'll teach me to get around by
myself."

His frankness touched my heart. I knew I was

wasting time, but two blind souls were passing their love to each other, and I hated to separate them.

"I have to go find the bad men, Farley, I wish I could visit longer, but I can't."

"Thank you for letting me touch Bobby Lee," he said politely, and put his arms around the dog and hugged. "I wish I could've seen what the robbers looked like, but I only heard them. Will Bobby Lee be able to find them?"

I took a deep breath. I was afraid to ask, not daring to believe.

"What did you hear?" I said carefully.

"Two people running. They got in the car in front of us and tried and tried, but it wouldn't start. Then they got out and got in the next car and drove away, real fast."

"I'm gonna put my head near yours for just a minute, Farley." I told Bobby Lee to rest. He removed his paw and sat. I crowded close to Farley.

"Point to the car they tried to start," I told him. I followed the line of sight from his pointing finger and saw an old truck parked directly in front of us.

"Now point to where the car was that you heard leave."

Farley moved his arm a few degrees and was pointing toward the adjoining parking space to the truck's right. The slot was empty.

"Were you able to hear which way they went?"

"Yes'm. They backed out and went that-a-way." He was pointing directly at the front exit onto Main Street.

"That's great, Farley. You did good and you've

been a great help. Thank you so much. You heard more than all the people on this lot saw. I'm very proud of you. I'm going to tell everyone how much you helped." I leaned over and hugged his small frame.

I saw P.C. and Farley's mom and sister heading back toward her car. I waited by the old pickup until he joined me.

"What gives, Jo Beth? The lady says her son is blind." He looked upset.

"Hold on, P.C. Farley's blind, but he was more observant than his mother and all the other sighted people on this lot. We have an earwitness to the getaway."

"A what?"

"You heard me. This truck belongs to the robbers," I said, indicating the vehicle in front of us. "They hopped in, and it wouldn't start. Then they stole the car parked next to it and drove out the main exit onto Main. Let's check it out."

He shook his head and followed me around to the driver's side. I stood on my toes, looked in, and saw the keys hanging from the lock.

"This truck?" P.C. laughed. "You know who owns this truck? Marcus Walter. He's a drunk. Probably sitting across the road in the Brown Keg getting pie-eyed this very minute. He knows better than to park out front; we'd just go in and take his keys. For the last four years he's been in our lockup more than he's been out."

"Henry Walter's boy? Tall, black hair, always wears white shirts and cowboy boots?" P.C. was nodding and grinning. "He's about four years younger than I am. Twenty-six? Twenty-seven?"

"He's twenty-seven. I saw his booking sheet about three weeks ago," P.C. agreed. "You telling me he's our bank robber?"

"Either that or someone tried to steal his pickup and it wouldn't start."

I looked at the truck again.

"P.C., check inside. Don't touch anything. If you're sure the pickup is in park, turn the key and see what happens. Wait," I said, having second thoughts. "Let me get a scent sample first. You can't get in there without leaning on or touching something. While I'm getting a sample, why don't you ask the folks inside the bank to step out here. I'll stand in the empty parking space, and we'll find out what kind of transportation the robbers lifted."

"I think you're barking up the wrong tree," he replied.

"We'll see. You got any better ideas?" I asked, in a mocking tone.

"I'll go round them up."

"Keep them on the steps!" I yelled to his retreating back.

After retrieving my backpack from the van, I went to the truck. I took out a package of sterile four-inch bandages and a pair of thin rubber gloves. I opened the truck door and ran the gauze lightly over the seat, steering wheel, and brake pedal. I then sealed it in a Ziploc and wrote *Driver* on the label. I reached down, felt under the seat, and pulled out a fright mask that was supposed to represent Dracula.

I grinned with pleasure and placed it in a gallon-size bag.

Bobby Lee and I moved to the center of the empty parking space, and I waved at the people standing on the steps. I walked to the other side of the truck, took a sample from the seat, and bagged a Frankenstein mask. I placed the scent bags in my pockets and held the fright masks. I heard P.C. and the others before I saw them. Feet slapping on the asphalt surface. I closed my eyes, and knew this was what Farley had heard about an hour ago.

"It was a 'ninety-four Jeep Cherokee," P.C. said. He was out of breath from his sixty-yard dash. Deputies Rigdon and Selph were with him.

"Belong to Mrs. Cruise?" I inquired with a smile.

"No," P.C. returned with a grin, "Pete Mayes. His wife was driving it."

"Good. I know they drove out there," I said, pointing toward Main Street, "but we don't know if they went left or right. Did you put out an APB?"

"They're checking with DMV now. We'll have the plate number soon."

"Well, do you want to try and track them or just wait until the stolen vehicle is found?"

"Down Main Street? Is it possible?" P.C. sounded doubtful.

"Maybe."

"Jo Beth, they had shotguns. I want to find Marcus and his partner, quick, before someone gets hurt."

"Bobby Lee will give it a try. Put two cars out

front, and have someone drive my van and follow
us. I don't want anyone running up my backside."

"Rigdon and Selph will drive point. I'll drive
your van. Give me five minutes to soothe some ruffled feathers."

 **15**

# Parading down Main Street
## *April 16, Tuesday, 12:15 P.M.*

P.C. took off to tell everyone they were free to leave. I told him to keep them off Main and not use the front exit. I turned to the two deputies.

"One car remains directly in front of us at all times. The other drives ahead and holds up traffic coming from side streets. Bobby Lee will have to decide which way to go at each intersection. After we clear an intersection, the traffic stopper can catch up, and we do it again at the next crossing. Understand?" They both nodded. "Never leave Bobby Lee and me exposed to traffic. We have some fast-and-loose drivers, and this street is the busiest. Just keep us safe."

I went to the van to dress in my suit. It was beautiful, a perfect day: mid-70s and a slight breeze. I hated to suit up, but the bright yellow color could be seen easier. I put Bobby Lee's

matching-colored pad around his girth and buckled
it. I strapped on my holster outside the suit. I had
no plan to go up against shotguns, but I feel better
when I can reach a gun quickly. Bubba was somewhere out there also.

When P.C. drove my van over and the two
deputies had both sides of the exit blocked from
traffic, I took the driver's scent bag out of my
pocket. I gave Bobby Lee two pieces of jerky and
let him smell the bag's contents.

He lowered his nose and began the search. He
sniffed the air and moved to the empty parking
space, then turned and started tugging me along,
straining forward in a left-hand arc. He stopped
after several feet, then turned right toward the exit.
He had just duplicated the movement of a car backing out and then going forward. It appeared that he
was mantrailing.

Bobby Lee was eager and picked up speed. He
entered Main Street and didn't even slow down.
When he turned left, I held him back, praised him,
and watched him jiggle-dance with excitement until
the cars were in place in front of us. All the flashers
were activated on the search-team vehicles, including mine. We resembled a small parade, traveling
the downtown main drag.

We were attracting attention. There were a few
whistles and people yelling questions. Not wearing
a backpack, I was able to keep up the pace without
having to pull back on Bobby Lee's lead. We
crossed three intersections without turning. I began
to tire from the fast pace and started talking to

Bobby Lee, slowing him down and pulling heavily on his lead.

I stopped his progress and ordered a rest just before we reached the next intersection. Holding up my hand to halt the vehicles, I turned and saw that we had collected a following. There must have been two dozen people, behind and alongside my van, keeping pace with us. P.C. was ordering them back onto the sidewalk before I arrived. The crowd, mostly teenagers and young adults, was reluctantly obeying, but P.C. was wasting his time. The minute we started up, they'd fall in behind us again.

P.C. met me and said softly, "Rubberneckers!"

I smiled. "If Bobby Lee crosses Wadsworth here, the next intersection is Sycamore Drive. We'll try leapfrogging. That should leave a few of our oglers behind. Tell your men."

Upon leaving I saw him reach for the radio mike. Bobby Lee went through the intersection. I pulled him off the scent, and we ran back to the van, with me yelling for him to retreat. It was six long blocks to Sycamore. We piled in, the point cars gunned it, and we raced after them, leaving our followers in the middle of the crossroads.

At Sycamore, Bobby Lee turned right. Traffic was lighter, and the connecting blocks were longer. We were moving out of downtown. Bobby Lee moved out of the street and turned into the parking lot of a convenience store. The men in front had to back up and turn around. P.C. was right behind me when Bobby Lee walked in a small circle near a parking space and headed for the front door.

"Does your dog need to pick up anything here? Do a little shopping?" P.C. said humorously.

"My guess is the bank robbers needed to pick up some beer. You said one was a drunk. Maybe they both are. Let's inquire."

I opened the door for Bobby Lee and he entered, ignoring the people, and sniffed his way to the large glass-fronted beer coolers. He paced down the aisle beside them and stopped at the section holding the Budweiser. There were several selections to choose from and at least eight feet of beer cases loaded with cans and bottles.

In southeast Georgia, way out here in the boonies, Budweiser is not only the king of beers, it's also the best-seller, almost ten to one over other brands. It's Bubba's only choice.

Bobby Lee turned and headed to the counter, where P.C. was questioning a middle-aged man who said he couldn't remember anyone buying beer in the last hour.

The man yelled for the teenager who was back in the cooler putting up stock. When he came up front, taking his own sweet time, the older man asked him if he remembered anyone. The young guy shook his head.

"Budweiser," I suggested. "Probably two six-packs. Possibly two men and they both had twenties."

"Oh, yeah." The older clerk spoke. "I remember now. Seems like hours ago now. I don't keep track of who comes and goes, or what they buy."

The teenager was nodding his head. I addressed

my next sentence his way. "Do you remember them?"

"Yeah." He was still nodding. "Marcus and Elton."

P.C. and I exchanged glances.

"Marcus Walter and Elton Davis?" P.C. asked, leaning casually against the counter and acting like he wasn't too interested in the kid's answer.

The boy agreed with another nod.

The older clerk finally awoke to the fact that they were being questioned by a deputy.

"I check IDs. Never miss a one. Those men were old enough to buy legal-like. I always look at the date on their license. Never miss a one." He was repeating himself in his haste to convince P.C.

"No problem. Just checking," P.C. assured him. He straightened, adjusted his hat, thanked them, and we got out of there.

Outside, we grinned at each other.

"How'd you know they used twenties?" said P.C.

"Elementary, my dear Watson. They needed money to buy beer, that's why they robbed the bank. Even drunk, they wouldn't have said to the teller, 'Give me all your ones.'"

"Can he find their scent back out on the road?" P.C. was eyeing Bobby Lee.

"Never fear, Superdog is here. Let's roll."

Bobby Lee and I waited at the curb until our escorts got their vehicles lined up. When they were in place, I put Bobby Lee back on the scent. On Sycamore Street he trotted along as if we were doing a field exercise. I should've drunk some liquid before we started. I was thirsty. After three blocks, P.C. tapped the horn once, and I pulled Bobby Lee back until P.C. eased up and was rolling alongside us.

"There isn't another intersecting road for a quarter of a mile. We're traveling parallel with the railroad line. Hop in."

I was having less trouble pulling Bobby Lee off the scent. He had caught on to the rhythm of loading and unloading. He didn't understand why we were doing it, just that it was part of today's routine. Repetition let him know that we would return to the search. I hadn't had to reinforce the scent for him. Truly, a great mantrailer.

I popped a can of Coke and offered it to P.C. He accepted, and I opened another for me.

"Doesn't Superdog get one?"

"Bobby Lee gets water at the next stop. You makin' fun of my dog, mister?"

"*Au contraire,* my dear, I have nothing but admiration for your gifted pooch." He had lifted his voice so I could hear. We were doing over sixty and the windows were open.

I yelled back, "Call him a pooch again and I'll kneecap you at the first opportunity!"

We were high on success and the adrenaline was pumping. We exchanged silly banter until we reached the next crossing.

I unloaded Bobby Lee and poured his dish full of water. He promptly lapped it dry. I filled it again and then gave him two pieces of deer jerky. He gulped the treat, drank half the water, and then began pulling me toward the scent. I picked up his dish, drained it, and tossed it in the van.

Bobby Lee scouted for the scent and turned right on Cow Shed Road, a narrow dirt trail that winds in and out of timber tracts and passes only one or two homesteads. It then leads to the county line, at least ten miles away. It was probably two or three miles to the first isolated house, or houses.

I pulled back and ordered Bobby Lee to load. Our point cars were now having to drive single file. I climbed back in and Bobby Lee settled in the middle on his pad. We bumped along, barely doing thirty miles an hour on the deep-rutted road.

"Stop," I called out. P.C. braked and looked at me.

"Back up. I completely forgot the turnoff to the old oil well. It's back a ways."

"I did too. You think they'd go there?"

"Well, it's isolated," I said defensively. "Hardly anyone travels that road now, but when I was younger that's where we went when we wanted to have a private beer bash."

"You wanna try it?" He was doubtful.

"The way my luck's been running lately, if we pass it up and don't check, surely to God it'll be the road they took."

P.C. began backing the van. I'm glad it wasn't me behind the wheel. I'm the world's worst backer. I weave like a snake.

Turning the van slowly into the overgrown road, hardly more than a path after all these years of neglect, it was evident that another vehicle had traveled it before us. Two thin lines of flattened vegetation gave credence to my supposition. My stomach muscles clenched.

"Looks like you may be right," P.C. commented.

"Bet your ass," I whispered under my breath.

I glanced behind us to make sure the two deputies were following. A reflection of light off chrome or glass reassured me they were there.

Some sixty years ago, an overly optimistic speculator had purchased the underground mineral rights to thousands of acres of timberland, most of them here in Dunston County. He had chosen our destination as the first place to sink an oil well. Running out of money before hitting pay dirt, he had folded his tent and silently departed in the middle of the night, leaving disenchanted several merchants who had extended him credit. I hadn't taken this road in over fifteen years.

"P.C., I think it's time to discuss some final points in this search."

"I'm all ears," he answered. He was concentrating on keeping the van in the middle of the narrow lane and didn't look up.

"At the first glimpse of the Jeep, Bobby Lee and I will have completed our assignment and we're history. My gifted mantrailer doesn't go up against shotguns, and neither do I."

"Rest easy, Jo Beth, we men will handle the shotguns."

I bit my lip, fighting to keep from making a feminist retort.

"This rule applies even if they hear us coming and take to the woods. Bobby Lee and I will not track them. I also will not let you goad me into participating. Prudence is a virtue."

"Understood." He sounded smug.

From all appearances we were nearing the end of the trail. The remains of the original drilling site consisted of a few rotting timbers and a concrete-covered base. All the metal pieces had·been carted away years ago. A tiny tin shack had rusted and fallen into an unrecognizable pile.

After straightening out of a curve in the road, we slowly moved forward. I saw the tail end of the Jeep protruding from some high shrubbery.

I unhooked Bobby Lee and tugged him back to a cage opposite Circe, patted the straw bedding, and said, "Load." He sprang into the cage, and I closed the mesh door.

P.C. had pulled up far enough into the weeds that the two cars behind him could pull abreast. When the motors were silenced, all that could be heard was the faint *ping* of overheated metal cooling in the spring breeze, a few bird chirps, and the lazy drone of bees.

"Good luck," I said softly to P.C. I pulled my gun and jammed myself behind the bulkhead and the driver's seat. Prudence had taken over.

# 16

## Two Drunks, Blood, and the Pillowcase Loot
### *April 16, Tuesday, 2:30 P.M.*

I heard P.C. exit the van and strained to hear the whispered conversation as the men formulated their attack. Only a phrase or two reached my ears.

I sat wedged in the narrow space. My shoulders were cramped. My gun was resting in my lap. I glanced at my watch and eyed the medium-green interior paint on the opposite wall about four feet from my nose. Only the small aisle leading to the cages was between us.

I thought about the fact that someone could get killed in the next few minutes. I gazed at my hands and decided tonight was the night I must spend some time on my nails. They were in pitiful condition. My wrist felt fine.

I checked the time. Two minutes had flown by. A crossword puzzle to occupy my mind would be appreciated. Mentally I started a shopping list. Opening my kitchen cabinets one by one, I tried to visualize their contents. After checking the refrigerator, I had a total of twelve items I needed, which I'd forget before I entered the store. I thought about a lot of things.

The deep-throated roar of a shotgun blast shattered the silence. I drew in a ragged breath. I wiggled my shoulders and worked my head above the seat just far enough to peer through the windshield. All I saw was an edge of trees and the sky.

Prudence was tossed aside as I grew bolder. I stood, clutching the gun, and looked everywhere at once. Nothing but weeds, trees, and brush. I thought I heard a faint voice calling "Over here!" but I wasn't sure. I listened.

A small figure in uniform appeared near the Jeep, waving tiny arms. He was over a hundred yards away. I jumped out the door of the van and began running, still holding the gun in my hand. Over the pounding of my heart and lungs, I heard a voice. I stopped.

"First-aid kit!" This time I heard the words clearly. It was P.C. I hauled butt back to the van and slung one backpack strap over my shoulder. It bumped against my leg with every returning step. I had hastily holstered the gun. With the deputy standing and yelling, I assumed the battle was over and someone was hurt.

As I drew near, I saw P.C. turn and, taking fast strides, run back into the weeds. I caught up with him and pounded along behind, running smack into

him when he stopped suddenly. This caused both of
us to stumble, lose our balance, and sprawl on the
ground. I grunted when my elbow landed on an
exposed root.

P.C. hauled me to my feet, cursing.

"Damn, Jo Beth, you ran into me like a freight
train!"

"You should've signaled!" I yelled. "I was looking where I was stepping!"

"My taillights don't work," he retorted.
"Rigdon's over here. He's been shot."

I stepped around P.C. and surveyed the scene.
Deputy Rigdon was lying on his side facing me and
clasping a handful of weeds. It was obvious he was
in pain. Sweat was pouring from his hair and tem-
ples, wetting his neck and uniform. I saw no blood
or holes in his uniform.

"In the back?" I whispered to P.C.

"In his tail!" P.C. thundered. "The damn fool lost
his grip on the shotgun, slinging it behind him as he
jumped a log. It landed on the butt and sent a full
load of birdshot skimming the right edge of his lily-
white ass!"

"Birdshot?" I couldn't believe my ears.

I walked around behind Rigdon and surveyed the
damage. The seat of his trousers was shredded,
with a few holes scattered in the upper right thigh
area. I knew many tiny pieces of metal were buried
in his flesh, but they were shallow and not life-
threatening. Painful, but very little blood loss.
Birdshot doesn't have the power to penetrate
deeply on a slant. If the shot had been dead on, it

would have blown his buttocks out of existence and killed him.

I couldn't believe Rigdon would face guns loaded with buckshot with a gun only holding birdshot.

*"Birdshot?"* I stood directly in front of P.C. as I posed my second request for enlightenment.

"He was using my gun," explained P.C. He sounded defensive. "I had it loaded with birdshot for the wood rats that plunder my gardening shed. I forgot to change shells when I racked it in my cruiser."

I snickered, clamping my hand over my mouth. I couldn't help it. How ironic. If P.C. had changed loads and put in the correct shells, Rigdon would have died instantly. The thought of what might have been sobered me. I lost the urge to giggle.

I took a Percodan from my medicine stash and held my bottle of water while Rigdon drank.

"Did you capture the bank robbers?"

P.C. was glowering at both of us. He didn't appreciate my laughing at his error with the gun, and he was still mad at Rigdon for scaring him so badly. I knew we were all remembering the sound of the gun exploding.

"Yes," he answered shortly.

I started digging out the rescue sled. P.C. held it open and Rigdon crawled inside and lay on his stomach. Deputy Tom Selph arrived as we finished.

"I have them both loaded," Selph reported to P.C.

"They give you any trouble?"

"Nah, they're both drunk as piss ants," he said

with disgust. "Davis started heaving the minute I put him in the cruiser."

"I hope you put him in *your* back seat," P.C. snapped.

"Nope, he's in yours." Selph gave P.C. a brief smile.

"Shit!"

"Who's gonna pull Rigdon out?" I tossed the question without looking up as I straightened and adjusted my backpack, but I already knew the answer.

"He is!" P.C. was indicating Selph.

While P.C. and Tom strapped Rigdon to the stretcher, I glanced in the windows at Marcus Walter and Elton Davis. They didn't seem concerned about their futures. Marcus gave me a bleary smile, and Elton had his head back with his eyes closed, sawing logs. I heard a loud snore as I turned away.

The only people who would feel pain from this comedy of errors was Henry Walter, Marcus's dad, who was a decent man, and, of course, Rigdon, with his riddled behind.

# 17

## Stalking Mr. Reptile
### *April 22, Monday, 4:40 P.M.*

"This cast is driving me nuts!" Jasmine complained.

I glanced up and watched as she dug energetically in its depths with the scratcher Wayne had made for her.

"It's only been on a week. The swelling is down and Doc Sellers says it's doing fine. You keep scratching like that, you'll have scars before it comes off."

I was admiring my accounts payable on the computer screen. Out of boredom, Jasmine had taken over my data entries, and all the paperwork was up-to-date. It was awkward for her getting up and down stairs. I feared she might lose her balance, so I had moved her in with me last Tuesday afternoon. The move was wise but not popular. She was feeling housebound and longing for her own four walls.

"I'm sure I can manage. I'm thinking about driving to class tonight." She was testing the waters.

One of her friends had been taping the lectures, and Donnie Ray had been running her homework assignments back and forth from the college.

"Doctor Sellers said you shouldn't drive with the cast on. You're doing so well. Do you think you should risk it?"

I put it like she had a choice. She knew damn well I'd put my foot down if she even attempted to get into her car.

"I guess not." She was annoyed, with me and the world in general. "How is Donnie Ray doing?"

"Wayne has him at the firing range as we speak. He says Donnie Ray isn't flinching anymore. He is not raising the barrel, but he still doesn't score well."

Donnie Ray was temporarily filling in for Jasmine as my backup. Not a backup, really; I was taking him along just in case. He wasn't handling a dog. He just walked with me, carrying a pack. I was teaching him basic things that would help him if he was ever lost. With Wayne having to cover Jasmine's sweeps that I didn't have time for, we were busy as beavers.

I had taken Donnie Ray with me for three excursions on Judge McAlbee's property during the past week. We had seen and heard nothing. We had trekked through the first plot in a straight line. The other two we had marched in an X pattern because they were smaller. I knew there were many, many acres we didn't pass through. The size of his timberland and old growth holdings was vast enough to

intimidate. I knew that, unless we got very lucky, I
might never discover what the judge had going in
his woods.

"You know what Donnie Ray told me yesterday?
He said when he carries a pack, his feet hurt, but
when he had his camera and equipment, they never
bothered him."

Jasmine grinned. "A clear indication he's bored."

"He's ready to climb tall trees," I agreed, "but he
needs the experience."

It was five o'clock. I stood.

"I saw Harvey go by a few minutes ago." The vet
was helping with the evening feedings this week.
"The trainers will be coming in soon. I'm going
over to help him. Need anything?"

"A chain saw would be nice," she said with a
grin.

"I'm gonna start hiding the sharp knives," I said,
laughing. "Don't you dare start whittlin' on that
cast!"

I walked across the porch and down the steps,
breathing the fresh smell of spring. My hot bath an
hour ago had loosened my tired muscles from the
day's hike. I felt good. Susan was coming to supper.
Since Miz Jansee was cooking this week, she had
promised to come often and help me cheer up
Jasmine.

Jonathan hadn't called. Maybe he realized it
wouldn't do any good. I started answering the
phone yesterday. I was tired of flinching when it
rang.

As I strolled toward the grooming room doorway,

I heard a hoarse shout from the direction of the kennel at the south end of the building. I whirled toward the sound.

Harvey was running across the courtyard waving his arms, eyes wide with fear. I froze. My gun was lying on the bed where I'd placed it when I undressed for my bath. I was out in the open. In the next second I fully expected to see Bubba, carrying a baseball bat, come charging around the building behind Harvey. *Careless* was glowing in my brain like it was written in neon. How could I be so careless?

"Don't go in there!" Harvey yelled as he drew nearer. "There's a huge alligator in the grooming room!"

"How big?" I shot at him.

"Monster," he croaked, trying to get his breath. "He must be fifteen feet long!"

I hoped that Harvey was exaggerating. Very old bull gators can attain a length of fifteen feet, but they are a rare sight. My twenty-two rifle wouldn't be any help. Oh, my God, the puppies. He was going for the puppies!

"Get Miz Jansee out of the common room and into my house. You stand on the steps and warn the trainers; they're due back any minute. If the gator starts toward you, get inside and close the door. Move!"

I ran toward the common room with Harvey at my heels. I veered to Wayne's office and heard Harvey calling Miz Jansee. I wanted Wayne's pride and joy, a 30.06 hunting rifle he had purchased last year. He kept it in a gun cabinet. He had paid much too much for it, just like his handgun collection. Men bought guns, even if they didn't hunt. If the cabinet was locked, or if he didn't have 150-grain hollow-point shells, I'd kill him with my bare hands.

The cabinet was locked. I yanked open his middle desk drawer and pawed through the objects, looking for two small keys on a ring. Nothing. I turned and scanned the large cork keyboard on the wall where we keep all the kennel keys. I spotted a small key on a ring. I fumbled it in the lock and prayed as I turned it. It was the right one.

I swung open the glass door, jerked out the rifle, and opened the breech. It was empty, naturally. Safe-and-sane Wayne. I opened three small drawers in the base of the gun cabinet before I found the shells. They were hollow-points.

I dumped them on the desk, picked up four, all I could grab with one hand, and started feeding them in the breech while I ran. I dropped the first one trying to turn it around, but I didn't stop to pick it up.

Running out of the common room, I raced down the tarmac and saw Harvey standing on the porch steps. He was yelling at two of the trainers coming in from the field. I didn't glance in their direction. At this moment, I felt that the money I'd spent on the inside fence surrounding the dog pens was justified. I had berated myself many times for what I considered a lapse in judgment and an unnecessary expense.

The trainers coming in from the field had a six-

foot fence between them and the gator. My eyes
were glued on the grooming room door. It was
opened first thing in the morning, and it stood that
way all day unless it was raining or cold. This was
where the gator had gotten in. I groaned when I
remembered we also left the back door open. The
back door led directly to the walkway in front of the
pens, and the puppy pens were less than thirty feet
from the open door.

I stepped slowly inside the doorway, looking
everywhere at once. The grooming room was large
with lots of places to hide, but if the gator was as
big as Harvey had described, he wouldn't be hard to
find. I reached with my left hand and slowly closed
the door behind me, leaned against it, and took a
couple of deep breaths.

The gator was now confined. With dismay, I
remembered how fast Harvey was running when
he'd entered the courtyard. If he hadn't closed the
south gate, the gator could exit there. If he had
jerked the gate hard and slung it open, it could've
come back and closed on its own. It was useless to
speculate.

"Time's awastin'," I said under my breath, to bol-
ster my courage. "Here I come," I added softly.

I looked up and down the length of the harness
workbench, under it, the shadowed corners, and
under the conveyor belt. I moved three steps till I
could see the closed door leading to the common
room. Miz Jansee kept it closed for the air condi-
tioning. The heat from the stove and oven warranted
it. Good. I advanced a few more feet, straining to

catch any movement. I checked the washing sinks, the storage area, the bags of dog food stacked on pallets, and saw that the door to the cleaning supply room was closed.

I heard a noise behind me, whirled, and saw Harvey tiptoeing toward me. I hadn't heard the door open or close. I was concentrating so hard on seeing, I wasn't listening closely.

"Get out of here," I whispered when he was close enough to hear me.

I turned my back on him and went back to staring at the floor. Now would be a bad time for the gator to come charging across the room. Harvey's almost silent approach had rattled me.

Harvey moved so close behind me, I could feel his warm breath on the back of my neck.

"My fear of losing my balls overrode my fear of being eaten alive," he whispered in my ear.

"Get out of here," I mumbled furiously. "If I have to back up suddenly, we'll both be on the floor. Get lost!"

"No way. Males are supposed to protect females. It's the rules."

"What are you gonna use to protect me?" I muttered with sarcasm.

"My dying breath. Shouldn't you be doing something?"

"I *am* doing something," I said through clenched teeth. "Stay behind me and shut up."

I took a few steps and stopped, listening and watching. Nothing. At least Harvey hadn't climbed up my backside when I halted. I moved a few feet to get a clear view of the back room and could easily see that the gator wasn't hiding there. Only scales and clipboards on the walls, with a long bare table where we placed the puppies as we inspected them.

I glided, trying to be silent and graceful, to the door and stopped suddenly, leaning my shoulder against the frame. I was lightly bumped from behind because Harvey couldn't stop his forward momentum. I gave him a silent glare and prepared to peek around the doorsill.

I heard a soft canine yelp, then growls and whimpers coming from the south side of the doorway. The puppies. Hearing them in distress made me reckless. I moved boldly through the opening and automatically faced left. It didn't matter at that moment, but the creature could now be behind me if I had mistakenly chosen the wrong direction.

Fortunately, I had turned correctly. I stared at the tableau.

The puppies had retreated back against their sleeping quarters, huddled in a quivering mass, facing the menace that was trying to reach them. Their instincts had signaled danger. Each one was trying to burrow deeper into the warmth of its siblings to escape the predator. I heard terror in the panicky bays of the adult dogs, who couldn't see anything but had smelled peril.

The bull alligator was clinging to the wire, his vast snout three feet above the top edge, his preposterous-looking short stout legs folded over the ridge bar that supported the weight of his grotesque body. The rear legs were on the walkway, pushing to gain leverage. A generous amount of tail rested on the path.

I raised the rifle, seemingly in slow motion, and fed all the knowledge I had observed into my brain. Three feet of snout, six feet of body, maybe two feet of tail. Between ten and eleven feet, and hundreds of pounds in weight. There was no way I could hit the killing spot—the brain—located to the rear of the jaws and centered just behind his raised and protruding eyes.

I had to knock him off the fence with my first shot. Even with their bulk, gators can move as fast as greased lightning. He was poised, silhouetted against the skyline, and in a direct line with the cowering puppies. In an instant, he'd be up and over the barrier.

I pushed against the fence, firmly holding the rifle at a precarious angle but not jamming it against my shoulder. It was the only safe trajectory I could choose to keep from hitting the puppies and the adult dogs directly behind them. The bullet would pass through the thick body and travel an inordinate distance before its velocity was spent. I knew the rifle's powerful kick would throw it up at least a foot.

I aimed at the lower body and unconsciously closed my eyes as I pulled the trigger. When I opened them, the gator was on his back on the pathway, not inside the pen. His stubby legs were clawing for purchase as his body writhed back and forth. The large tail was slashing in arcs, striking the wire fence, the wall of the kennel, and then the wire again.

I had forgotten to breathe. My flesh was aching from the recoil of the rifle where the butt had slammed into my shoulder, and I was deaf from the explosion.

I started forward to close the distance for my next shot. The gator was only wounded—and far from dead. I saw the gaping hole I'd blown through the middle of his body. The recoil had forced the barrel upward, as I thought it would. The same thing had happened when Bubba had tried to teach me to shoot years ago. He had laughed at my inability to hold the gun on target and hadn't warned me about the recoil. My shoulder had been black and blue for a week. Even with my hard-earned knowledge, I knew my shoulder was damaged.

Harvey grabbed me and halted my forward movement. I saw his lips moving, but I couldn't hear what he was saying. I angrily tore loose from his grasp. I had to finish off the monster before I could rest. He could still move quickly and get away and was now even more dangerous than before.

I turned back to the gator and froze. Harvey's momentary distraction had given the creature time to manipulate his legs and right himself. He was standing up and pointed in our direction.

In terror, I threw the gun to my shoulder and fired at the same instant. I commanded my eyes to remain open. This time when the gun's recoil knocked me backward, I took a fast step and quickly regained my balance. I had missed. He was still on his feet. A ray of the setting sun lay across his snout, reflecting beady eyes the color of rubies.

Number one, I calmly counted, had blown him off the fence. Number two had missed him completely. I had loaded only three shells. One shot remained. I stared across the thirty feet of space that separated us from the primeval killer.

I was thankful this rifle was a semiautomatic and not a bolt-action like the one Bubba had made me fire a few times. Right now I didn't have any time to spare.

I sighted down the barrel, looking for the gator's eyes. I lowered the rifle six inches, took a breath, let out half of it, and squeezed the trigger just as the gator charged. I watched him as he seemed to loom larger than life before Harvey jerked me backward. He swore later that he didn't want the gator's thick ridged tail slicing into me as it thrashed in the monster's final throes, but I have a different theory. I think Harvey was preparing to haul ass and didn't want to leave without me.

I leaned weakly against the fence when Harvey released me. My legs were wobbly, and I slid my butt down the chain-link mesh and sat on the walkway. We looked at the gator.

"Is he dead?" Harvey's voice sounded thin as tinfoil and seemed to come from a great distance, but I knew it was my ears. They hadn't recovered from the tremendous assault of sound.

"Dead, dead, dead," I pronounced, and promptly started bawling.

"Hey." Harvey squatted beside me, patted my shoulder, and offered his handkerchief. I didn't see it because I was blindly groping for tissues in the

pocket of my jeans. I wasn't having any success; the
jeans were tight and I was bent in the middle. He
started wiping the tears away, and I sat there and let
him. I was too damn weary to protest.

I saw two heads peeping around the south end of
the building: Wayne and Donnie Ray. I raised my
fist and gave the all-clear signal and beckoned them
forward.

They both stared in awe at the dead alligator.
They came toward me, with Wayne signing and
Donnie Ray biting off his words in haste. I finally
made out what they were asking. Seems they had a
mutual request.

"Can we have the hide?"

I choked on laughter.

# 18

## Too Close for Comfort
### April 23, Tuesday, 10:20 A.M.

I returned to my game plan and was once again searching McAlbee's acreage for wrongdoing. By 10 A.M., Donnie Ray, Circe, and I had trekked a three-mile stretch of planted pines. The dew had dried, and we had halted to change shoes and socks. We were both sweating like horses after a long workout. We drank from our canteens. Circe was lying in a shallow ditch near me, cooling her belly in the water and occasionally lapping the dark liquid between her front legs.

I was sitting with my back propped against a pine tree and trying to summon the energy to pull off my shoes and change. Staring idly through a small opening in the trees, I saw an open space ahead with tall golden wheatlike grass moving gently when a small amount of air stirred. The tops of large trees were undulating in a good breeze, but we weren't feeling much of it at ground level. Something moved in the tall grass. I watched the spot and saw a bird walk slowly into the sunlight. I sat up straight and whispered to Donnie Ray.

"Don't make any noise. Scoot over here. I want to show you something."

He inched forward and peered through the opening.

"What are they?" He spoke with his voice lowered.

There were now two birds, about five feet tall; they would weigh at least fifteen pounds. White feathers with a small red patch crowned their heads. They stood on pipestem legs so long and thin you wondered how they kept their balance.

"Sandhill cranes," I answered. "I'm surprised we got this close. They're called watchmen of the swamp."

"Why?"

Circe stood and began shaking the water from her pelt. Then she snorted and crashed up the bank to lie in the shade.

Horrendous cries shattered the silence. The noise could be heard for miles. The large birds spread their wings, folded their long thin legs under their bodies, and swept away, calling their raucous alarm over and over. Donnie Ray jumped like he'd been shot. The noise slowly faded. I laughed at his antics.

"Why did they do that? It's sure loud enough," he complained.

"That's their job. They warn other animals, alerting them to our presence. Other cranes take up the cry and pass on the message. Their signals are like jungle drums."

"They must have heard Circe," he guessed. "I'm surprised the hunters haven't killed them all off."

"They're hard to kill. They're extremely wary and have amazing vision, two attributes that all creatures great and small should have, including us. Change your socks."

We reached the far side of the woods in time for lunch, rested awhile, and then shifted over about three hundred feet and began hiking back toward the van. We saw a few critters, spotted a rattlesnake sunning in the path before us, and made a wide detour. We didn't reach the van until 5:30 P.M. Stripping off our rescue suits, we loaded Circe, climbed in our seats, and slumped in exhaustion.

"Took longer than I planned."

"My feet are ruint," Donnie Ray said with clarity. "I'll limp for the rest of my life."

"Nah, after the first five miles tomorrow, they'll work fine."

"Please don't tease me. I mean, yes, say you're teasing me; you aren't really gonna make me walk all day tomorrow, are you?"

"We'll see," I answered enigmatically.

Donnie Ray groaned.

I lit a cigarette and drove us out of McAlbee's territory, turning down a dirt road that would take us into Perce Camp Break and home.

Donnie Ray spotted the man first.

"Who's he?"

"I have no idea. I didn't think anyone lived around here."

The man was on the left side of the road, trudging along toward us and not looking up.

I stopped about fifteen feet from his position. He was tall and thin, looked to be in his early seventies, and had wispy white hair and a long thin beard. He was wearing overalls and a long-sleeved white shirt. When he was abreast of us, he hesitated and stared.

"Can we give you a lift, sir?" I said, smiling.

"Who're you?" He didn't smile or even pretend to tip his worn felt hat.

"I'm Jo Beth Sidden, sir," I said, thickening my accent. "My daddy was Arthur Henry Stonley, and my mama was Sue Ann Flowers. My mama's daddy was Archibald Flowers."

I had run out of relatives. You identify yourself by giving your pedigree to these older inhabitants. They judge you by your ancestors. You're supposed to keep going until you can produce someone the other person knows. I saw his expression soften, and he drew off his hat.

"I knew an Archibald Flowers who farmed over in Dunston County years ago."

"Yes, sir," I replied. "He was my granddaddy. Died in 'seventy-four."

"That's the one. Good man." He parted his lips with a small smile.

"Do you live around here, sir? Me and my friend are simply parched. We both would appreciate a drink of cold well water."

You have to make it sound like they are doing you a favor, not vice versa. Proud, independent people.

"I've got the coldest well water around. My daddy sank the well in 1897, and it's never gone dry." He sounded more gracious with each passing minute. "Y'all will have to turn around and go back a ways."

"We sure'll be grateful," I said with humility.

The man started around the front of the van. I glared at Donnie Ray, and he scrambled for the back. The man crawled in and sat stiffly in the passenger seat.

"My name is Pilter Phelps." He didn't offer his hand.

It was my time to find a connection.

"I know a James Phelps. He's a game warden in the Okefenokee Swamp at the Fargo Landing."

The old man slapped his thigh and showed me a toothless grin.

"He's my brother Homer's boy. There's one older and one younger than him. James married Leon Stritch's youngest daughter."

I turned the van around, went back the way we came, and followed his directions. The road he indicated was almost hidden, having a shallow curve. The driveway looked like a turnaround, not the entranceway to a house.

On the drive, Donnie Ray and I listened to a litany of Pilter Phelps's kin, dating back almost to the Civil War. The clearing that comprised his homestead was less than an acre. The small dilapidated house had never seen paint and looked ready to collapse with old age. A few chickens scratched in the weed-covered dirt, and a goose ran around the yard squawking her raucous cry that intruders had arrived. Years ago, most homeowners used these birds as early warning systems.

"I 'preciate the lift home," Phelps said, as he led us to the back yard and the old-fashioned covered well. "My fuel pump finally quit in the truck. Y'all will be passin' it when you get up the road a ways. I hope them heathens don't bust out the windows in it 'fore my nephew gets here. He comes out and checks on me 'bout ever' week or so."

"Having some trouble with your neighbors?" I asked idly, as Donnie Ray and I were drinking his well water. He had dropped a bucket in it and had brought up cold nectar.

"Them furriners ain't no neighbors of mine," he said quickly, spitting on the dirt to show his disgust.

"Foreigners?"

"Yep, and heathens to boot. They're meaner'n snakes, specially on weekends when they're liquored up. They throw beer cans in the back of my pickup when they pass me on the road, hollerin' and cuttin' the fool. Had me a ol' blue-tick bitch. She didn't bother nobody. Found her run over down the road a while back. They didn't even put her out of her misery. I had to do it. Didn't see it, but know they did it."

I expressed sympathy for the dead hound. This was beginning to sound interesting.

"Did you report these foreigners to the sheriff?"

"Nope. Still try to take care of my own business and nobody else's. Paid the judge a visit. He said he'd speak to them, but it didn't do no good."

"These foreigners live on his land?"

"Yep. Somewhere around Possum Crick. Ain't been down there and don't plan to. Them kind would stick you with a knife as quick as a wink. My papa didn't raise no foolish young'un."

When southern manners permitted, we left with "Y'all come back, you hear?" ringing in our ears.

When we arrived at the battered pickup that belonged to Pilter Phelps, I pulled over.

"Can you tell me the year and make of that truck?"

"That piece of junk?" Donnie Ray stared at the truck. "Why?"

"Hustle your buns over there and write down the make and model. Look under the hood or something." I handed him a pad and pen.

He inspected the truck, wrote something down, and returned.

"I've got it," he said. "You're gonna send Wayne and me to a parts store in the morning to buy a fuel pump. Then we come out here and install it, at least Wayne will. Then we deliver it to old man Phelps, thus doing your good deed for you."

"It'll give your sore feet a rest."

"How'd you know?"

"Know what?" I thought I knew what he was getting at, I just wanted to know his deductive reasoning.

"All I saw was an old man walking down a road. Tell me what you saw."

Well, fair's fair. "On a spring afternoon, I saw an elderly man, neat and clean. The white shirt was spotless. This meant that he takes good care of himself, or his wife does, and he wasn't senile or dotty. It also meant he didn't make his own home brew and lie around drinking it all day like a few people who live out here. He's a proud man. He didn't try to flag us down and ask for a ride. I saw him glance in back when he climbed in the van; he didn't miss a trick. Did you notice, he didn't ask one question about what we were doing out here or mention Circe?"

"Maybe he was being polite."

"Bull. No proud man would open up to strangers about his troubles. He volunteered all he knew about the foreigners, hoping that we were out here looking for them. He knows they're a bad lot and wants to get them out of his neighborhood. He saw Dunston County on the door panel; we're five miles into Gilsford County. We also didn't ask him any pointed questions. He knows we're search-and-rescue. He saw the suits."

"Good deducing," he said with a grin.

"Thank you," I said, and nodded politely. I didn't hear a whisper of sarcasm in his praise.


Susan entered the common room with Hank in tow. We were having a couple of beers before supper, at least I was. Wayne and Donnie Ray were drinking Cokes. Jasmine and Rosie were having white wine, and Chief Clemments was drinking bourbon.

Susan drew me aside. "I hope you don't mind that I brought Hank. You two are friends again, aren't you?"

"We're buddies, and I'm glad you invited him. You're looking spiffy tonight."

"I had to go shopping for spring. Didn't have a thing to wear," she declared.

"Poor baby," I crooned in mock sympathy.

She laughed. "How's Jasmine?"

"Disgusted with her cast. Annoyed that she can't levitate up and down the stairs. Peeved that I won't let her drive or attend college classes yet."

"I'll cheer her up," Susan vowed.

"You'll earn your supper tonight," I cautioned.

Hank sat at my right at the supper table.

"How's the Balsa City Arms fire investigation progressing?" I asked Chief Clemments.

"After Rosie proved it was arson, we established that kerosene was used for fuel. That's it. A couple of winos who lived there said they saw two spics hanging around before the fire, but they're hardly credible."

"Cleopatra did all the work," Rosie said quickly. She had seen me flinch when Clemments uttered the word *spic*. "All I did was hold her lead and try to keep up with her. And Simon knows he's among friends when he calls Hispanics spics. Downtown he refers to them correctly, don't you, dear?"

Our esteemed fire chief just grunted and didn't look up from his plate. I saw Rosie's expression and knew he was gonna get it when she got him home.

The arson of the Balsa City Arms and Clara Ainsley's murder probably would go unpunished, unless McAlbee confessed to the crimes, and that would be a cold day in hell. But I just might find out what was going on in the woods. That would sink him, maybe.

I turned to Hank. "I ran into an old man today who knew my grandfather, Archibald Flowers. He lives over near Possum Crick in Gilsford County. He told me a bunch of foreigners were harassing him. You heard anything?"

"Not about the old man, but some two weeks ago we got a tip on a bad knifing at an immigrant workers' camp out near Possum Crick. I passed it on to Sheriff Scroggins, but nothing will come of it. Those people bury their own dead. Half of them are illegals. You can send the immigration people out there, and they disappear into the pines and are back a week later. I did mention it to Judge McAlbee, however."

"What's McAlbee got to do with it?" I asked, innocent as a lamb.

"He owns the property the camp's on."

"Oh," I remarked, and promptly changed the subject. If I messed up in the future, I didn't want him remembering this conversation.

The Great Alligator Stalk was related to Hank by Wayne and Donnie Ray. Donnie Ray spoke for Wayne and used exaggerated hand gestures. I ate as they described the hunt to Hank.

Wayne and Donnie Ray escaped as soon as they were finished with their meal. We moved from the table to the lounge area, relaxed, and enjoyed our after-dinner drinks.

Hank danced with Susan, then returned to the couch where I was sitting and dropped down beside me.

"Well, now you slay dragons *and* alligators. Your courage knows no bounds. I'm in awe," he remarked. "'Course, that wasn't the picture I drew from my men's description of the Great Bank Robbery."

"Quit your teasing. I was scared witless both times. At the robbery, I'm glad I hid. If I hadn't, Rigdon might have popped me instead of himself. And P.C.? He doesn't have any room to talk, showing up with birdshot to capture armed and dangerous men."

We both laughed. He leaned close. "I understand your police chief has been given the chop. Sorry it didn't work out."

My face flamed. Susan. Ah, well, a friend is a friend even though she doesn't know when to button her lip.

Hank pulled me to my feet just as an upbeat George Strait song began playing on the jukebox.

"I'm too tired," I complained.

"It'll loosen you up," he said, and grabbed Susan on the way to a clear area on the dance floor.

The three of us faced our audience of three and line-danced to the country beat. We received applause and a shrill whistle from the fire chief. There was no call for an encore. I bowed to Hank and Susan and visited the can.

Susan and I walked Miz Jansee to her car. When

we returned, Hank and Clemments were discussing the Atlanta Braves. We went over and joined Rosie and Jasmine.

Jasmine pointed to the phone. The message light was blinking. When I dialed my code, I heard Bubba's whiskey-soaked words. "I'm coming for you, bitch."

I hung up as soon as his voice penetrated my consciousness and stood there with my back to my guests until I could regain my composure.

"What's wrong? Who was that?" I wasn't aware that Hank was beside me until he spoke.

"Bubba." I managed to sound calm while seething inside. "Just a reminder that he's still out there, free to stalk me. He'd waited so long this time, I was beginning to believe he's tired of the prison routine and may want to remain outside for a while. What do you think?"

"I think he's nuts to put a threat on tape, and him with a valid restraining order on file. Save it. I'll have a chat with him tomorrow."

"I've already erased it," I lied. "You know it will only make matters worse if you confront him. You might make him escalate his plan of attack. Leave it be. I'm coping with the status quo."

"I sincerely wish I could match evil with evil and blow the sucker away," he said with feeling.

"That makes two of us," I agreed.

# 19

## A Whole Lot of Shakin' Going On
### *April 24, Wednesday, 10 A.M.*

I was down on my knees in front of Violet, about to lose my temper.

"Sit, you're a bad girl. Sit!"

She plopped her butt to the floor, obeying me with no hesitation. I glanced at Rachel. She was sitting in the classic pose, head down, deepening her wrinkles and looking like a petulant buzzard. I rose, dusted off my knees, and gave Tim an embarrassed grin.

"They're full of high jinks this morning."

"So I see," Tim said, amused at my discomfort.

I had come to Cannon Trucking Company this morning to pull a surprise sweep. This was the maiden workout for Violet and Rachel. At nine months old, they were showing they weren't as prepared as I'd thought.

Tim Fergerson was second-in-command in security. As always, he was immaculately turned out: tailored uniform, every hair in place, looking ready for the impromptu inspection. He was just under six feet, brown hair and eyes, clean-shaven, and able to blend into the woodwork, if he so desired. At thirty-five, he was doing well in his second career. His first had ended on a high-speed chase when his patrol car slid under a semi's trailer. He could walk all day, but he couldn't run fast enough to pass muster with the Waycross police force.

I took a deep breath, turned my back on the dogs, and started to walk away. I gave a tug on the leads and signaled the command to follow. I heard movement and toenails clicking on the parking garage floor. Then I was hit from behind by ninety-five pounds of exuberant dog and driven to my knees again.

With a half turn, I grabbed Violet's forelegs and wrestled her onto her back. This is not an easy feat to accomplish when the dog is a bloodhound in a playful mood, twisting and squirming to regain her balance. She had found a wonderful new game.

I held her down and managed to get a knee on her stomach. I put my face above hers and gave her my meanest growl. I howled my superiority in her ear. I was demonstrating that I was the Alpha bitch, letting her know who was boss. I straddled her, grabbed her jowls, and growled some more.

Violet's happy expression faded. This new game wasn't so wonderful anymore. She looked worried. I had proved my point. I released her and gave a sharp command to retreat. She moved back and plopped down beside Rachel. Her head was canted downward and she looked dejected.

Tim was trying to suppress laughter and doing a lousy job. I saw his lips twitching from his efforts.

"Just establishing my rights as leader," I said smoothly, trying to act unruffled.

I picked up the leads, ran my hand through my hair, wiped my sweaty palms surreptitiously down my jeans, turned, and gave the command to follow.

Oh, no! The first blow sent me to my knees and the unexpected second lunge completed the rout and put me flat on my face, sprawled in disarray. Both Violet and Rachel were licking and drooling, nudging and pushing, dancing with delight. I regained my footing and wiped my face with a tissue.

"Go ahead and laugh. I know you're dying to," I snapped.

"Who me?" Tim howled his glee.

I admitted defeat, loaded the miscreants, and waved at Tim as I started to back the van. He was still laughing.

When Wayne and Donnie Ray returned from delivering Pilter Phelps's now-running truck, I told Wayne about the morning's fiasco.

"They haven't given me a minute's trouble," he signed with surprise.

"Nope, they wouldn't with you. It's the Alpha bitch thing. I'll have to spend a lot more time with them. And Jasmine has to learn how to control them also. We're the ones who handle them on searches.

Pairing a male and female would stop it, but I might
need both of them together in the future. With three
females working together, they'll constantly fight for
control, I suppose. Better to see the problem now and
not during a search-and-rescue."

After lunch I went to the office and called Susan.

"You busy?"

"Not in the least. I'm reading. All my customers
think because I sell books, I automatically know
what's between the covers. They look shocked
when I say I haven't read a certain book they ask
questions about."

I told her about Violet and Rachel's acts of rebel-
lion. After her laughter, I worked the conversation
back to her customers and my reason for the call.

"Being only a block from the courthouse, you
must get a lot of walk-ins from there. Didn't I hear
you mention a while back that Layton from the barber shop was a friend of yours? I can't remember
his first name."

"James? He's a good friend. He owns the shop."

"How close are you two?"

"I haven't slept with him, if that's what you're
asking."

"That wasn't what I meant and you know it," I
said, chiding her and chuckling over her answer.
"Do all your thoughts end up in the bedroom?"

"Only when I'm awake or asleep," she clarified.

"Okay, let me try to rephrase my question. If he
knew a funny story about someone, would he
repeat it?"

"Of course. Wouldn't anyone?"

"Now here's where we separate the men from the boys. If you told him a funny or unusual story and cautioned him not to repeat it, would he keep it secret or blab it around town?"

"It would depend on the story," she said, after thinking it over. "If it was *really* funny or juicy or unusual, he would make everyone swear they wouldn't repeat it and promptly tell them."

"Well," I said gloomily, "that's the last of the what-ifs. I'll have to think of something else."

"Sidden, if you trusted me more than you do a casual acquaintance, you wouldn't have to beat around the bush when you asked for a favor. My feelings are hurt and I'm highly pissed. I'm gonna hang up now." Her voice was shaky.

"Susan, you do realize you're my best and closest friend in the whole wide world, don't you? You must also know what I'm feeling, knowing that being my buddy is what put Leroy in that damn hospital bed. I try to help people and end up getting them or someone else badly hurt. Tell you what, I'll tell you the whole dangerous, grizzly tale. Just dump it in your lap. Then when you get killed, after telling one person, who will of course pass it along, I'll not shed a tear. I'll get me another confidante and you'll be pushing up daisies. Okay?" Now *I* was pissed.

Silence. "Sidden, I know I sometimes tell things I shouldn't. It just slips out when I put my mouth in gear. But knowing it could get me killed, do you think I'd be that foolish? Anyway, I doubt you know something that could get anyone whacked. Do you?"

"Susan, you're absolutely right. I was just joshing you. What could I possibly know that could get somebody rubbed out? I didn't think you'd buy it. Listen, I have a pot boiling over. I'll talk to you later."

"What's boiling over?"

"My temper," I yelled as I slammed down the phone.

Jasmine clumped in from the guest room and fell into a chair. "I couldn't help overhearing your side of the conversation. You were yelling," she said quietly. "Problems?"

"Susan is so irritating at times," I said, still smarting because I couldn't make her understand.

"I know someone exactly like that," she remarked solemnly.

"Don't *you* start on me, Jasmine. I'm not in the mood." I rubbed my face and rotated my shoulders, relieving the tension.

"You want her to be something she isn't. Cherish her friendship and leave her out of your adventures. Use me. Can't I do what you wanted Susan to do?"

"Nope."

"Sure?"

"All right, all right! I'll tell you. Maybe we can figure something out. Susan is a friend of the barber who cuts McAlbee's hair. I'd figured out a couple of scenarios that could have worked, except I realized while I was talking to her that she wouldn't believe the danger and screw it up."

"What did you want her to do?" Jasmine said patiently.

"Get some of McAlbee's hair when he gets his next haircut. You know how barbers remove the clippings on the floor after each cutting? Layton could sweep up the judge's hair and save it for Susan."

"What would be Susan's story for wanting the judge's hair?"

"That's where it gets sticky. Any excuse she offered would be unusual, or funny, or weird. Layton would spread the story, and it would find its way back to McAlbee. Small-town gossip on a spring afternoon."

"What would she tell the barber?"

"Number one, that she had a bet with a friend for one hundred smackers that the judge dyed his hair. She had someone who would test it for twenty dollars, so she'd make eighty bucks profit. She could offer Layton twenty for collecting the clippings. I thought maybe it would make him an accessory— working against the judge—and he'd think twice before repeating the tale."

"What's number two?" Jasmine asked wryly.

"That was the best one!" I exclaimed, defending my idea. "If you think it won't fly, I know you're gonna love the others."

"Try me."

"Something along the lines of making wooden figures to sell at the Swampfest Jubilee and needing black hair to paste on them. She has a booth every year where she sells books about the swamp. Why not add carved art or totem-pole replicas? It's feasible."

"Any more?"

"Number three is off the wall. I knew it was too weird as soon as I thought it up. Forget it."

"Not a chance. Let's hear it."

"Susan has a friend whom the judge treated dirty. She's helping her get what she needs in order for a witch out on Highway 301 to fashion a juju doll and lay a curse on him."

Jasmine tossed her head back and roared.

I kicked back, placed my feet on the desk, and closed my eyes. I knew they were ridiculous suggestions, but they were all I could dream up.

"I'm dying to know why you think it necessary to collect hair from the judge and how you plan to use it."

"After that horse laugh?" I asked, pretending to be hurt. "I think I'll keep my suppositions private, thank you very much."

"I won't be able to sleep nights," she said. "I won't be able to eat, and I'll lose weight. You'd really hate that, me being slim and willowy."

I sat up and grinned.

"You listen this time, and don't hoot until you think about what I've observed. When Gilly was talking to me, I looked at her jawline. You know how everyone around here searches for any resemblance to relatives? The minute Gilly said she was illegitimate, I started playing the game, Who's the daddy? Her jawline looked familiar. I had only seen her mother that one night. But I didn't think that was the answer. After examining my memory, the obvious answer is McAlbee.

"Picture this: A lonely widower is upstairs, with a young and inexperienced servant who would've looked up to him and felt sorry for him when his wife died. Now remember Gilly's jawline and conjure up McAlbee's. Ring any bells?"

Jasmine was silent for a long time. "You could be right. Gilly could be his daughter. So what? I suppose the hair's for a secret DNA test to prove it. How does it connect to your current mystery about what McAlbee was doing in the woods? And allegedly murdering or having her mother killed and attempting to toast Gilly? Also, I don't think she would thank you if you present her with a father who destroyed her mother and wished for her death."

"Jasmine, I can't let the bastard get away without paying for what he did to them. Keeping them both in his house, working them hard without mercy or kindness, and never acknowledging his daughter. I want to nail the bastard."

"How would proving his paternity nail him?"

"McAlbee is arrogant about his aristocratic ancestors. If I'm successful in uncovering his illegal activities, he'll face disgrace and possible jail time. He will no longer be a leader in this community, but he'll still have his aristocratic standing.

"Those highborn snobs will turn a blind eye to any of his nefarious deeds, but they would *never* forgive him for planting his seed in his live-in servant. It's the unforgivable sin—sullying the lineage. He could face anything but scorn and ostracism from his peers. I predict he'll be gone within the month if he's completely unmasked."

"I still don't see how Gilly benefits."

"If and when this happens, I'll have enough proof so Gilly's lawyer can contest his will and demand a court-sanctioned DNA test of his remains."

"God, you do plan ahead, don't you?"

I was hurt. "I don't deserve that remark."

"I'm sorry." She shook her head. "It just sounded so ghoulish. I know you have honorable intentions, and I apologize."

"Honorable," I mused. "I'm not honorable. I lust for retribution. That's more my speed."

"Not so. I meant it," she said with a smile.

"You're just trying to make me feel guilty for welshing on our bet and weaseling out of attending a semester of college."

"True, true," she agreed.

After supper I called Glydia. "Jo Beth. Are you busy?"

"Just waiting for your call. I have good news. Leroy's neurological studies came back today. They confirm no permanent nerve damage. And his orthopedic surgeon says no permanent injuries to bones, joints, or muscles. He's gonna walk again when he heals and goes through rehab therapy."

I closed my eyes and gave a sigh of relief. "That's great news, Glydia. How's Peter? Has he had any more nightmares?"

"He's had two sessions with a children's therapist. He seems better. Josh is taking him twice a week at seven o'clock. Afterward, they go out, just the two of them. Have a burger or pizza and talk. Frankly, I think the extra time alone with his dad is doing more good than the therapy. So far, he's sleeping like a log."

"That's wonderful. I'll let you go. I know you're busy. I'll call tomorrow night. Bye-bye."

"Take care."

At dawn, Donnie Ray and I had finished with our disguises and loaded the battered old pickup we use for hauling garbage. I had recently bought Wayne a new one. We were five miles deep into Gilsford County, heading for Possum Crick. It was first light, that short period of time you can make out vague shapes in the darkness but the sun hasn't even painted a faint blush on the eastern horizon.

"No one goes to work this early," Donnie Ray complained.

"Illegals do. Their sponsors want to get every minute's worth of work they can out of them."

Circe was sitting between us, eyes lidded, leaning heavily on my shoulder and swaying with the motion of the truck. Our rescue gear was in back, lashed down and covered with an old paint-splattered tarpaulin.

Donnie Ray's naturally blond hair was a dull, lifeless medium-brown. He had almost rebelled, but I had forced his head under the kitchen faucet and applied the rinse. I told him not to be such a baby; it would wash out in three days if he shampooed each morning. He had reminded me that I hadn't put a rinse in mine. I reminded him that I signed his paycheck, and so it went. Actually, I had no idea how long it took before his hair would be blond again. I hoped my guess was close.

My hair and ears were covered with a faded scarf tied tightly on the back of my neck. My tinted glasses were lying on the dash. I'd don them at first sight of a foreigner. My makeup looked like it had been applied with a trowel. Lots of heavy dark base, deep red blush, and lip gloss. My dangly earrings consisted of a peach, about half the size of a real one, with peach blossoms cascading down at least four inches. I wear them with my Scarlett O'Hara costume, when common sense goes out the window and we consenting adults go trick-or-treating on All Hallows Eve.

Donnie Ray resembled an escapee from juvenile detention. The two tattoo transfers from a children's cereal box on his forearms looked real. I had also drawn a pencil-thin mustache on his upper lip. Wearing ratty jeans and faded T-shirts and riding in a dilapidated truck, we should be able to pass muster.

I glanced at Donnie Ray and saw the white blur of a bandage on his cheek.

"What happened to your face?"

"Nothing. I read somewhere that a Band-Aid on your face draws attention and makes it harder for people to describe features. They see gauze instead of face—I hope. I don't want those dudes to get a good look at me."

I suppressed a smile. He was enjoying this caper, even though he wouldn't admit it for the world.

"Tell me again what we do when we run into them." He sighed wearily.

"We avoid them, kiddo. We sneak up on their camp and then fade into the brush, try to observe and possibly follow them. I figure they're driven to wherever they work. Illegal dealings wouldn't take place close to their camp, in case immigration comes calling."

"What if they're not driven?"

"Stay loose, partner. We'll see what happens and improvise."

"That's what I'm afraid of, you saying wait and see," he muttered.

"File a complaint with management."

"And get overruled," he said with disgust.

"You got it."

After consulting the map, I turned down a well-used dirt road and slowed to a crawl. There were many tire tracks. This meant that here in the boonies, out of hunting season, someone lived nearby.

I was looking at tire prints when Donnie Ray said, "Look, lots of lights!"

I quickly doused my headlights and shoved the gear lever into reverse. I backed slowly, taking in what I could see before I stuck my head out the window to check where I was headed.

"You're backing into the ditch!" Donnie Ray yelled.

"Nonsense. And don't yell."

Just in case he was correct, I quickly turned the wheel hard the opposite way and added some gas.

Donnie Ray screamed, just as I felt the bump and the left back wheel dropped.

"Don't make those terrible sounds," I told him softly. "What's the problem?"

"You're in the ditch!"

"That's impossible. I turned the wheel—"

"Not the *right* ditch," he said distinctly. "You missed the *right* ditch. You're in the *left* ditch. Can I drive?" he pleaded.

"If you insist."

I hopped out with alacrity, and we quickly traded places.

Backing the truck easily—in a straight line—and moving thirty miles an hour, Donnie Ray quickly reached a turnaround. He backed in, drove out, and headed off the way we had come. I was watching for side roads. "There's one leading left," I cautioned.

Donnie Ray stopped.

"There's a place to hide about a hundred yards back on your right," I told him.

We were going to find the closest turnaround and hide the truck, then lie in wait for the workers to see which way they turned and try to follow them.

Donnie Ray backed in about thirty yards and we hopped out. I put on my gloves to keep from smearing my palms with pine tar. We broke several limbs off the surrounding pine trees and used them to camouflage the truck. This blurred the dark hard edges of the chassis and effectively hid it from anyone passing on the main road.

"Suit up," I ordered.

"Just to observe?"

"We'll be lying on our bellies, covered with straw, in the early morning when snakes are still feeding. You want to try it just in jeans and a T-shirt? Get real."

We dressed and walked to the road under cover of the trees. I tied Circe farther in where she couldn't be seen. We lay down behind some bushes, pulled straw over our backs and legs, and hid our heads. We clutched our binoculars and waited.

"Remember, count the occupants and observe as much as you can. They probably speed like maniacs on these back roads. I'll take the first one, you the second, and so on. If it's only one vehicle, you count heads and I'll look for details."

It was full daylight when we heard their engines. I was glad. I'd wondered about headlights reflecting off our lenses, but they weren't on. In the straight stretch before us, four vehicles headed toward us. I raised the binoculars and watched the lead vehicle approach and get life-size in my eyepiece. As they skidded to a stop, just past our position, I was still counting bodies.

I held my breath and lowered my head until the binoculars were just above the roots. I peered out at the trucks stopped in front of us, not thirty yards away.

The passenger in the front truck opened his door, alighted, and started walking directly toward us.

# 20

## ¿Habla Español?
### April 25, Thursday, 6:15 A.M.

I stared at the man who was casually urinating on
the dirt less than thirty yards away and decided he
was no gentleman. Each of the four vehicles in the
caravan had a woman as a passenger. Even if they
were wives, sisters, or other close relations, he had
to be embarrassing them with the crude display of
his dillywhacker.

The caravan consisted of three old trucks and one
battered car that was manufactured in Detroit in the
days when big was considered better. Each vehicle
held four males and one female. All were in their
twenties or early thirties and appeared to be of
Hispanic origin.

They roared away and I decided not to follow
them. I stood and walked out in time to see them
turn right a few hundred yards ahead.

Donnie Ray was stripping off his rescue suit.

"Aren't we gonna follow them?"

He had noted my leisurely stroll back from the road, and I wasn't touching the zipper of my suit.

"I'm guessing the women were along to drive the cars back. When they return, we'll pay them a visit."

"You're just gonna drive in and question them?"

"Not exactly. We'd planned to follow them and watch the first turn, then come back tomorrow, hide, and watch the second turn, and so on. Right?"

"Right."

"Well, we already know where the first turn is, so we haven't wasted today. If the women return within the hour, we'll go in and pretend we're lost. I'll distract them while you carve some notches on their tires. Then tomorrow we'll be able to follow them right to their workplace."

"Sounds dangerous."

"Living is dangerous, Donnie Ray. You could slip in the shower, take a header down a flight of stairs, or piss off your employer—life is dicey. Who knows?"

He decided I was kidding and grinned.

"What if you're wrong about the women being the drivers?"

"Then we fall back on our original plan. You're turning out to be a worrier. Let's eat."

I had made sandwiches. His was peanut butter and jelly on white. Mine was peanut butter and banana slices, also on white. We each drank a Diet Coke, and I smoked.

Donnie listened to his music, using earphones,

and tried not to rock the old truck with his body movement. I drank and smoked and waited.

After thirty minutes, we suited up and assumed our original positions at the tree line. We had no sooner gotten settled when a car approached, leaving the camp. It was full of small children and a woman was driving.

"Taking the kids to the bus stop," I told Donnie Ray.

"It's too early for that, isn't it?"

"Out in the boonies, even kindergartners have to rise before dawn. When the woman puts them on the bus, they probably have at least thirty more miles of commuting to school. I have a friend who lives in Fargo. Her kids spend almost three hours a day traveling from home to school and back. They go to the county seat in Homerville, thirty miles away."

It was another twenty-minute wait before we heard engine sounds. We watched the four vehicles come by at a more modest speed.

"I counted two men in addition to the drivers," I said.

"That's all I saw. Who do you think they are?"

"My guess is night guards. Let's give them an hour to eat and get tucked in bed before you start carving on their tires."

Donnie Ray grunted his reply. We took off our suits and prepared to wait another hour.

I punched Donnie Ray when it was time. We pulled the pine boughs from the truck and threw them into the woods.

Driving slowly, he pulled out and turned left.

"Remember, get out and lean against the car until I get into a conversation with them. Let them look you over first. Act like you're bored. Park as close to the other cars as you can."

"Yes, yes, I got you," he said.

He was uptight, and I had a few butterflies in my gut too. The clearing was on the left, with a small cluster of shacks in a row. They were unpainted and didn't look over a couple of years old. I counted eight small cabins with minuscule stoops and cement blocks for steps. I saw smoke rising from tin flues extending out from the side of each building instead of the roof. The early mornings were still in the high 50s, so those uninsulated walls meant they still needed heat in the cabins.

Clothes were hanging to dry on wires strung between pine trees. There were nine well-used cars and trucks in the small clearing, parked like herded cattle. Only one ramp crossed the ditch. All vehicles had to back out, so they left them close to the driveway.

Donnie pulled up on the ramp, close to the tailgates of two trucks. I hopped out. I was chewing two pieces of gum. I thought this mouthful might help distort my face and voice.

"Hello!" I called cheerfully as I approached the closest stoop. "Hello?"

The wooden door was jerked open. A woman held the screen open and rattled off something in Spanish.

"I seem to have gotten lost," I said, ignoring her

incomprehensible greeting. "I'm trying to locate a man by the name of Pilter Phelps. Does he live here, or have I come too far?"

The minute I started talking she began her fast Spanish, pointing to herself and shaking her head back and forth. Only an idiot would keep on talking and ignoring these signals that she didn't speak or understand English, but that's just what I did.

"I guess you're trying to tell me you don't speak English, and I sure don't understand Spanish. Does anyone here speak English? English?"

She turned her head and yelled something to someone inside. Then she repeated her words in a louder tone. She turned back toward me and gave me a troubled look.

She appeared to be in her early thirties, with long black hair, dark eyes, and a smooth olive complexion. A look-alike appeared beside her, about half her age. She had the sullen pout that only teenagers can project so vividly.

"What you want?" she asked, as if she couldn't care less about my answer.

I had seen her take a quick glance at my truck and my unconventional attire. I wasn't law, immigration, truant officer, or social services case worker. Her countenance showed contempt.

"Oh, good, you speak English!" I said with a laugh. "I seem to be lost. Oh, my goodness!" I said suddenly. I started to slump and clutched at the screen. "Maybe I should sit down. I feel dizzy!"

For the older woman's comprehension, I patted

my stomach and made a rounded gesture to indi-
cate I was just a teeny bit preggy. I knew the petulant girl wouldn't care if I toppled over in a dead
faint.

Mama's expression softened from worried to compassionate. She took me by the shoulders, walked me
inside the door, and indicated that I should sit on the
couch. I slumped, trying to act faint. I decided to fan
myself with my hand.

While the woman went to get some water, the girl
stared at me with hard eyes. I scanned the room with
lowered eyelids, using my fanning hand to shield
my interest. The single-room cabin was immacu-
late, which was all you could say about it. Two worn
upholstered chairs, a couch, and a double bed.
Orange and peach crates, used as kitchen cabinets,
stood beside a single standing sink with a faucet and
an ancient stove. A small table and chairs stood near
the sink. Religious pictures of Mother and Son and
a plain wooden cross decorated the walls. I didn't
see a bathroom. It could be on the back porch.

The woman returned with the water. I drank it
and smiled gratefully.

"You feel better to go?" The girl made herself
smile, but her heart wasn't in it.

I stood. "The quick Peter brown Piper fox peck
jumped over pickled lazy peppers dog."

Susan and I had twisted those two little bits of
nonsense together one stormy afternoon in the fifth
grade and, with tedious rote, had burned them into
our minds forever. I was amazed that I didn't twist
my tongue almost twenty years later.

I patted Mama's shoulder and left the girl frowning over my mystery message.

Donnie Ray had the motor running when I hopped in beside him and Circe.

"Did you have time to notch at least two tires?" I asked, as we roared down the road, kicking up dust.

"I notched the back left tire on all four vehicles we saw this morning. I had enough time to carve my initials! What took you so long? I was getting ready to go in after you, waving my gun! Christ!"

"Don't cuss. I met a nice lady and a snotty teen. Did you see anyone else?"

"A man came out of the third cabin down and entered the fourth one after I got back in the truck." Donnie Ray was calming down. His voice was back to normal.

"Did he seem suspicious?"

"He had his head down. I don't think he even saw either the truck or me."

"Good. Take us home, partner." Circe leaned her body against me and dozed all the way.



"I feel as useless as a bump on a log." Jasmine recited the old adage in a melancholy whisper.

"Stop it!" I said, sounding severe. "You were honorably wounded during battle. Your commander orders you to relax and heal and quit feeling sorry for yourself. Jeeze, am I gonna hear this for four more weeks?"

Jasmine flashed her teeth. "You're going on my sweep. I've been doing that search for almost eight months now. A new plant manager has been transferred in since you were there. He's tall, dark, and handsome. Tell him I said hello."

"Better yet, I'll tell him you're inviting him to supper here tomorrow night."

"Don't you dare!" She pushed up straighter in the chair. "Please, Jo Beth, I was only kidding. Promise you won't!"

"Why not? I think it's a great idea."

"I'll tell you," she said, her dark eyes flashing. "One, he's probably asked the girls working there about me, and you know how happy they were to fill him in on my past occupation. Two, he's never made any move on me; and three, he wears a wedding ring."

"Okay, how is this? First I ask him if he's married, and if he says no, I ask him if he likes you. If he says yes, *then* I invite him to supper tomorrow night."

"Please don't."

I looked at her and saw tears running down her face.

"Hey, Jasmine, I'm sorry." I grabbed the tissue box and sat on the edge of the ottoman where her encased leg was elevated. "You know me, always putting my big foot in my mouth. I was just ribbing. Honestly."

"I'm down and feeling blue," she said, sniffing and wiping her face. "Pay no attention."

"Forgive me?"

"Only if you'll forget what I said about him."

"What's his name?"

"Bradford Williams. He's from a small town in Illinois. He mentioned a sister once. He has a degree in business administration. That's all I know about him."

"Do you like him?"

"He seems very nice." She was hedging. I could tell she liked him, but I couldn't push her.

"Interesting conversationalist?"

"Jo Beth, he's knowledgeable about anything you mention. He's witty, urbane, and his voice flows like warm honey."

"How's his bod?"

Jasmine smiled. "I think he lifts weights or has a rowing machine or something. He's muscled, but they don't bulge. He's smooth and wears beautiful clothes."

I watched her as she talked about him. She was like a young girl experiencing her first flush of love. Because she was working the streets at twelve, she had missed childhood and teenage crushes and any chance of falling in love. After she retired at nineteen, she hadn't wanted men. Now her sexuality was battling with her religious beliefs and her feelings of unworthiness. I'd check out this dude she was so interested in. See if he was good enough for her.

At a little after four, I pulled into the Azalea Cotton Products parking lot, directly in front of a little-used side door. The plant manager was standing outside waiting for me. He walked over as I unloaded Pocahontas and Stanley.

Jasmine was correct, he was a hunk. His mocha complexion was flawless. Tall, slim, with average shoulders, he walked as if every joint had just been oiled. His eyeglasses were gold-tinted and added to his good looks. He was an eight plus, maybe even a nine. There are no tens on my scale.

"Ms. Sidden? Thank you for calling and alerting me. Ms. Jones has spoken of you often. I'm Bradford Williams, plant manager." He extended his hand.

I smiled at him and we shook. "Jasmine only told me about you less than two hours ago. I guess you know we Southerners are informal. I'd like you to call me Jo Beth."

"I'm Bradford."

His smile could melt polar caps. No wonder Jasmine had finally thawed.

"What wonderful names do the dogs have today? I've really enjoyed learning about your bloodhounds. They're very talented."

"This is Pocahontas," I said, rubbing her ears, "and this is Stanley," I said with pride.

"Stanley? No, please, give me a minute." He closed his eyes.

We stood in the mild sunshine, while he gave it some thought.

"I'm drawing a blank. I give up."

"As with Dr. Livingston," I told him.

"Of course. I did think of Erle Stanley Gardner but didn't suggest it."

"I'll name a future sniffer Erle in your honor."

"Thank you. You didn't mention during your phone call the reason Ms. Jones didn't come today. I trust she's not ill?"

Aha! He was interested—or maybe he was just being polite. I wiped away cheerfulness and donned a solemn expression.

"Jasmine was injured in a search-and-rescue mission about ten days ago," I said softly.

Concern flooded his face like an incoming tide.

"Wh-what happened?" he stuttered.

Oh, how sweet. He stammered when he was anxious. What an endearing flaw. A definite nine.

"She fractured her left leg in the field. She's in a walking cast and climbing the walls from being housebound. Four more weeks and physical therapy before she can start her sweeps and attend her college classes."

"I didn't know. Tell her I was asking about her. Perhaps I could send flowers?"

"Ah, Bradford, the gesture might be misunderstood. Better not." I glanced pointedly at his ring finger.

He laughed. "Jo Beth, I have to confess. You southern belles overwhelm me. It must be the warmer climate. The first week I was here I received some embarrassing offers from workers in the plant. Company policy dictates no dating employees. I visited a pawnshop and purchased a wedding ring. Is that what you meant?"

"Something like that," I said lightly. "Let's go sweep."

We entered the cutting room, and the high whine of producing machines filled our ears. Soft rock-and-roll music was pouring out of speakers located high on the crossbeams. The constant music would drive me up the wall, not to mention the high screech of machinery. Pocahontas and Stanley went to work after sniffing my samples of marijuana, crack, and LSD.

They chomped their jerky and took another inhalation over the bags' contents. They knew the drill. Noses to the floor, they started their figure-eight search pattern. The noise would rise and fall as we passed. Sewing machines stopped, then slowly started up again. Some sat and gaped. They liked to watch the dogs to see who was holding and who got caught.

Pocahontas scooted under a table loaded with stacks of T-shirts and briefs waiting to be stitched. Empty cartons were stacked underneath to hold the finished product. I handed Stanley's lead to Bradford, commanded the dog to stay, and crawled under the table.

Pocahontas was pawing an empty carton and trying to crawl inside it. I put my hand in the opening and drew out a green leather wallet, then backed out from underneath the table and stood. The girl at the closest machine stared at me in defiance. A tote bag was by her right foot. I gave the wallet to Bradford. He flipped it open, checked the driver's license, and offered it to the girl.

He leaned over and spoke near her ear. She got up and left. I relieved him of Stanley's lead.

"What did you say to her?"

"To open her purse for inspection or punch the time clock and wait in the office for her pay." He shrugged. "Why do they keep on doing it? They must need the money, or they wouldn't be working. They know they're subject to automatic dismissal if they bring drugs into the plant. In the four months I've been here, we've lost eleven employees. Some had five years or more invested in the pension plan."

"Many are hooked, and others think they'll never be caught. Take your pick. Jasmine and I have heard some weird excuses. One woman told me she held it during school hours for her fourteen-year-old son so he wouldn't smoke on campus. Then she returned it to him each afternoon after classes."

We worked our way through the plant and finished up near the front office. We found three rolled joints lying in the aisle of the storage room where someone had obviously tossed them. Of course, no one had seen anything or knew who had done it.

"I'll flush them," I said, when he handed them to me.

"Would you like something to drink?" I had the feeling he wanted to pump me about Jasmine. I knew I wanted to ask him some questions.

"Sure. A Diet Coke, please."

"Meet you in my office," he said.

I went to the washroom and flushed the cigarettes. Street value was now five bucks each. I knew the sewing machine operators were on piecework; after they'd earned the minimum wage they were paid extra. I wondered how many briefs or T-shirts they had to stitch to be able to buy the joints. I pulled off my gloves, tucked them in my back pockets, and washed my hands.

The dogs and I entered the office just after five. They flopped on the carpet and I sat in a chair. Two Cokes were on Bradford's desk, but he wasn't behind it. I heard water running, and then he entered from a door at the far wall. An Oriental screen was sitting at an angle in front of the entrance. In his haste to return, he hadn't closed the bathroom door.

He smiled and handed me a Coke. I pulled the tab. Stanley rose to his feet in one smooth motion and was halfway to the screen before I caught on.

"Hey!" I yelled. I lunged for his trailing lead and missed. "He's forgotten his manners," I said over my shoulder, and hurried to catch him before he drank from the toilet. He had obviously smelled water and was thirsty.

I was wrong. Stanley started whining and scratching at the built-in storage closet. He was baying his mournful call of success. He wasn't after water.

"Bradford!"

"Wh-what is it?" He was behind me, trying to peer over my shoulder at Stanley. "What's he doing?"

The dogs don't bay inside a building as a rule. There had to be some heavy drugs in that cabinet to make Stanley act this way.

"I think someone has stashed a stash in your executive washroom," I said, finding humor in the situation. "Under the boss's nose, so to speak."

"I lock my office door when I leave at night. It has to be the day shift, and they go home at three."

Stanley was still baying loudly and about to

break a toenail on the paneled cabinet. In the small room it sounded twice as loud and seemed to vibrate off the tiled walls.

I pulled him back, yelling "*Retreat,*" and man-handled him away from the opening. I jerked open the latch and peered inside: towels, soap, wash-cloths, personal grooming items belonging to Bradford. A white bathrobe, slippers, and a change of clothing hung to one side of the shelves. I pawed the towels aside and moved boxes of tissues. My eyes traveled to the bottom shelf. I leaned closer and saw a beat-up black lunch box behind several rolls of toilet paper.

"You own a black lunch box, Bradford?"

"No."

I sat down on the floor, drew it between my legs, and opened it. Stanley was trying to work his head under my arm. We both smelled the fertilizer and fuel oil the same instant. I lowered the lid carefully and gently placed it on the shelf and pushed the panel closed. Scooting backward on my ass, I used the wall for leverage to stand and pulled Stanley close.

"I hope to hell you're current on fire drill proce-dures, Bradford, because we need one—right about now. You have a fire bomb in your closet. We have to evacuate the building!"

# 21

## Glow, Little Glowworm, Glimmer, Glimmer
*April 25, Thursday, 5:15 P.M.*

Bradford whirled and grabbed the phone. After he dialed some numbers, the fire alarm and a recorded message began. He fumbled out his keys and started gathering disks from a computer table.

"I'll call the sheriff's department. You call the fire department!" I yelled, heading for his secretary's desk. I had to bellow to be heard. The instructions being sent over the PA system were bouncing around in my ears.

"The alarm is wired directly into the fire station," he called, heading for the safe.

"I'll meet you outside," I screamed, and he nodded his understanding. I had to get the dogs out and move the van.

I ignored the milling crowd gathering on the parking lot. I turned on my flashers and siren and backed the van out and onto the street. After I was clear, I called Hank on the radio.

"I'm en route," he answered, butting in on my transmission to the county dispatcher.

I gave the dogs some water, the balance of the jerky, and lit a cigarette.

Chief Clemments arrived first in his shiny red car, with three fire trucks hot on his heels. Hank pulled up beside me, turned off his siren, left his lights flashing, and joined me.

"You working arson now?"

"Nope. We got lucky. I had Stanley along. Rosie trained him in arson for two months before I moved him over to search-and-rescue. She had too many in her class. He retained the memory of fuel oil and fertilizer, I guess. Pocahontas didn't blink an eye. She had no idea what all the excitement was about."

"Was it a professional job?"

"Listen, when Stanley and I got a whiff of the contents, I gently closed the lid and scrammed. I didn't inspect it. Wouldn't have been able to tell too much anyway, because I don't know beans about it. Rosie's the expert on arson."

Bradford worked his way toward us, and I introduced him to Hank.

"Your company trying to downsize, or have you fired one too many lately?" I asked Bradford.

He looked grim. "We've had union thugs in town for three weeks. They're trying to organize the plant. I've reported them twice to union headquarters. They've been threatening my key workers who are in line for management for trying to give others the truth about the union."

"What's the truth?" I knew he was for a nonunion shop, I just wanted to hear why.

"They won't get any more money with the union than they're getting right now. In fact, they could lose some of their benefits. We give more than we're required to, so if the plant votes for the union, we can take away the freebies."

I shrugged. I wasn't going to get embroiled in union versus nonunion. There are good and bad on both sides.

Hank questioned Bradford and said he'd take a full statement when the present actions were cleared up. Bradford excused himself and went to speak to the fire chief.

"Hank, do me a favor. When you talk to Bradford, tell him about Jasmine's former occupation. Spell it out."

"Why?"

"Jasmine is falling for him. I don't want her hurt if he can't handle the truth."

"She'll tell him the first time they date."

"I know. But this way, if he shies and runs, she doesn't have to tell it and still lose him."

"Are you sure?"

"Trust me."

"Don't make me laugh," he muttered under his breath. We traded grins.


After supper, Jasmine and I were back in my office killing time. I had brought her a large jigsaw puzzle and emptied all the pieces on a low square coffee table. We were patiently turning them all over before we began.

"Don't take them apart!" she cried, as I separated several pieces that were still hanging together.

"It's cheating if you don't start from scratch," I declared.

"No, it's not. It's a bonus."

"I have to call Glydia. Don't cheat while I'm gone."

"It's not cheating!" she yelled.

After Glydia gave me Leroy's current condition and said he was improving daily, she laughed.

"Did you hear what the boys at county are getting Rigdon for his birthday?"

"No, tell me," I pleaded.

"They got all the birdshot that Emergency picked out of his rear. They had the pellets tinted gold and then mounted on the bull's-eye of a dart board. It spells out BANK ROBBERY EVIDENCE."

"He'll treasure it always," I said with a laugh. "Glydia, I need a favor."

"Just ask."

"I have to warn you, this is dangerous. You have to do it so it can't possibly be traced back to you. I wouldn't ask you, but I can't think of any other way."

"Jo Beth, you know I'd walk barefooted across hot coals for you. Quit pussyfooting around and tell me what you need."

"No, I have to be certain that you understand the risk. If you can't manage it without getting caught, tell me, and we'll forget it. Will you promise?"

"My solemn oath," she intoned. "Now cut the shit and lay it on me."

"I need a small vial of Judge McAlbee's uncontaminated blood. And he can't be aware that you had anything to do with taking it."

Glydia sighed. "Jo Beth, for a small-town girl who raises dogs, you sure lead a colorful life. Your teeth giving you any trouble? They're not *looking* pointy. You're not growing fangs, are you?"

I spurted laughter. "I'd like to bite him, but not for his blood. He can't know that you're the one who wants it, Glydia. If he hears your name, he'll know I'm behind it. That's when the game will become deadly."

"Off the top of my head, I can't see a way right this minute. Let me think about it. I'll have plenty of time tonight. I won't be able to sleep a wink trying to figure out why you want the judge's blood. Call me tomorrow night?"

"I will, and take care."

"You bet."

Jasmine had overhead my conversation. I went back and joined her and the puzzle. We were sitting on the floor eating plain popcorn. To me, it's better with salt and dripping with butter, but with Jasmine in residence it remains unadulterated.

Again, at dawn, Donnie Ray, Circe, and I were parked back a ways in a turnaround waiting for our work force to roar by. We were in the puddle jumper, my old worn truck. Broken pine branches hid us. I was drinking coffee. I'd decided we didn't have to suit up and lie on the dirt, we could see well enough from here. The small turn-in ran parallel with the road for a few yards. We could see the vehicles and the occupants clearly enough.

It was daylight when they passed, like yesterday. It was in the mid-50s this morning. I was wearing an old ratty sweater, the huge peach earrings, and my hair was bound. Donnie Ray's dull brown hair looked terrible in the dimness of early dawn. I sure hoped the rinse would disappear when we finished this caper.

I was feeling bad about my sharp words to Susan. I'd call her today and apologize and invite her out to supper. Miz Jansee didn't work on the weekends. It would be pizza time. This way she'd get a balanced meal.

I heard the caravan approaching and punched Donnie Ray. He was listening to music through earphones. They appeared from our left, going fast, and were in view long enough for us to see that they were the same vehicles as yesterday.

We'd have to wait until the drivers returned before we could attempt to track the bad guys to their workplace.

Circe was nodding on my shoulder. She liked this new game we were playing. Anytime the truck was in motion, she was heavy-eyed and ready to catch some z's. Bloodhounds can grab a nap, even standing, if they can find something to lean on.

The women returned. I wondered if the compassionate woman of yesterday was among the drivers.

When the dust cleared, we pulled off the covering foliage, drove out, and turned right.

Only deep gray shadows surrounded us. Not daylight, not darkness. Everything was blah and barely visible.

"Sky looks funny," Donnie Ray commented.

"I know," I said anxiously. "We have a thirty-percent chance of rain."

No sooner had the words left my mouth than widely scattered drops pelted the windshield.

"Shit. Speed up a bit. Maybe we can outrun it."

"Sure," said Donnie Ray. "Sure 'nuff."

It started pouring. A sudden gust of wind blew across the trees, which were laden with a dark curtain of rain. The pines bent in supplication, then moved upright as the wind suddenly turned and pushed them from a different direction. Lightning lit up the landscape; only seconds later, thunder roared and shook the static air.

We watched our spoor disintegrate before our eyes with the aid of the headlights' beams. First dimples appeared on the dusty road, then tiny rivulets of water ran to lower positions and joined other tiny fingers of liquid. Unfortunately, all these changes taking place were ruining the impressions of the tire treads we were trying to follow.

Donnie Ray slowed to a crawl. The windshield wipers couldn't keep up with the flow pounding against the glass.

I looked behind us and couldn't see diddly-squat.

"Turn around, Donnie Ray, it's useless. I want to get off this road while the rain is still washing away tracks. One lone set of tire treads might make them suspicious."

A wasted morning. Tomorrow was Saturday. The seminar started on Monday, and the trainers were arriving Sunday afternoon. I was running out of time to help Gilly find some answers. On the way back the rain suddenly stopped. It was as if someone had turned off a faucet. Dark clouds made the false dawn disappear. It was dismal, dark, and dreary, and so were my spirits. We got home in time for breakfast.

I called Gilly. She was happy, enjoying her new-found family and being needed in the busy household. The only time she mentioned Jonathan's name was near the end of the conversation.

"Miz Jo Beth, Mr. Jonathan sure does miss you. He doesn't do much smiling nowadays."

I made a noncommittal reply and ended the visit. Jonathan couldn't possibly miss me half as much as I missed him. I yearned to hear his voice and feel his touch. Next time, I'd listen to my pragmatic mind instead of my blithesome heart.

Jasmine was hooked on the jigsaw puzzle. I went over, folded my legs, sat, and admired what she had accomplished so far.

"You have all the edges!"

"I'm missing two pieces right here." She pointed to the gap I'd missed. I studied the picture on the box. It was two white fluffy-haired cats with a background of variegated flowers.

I studied the mass of separate pieces.

"Yesterday, when you were telling me about what

happened at the sewing plant, you never mentioned if Bradford asked about me."

"We had our hands full," I said, pretending I was engrossed in the puzzle. I was going to make her dig for the answer she was seeking.

"Before you found the fire bomb, when you first arrived, he didn't say anything?" She was trying to seem casual.

I stared at the puzzle and pretended to be deep in thought.

"Maybe, I can't remember." I hesitated. "He said . . . no . . . nope, can't recall."

"Have you ever been kicked by a person wearing a leg cast?"

She struggled to rise and I started laughing.

"Okay, your threat of physical violence has made me remember. He inquired, and I told him your leg was in a cast. You sat around all day in a tattered bathrobe, your hair uncombed, and whined and whined." I jumped up and ran for the door.

She braced her hands on the coffee table and ottoman and rose as she spoke. "There is nowhere you can hide where I can't find you. Prepare to die!"

"He asked why you weren't there. I told him your leg was fractured and he showed great concern. He wanted to send flowers, but I told him it would be a bad idea. I stared at his ring finger so the schmuck wouldn't miss my point. He aw-shucked, shuffled his feet, and admitted it came from a pawnshop. He wears it to help fend off unwanted advances from his vixen crew.

"I told Hank to fill him in on your previous occupation. I called Hank a few minutes before I started working on your puzzle. You know what Hank said that Bradford said?"

I continued without giving her a chance to open her mouth. She was staring at me with trepidation, yearning for, yet fearing to hear, the answer.

"Hank said Bradford was surprised when he asked him if he could forgive you. 'Forgive her? For what? Whatever happened before I met her is her business.' That's an actual quote, by the way. I made Hank repeat it word for word.

"I'm going over to help Wayne and Donnie Ray with the evening meal for the dogs. Oh!" I suddenly exclaimed. "I forgot. I also called Bradford, after speaking with Hank, and invited him for supper tonight." I made a point of consulting my watch. "Which is one hour and twenty minutes from now. See ya later."

# 22

## Searching for the Answers
### *April 27, Saturday, 8 A.M.*

We were up at dawn again, and so far we'd followed yesterday's moves. The workers were in the woods and the drivers had returned. We waited an extra thirty minutes. If they had posted a lookout, it wouldn't appear that we had backtracked the women going home.

The skies were clear and it was already heating up. The ground had been fairly dry yesterday before the two inches of rain from the thirty-minute thunderstorm. Most of the precipitation had soaked in and left the ground firm. A few deep tire ruts were lined with dark gray mud. These were the vehicle tracks from the women picking up their passengers after the downpour. Their tracks from this morning were clearer and didn't cut too far into the drained soil.

When you knew what to look for, it was easy to

spot the small triangle that Donnie Ray had cut into
their tires. I was sure no one from the cabins had
noticed the notch in their tracks. We were going
slowly enough to read them while driving.

"Remember, we keep going when we find where
they entered the woods. They may or may not have
a guard, but we'll act as if they do. I'll do the talking if someone steps out and challenges us."

"Understood," Donnie Ray said, drawing a deep
breath. He was uptight. This is good when you need
to keep your wits about you.

The air was washed clean from the wind and
rain. The ever-present swampy smell was interlaced
with fresh early blooms of wildflowers and just
plain old weeds.

"The tracks end up ahead," Donnie noted.

We kept traveling the untracked road at the same
speed. I raised my hand as if to scratch my head in
order to hide my speculative stare at the turnaround
they had used. The tire tracks were clearly
delineated. Vehicles had cut in and backed out many
times from this location. They ran a sloppy operation. Any observant person—which covered
hunters, local residents, timber-company line riders,
and many others—could read the signs.

We drove a half mile farther, and Donnie Ray
turned in on a small three-path road. We had traveled a hundred yards or so when I spotted the perfect hiding space for the truck.

"Pull up and back in there," I directed, pointing
to his left.

Three trees were missing, and Donnie Ray straddled the planting mound worn down by time. The oil pan didn't scrape. When we were clear of the three-path by about six feet, he stopped.

"Am I far enough back?"

"I'll check," I said, opening the door and disturbing Circe's nap. She sat up and yawned. I walked to the edge of the woods and looked both ways.

"You're fine."

He shut off the motor, and we both listened in the silence. The truck seat squeaked as Donnie Ray alighted. I unhooked Circe's safety ring, attached her long lead, and directed her to the ground. She selected a spot, peed, and I tied her to a tree.

We unloaded our equipment and placed it on a planting mound. Using knives, we removed limbs from pine trees and used them to cover the truck on the front and sides so anyone traveling on the three-path couldn't spot it.

Donnie Ray was pulling on his rescue suit. I donned mine, and then we got into our green and brown camouflage jumpsuits. This was one search where we didn't want to be seen. I was glad it wasn't hunting season. Anyone entering the woods in clothes designed to hide them should remember they are also hidden from other hunters. Some rifle- or shotgun-toting opportunists are trigger-happy. If they hear or spot movement, they fire before they check their target.

I packed my pockets with things I'd need on the trail. We strapped on our packs and added caps. I gave Circe a treat and told her this was a silent chase and I would direct her. She's good, but I knew I'd be constantly correcting her direction. She doesn't like a straight-line march. She wants to explore any scent that smells interesting, especially when she hasn't been given a specific odor to track. My arms would ache within the hour, and if it was a long search they'd feel dislocated from their sockets before we finished.

You can't physically pull a 125-pound blood-hound straight if he or she wants to take a side trip. You signal the correct way, feed a treat, and hope the dog will agree with your choice. A short journey can be exhausting if the bloodhound is in a playful mood.

My compass was on a chain around my neck. I consulted it and planned the excursion. The order of the day was to skirt the guard and find the men. Maybe we'd get lucky if they used the same trail day after day; if we could intercept it somewhere toward the interior, we'd have it made. If not, we might do a lot of zigging and zagging and still not find anything.

We started out, walking as quietly as possible through the trees. The first leg was easy going. We were less than three hundred feet in from the dirt road. I was trying to slant our progress so we would cross their path by traveling southeast. If they frequently changed the way in, we could miss them, but remembering the well-worn ground where the women made their turn each morning, I doubted they would be that cautious. One can hope.

After progressing inward about five hundred

yards, I called a halt. The pine-needle-covered path was helping to silence our passage, but we were still making too much noise by trying to match Circe's fast pace. Our feet would land on a piece of dry wood, and the result was a noisy crack. We inadvertently bumped into obstacles in our haste. I leaned against a tree to catch my breath.

"We have to slow down a little. We're making too much noise," I said in a low tone.

"That won't break my heart. My feet hurt already," he replied.

I shortened the lead, thus keeping Circe closer, and we started again. She was enjoying herself. She could keep up her fast trot all day and still be perky.

We covered the next quarter of a mile more slowly. The foliage grew thicker and harder to penetrate. Vines, short scrub-oak growth, and palmettos with their razor-sharp fronds grew in dense clumps. We were forced to zig and zag, making frequent detours around small cypress ponds.

I called a halt. I slipped off my pack, sat down on a planting row, and leaned against a tree. It was ten o'clock. I was too tired to feel hungry, but I needed something in my stomach. I munched on a granola bar.

Circe moved closer. I ignored her silent request for a bite. She had already eaten almost half a bag of jerky. I had brought two along, anticipating she'd be difficult to keep on a true compass heading.

Donnie Ray ate two sandwiches with obvious relish. Ah, youth! I longed for a cigarette, but in this damp air the smell would hover like a blanket. We should be getting nearer to where the men did whatever they did. I raised my canteen and drank water. As I lowered it, my eyes picked up movement. It was a man, about thirty feet away, walking along a path. He was going in the opposite direction.

I grabbed Circe's lead, drew her close, and put a hand over her muzzle. I looked at Donnie Ray, who wasn't looking at me. I went to my knees and started crawling in his direction, encumbered by my tight hold on Circe. He glanced my way and frowned; then his eyes grew wide. I motioned him down. He rolled over on his belly and stared at me. I finally closed the eight feet between us.

"A man in the path ahead," I whispered. "About thirty feet and to the left. Hold Circe. I'm going to take a look."

He took the lead. I unbuckled my pack, dropped it, and pushed it out of sight behind a small shrub. I shifted a glance back to Donnie Ray and Circe. He was lying in a rigid position with his hands clasped on Circe's harness and her flews. He should do okay the few minutes I'd be gone. He wasn't a trainer, but he had been around the dogs for a year now, feeding, exercising, bathing, and grooming them.

I crawled about ten feet, then stopped to listen and watch. Nothing. Was the man a guard or part of the work force? I put my bulk behind a tree and eased up to a standing position. Straining my eyes, I tried to look everywhere at once.

Pulling off a glove, I rubbed my eyes to relieve the tension. Then I started quartering the area, looking and watching. Nothing moved. I blinked and began a sweep of the view again: woods, the edge of a cypress pond, and a path. I could see only short sections between the trees where growth didn't block my vision.

They had matted and killed the weed growth, making a well-marked track. I glanced up at the tree cover. It was sufficient to hide the path from the air. I was standing in a planted area of trees, but old growth was directly ahead. One blended into the other without any openings between the treetops. It was a tiny bit of canopied forest. Out here in the boonies, it was a good place to have a covert operation.

I started downward and began to crawl to the next tree. I heard the rustle of bushes behind me and whirled. Circe was trotting toward me, dragging her lead. Happy that she had slipped her bonds, she pranced and wiggled and slung her head. My heart was in my throat. I reached for the treats, dug out two, held them in my hand, and prayed.

This was a nightmare unfolding. From the first day I'd worked in this swamp, I knew that a dog should never be free to roam here. Circe was dragging her lead. Bloodhounds can be capricious, ornery, or mischievous as children. They have a sense of humor that rivals a clown's. I couldn't lunge at her or go for the lead. If she bolted, she could easily romp for several miles, or until her lead was snagged on a root or tough vine and halted her progress. Then she couldn't return, even if she tried.

If she ran away, there was no way I could find her. Even if I had another dog, I couldn't mount a search for her so near the men's presence.

Circe eyed the treats in my palm. She took two steps and stopped. She started wagging her tail, sweeping it back and forth with wild abandon. Oh, my God, she thought I was playing a game! It was all my fault. I had always overtreated the animals. Wayne, Rosie, and Jasmine had fussed at me at one time or another. I was a softy and couldn't resist their imploring looks.

Circe had half a bag of jerky in her stomach. She wasn't sated—it's difficult to fill a bloodhound's gut—but her constant edge of hunger was blunted. She could afford to play and not rush to grab a bite. I brought the treat to my lips and pretended to eat it, then lowered my hand for her. She took a step closer, still wagging her tail.

I forced myself to turn my back and hunch over the treat. I wiggled my body and popped my elbows back and forth. Bloodhounds are also very curious. I sat and sweated and hoped she would investigate what the silly handler was up to.

I imagined her sailing by me, picking up the man's smell, and trotting into their camp for a few pets and hugs. Bloodhounds enjoy people and, unless they're abused, don't act shy around humans. In her unexpected freedom, she could also forget her silent commands, and whine, deep-cough a bark, or let loose a bay of happiness.

I peeked under my arm at her. She ran the few steps that separated us and ate the treats in my outstretched hand. I dropped my arm around her neck, dug my gloveless fingers under her harness, and closed my fist in a death grip. I bowed my head on her shoulder and felt weak-kneed from eased tension.

I secured her lead in my left hand, wrapping the loop twice. I crawled back to Donnie Ray. He had lain in the path and watched helplessly, knowing I would be furious. He gave me a sickly smile.

"Sorry," he whispered. "She tore out of my grasp. She caught me by surprise. I didn't know she could move so fast!"

"It happened. Just make sure it never happens again. I grew old and feeble in the five minutes she was free."

"Both of us," he concurred.

I smiled my forgiveness. He was a good kid, and now contrite, so I knew he was aware of the danger.

"Stay here hidden with Circe. I'm going to take a look around, maybe get some pictures. Take off your pack now. If you hear me yelling and screeching, that's the signal to run like a striped ape. Take Circe and leave the packs. When you're clear, call Hank. Then go to Perce Camp Break and wait to guide him in. Got it?"

"Why can't I go take pictures and you wait here?"

"Because I'd be tossed out of NOW."

He barely moved his lips. "Fat chance."

I grinned and moved off. I crawled most of the way, only standing when the birds were quiet and I could hear no rustling in the undergrowth. I tried to keep parallel with the path, but back far enough not to be seen.

I picked my way quietly, testing each hand and

knee pressure first before adding my weight. My stealth paid off. I raised my head to check my progress and saw a sleeping fawn curled in a small protective ball. The mother would be close by, unless the baby was one of the unfortunate ones who lost its protector before it could fend for itself. I wished it well and continued my snail's pace.

The slow journey was grating on my nerves, my patience wearing thin. I'm brash and quick to charge, not creep. I placed a hand forward and froze. I heard voices. That meant I was too close. I fought the urge to scoot backward into thick brush and focused on listening. They were speaking Spanish, and then I heard laughter.

I eased upward behind a tree until I was on my knees. I turned the bill of my cap backward and peeked around the tree trunk. Christ, I had crawled right into their camp! A man was sitting on a wooden packing crate with his back to me. He was peeling an apple with a pigsticker. The blade was at least five inches long. He was paring off the skin in a continuous strip. I eased my head back until it was hidden and glanced up at the trees. During my crawl I hadn't looked up. A bad mistake. My low restricted view had kept me from spotting the camouflage netting covering the area surrounding me. I was practically sitting in their lap. My mouth was dry. I decided this was not the time to sneeze.

More Spanish words, dulcet and slow. It didn't sound like "Yes, yes, I see the gringo bitch cowering behind the tree, let's go grab her," but I couldn't be sure. I took shallow breaths and breathed with my mouth open. I didn't have to worry about swallowing insects; there weren't any around. They probably had a backpack sprayer and used it often to keep the pests at bay.

I turned my head slowly until I could see the man. Moving only my eyes, I counted three more in front of two small huts. That accounted for five men out of sixteen. Maybe one was a guard. Where were the other ten? Out planting marijuana? Learning to survive in a jungle?

They could be revolutionaries, but they didn't look the type. Of course all of them were young, but some were fat and others skinny. The camp wasn't neat or squared away like most things involving the military. I could be wrong. I had never seen a revolutionary group in training. But Judge McAlbee wasn't the type to lend his support for a cause. The only cause he'd rally behind would be his bank account.

I peeked out from the left side of the tree, which gave me a different view. Three men appeared from inside a small hut. They were in the process of pulling down white gauze masks that had covered their mouth and noses. After the masks were around their necks, all three lit cigarettes.

I knew they weren't performing surgery. That narrowed the field of illegal activities. No masks were needed for marijuana. This was a lab. And I had a pretty good idea what substance they were manufacturing in their messy little camp out here.

What they were brewing was a killer-diller. I tried to remember all the names of this new illegal drug of choice: crank, speed, ice, or poor man's coke. The chemical name is methamphetamine. Wayne and I had attended a DEA lecture in Waycross last year. It was a day-long seminar for drug dog handlers and special law enforcement officers.

Georgia lags behind other states in almost all categories of endeavor. This drug was one of our slower accomplishments. In 1994, seizures of methamphetamine by dosage were up 88 percent over the previous year. And the doses were more powerful—purity jumped from 46 to 72 percent in only two years.

Georgia was finally catching up. I had never seen or found any evidence of it in our county. Neither had Hank. Either these boys believed in the saying "Don't shit in your own nest" or they had just begun their operation.

Like cocaine, meth is a powder that can be snorted, smoked, or injected. It gives an exhilarating and long-lasting energetic high. The DEA said users can go as long as nineteen to twenty days with no sleep. They become walking and talking weapons, very dangerous and paranoid. The drug spawns a "speed psychosis."

Meth costs half the price of cocaine, and even amateur chemists can manufacture it. These guys didn't look like chemists, but looks can be deceiving. Anyone bright enough can cook up a batch. In the late 1980s, the amateurs figured out how to make methamphetamine from a legal drug, ephedrine. That's when street prices dropped to half that of cocaine or less. Sales soared all over the country. Now we have it here.

This was all I knew courtesy of the DEA, but I remembered reading a magazine article recently. Of 100 women recently booked into the Minneapolis jail, 75 had methamphetamine traces in their urine. Even in rural southwest Missouri, twelve meth labs had been raided in the last two years.

Now it was being manufactured in my back yard. This in no way falls into the category of marijuana. This was a whole different ball game. There would be no understanding or looking the other way by me. This drug can kill and turn people into nutso killers. I had to get this lab raided and the operation totally destroyed. Linking it to McAlbee might not be possible. It would be up to the big boys to prove his connection with this group.

I was beginning to see how naive I'd been in thinking I was going to prove McAlbee murdered Clara Ainsley. Her note would cast suspicion only. Unless the judge confessed, which was highly unlikely, there were no legal remedies at hand. I had thought this drug action on his land and the note tying him to something wrong out here would be enough.

Regardless of whether or not my actions snagged the judge, I had to act on this lab. I also had to quit cogitating and get out of this immediate vicinity without getting caught. I pulled out my camera from a zippered pocket. I'd take enough pictures to prove this lab existed. After that, who knew?

I took another careful scan of the scene and saw

nothing to scare me anymore than I already was. I just had to do it and quit stalling before I lost my nerve. Raising the camera, I started from my left viewpoint, moving it just a fraction after each click and trying to overlap each exposure. I took picture after picture. The small motorized sound of the film being advanced sounded like a tidal wave approaching.

I pocketed the camera and took another survey. None of the men were jumping up and down and pointing in my direction, so I decided they hadn't heard anything. Now to get out of here. . . .

It took what seemed a week to get back to Donnie Ray and Circe. I kept forgetting to breathe.

"What took you so long?" Donnie murmured in my direction, looking like he was lying on pins and needles instead of pine straw. I almost smiled. Little did he know.

Circe was wagging her tail in greeting. I reinforced the command for silence and added the signal to retreat and load up. Donnie Ray and I carried our packs for another fifty feet before putting them on. I wanted to put some distance between us and the working chemists.

On the return, Circe would backtrack the same way we had entered. I stopped her often to listen for a possible guard. When I figured we were about halfway between the lab and the truck, I called a halt to rest. I took some cautious breaths and felt somewhat relieved. So far, so good.

We removed our packs and slumped to the ground. I had tied Circe ten feet away before digging for a cigarette. The pressure I'd been under had created the need for a nicotine fix. It had been hours. Donnie Ray drank from his canteen.

I heard a low moaning noise from Circe. She was rigid and listening to something we couldn't hear. With each inhalation she released a small whine. I took a drag from my cigarette and stubbed it out. I signed to Donnie Ray to listen and be very quiet. I crawled to Circe and put an arm around her in case she became excited and vocal.

Bloodhounds do not fear man. To them, mantrailing is finding a friend. Unless a dog is abused by a human being, it will not shy away and whimper. Circe had smelled the approach of some animal. Not many species out here could cause her to whimper. I checked the short list: a sow with piglets, a wounded or cornered bear. I could think of nothing else. They would love to trail possums, coons, rabbits, and deer. It's not allowed, so with reluctance they usually give up an interesting scent. Occasionally they'll rebel and pick up a trail, but never would they whimper, shake, or do anything to give away the fact that they are misbehaving. Her inherited senses were warning her something was out there that she didn't like.

Then I heard them. The hairs stood on my arms, and I felt a scatter of goose bumps.

"What was that?" Donnie Ray whispered with alarm.

I listened to the high-pitched yipping and yapping. The feral howling is one of those truly wild sounds. My genes from ancient cavemen made me dread the calls.

"Coyote," I softly replied. "God's dog."

"I thought you and Wayne were joking last year when you said you saw some. Don't they belong out west?"

"They started making tracks east in the last century. They reached Florida's panhandle in the 1970s. Now we have them living in every one of the hundred and fifty-nine counties in Georgia. Like them or not, they are here to stay."

"Do they attack people?"

"Not if there's sufficient food around."

I listened to the wild sounds that surrounded us and hugged Circe tighter.

"Do they eat dogs?" Donnie Ray had noticed Circe's agitation.

"They'll eat dogs and cats. Some aggressive breeds of dogs have been known to kill coyotes, but bloodhounds aren't in that category."

"Would they attack Circe?"

"Coyotes raise their young in families. Sometimes, when food is scarce, several families will hunt together by forming a pack, like wolves. Carry your rifle. I don't like what I'm hearing. I don't know enough about their habits to guess whether they would or wouldn't attack. You take the lead."

I pulled my .22 semiautomatic rifle from the scabbard. I carry it for snakes. It holds eighteen rounds of .22 longs.

"Don't shoot, unless you see one definitely commit to a run at Circe."

We started back. Circe didn't run in front as usual and was happy to have Donnie Ray lead, with me in the rear. She kept turning her ears to pick up the feral sounds. She emitted a guttural noise with each breath, as if she were growling comments to the predators, but I compared it to a person whistling in the dark to allay fear.

We made it back to the three-path road in record time. We walked in the shallow ditch to cover our footprints and scuffed and smoothed out our tracks as we approached the hidden truck. I cleared the passenger side and loaded Circe before I took off my pack. Safely in the truck she gave me a big sloppy grin as if to say she hadn't really been worried.

After scattering the broken branches among the foliage, we stowed our backpacks under the tarp and drove out to the road.

"Did you see one? I didn't," Donnie Ray said with relief.

"Nary a one," I lied. They are very good at using foliage to disguise themselves, but back in the shadows I had spied two.

"Describe what they look like," Donnie Ray asked me as he drove. "One of these days they might show themselves."

"They look like a cross between a fox and a German shepherd, stand knee-high, and weigh between thirty and forty pounds. They have a tawny gray coat, with white fur around the face and muzzle, and a thick, bushy tail. They are often mistakenly confused with wolves."

"Now I'll know what to look for," he said with satisfaction. "I knew generally, but you painted a vivid picture."

I gave him a smile. What I hadn't told him, from the scanty facts I was aware of, was that they howled, yipped, and yapped from dusk to dawn, their natural feeding cycle. To have surrounded us in early afternoon and sing their wild and chilling song, they were hunting and obviously hungry.

# 23

## Boots Are for Walking, Phones Are for Talking
### *April 27, Saturday, 4 P.M.*

When we returned home, Donnie Ray and Wayne unloaded the truck.

"I'll be back from town about six-thirty with pizza, or do you two have other plans?"

"We'll be here for pizza," Wayne signed, and Donnie Ray's energetic whistle of approval rang in my ear.

"I'm taking the grocery list Miz Jansee left yesterday. When I get back, I'll honk the horn. I'll need help."

"We'll start the feedings early so we'll be finished," Wayne signed, and Donnie Ray agreed with less enthusiasm.

I took a shower. Jasmine followed me to the bedroom and played with Rudy and Bobby Lee on the bed while I dressed. I told her what had happened in the woods and asked her about last night.

"So, how do you like Bradford? Is he a good conversationalist?"

I hadn't had a chance to pump her. After supper, she had taken him upstairs to show him her apartment. His roses were displayed in the common room on a large table in front of a mirror. Hearing his car leave at ten o'clock, I had peeked out the window. Wayne had gone behind him to lock the gates, so I knew he hadn't spent the night. I hadn't really expected him to get an offer to stay over. She was still in bed when Donnie Ray and I had left before dawn.

"He's nice. I think he had a good time. I know I did. Do I really look as awkward as I feel in this dang cast?"

"You'd look lovely in a barrel, Jasmine. The cast didn't detract from your appearance. You were cool and poised."

"I felt like a hippo, clumping around."

"I don't think Bradford even saw the cast. Once, when you went to the rest room, his eyes followed you to the door. He wasn't aware that everyone was watching him watching you. Susan whispered to me that she bet he wouldn't have heard a cannon going off, his attention was so focused."

"Really?"

"Really. Susan gave him a score of ten."

"Susan gives any man who's six feet tall, breathing, and isn't cross-eyed and knock-kneed a ten. How did you rate him?"

"From me, he gets a nine and a half. You know

there aren't any tens on my scale. All of them have at least one flaw. I haven't seen Bradford's yet, but I know he has one."

"I guess so," Jasmine agreed, but I could tell she didn't mean it. She was gone on the guy.

I drove the van to run my errands. Jerry opened the door of his shop for me at ten minutes till five. My camera, still loaded with the film I'd shot, was in my hand.

"Just made it, Jo Beth. I've been hovering over the lock for five minutes. Another five and I would've locked up and pulled the shade."

"Important date?" I asked.

"I should be so lucky. Nope. Just tired of these walls."

"Damn. I was gonna ask a big favor, Jerry. I have a roll of film I need developed yesterday. You know how it goes."

"Hey, Jo Beth, why is it you always have a reason to rush? Other people can wait to see their pictures, and so can you. They'll be ready Monday afternoon after two."

"I really need them now, Jerry. I wouldn't ask if it wasn't important."

"Yeah, yeah, not a chance. I won't let you con me. It's pictures of the dogs, right?"

"I think I've found a meth lab. I need the pictures as proof to make the DEA act. Knowing how you feel about drugs, can I count on you not to tell anyone what's on the film?"

"My lips will remain closed, and so will the lab. See you Monday."

"How's Alyce?"

A few months ago, I'd found amphetamines in Jerry's twelve-year-old daughter's school locker. I had palmed them and alerted Jerry, and she'd had three months of drug rehab in Jacksonville. I'd heard recently she was back home and making decent grades. This was one time I felt sleazy applying my quid-pro-quo polite blackmail.

"She's doing great and I've had a heavy week, or you wouldn't have to remind me of the favor I owe you. Sorry. Gimme your film and come back in an hour. It'll be ready."

"I regret—"

He held up a hand. "We're both wimps. Git!"

At Winn Dixie I maneuvered two laden baskets to Annette's checkout lane.

"Hi, Jo Beth! You got company coming?"

"A seminar starts Monday. Six new trainees and six trainers."

"Don't you still plant a garden and can the vegetables?"

"Yep, but my toilet paper and paper towels didn't come up, and I'm having trouble finding seeds for salt and aluminum foil."

"You're right. Half the grocery bill nowadays is inedible."

"How's your husband coping with a fourth daughter instead of a son?"

"He's planning a world-renowned girls basketball team. I told him if the team required more than four girls, we'd have to adopt. This baby factory is permanently closed."

After picking up the pictures, I returned home. Wayne and Donnie unloaded.

"Be sure and put this stuff in its proper place. I don't want to upset Miz Jansee."

I parked the van in the garage and drove the car to the pizza parlor.

After supper I left Jasmine, Wayne, and Donnie Ray working on the jigsaw puzzle and went to the common room, where I'd have privacy for my calls. First, Glydia to check on Leroy. All was well. My next call was to Judge Constance Dalby, chief justice of the Tenth District, which includes Balsa City. She was Judge McAlbee's boss.

I had first met Judge Dalby last April after Wade Bennett, my lawyer, called and asked her to attend my bail hearing. She was Wade's late father's love of yesteryear. Her presence in the courtroom had forced Judge McAlbee and Assistant District Attorney Charlene Stevens to treat my case correctly. This had foiled their scheme to throw me in jail. Constance resented having to censure a judge in her own district, but she had been fair and wished me well. I knew this time she wouldn't be so accommodating. When Sheri, Wade's fiancée, and I had dug up Wade's father's stash of illegal gains, I found out that the container for the loot was fired by Judge Dalby's lily-white hands in her own kiln. That was when I realized I had enough on her to blow her out of the water, should I ever need the ammo. Now I would try to secure her help without stooping to blackmail. I do try to be good; it's not my fault they won't let me.

I was calling her on a Saturday evening at her home. Not an auspicious beginning. It took six rings before she answered. I hoped to hell she hadn't been in the tub. Blackmail will only go so far.

"Judge Dalby, this is Jo Beth Sidden. I met you last year when Wade Bennett introduced us."

"I remember you, Ms. Sidden," she snapped. "What do you want?"

"I'm sorry for calling you at home, but I need to contain this information I'm about to tell you to as few people as possible. Judge McAlbee's housekeeper, Clara Ainsley, supposedly fell down a flight of stairs at the judge's house about three weeks ago. Her daughter, who lived on the premises with her, found a note that Mrs. Ainsley had secreted in her Bible. She knew she was going to die and warned her daughter not to accept the news of her death as accidental. She tells in the note about being taken into the woods and seeing too much. She asked her daughter, Gilly, to contact me. After her mother died, Gilly moved into an old resident hotel and it was torched the next day. I sent Gilly away for her own safety and started investigating—"

"Ms. Sidden, don't say another word! This is absolutely the most outlandish story I've heard in years! If you think you have knowledge of any malfeasance in regard to Judge McAlbee, you go through the proper channels. I interceded once in your behalf because an old friend asked for my help. I want you to know, I've regretted it ever since. It won't happen again. Do I make myself clear?"

"Perfectly. Where do you suggest I start?"

"Don't act coy with me, young lady. I'd suggest you take your ridiculous accusations to your local sheriff. I remember you calling me last summer and urging me to call the governor and recommend that Cribbs be appointed until elections could be held. I did call the governor, but not because of you. I investigated and he seemed a viable choice."

"And if the sheriff believed my tale, who would sign a search warrant? Judge Greison is scared to death of McAlbee. That means the sheriff would have to go to another county seat judge, who would laugh at his request. His only alternative would be the state attorney general's office, and they, in turn, would call you before they even considered investigating. I want to catch Judge McAlbee and his cohorts in the act, so to speak. To do that quickly and efficiently, I'm cutting out the middlemen and going directly to the top of the lineup. Do I make myself clear?"

"You will not speak to me in that tone. I will make sure—"

"Listen, Constance," I broke in. "I'm giving you a chance to contain the damage to your district when the dirty dealings come to light. You'd better listen—or get burned."

I'd heard her startled gasp when I used her first name, but I plowed on. I knew I had to shock her or I would lose her.

"I also want to mention that I really didn't understand or appreciate your artwork, but that wasn't the reason I busted your crude statue of a pig one day last fall, right on Wade's garage floor. Sheri and I haven't told him, but we could still change our minds and rectify our omission. It's up to you, and the way you handle this call."

I listened to a prolonged silence. I would've had time to pop into the kitchen and fetch another beer.

"You do not have my permission to tape this call," she said, forcing out the words. "Therefore, any recording—"

"Relax, judge, this conversation is just between you and me. You would never have heard these words if I had any other avenue to choose. Most of us will bend the rules when it's the best solution for everyone concerned. It's a crime only if you get caught."

"What do you want?" Judge Dalby's patience was wearing thin.

I don't imagine anyone had ever before tried to blackmail her into cooperating in the investigation of one of her judges. Usually, the good ol' boys in politics only use it to get someone *out* of hot water.

"Tomorrow or early Monday morning you'll probably receive a call from our local state attorney's office. They'll be requesting a search warrant for Judge McAlbee's house and grounds, plus any large tracts of planted timber recorded in his name at the courthouse. They'll want permission to gather any evidence they find that points to his guilt in the death of Clara Ainsley, the Balsa City Hotel arson, and in a conspiracy to manufacture various illegal chemicals, namely methamphetamine, being produced on his property with his knowledge."

"That's much too broad. I could never sign that," she asserted. "What proof will they have?"

"The sworn testimony of a reliable witness— that's me—and also the directions to an operating meth lab from a gifted bloodhound. Her name is Circe, and she's qualified to testify as an expert witness."

"It's still too broad a statement. The warrant would be illegal and thrown out, along with all your evidence. It would be fruit from the tainted tree." She sounded smug.

"I'm sure the attorney general's office will state what we require in better legal language than I have," I said softly. "Also, you are to make sure that whatever we find can be presented in court and *won't* be tainted."

"If I do this, do I have your word that you will never contact me again—for anything?"

"The only time I'll ever bother you is if some good guys need help that only you can supply. You have my word."

"That's not satisfactory!" she said imperiously.

"Good night, judge." I broke the connection.

My next call was to James Carmichel, chief state attorney in our local office. One of his twin sons, Rodney, worked at the kennel during the summer by helping to lay trails for training. James and I had worked together in the past. It took me over an hour to tell him my story and work out the details of staging the raid and search.

The hardest point to sell was the total cooperation of Judge Constance Dalby. James couldn't believe that she wouldn't stonewall the whole operation. His parting shot mirrored his doubt.

"I hope to hell you know what you're talking about!"

"Trust me."

The last call was to Hank. I always do the easy things first. Bennie Tatum was dispatching. He finally got Hank on the radio out at Porky's.

"What is it, Sidden, I'm up to my ears tonight." He didn't seem happy to hear my voice.

"Big trouble?"

"Your ex, Bubba, was reputedly involved in an altercation out here less than thirty minutes ago. Natch, when we got here, Bubba's not visible. No one has seen or heard anything. Half the men out here won't even admit to knowing who he is."

"Typical," I commented. "When you can cut loose for a few minutes, call me back on a secure phone, not the radio."

He groaned.

"You're gonna love this, I promise."

"Why don't I believe you?"

I had just taken the first sip of beer number four when Hank called back. As I laid out the plan, he began to find fault.

"You know I can't go into Gilsford County without Sheriff Scroggins's approval!" he bellowed.

"I know that, Hank," I said, soothing his ruffled feathers. "I'll call the sheriff tomorrow. Either he or one of his representatives will be there. If it's not Scroggins himself, the deputy won't be told anything but the staging location. I don't want any leaks on this. There're a lot of people out there who would love to make points with McAlbee."

"That's your opinion," he countered.

I sighed theatrically into the receiver.

"The difference between us is I'll admit there's a lot of skullduggery going on within the departments and you won't."

"Prove it," he said, softening his voice.

"Oh, for the time to try!" I countered.

"You didn't mention the GBI in your grandiose scheme."

"I don't want them in on this. You know how they hog the credit. John Fray would dig in his heels at every turn. He hates me, and believe me the feeling is mutual!"

"I won't be part of this without them," he stated. "I have to work with these guys year round. If I dick them on this, they'll find ways to cut me out of the loop. I wouldn't know what was going on in my own county."

"Hank, please," I pleaded, "they'll screw it up, I know it! James went along with not inviting them. Why can't you?"

I didn't mention the protracted battle I'd fought with James before he reluctantly agreed with me.

"Sorry. No GBI, no Dunston County."

Shit. I tried to think of what to say to convince him. I realized I didn't have any ammunition or anything to bargain with. Wait, maybe I did.

"Tell you what I'll do," I coaxed. "I'll give you the entire story of the Cannon kidnapping, chapter and verse. How about it?"

It would be safe enough now to tell him. The elder Cannons had moved away. I hadn't kept track of the sons, but I could see no way that Jasmine and I could be implicated at this late date.

"Let me see if I understand you," he said slowly. "You'll tell me everything if I agree not to notify the GBI and have them present?"

"Yep, the true scoop." Maybe things were looking up.

"No deal," he said, laughing. "I forgot to mention it, but I know all the answers already."

# 24

## Just One Big Happy Family
### *April 29, Monday, 8 A.M.*

We had a nice day for a search-and-seizure: 63 degrees, but it would be in the 70s soon. A spring breeze was blowing from east to west. I wore a denim jacket over my T-shirt and jeans. We were gathering at Pauley's old tobacco barn, just inside the Dunston County line.

Hank was already there when I arrived. Donnie Ray was ecstatic that he was allowed to come and tape the search. I had given him the rules to follow on the way over.

"Stay out of the way of the DEA boys. They have swelled heads and think they're hot stuff. I don't know how good they are with their riot guns, but don't get in front of them. They try to act like a SWAT team and will be loaded for bear. In fact, it would be wise to watch your back with everyone here. I don't know who the attorney general's office will bring and who Sheriff Scroggins will send. These guys thrive on the excitement of the chase and enjoy the adrenaline rush."

"Sounds like someone I know," Donnie Ray answered as he stared out the window.

"Listen, my man, don't get cute with me this morning. I'm going to do you a favor and let you earn some extra money to add to your new truck fund."

"I'm all ears," he said, looking eager.

"Here's how it goes. As soon as you start taping at the staging point, most of the men will start strutting like peacocks. Waste some footage. Ask all of them to pose in groups and then individually. If this goes down smoothly, every blessed one of them will want a copy of the tape. Let them know you'll make one. Spread it on thick. Don't mention price. We'll figure that out later when we see what we've got. We'll go easy on Hank's men, charge the attorney general's office a reasonable amount, but we'll gouge the DEA without mercy. Reimburse me for the cassettes, and you get to keep the rest."

"You really think they'll buy a copy?" Donnie Ray couldn't believe his good fortune. He saw greenbacks floating before his eyes.

"The more macho they are, the quicker they'll buy. Be sure and get everyone's name and address. You'll want to identify each one on the tape."

"Gotcha," he said. "It's cool!"

I watched Donnie Ray as he strolled slowly past each car. He spoke to the men and scribbled hastily in a notebook. The heavy video camera rested on his shoulder. I was enjoying the byplay and standing far enough away so I couldn't hear them, just see their reactions. The minute Donnie Ray turned on the camera they were sucking in their guts, posing, and trying to look mean and handsome all at the same time.

I unloaded Circe so she would see and smell the men who were going on the hunt. I wanted her to be able to tell the good guys from the bad guys. Hank's men had come in twos and threes and in six cars, not counting his. He had brought fourteen deputies. I wondered who was minding the store.

Hank strolled over as I was fastening Circe's lead to the bolt on the side of the van.

"You gonna put me in the movies?"

He was as amused as I at the reaction from the men to Donnie Ray's camera.

"You'll have to stand in line. Donnie Ray is casting for an epic, *Great Meth Raid in the Piney Woods.*"

"This was your idea, I bet."

"Aw, shucks, t'wern't nothin'," I replied shyly, kicking up dust with my toe.

We both turned when we heard the new arrivals. James Carmichel, chief state attorney from the Balsa City annex (a.k.a. two back rooms in the post office) had arrived. His caravan consisted of four cars carrying six men. One was a state investigator I had worked with in the past. The other five were mystery guests. Two of them were wearing slacks, sport coats, and ties. I glanced at their shoes, turned my head, and snickered. Lord, they had on tasseled loafers! They had to be lawyers from his office.

"We already have the lawbreakers outnumbered," I said wryly. "Let's send them a fax, telling them of our strength, and go home. They can surrender themselves."

"And miss all the fun?" Hank mused. He instantly sobered. "I just had a horrible thought. I bet every one of these dudes is packing a weapon."

"Perish the thought. Do you have an extra bullet-proof vest I can borrow? It does remind me, however, of trying times. I trust you left Deputy Rigdon on traffic control or guarding the bank?"

Hank grinned. "No, he's here and coming along nicely. He's learned how to swim, taken an auxiliary powerboat course at Saint Mary's, and doesn't have to sit on a pillow any longer."

Carmichel was making his way toward us. He stopped and turned when John Fray of the GBI and his band of merry men arrived like speeding bullets. They kicked up so much dust from their flamboyant arrival, I had to fan to keep it out of my nose. Fray's entourage consisted of four cars and seven men. Probably two were actually GBI agents. The rest would be off-duty sheriff's deputies, highway patrolmen, and policemen.

"They probably hid down the road until everyone arrived so they could make a grand entrance," I told Hank.

Carmichel joined us. He was a tall black man wearing glasses and a sweet smile.

"Good morning, Jo Beth, Hank." He shook hands with Hank and gave me a hug.

"Now I know where your son Rodney got his wonderful way with women," I told him. "All the female trainers at the kennel fight over him."

"He just became a teenager. Can't wait till he attends college. Then he can teach his ol' dad some new tricks."

John Fray strode up and slapped a clipboard on the hood of my van. He is short, only about five feet four, and has a slim build. He has dark hair and eyes and looks every day of his forty years. I found myself wondering if he would have been less aggressive had he grown to six feet. But I know other short men with pleasing personalities and a firm grip on life. I decided that his height had nothing to do with his unpleasant attitude. He was simply an asshole.

"Morning, men. Let's get this briefing started." He unfolded a map and spread it on the van's surface. "Give me the location of the raid and what you expect to find." Fray looked directly at Hank. "I can appreciate keeping the knowledge on a need-to-know basis for civilians and other personnel, but I am the GBI, and I resent being left in the dark until the last minute." He stared coolly at Hank and ignored Carmichel and me.

"I'm the one who's holding the location and what we expect to find," I told him, sweet and proper. "Hank insisted that you be present, so you can thank him later. Right now, we'll wait until everyone arrives before starting the briefing. Also, we have to wait for the dust to clear. You kicked up quite a bit, speeding, skidding, and such."

Ignoring me, Fray put his hands on his hips and divided a glowering scowl between Hank and Carmichel.

"Will one of you explain how this . . . this *dog handler* seems to be running the show?"

"Surely," replied Carmichel in a smooth voice. "Miz Sidden found the illegal activity, and she's the expert here on terrain and local inhabitants. She secured the search warrant from Judge Dalby in Waycross and called us in. She's in charge of the proceedings this morning. She'll lead us—and brief us."

I'd been watching Fray's expression. When he heard the judge's name, he didn't exactly flinch, but I saw some of the resolve melt from his face and stance.

"Who's missing?" he snapped in my direction.

"Me? You asking me?" I asked, like I wasn't sure.

"Yes, *you*. Who's missing?"

"We have to wait for Sheriff Scroggins or one of his deputies." I said the words politely.

"We're going to search in Gilsford County?" He was thunderstruck. "What's Cribbs doing here?"

"Careful." I was being cheerful and carefree. "You're biting the hand that invited you. We need Sheriff Cribbs. He's also an expert in the woods. Are you? His men are poised at other locations to be searched, along with some of State Attorney Carmichel's men."

"Whose names and what locations are on the search warrants?" He questioned me bluntly, all business.

I was lighting a cigarette. I took my sweet time and drew in a leisurely drag before I responded.

"Judge Sanford J. McAlbee's chambers in the courthouse, his residence, and immediate grounds. Out here, we'll be raiding a lab located on Judge McAlbee's land. Methamphetamine is being manufacturing as we speak."

"You're crazy!" he yelled. He stared at the three of us.

At least, when I dropped the name of my surprise suspect, I got his undivided attention. He stared at me, shaking his head, denying the possibility of McAlbee's involvement.

"This will mean your jobs! How could you do something so stupid!" Fray shared these pithy observations with Hank and Carmichel. Neither responded. They stood relaxed and observed his reaction.

"I'm leaving," he said. He shook his finger in my face. "I'm not any part of this, and I will inform the judge of this fact—immediately!"

"I'm afraid not," I said gently, looking into his eyes. "After your threat to circumvent this crucial search, if you attempt to leave, use the radio, instruct anyone else to do so, or impede this investigation in any way, I'll be forced to place you under citizen's arrest. You don't have to participate in this raid, but you can't wreck our chances to make legal arrests and secure evidence. Did I explain these facts clearly enough? Do you understand me?"

Fray stared at me as if I had suddenly sprouted two heads and spoken Dutch.

"You're going to arrest me?" He was in shock.

"What part of 'arrest' do you not understand?" I returned.

"You men heard her?" Fray asked, with a grimace.

"I did, yes," said Carmichel.

"So did I," Hank stoutly replied.

"Well, now, missy, you're the one that's under arrest for threatening an agent of the GBI," Fray informed me. "How does that grab you?"

"I'm afraid you're mistaken, Fray. You will remain with us here until we have completed the search. Then you're free to leave," Carmichel said.

"My sentiments exactly," Hank replied, folding his arms on his chest and staring at Fray.

"You'll regret this," Fray sputtered. "I'll have you both brought up on charges!"

"That's your privilege," Carmichel informed him, with an implacable stare. "In the meantime, I would appreciate your handing me your weapon and submitting to handcuffs until we have finished our business. Sheriff Cribbs, would you please place handcuffs on Agent Fray?"

"I surely will," Hank replied. His voice sounded hoarse. I could empathize. My own throat was very dry.

Fray took two quick steps backward and changed his tune.

"That's not necessary, men," he said, with an

ingratiating grin. "I was shocked by who you were accusing. I made a couple of silly statements. Let's forget I ever opened my mouth. I will not cause any trouble. You have my word."

Another car pulled into the lot. I glanced at the Gilsford County logo on the door, then at the occupant as he alighted.

Sheriff Scroggins had sent Deputy Sergeant Tom Lyons. I groaned mentally. Lyons was a self-centered opportunist I had tangled with last year. He wanted to run for the office when Sheriff Scroggins retired. His only hope of achieving this goal was the endorsement of the sheriff. I was a friend of the incumbent, so Lyons tiptoed lightly in my presence, but I knew he didn't like me.

Deputy Lyons walked quickly toward us and displayed a wide smile. He had finished shaking hands with the men, excluding me, before he felt the tension-laden air. It was so thick it could've been sliced with a knife.

"Is something wrong?" His glance searched each face for a clue.

Carmichel spoke. "Agent Fray has just learned that our target is Judge McAlbee. He refused to participate and has threatened to warn the suspect before we search. We are holding him until after the raid is completed. Do you have any qualms about assisting us?"

I felt a little sorry for Tom. He's a political animal who doesn't dare take sides with warring factions. You could almost see the wheels spinning in his mind. He wanted to remain on top of the fence, not choosing either side, until he could decide who would be victorious.

"I know none of the facts. I take orders from the sheriff. I feel I should call him and let him make the decision," Lyons finally stated. His eyes darted over the three male listeners and finally landed on me.

My lip curled in contempt. "Best hedging I've heard in years, Tom. You must love crawfish."

His face suffused with color, and he clamped his lips shut, fighting the urge to retaliate.

"Just your presence is sufficient," Carmichel said with disgust. "We'll make a note that you were under orders to attend. You can't *report* to the sheriff. You'd just be airing the information we're trying to keep quiet." He turned to Hank. "Let's gather the men."

Both of them strode into the open a few feet, gestured to the men, and returned.

I handed the packet of photos to Carmichel. "Give these to Hank when you finish with them."

When the men gathered around the van, I explained where we were going, how many men to expect, and what the camp looked like. I didn't mention the judge's name.

"We'll stage a half mile before we reach their entrance, and Sheriff Cribbs and I will take out the guard if they have one posted. We'll call you in on the radio when we're in place. Walk very carefully. A dry bit of wood sounds like a springing bear trap if you step on it. You'll know when you reach the camp. The whole area is under heavy camouflage netting. Keep low, and don't be afraid to crawl. You'll make less noise. Any questions?"

If they had any, they didn't ask. Hank gave the pictures to a deputy. He looked and passed them on.

I stood close to Carmichel. "Try to keep them quiet, James. I didn't see a single weapon on any of the men in the camp. Tell them not to shoot unless someone shoots at them first. I'm afraid they might hit Circe or Hank and me."

"We'll cover you, Jo Beth, rest easy," he said with a smile. "This is better than sitting behind a desk and trying cases. I can feel like Rambo, even though there's no physical resemblance."

I laughed and loaded Circe.

I turned on the ignition and pulled out, heading for the rendezvous. I passed Donnie Ray filming us leaving. I stopped half a mile down the road. The last car, containing Deputy Rigdon, roared up beside me and Donnie Ray hopped out and climbed into the back of the van.

"Go!" he yelled and secured the van door. I started the long procession again. He climbed in beside Circe and me and fastened his seat belt.

"How's business?"

He was bubbling with enthusiasm. "When I took their names and addresses, I made them give me a deposit, at least the ones who had twenty bucks on them. I got nineteen orders already!"

"The deposit is a detail I overlooked. Good thinking. How much cash did you collect?"

"Three hundred and eighty bucks!" he yelled.

"See, it's also gonna help you with your higher math."

"Do you know how many men and vehicles are behind us?"

"I do, but you tell me."

"There're thirty-one men and sixteen cars, not counting the van and us. I bet I can sell thirty copies of the tape!"

"I don't think so. Fray and Lyons are not participating. I don't think they'll want one. . . . I just had a thought. Fray is so vindictive, he just might try to grab the tape as evidence so he can get it for free and save his men from having to buy copies. Be sure and make a tape editing out Fray and every one of his men. Leave it out and hide all the other copies. Don't sell any until everyone pays in full. Then you can mail them all at the same time so no one can make copies. That way, if he is cheesy enough to get a search warrant, you won't lose any money."

"Boy, Jo Beth, I'm learning a lot from you!"

I frowned and then cleared my expression. Wayne would teach him the right things to *do*. My advice could help him learn a little more about *people*. He was very naive. Since he'd been shorted in the muscle department, he could use guile to implement his defenses.

"I've decided to leave Circe with Carmichel. I want you to stay close to him in case he needs advice. Carmichel isn't a woodsman, and he might have trouble finding the trail. I want to make sure that the main force will be behind us, not wandering around in the woods. I'll leave a scent article with you, and you can show him how to use it. Circe will come directly to me when you put her on the trail. Okay?"

"I was hoping to tape you and the sheriff taking out the guard." He was disappointed.

"No way. If we have to sneak up on him, we don't need you stumbling behind us."

I slowed down at least a mile before we reached our destination. I didn't want the sound of all these motors alerting them. We crawled along at fifteen miles an hour until we reached the half-mile mark I'd chosen. Hank pulled up beside me, and the others started parking behind us, two abreast. I sure pitied anyone who came along and wanted to get past. There was water in the ditches on both sides of the road, even small sloughs. This part of Gilsford County borders directly on the swamp.

Donnie Ray and I climbed into our rescue suits. I added the camouflage jumpsuit after I'd strapped on my .32. I might have to crawl in mud, and I didn't want to get any moisture in its mechanism. I noticed Hank and his men pulling on twill jumpsuits with SHERIFF'S DEPARTMENT in large Day-Glo letters, front and back.

"Donnie, get Hank your camouflage jumpsuit. It's loose on you. It will probably fit him."

Fray's men were stepping into the most prized outfit around, the dark-blue twill jumpsuit with bright yellow Day-Glo GBI initials emblazoned front and back in foot-high letters. They had matching caps, which they put on backward just like all the assault teams they'd seen on TV.

Carmichel's men looked like laborers reporting for work at the sawmill. They didn't have any special unit wear in the state attorney's office. They were attired in blue denim jackets, heavy long-sleeved shirts, and the stout boots I had advised Carmichel to instruct them to wear. The two dudes in jackets and tasseled loafers were standing around watching the other men dress.

I walked over to Carmichel. He was wearing an old hunting jacket with matching pants. Both were a dull shade of olive-green, faded from many washings. They had large roomy pockets everywhere a pocket could be sewn.

"I thought you said you weren't a woodsman." I was looking at his apparel.

"I'm not," he countered. "I wear these when I go fishing. I hunt savvy fish, not doe-eyed animals and helpless birds."

"Savvy fish?"

"They must be very smart. They have evaded my hooks for many a year."

I smiled. "Are the dressed-up dudes planning on attending this picnic?"

"One is an aide from the governor's office. The other is an investigator from the governor's ethics committee. That clothing is all they brought. I tried to loan them some, but they declined. Said they'd just observe."

"Are they observing from the road here, or in person inside the swamp?"

"I believe they're tagging along."

I walked over to where the governor's men were.

"Gentlemen, I suggest you stay by the cars and remain dry. Your threads will be ruined in the first hundred yards, and you won't be able to preserve your footwear. It's messy out there."

"We'll manage," one said quietly.

"Thanks for your concern," added the other.

I wouldn't let my eyes travel to their loafers. I didn't want to snicker. It wouldn't be classy. I nodded and smiled.

I found Hank. Donnie Ray's camouflage suit was three inches short in the sleeves, and I could see at least five inches of Hank's pant legs.

"Got enough room?"

"Plenty. I didn't know we had to surprise a sentry, or I would've brought my hunting outfit. This will work."

"Ready?"

"Ready."

I gave my backpack to Deputy Rigdon. He agreed to bring it in later for me. Looking for the guard and taking him out of action would require stealth. I needed to move quickly.

Donnie Ray brought me a Ziploc bag. I unzipped both suits, lifted my T-shirt, and untied the large bandanna I wore next to my skin. I tucked it into the bag and introduced Carmichel to Circe. I gave him the jerky treats and explained how to use the bandanna. I showed him how to loop her lead around his wrist after he pulled on gloves.

"Give us thirty minutes. Signal your men in town

and come in. We'll find the guard, if any, and wait at the edge of the clearing. The timing should be about right so one location can't warn the other."

"Good luck," said Carmichel.

Hank and I entered the tree line and traveled straight back for several yards until we felt we were deep enough to be hidden within the trees and shrubs. Then we started angling over to intercept the path.

It was now close to ten o'clock. I tried to imagine the expression on Judge McAlbee's face when the men walked in with search warrants. He had signed hundreds of them, but I doubt if he had ever been on the receiving end of one before.

We had no breeze. The sun had heated the air, and the swamp air felt steamy and stale. Mosquitoes and other flying insects were routinely wiped away without conscious thought. We stopped often to get our bearings. I made Hank sit and rest for ten minutes and drink water. He didn't want to stop. I wouldn't admit it to him for all the tea in China, but his fast long-legged stride through the brush and his quiet dodging of vines and circling of merkle bushes were wearing me down.

This area we were traveling through was planted in slash pines, about ten years old. The underbrush hadn't been control-burned in at least three or four years. Most of the scrub growth was almost five feet high. We didn't have to crawl; we were able to negotiate the terrain by hunching over. Even without the pack, I couldn't travel as fast hunched over as upright. Hank had moved out in front, taking the lead and setting the pace.

"Am I going too fast for you?" he whispered.

"Not at all," I answered, cool and calm, trying to regulate my breathing so he wouldn't hear me panting like a dog.

"Wait here a minute. I'm going to move over about six rows of trees and listen. I thought I heard something to the right just as we stopped."

"Don't get lost," I whispered softly in his ear, half serious and half in jest.

He moved off, and the green foliage swallowed him. I was alone. I fought off the urge for a cigarette. I couldn't smoke one and have smog hovering over me when Hank returned. I also knew the evidence would linger above me, with no wind, and could be detected by a nonsmoker from several yards away. All these facts didn't diminish the craving, just gave me something to think about as I tried to quiet my breathing. I had to stop these cigarettes. They were robbing me of stamina and the ability to tromp over uneven ground without breaking out in a sweat.

I kept my eyes on patrol and my ears cocked for Hank's return. Small birds flitted back and forth in the bush, singing their cheerful songs as they played and flew around in short flight patterns. My breathing returned to normal. I glanced at my watch. I hadn't checked the time when Hank left, but it seemed he'd been gone at least five minutes. I would give him five more, then go investigate.

No, I shouldn't move. I was in a known position, at least not moving around. If I left to try and find Hank, we both could be skulking around in the bushes, playing ring around the roses, when the full task force came in with Circe leading in full cry.

I couldn't just sit here either. I peeked around the brush, hoping to see Hank moving swiftly toward me in his crouched stance. Nothing. I decided to move over six rows of trees, just what Hank said he planned on doing, and then return. Maybe by that time I'd bump into him, or he'd be here sweating *me* out. It beat inactivity.

I moved over one row, crouched, and listened. Nothing moved. A crow cawed, warning others I was on the prowl. I ducked my head and moved two more rows before I stopped to listen. I heard something to my right. I flattened myself behind a pine tree, trying to hide my body behind its skinny girth. I moved slowly, angling to the right, and squeezed close to a titi bush. Its abundant runners of new growth were heavy with buds. I moved two small branches, edging my head around to peer down the next row of trees.

There were dark marks on the ground. Two parallel shallow ridges, two feet apart, leading to the right. My eyes telegraphed the facts to my brain, and my brain told me what they were: drag marks from heels. Someone had been dragged, their legs useless, and their heels had dug the narrow furrows. I drew my head back within the cover of the titi limbs and started backing around the bush.

I backed into rough hands and a smelly shirt. I kicked behind me but hit nothing but air. When I had launched the kick, I had been vertical. Now I was on the way to the ground, face first. I hit the dirt hard and felt smothered from the fierceness of the blow and the fact that my face was pressed into damp, packed straw.

I knew that my gun, resting above my left breast, had left an indelible imprint on my chest. I grunted as I felt the air being knocked out of my lungs. As I struggled to breathe, my arms were jerked behind me and bound with a stiff, textured rope. A heavy knee was pressed into my back.

I was fighting to turn my head away from the suffocating straw. At that moment I was unceremoniously jerked up by someone with a grip on the back of my collar, which lifted me two feet from the ground. I was being hauled face down, inelegantly, like a helpless puppy being carried by the scruff of its neck.

I watched the ground moving beneath me, trying to regulate my breathing. I was wrong about the tracks I had seen earlier. It wasn't the shoe heels making marks, it was the toes. I bet my marks weren't as neat as Hank's because my knees kept bumping over the planting rows and causing my feet to flop around.

I was dumped on the ground and turned over, and a filthy rag was crammed into my mouth. I smelled grease, fuel oil, and God knows what else. It triggered my gag reflexes. I fought nausea—tooth and claw—until I had it under control.

I could see my captor for the first time. He loomed over me, tying some kind of leather thong across my mouth to hold the dirty gag in place. It bit into the edge of my lips.

I tried to form a mental image of his face so I could recognize him later—if I got the chance. Everything about him seemed large and exaggerated. I tried to calm myself, thinking, No one's this big! He looked big because of my fear and my feelings of helplessness. You definitely would not want to meet this Hispanic hombre in a dim alley. He looked intimidating and implacable in the generous sunshine of the April morning.

He straightened. The treetops, swaying in a gentle breeze, and the sky came into view. If I was brought here, wouldn't Hank be nearby? I turned my head to the right and saw two men standing close talking in Spanish. I had heard them before I saw them, but the words weren't recognizable to my ears, so I was slow to react. I looked to the left, and Hank was lying less than four feet away, bound and gagged just like me. His face was turned my way, but his eyes were closed.

I heard an improbable sound in the morning stillness. A lawnmower out here? As the noise grew louder, I turned in its direction. It was a small narrow tractor, the kind lumber companies use in timber tracts to cut the brush. It stopped six feet from where I was lying. By cutting my eyes sharply and hunching up the back of my neck, I could see it had a metal cart attached. The man driving left the motor idling, and all three men started toward Hank and me. I closed my eyes. I didn't think I wanted to observe what happened next.

# 25

## Useless as a Fur-Lined Syrup Pitcher
*April 29, Monday, 10:30 A.M.*

I heard the men as they approached. One grunted when he picked up Hank. More movement, silence, and then a thump. I winced. They must have just slung him into the cart. I braced myself, then decided it would be better to relax my muscles. I couldn't stand the suspense and peeked through squinted eyes and saw their bulks in a blur as they grabbed me by my bound arms and unfettered legs.

My nerves were as tight as a cocked crossbow as I was plunked onto the metal surface. My neck cracked and stars floated in my darkened vision. My back was arched over some part of Hank's anatomy, but I was too sick to care. I felt swimmy-headed and, again, had to fight nausea.

The engine noise grew louder and I sensed movement. I carefully opened my eyelids a crack and watched as one of the captors walked alongside the tractor. His shirt color and bulky body confirmed that he was the hulk who had bound and gagged me. Wait till I get my Hanes on you. I felt like giggling. Hanes? Shades of TV commercials. I meant hands. I was losing it. I was on the bubble of roaring an endless primal scream that couldn't be voiced.

Tears were oozing from beneath my eyelids. Great. Stop up your sinuses by sniveling and you won't be able to draw in air. I tried to relax my raspy throat by taking some calming breaths and also wrest control from my panicky mind. That's better.

It seemed like eons since my capture, and I felt at least thirty minutes had passed in real time. That meant the posse was on the move, with Circe leading the way. She would find me. The thousands of microscopic dead skin cells my body was sloughing into the air every second would leave a scent trail five feet wide. Circe would detect my scent as easily as a cartographer reading a road map.

I hunched my shoulders and moved an inch or two. This relieved some of the pressure on my neck. I tried gripping and releasing my hands. The rope was cutting off circulation. I could feel a dull thudding pain beginning in my wrists. My fingers brushed against something just out of my reach. I hunched upward a little, strained, and felt flesh. Was it an arm, a face, what? My fingers were numb, and I couldn't easily identify what I was touching. I fumbled and felt fingers. Hank and I were back to back. My grip was weak, but I forced strength into my hands and squeezed.

The ride was rough. A whole lot of bumping and shaking was going on. With all the movement, I couldn't tell if Hank returned the pressure. I tried again and thought I felt something from his fingers. My spirits soared. I had refused to speculate on his condition. I didn't know if he was unconscious and concussed, dead, or simply playing possum.

Two men had taken Hank and me down. The third one came with the tractor. This meant they had a way of communicating with one another. The meth lab had much more security than I had originally thought. Now I knew why I saw fewer than half the workers in the camp on Saturday. I bet they had two-man patrols on all frontiers: north, east, south, and west.

Another operation was probably going on somewhere near. The tractor wasn't needed at the meth camp. This cart we were in reeked of fertilizer: specifically, bat and bird guano. I had smelled enough of the locally preferred nutrient at the many pot patches I had discovered that I recognized the odor.

The seemingly endless journey was finally over. I heard the tractor stop and all movement ceased. They began to speak in Spanish. It was loud, urgent-sounding, and incomprehensible. There are times when a second language could help one's career, and this was one of them. The conversation ended. I looked through squinted eyes and saw hands reaching for me.

I couldn't help it, my muscles tensed and locked. I felt vulnerable and breakable. This time I was placed none too gently on a higher surface. I was afraid they were separating us, but then I had the perception of Hank being placed beside me. Terror eased somewhat when I turned my head and looked. It was Hank. I half turned on my left side and scooted backward a little. My tied hands made contact with Hank's. No one shouted in Spanish or shoved me rudely away from him, so I decided no one was watching. I opened my eyes wide and took in all I could see. I was in a truck! It was a large beat-up flatbed with a scarred and splintered floor. I was looking out between paint-peeled stakes that formed the sides. My theory that they didn't have any getaway wheels out here fell by the wayside. I looked above me, and the trees overlapped the truck. This wasn't the road we had traveled earlier. This passageway was narrow, with close tree growth just inches from the side of the vehicle. They had a bolt hole *and* motorized transportation. Live and learn.

I angled my neck as far as possible in all directions. Hank and I were alone, as far as I could tell. I couldn't see in the direction of the cab. I was busy trying to massage Hank's fingers. They were swollen and felt like stuffed sausages. Poor circulation. His hands were icy.

I turned sideways and rolled onto my knees. My head and shoulder pressed into Hank's side. Butting him with my head to get leverage, I straightened into a kneeling position. My brain was reeling with facts. We were temporarily alone, and our feet weren't tied. Hank's gun was missing, but I still had mine. The pocket of my rescue suit held a sharp knife with a three-inch blade. I added up these facts and opted to try to escape.

I twisted off my knees onto my butt and pushed my feet in Hank's direction. I kicked him hard enough to get his attention. I rotated my shoulders in a position where I could use an elbow to turn him over. It didn't work. I hunched closer and pushed the other way. I couldn't budge him. I was sweating. All the while I'd been clenching and unclenching my fists to get the blood circulating back in my fingers. I leaned close and studied the rope tied around Hank's wrists. I viewed the knots, turned my back, and inched backward until my groping fingers found his.

I didn't know how much time I could waste trying to get his hands untied, but I had to try. I drew on my memory and picked at the knots to loosen and ease them apart. I got one loop free, and my heart started pounding. I worked to release the second, then the third. I knew I'd used only two or three minutes, but time was passing so quickly. Where had the bad guys gone?

I finally released the last knot and the rope was free. He didn't try to move his hands. I knew they must be asleep, and it would be painful, but why wasn't he responding? I worked myself back onto my knees, strained upward, and rose to my feet. With a dizzying turn, I checked the landscape in all directions. I fully expected to see bodies hurtling at me to thwart my progress, but I didn't see or hear a thing.

I stepped over Hank so I could look at his face. He was lying half propped on his right side. His eyes were open! My heart sang, then sank. He was injured. They must have knocked him out. A concussion would be my guess. He wouldn't be able to untie me. I learned over his face and stared into his eyes. His gaze focused on me, but it was blank, with no sign of recognition in his expression. He could possibly respond to a loud voice, but who could speak? I was getting panicky again.

I turned full circle to check for our approaching captors, but the coast was clear. I walked to the stakes on the side and started working one of the boards between the thong and my cheek. The board was half-inch pine. Prolonged exposure to the elements had bubbled the paint. I kept pulling back and forth until I had pushed a small amount of wood from the stake between my face and the leather strap. As I worked, I felt the bond loosen a little.

My cheek was bleeding. I probably had embedded a wooden splinter, but I was more concerned with getting free than a cut face. I worked the thong down toward my chin. I closed my eyes and gave a lunge upward and the thong pulled free. I pushed with my tongue to eject the wad of rag, but it was firmly packed. I caught the edge of the material on a post and jerked sideways. It finally popped loose.

Now all I had to do was to get my hands untied, grab Hank, and run like a striped ape. Yeah. Sure. I ran my tongue around my arid gums and tried to work up enough moisture to speak. I leaned over Hank's ear.

"Hank, can you hear me?"

I was trying to sound loud enough for him to hear and soft enough my voice wouldn't carry.

"Hank, nod your head yes or no. Now!"

I watched closely and saw his head turn. It was moving! He might be out of it, but he was responding to simple commands.

"Move your hands. Put your hands together in front of you. Move your hands now!"

It was as if I were coaxing a recalcitrant child. His hands moved, then stopped. I repeated the command over and over. He slowly got his left hand in front of his body. His right hand was beneath him and wasn't moving. I pushed him over with my foot and kept prodding him with my voice to continue. He brought his right arm around after several false starts.

This was taking too long. The loudly ticking clock in my mind was signaling disaster with each passing second.

"Sit up, Hank. Sit up now!"

I decided to try a new approach. Get the hell off the truck and out of sight. When they came back, they just might leave without us. Surely the posse should be surrounding the lab camp by now. Nope. Circe should be leading them directly here to me. Still, we'd be easier to find if we hadn't been hauled somewhere else in the truck.

"Sit up, Hank! Sit up!"

Maybe I could give the instructions in stages.

"Lift your head, Hank! Lift your head!"

His head barely cleared the flooring, but it was up.

"Push down with your hands. Push your hands down on the floor: now!"

Hank moved his hands in position and applied pressure. I saw him flinch and then hesitate.

"Push down now, dammit! I know it hurts, but push!"

I was turning cranky. He was so slow. I was losing it again. I took a deep breath and tried another tactic.

"Please, big boy. Come on, Hank, you can do it for Mama. Push!"

His body was rising.

"Sit up, sweetheart, sit up. Come on, Hank, sit up!"

He was sitting. I moved and put a knee in his back, not only to help support him but to nudge him forward.

"Scoot, Hank. Lift your butt and scoot! Come on, scoot!"

He inched forward, and I pushed and prodded him, cajoling and urging him on. After what seemed like days, his legs were dangling down, and he was poised on the edge of the flatbed.

"Slide off and stand, slide off and stand!"

I chanted the refrain as I eased off the truck. I managed to keep my balance and stood directly in front of him.

"Slide off, damn you! Please slide off: now!"

He came off the truck, limber and loose. I tried to block him so he wouldn't fall. I almost lost my footing, but both of us managed to remain upright.

"Hook your hand inside my elbow," I told him. "Hook your hand."

He had to stoop a little, but he was finally able to do it.

"Hold on, big fella, we're getting the fuck out of here. Walk!"

I got him thirty yards into the brush and behind some large shrubs. Now to retrieve the knife. Step by step I ordered, cussed, and begged. He unzipped my jumpsuit and got it off my shoulders, but he couldn't undo my belt. My voice was now raspy and hoarse from trying to whisper urgently to him.

He finally worked his hand inside my rescue suit below the belt, pulled the knife free, and dropped it. I set him down and ordered him to pull on the elastic cuff at my right ankle. The knife fell into the weeds. I stepped back, pointed it out with my toe, and urged him to open it. I was whimpering with frustration.

I sat down between his legs with my back turned to him. I held up my bound wrists and choked out his instructions. He managed to nick my left wrist twice. Was he was sawing on the wrong rope? I had visions of him opening a vein and me bleeding to death out here. I felt a warm trickle of blood running down my palm.

When Hank dropped the knife the third time, I blew my cool. Pulling my arms apart and straining,

I put pressure on the partially severed rope. My vision blurred until I only saw a red haze. I felt the fibers part and my hands were free. I pulled them forward and inspected the damage. Sure enough, Hank had been slicing away on the rope embedded in my left wrist. The arm was slick with blood, but the nicks weren't deep.

I pushed Hank onto his back, unzipped his suit, and found his handkerchief. I wiped the excess blood on his suit and bound my cuts. I awkwardly tied the knot with my teeth and right hand. I cut the strap across Hank's mouth and pulled out the filthy gag. He lay there quietly, relaxed, and made no moves on his own. I helped him into a sitting position. Water was next. I glanced at the time and almost dropped the canteen I was in the process of opening. It was ten after eleven. I thought my watch had stopped. Bringing it to my ear, I heard its faithful ticking. I checked the position of the sun overhead and decided it might be correct. Only a little over an hour had passed since we had left the group.

I drank water, helped Hank sit up, and made him swallow some. I didn't know if he should, but it was getting hot, and we had been through a lot.

"Taste good?"

"Good."

His answer came as a total surprise. I had grown used to him being unresponsive.

"Feeling better?"

"No."

"Don't worry, everything works. You were clobbered. We're still in the woods, but we're free."

"Tired."

"Join the club. So am I, but we have to move, and soon."

I knelt in front of him, parted his dark hair, and looked for an injury. It didn't take long to find. He had a lump near the back of his head on the right side as big as half a walnut. There was crusted blood around the cut, but it had stopped bleeding. I didn't mess with it. It needed cleaning and a bandage, but I didn't have anything to work with.

I stood at the tree and peered at the top of the staked truck body. It was all I could see. I lit a cigarette. To hell with the smoke. If anyone came to investigate, I'd shoot them. I was good and ready to inflict some damage. I moved the air around a bit with my hands. I didn't want to send a pencil-size smoke signal straight up into this dense air without a breeze blowing.

After I finished the cigarette, I drank more water and helped Hank to his feet. I placed him to my left in order to leave my right hand free and wrapped his right hand around the button-down strap on my shoulder.

"Hold on and walk, partner."

I gave the truck a wide berth. We worked our way back to the trail where we were brought in, turned, and started backtracking. I stayed a good twelve feet off the path and traveled parallel to it so we could remain hidden.

I was now worried about the task force. Something had gone wrong. Circe would have led them to me by following my scent in the same direct line that Hank and I had traveled. If they had started out thirty minutes after we did, and forty-five minutes had passed, they were thirty minutes late in arriving, more or less.

There was only one possible scenario that could have unfolded without the good guys being in trouble. When Hank and I were in the cart, the route we'd traveled might have passed close to the lab. If this happened, the posse following the same way might have stopped to raid the lab, thus being late in rescuing Hank and me. It was one possible explanation. If this was what had happened, Hank and I might now be heading for the lab. Either way, we should meet up with the good guys soon.

We weren't making good time. I stopped every few minutes to let Hank rest. I was worried about his injury. I couldn't just wait until we were found, and I couldn't leave him here and go on without him. I didn't know if moving him was causing him more problems, but I didn't like any of the other choices.

The principals of the task force were carrying radios, but I couldn't break radio silence. It might put them in jeopardy, if they were still hidden or searching for us before they raided the lab. I mulled over the options. I decided to give them thirty more minutes. If we hadn't connected by then, I'd try the radio. As much as Hank and I had been bumped around, the radios in our leg pockets might be broken or not working. I reached down and fingered mine through the material of both suits, but decided not to pull it out and test it until I was ready to call. I stopped again to let Hank rest.

"How do you feel, Hank?"

"Peachy."

I searched his face. His sense of humor might be returning, but the inflections in his voice and his easily read expression revealed nothing.

We started up again. We trudged from tree to bush and bush to tree. I led Hank around puddles, cypress knots, tree limbs, and vines, trying to keep us vertical and unharmed. I now could empathize with the Flying Dutchman. He was cursed to sail the high seas forever, never allowed to enter a port and end his journey. I felt doomed to stumble through Okefenokee with a semiconscious partner, never allowed to reach my destination.

I stopped to listen. Carmichel stepped out from behind a tree about twelve feet from us. I suppressed a scream and jerked Hank closer. He stumbled and I struggled to keep us upright.

"It's about time you showed up!" I snapped, angry that he had caught me unawares.

"Sorry I startled you, Jo Beth," he whispered softly.

I was aware of the others coming into view, but I focused on Carmichel.

"What happened to Hank?" Carmichel questioned, staring at the hunched and silent form clinging to my arm like a child.

"He's hurt. Probably concussed. We were captured, trussed, and carted away to a truck, but we managed to free ourselves and get back." As I spoke, my eyes scanned the men who had moved forward.

"Where's Donnie Ray and Circe?"

He assumed a defensive stance and looked embarrassed. "I'm afraid we had some trouble too. The governor's ethics committee representative sprained his ankle. I sent Donnie Ray back to guide him out to the cars. No one else thought they could find their way back without getting lost. The governor's aide accompanied them."

"Donnie Ray took Circe with him?"

"No, I'm afraid not. Not five minutes after Donnie Ray left, I tripped over a root and fell. Circle pulled free and ran off. I'm sorry. I must have released the lead to catch myself."

"Trailing her lead!" I whispered, to complete my thought.

"What's the next move?" Carmichel seemed anxious. Okefenokee doesn't intimidate some people until they are stranded, not knowing which way to go and what misfortune might befall them.

I ignored his question and started digging for my radio. I figured I had a fifty-fifty chance of reaching the Dunston County sheriff's department. We were thirty-five miles away, plus most connections are iffy in the swamp.

I tried twice without success. I looked around for Lyons.

"Where's Tom?"

"Right here," he said, walking forward.

"Try to reach your dispatcher. Request an ambulance from Balsa City with a doctor on board. Explain that the sheriff received a blow to the head and is acting goofy. Have him stay on the line for another message."

Tom reached the Gilsford County dispatcher on the first try. We waited until he was back on the line. I gave Tom my number and told him to instruct Jasmine to send Wayne with Caesar and Mark Anthony. I listened as Tom gave the dispatcher implicit instructions on how to guide the ambulance and Jasmine to our location.

"James, I'm taking Hank out to the road. Your men can come with me or stay here and wait until I get back, or you can try to find the trail to the camp. To help you make your decision, I'll be looking for Circe when I return. She takes priority here. Her life's on the line. She's snagged her leash on something, or she would have found me by now."

"Are you saying you're abandoning the raid?" His voice was quiet, but he looked like he couldn't believe his ears.

"Yep, that's what I'm saying. I have to find Circe first."

"A dog over the raid?" He wanted to make sure he wasn't judging me or the situation wrongly.

"You got it," I said, nodding.

"Jesus!" He hesitated. "We'll go with you. It isn't feasible for us to stumble around in here hoping to find them. We'll follow you out."

"Wait a minute. Let me say something." Tom Lyons stepped closer and looked at both of us. "I can lead the search in this swamp, and we're sure to cross their path sooner or later. That's better than just giving up."

I looked at Carmichel.

"It's your decision, James. If I can locate Circe quickly, I'll find you and help."

"That's mighty white of you," Tom said, sneering. "Such compassion and sense of duty. Women!" He shook his head in amazement at my actions.

I ignored him and looked at Carmichel. "James?"

"I believe we'll continue on. Deputy Sergeant Lyons thinks he can guide us in."

I turned. "Rigdon?"

"Here!" he said, coming toward us.

"Remove the backpack. I need something."

I helped him by lowering the pack after he got the waist cinch undone. I pulled out a sterile gauze pad and a Ziploc.

I gave the dressing to Carmichel.

"Open it and wipe your face and hands. Rub it around your neck."

He ripped open the packet and started dry-washing his hands and face.

"What's this for?"

"After I find Circe, I'll come looking for you. It's your scent for the dog to follow." I placed the pad in the bag and sealed it.

"We'll be okay, Sidden," Tom said sarcastically. "You go find your doggie." I saw sneers and heard a couple of chuckles from the onlookers.

"Rigdon, I want you to come with me. Take Hank and help him. I'll lead the way."

I put on the backpack, adjusted it, and turned to James.

"Good luck."

"We'll make out fine," Tom said, straightening and looking confident.

"I hope you don't have reason to regret those words."

# 26

## The Vultures Gather for Road Kill
### *April 29, Monday, noon*

I led the way and Rigdon followed, his arm protectively around Hank. I hoped desperately that I could get us out without Circe's assistance. If Donnie Ray could do it, I could do it. Hell, the way things were going, Donnie Ray could be leading the governor's men around in circles, trying to find the road. The sun was directly overhead and not any help for dead reckoning. Like me, Donnie Ray had a compass hanging around his neck. I just didn't know how effective he would be in using it.

My heart fluttered when I started counting up bodies and assessing just how much of this task force was in shambles. Did Donnie Ray reach his destination, or was he lost? Circe was tethered with her leash caught on something somewhere in this area, but where?

By calling for Wayne, I was pulling him away

from the first day of the seminar. This left Jasmine, her movement restricted by a cast, to deal with six trainers and six trainees.

Twenty-six men were being led by Tom Lyons, who probably didn't know zip about the swamp. Then there were the sixteen illegal workers. Where and what were *they* doing? The two who had captured Hank and me had disappeared along with the tractor driver. I reasoned they'd gone to warn the others. Then they would all escape via their bolt hole in the flatbed truck. Anything was possible in this mishmash. Maybe the three had started back to warn the others, changed their minds, and returned to the truck. When they found out we were gone, they probably panicked and fled. I knew I shouldn't ask if anything else could go wrong. I was afraid I might find out the hard way.

Every time we stopped to rest, I called Circe's name, only to hear it echo in the swamp. I was praying she would hear my voice and howl in frustration, thus giving me a chance to find her. It wasn't a very viable plan, but what were the options? The odds on just walking through the swamp and accidentally running into her weren't too great.

Hank had answered Rigdon's questions during our rest period. His responses heartened me. He almost formed complete sentences, not just the one-word replies I'd received earlier. He seemed to be coming out of his fog. Maybe tramping in the swamp wasn't hurting him after all.

I consulted my compass and tried to keep us on a direct course of north-northeast. We had to detour around sloughs, thick brush, and vines that completely blanketed some areas. If we were traveling out, fairly faithful to the path coming in, we also had several cypress ponds with thick growths of cypress trees to negotiate.

I was angry at myself for not bringing a brace of bloodhounds. I had good reasons to bring only one dog, but they seemed pretty flimsy in the bright sunshine of this—so far—disastrous day.

I drank water and held the canteen for Hank. His hands came up to help brace the container. Things were looking up; his motors skills were returning. Rigdon had his own water.

"Deputy, I don't know your first name."

"Charles."

"Charles, are you all right?"

"Yes. Why?"

He was wiping his sweaty forehead with his handkerchief and swiping ineffectively at the flying insects. Among them were midges, which are tiny pests that love to investigate nose cavities. There were early yellow flies, staunch horseflies, mosquitoes that feast on your blood, and, last but not least, minute sand flies that dive-bomb at your ears with their kamikaze buzz.

"Your face is as red as a beet. You look ready to explode. You don't have high blood pressure, do you?"

"I could have by now. I'm hot, tired, and too pooped to pop. How much does that backpack of yours weigh?" He was trying to regulate his breathing.

"Thirty-two pounds."

"My lord, no wonder I'm beat. I lugged it to hell and back coming in here. I was ready to hide it behind a bush and tell you it was stolen."

"But I'm carrying it now," I pointed out.

"Thank God!"

I smiled. "Come on, we have to get our sheriff to the ambulance."

Rigdon pulled Hank to his feet, and we continued walking. Why hadn't we met Donnie Ray coming back? I hoped he hadn't gotten lost trying to find his way back to the men.

In addition to circumventing small cypress ponds and dodging thorny vines, the three of us also tried to evade the razor-sharp fan-shaped fronds of palmettos. It was an exercise in futility, because sooner or later they get you. I had a cut above my brow and a stinging scratch on my neck. The other two faces looked on a par with mine. Hank and Charles also had drops of blood on their light-colored twill jumpsuits because their legs weren't as well protected as mine.

We reached the edge of the tree line at twelve-forty-five. I couldn't see Donnie Ray or the two government men in either direction. I never knew how much I would miss my working canines. Circe would have known the right direction and would have trotted off to meet up with the men. I had to decide whether to go left or right. The dirt road curved, which didn't allow me to see very far ahead. Sometimes for miles these woods look exactly alike.

"Charles, I need you to go left. I'll take the

right. I don't know if Donnie Ray is waiting by the side of the road with the governor's men, or if they decided to hike back to the vehicles, which were a half mile or so to the left. We'll leave Hank here for a few minutes until we connect with them."

We set Hank down in shade beside a large titi bush.

"Hank, Charles and I are gonna split and try to find the other men. Wait here. If you see the bad guys, crawl behind the bush."

"Don't forget where you left me," he said, trying for humor. He was weak, tired, and possibly suffering from a concussion. You had to admire the guy.

I broke a small limb off the titi bush, walked with Charles to the road, and placed it on the edge.

"What do I do if I find them?" he asked.

"I'll only go around two curves, or about fifteen hundred feet. I don't think they'll be beyond that point. If you find them, tell the brass to stay put and send Donnie Ray after the van. He can bring it back here and load us. The ambulance should be arriving within minutes. If you don't find them, go get the van yourself and bring it here."

I unzipped and handed him the keys. If Donnie Ray had gone for the van, he knew there was a spare hidden under the back bumper.

"I'm going."

Charles straightened his shoulders and started out, taking long purposeful strides. I smiled. He wouldn't be able to maintain his rapid pace, but he'd keep it up at least until he was beyond my view. Everyone, including me, wants admiration for their efforts.

I turned and began hoofing it back to the right. I rounded the first curve. Nobody was waiting so I trudged on to the next one. I didn't think they could be any farther right. I'd turn around after I saw the next expanse.

As I came to a straight stretch of road, three figures left the tree line, one limping. I straightened my shoulders and strode toward them, trying to look heroic without a white horse. I was coming to their rescue. Go figure.

Donnie Ray ran the last few yards and reached me first. The other two stopped.

"Jo Beth, they wouldn't let me leave," he whispered. "I was gonna go back and hunt for Circe, but they threatened me with legal action if I abandoned them out here. That's exactly how they put it!"

"Oh, yeah? Rest easy. They're just scared of being left alone in this wilderness. I've sent Deputy Rigdon for the van. Go back and stay with Hank. He's injured and possibly has a concussion. I put a titi limb on the road as a marker. Stay with him until the ambulance arrives. Send Rigdon to pick us up. We'll stage where Hank is now. That's where I came out of the woods. Wayne is on his way. Then you'll go with him to lead the men in. I'll go look for Circe. Got it?"

"Yes'm. What happened to the sheriff?"

"He and I were captured, but we worked ourselves free. Have you got your gun?"

"Yes'm." He patted his holster.

"Guard the sheriff and watch for Wayne. He won't be carrying a gun."

He nodded. "I know."

"You did good. Now scram!"

"Yes'm." He turned and started trotting down the road.

I walked forward until I reached the hot, sweaty, scruffy-looking duo. They had their coats over their arms. Their sleeves were rolled up, and they were flailing away at the insects. Not at all the coolly competent well-dressed men I had seen earlier.

I extended a hand toward the first one. "Jo Beth Sidden," I said crisply. "I'm the dog handler. We'll have the van here shortly." Shaking the second hand, I said, "It's best if we wait in the shade." I indicated the woods they had just walked out of.

The brown-haired one was a little taller than I. He had a clear complexion, weighed about one sixty-five, and appeared to be in his mid-forties. He stared at me and rasped out a demand.

"What is going on? I've never experienced such a balled-up operation in my entire career in the governor's office." He seemed ready to bite the head off a nail.

"Are you the governor's aide?" I asked politely.

"No, I am," replied the blond.

He was in his early forties, almost six feet tall, and weighed in the neighborhood of one seventy-five. I supposed his nice-looking tan came from a lamp or a golf course.

"Andrew Phillips. I'm the governor's aide. This is Jerome Watson," he said, indicating his partner. "He's a member of the ethics commission. He sprained his ankle."

I looked at Watson's ankle. "Looks swollen. Let's get in the shade and I'll wrap it."

"Are you qualified to administer medical procedures?"

He was angry, frustrated, and feeling mean and nasty, a typical bureaucratic tyrant out of his milieu and trying to throw his weight around.

"Heavens, no!" I said, laughing. "I handle dogs. Just a good Samaritan offer. Forget it."

I fished out a cigarette, got it going, and walked toward the woods.

"Where are you going?" Watson roared.

I didn't bother to reply or turn around. I found a dry sandy clump of dirt at the edge of the tree line that was in the shade. I unhooked my pack, placed it beside me, and watched the men.

Watson seemed to be uttering threats in my direction, and Phillips, a political animal, looked like he was trying to be tactful. I was afraid Phillips's patience would wear thin before he got him placated and back to civilization. They came toward me. Watson was limping and leaning heavily on Phillips.

They arrived and sat a few feet away. I ignored them and continued smoking.

"How long before they pick us up?" Phillips was trying to get some dialogue going.

"It all depends. If the ambulance can find us, and

we can get the sheriff squared away, it shouldn't take long. The van will be here soon."

"I want the EMTs to take care of my ankle when they arrive." Watson was looking at Phillips and ignoring me.

Phillips raised his brow and cocked his head in my direction. I couldn't resist.

"I doubt the ambulance will come this far. They'll pick up the sheriff and roll."

"What happened to the sheriff?" Phillips asked.

"He got hit over the head by one of the opposition. I think he has a concussion." I didn't mind conversing with Phillips. He was trying to be decent.

"Listen, you, I don't like your attitude, and it'll go in my report to the governor!"

Watson was spoiling for a fight. I should have let it go, but, unfortunately, I don't always do the right thing. I was feeling a little ornery myself.

"Golly gee whiz! I bet that scares people in Atlanta!" I gestured toward my heart and widened my eyes excessively. "'Course it doesn't mean shit down here in the Okefenokee." I drank some water and lit another cigarette.

Watson was furious. "I'll make it my business—personally—to see that you find out just how much it can mean!" he yelled, leaning forward and shaking a finger at me.

"It's not wise to threaten your only means of getting out of this swamp anytime soon. I'd keep that in mind," I told him in a mild voice.

He wasn't worthy of trading insults. I was wor-

ried about Hank and Circe and the task force. There
were some forty-five men wandering around in the
swamp behind me. I needed to get back in there and
try to sort out who was doing what to whom. I tuned
out the two men and dug into my pack for a granola
bar.

I heard the van before they did. Phillips had his
head near Watson's, listening to his muttered comments. I rose, drew on my pack, and went striding
out to meet Donnie Ray. I didn't look back.

Donnie Ray stopped level with me. Rigdon was
sitting beside him.

"The ambulance arrive?"

"The sheriff is on his way to the hospital," Charles
replied. "I told Dr. Sellars about Mr. Watson's ankle.
He said it could wait. He needed to get the sheriff
back ASAP." He looked toward the tree line. "They
okay?"

"Watson's being obnoxious, but Phillips is a regular guy." I motioned to Donnie Ray. "Go up and
turn around." Charles moved into the aisle and I
hopped in, pack and all. I sat forward on the seat
and braced my hands on the dashboard. Donnie Ray
stepped on the gas and we went forward. I watched
the slow-moving duo without turning my head.
They stopped. Then both began waving. It wasn't
fun to see the boat pull away from shore when you
wanted passage off Devil's Island. I was exacting a
little retribution for Watson's attitude. All too well, I
knew his venom could give me trouble. I was just
too stubborn to back down and eat crow.

Donnie Ray found a turnaround and we started

back. I was in the back of the van with my pack off, filling my canteen, when we stopped to pick up the governor's men. Rigdon and I were joined by Phillips, who had let Watson crawl into the front. I opened the back door and let him in.

"Sorry for being so snotty back there," I said. "Your friend brings out the worst in me."

"Business associate, not friend," Phillips replied in a low voice. "I'm sorry he was rude to you."

"No harm, no foul," I replied with a smile.

Donnie Ray stopped the van at the titi limb marker. I saw my second van approaching. Wayne had made it.

"Sorry I can't get you out of here right now. I'll leave Deputy Rigdon with you. We'll need both vans." I fished in my backpack and removed some alcohol wipes, a three-inch Ace bandage, and two extra-strength Excedrins. I gave them to Phillips.

"After we leave, take care of his ankle."

"Thanks."

"You're welcome."

Donnie Ray, Wayne, and I conferred at the edge of the tree line. Wayne had Mark Anthony and I had Caesar. I signed and spoke.

"Let me go first. Give me five minutes to get ahead, then follow. Donnie Ray, you call for Circe. I could kick myself for letting her ride in the front, or we could have used the straw from the cage to get her scent. We can't use a seat wipe. The seat has been contaminated with people odor, and Bobby Lee rides there all the time.

"I don't know if the dogs will realize it's Circe we're looking for. I hope her name registers with them, but I doubt it. This has never occurred before. Frankly, I'm experimenting. Any suggestions?"

They both said no. I knelt beside Caesar and whispered in his ear, "Where's Circe? Find Circe? Go find Circe!" I exaggerated my emotions and acted excited.

The bloodhounds' word understanding is very limited. They also use human emotions as a clue to what's expected of them. On a scented human search I ask, "Where's your man? Where's your man?" over and over. I was substituting Circe's name, hoping they would connect her to the search. I had no idea if they could and didn't hold out much hope of success. It was all I had, so I had to run with it.

Caesar listened to me and then stared at the closest bushes as if he knew exactly what I wanted. Pulling me along, he galloped forward with his nose lowered. He stopped and sniffed and looked up at me, totally bewildered. Over thirty people had tromped on this ground, leaving a mixture of their flaking skin cells, lint, and individual body odors.

For the first fifteen minutes I called Circe's name, hoping she would smell Caesar and sound off. Nothing. I hated to stop and rest. Repetition is the name of the game with bloodhounds. Repetition and patience. I feed Caesar a jerky treat, repeated my refrain, and we started once again.

I didn't worry about the lab workers hearing me. I decided they had all split. The legals would be back at their small abodes, trying to look innocent. The illegals would be hiding out in the woods, afraid of deportation.

The sunlight dimmed and I checked the sky. A gray overcast was moving in. There were only a few dark clouds, but still we were going to be without the sun in just a few minutes. I hadn't thought to check with Carmichel to see if he had a compass. When Donnie Ray had been with him, he'd had the use of one, but Donnie Ray was now five minutes behind me. Damn. Another detail I'd overlooked. It's fairly simple to tell east from west and north from south when you have the sun overhead.

I called Circe and moved on. I didn't run into any bad guys or good guys and didn't hear a peep out of her. I was uptight, and Caesar could tell. His movements became jerky, and he switched from one side of the path to the other. He was shivering in anticipation or anxiety, I couldn't tell which, and I was losing steam.

I brought Caesar to a halt with the order to rest. He flopped down in the path, panting. I sat on a small rise of dirt and tried to control my despair and ease my breathing. Suddenly Caesar looked into the distance and stiffened. He rose and raised his head. A large moaning bay came forth. I stared at him and listened. A faint answering bay. My heart fluttered and I froze. I was hoping she would repeat the howl.

When Caesar and I heard it again, we were both ready to go. He headed toward the southwest and I let him lead. He was going in the direction where I thought the call from Circe had originated. Then Caesar turned right and was heading directly west. I hesitated and was rudely jerked. It took several fast steps to keep from sprawling on the ground. My calculations were more to the southwest.

I thought Caesar was going in the wrong direction, but his nose and ears were several thousand times more powerful and efficient than mine. If he understood we were trying to find Circe, then we had to go in his direction. I'd have to trust him.

I checked the time: 1:30 P.M. I had four good hours of sun left. Even though it was behind the clouds, it could return within minutes or remain hidden until first dark. Georgia crackers are used to the constantly changing weather conditions.

I remembered an old joke about a farm lad walking down the road on a scorching July day. This was in the early 1950s before air-conditioning in cars was common. He was given a ride in a big new car. He marveled at the cool temperature. The driver asked him where he was going.

"Well I'm supposed to go pick butter beans, but the weather's turned so cool my pappy will probably kill a hog." That's Georgia for you. If you don't like the weather, wait fifteen minutes. It'll probably change.

I followed Caesar. He was now half trotting, stopping only occasionally to listen. Circe didn't repeat her call, but Caesar raised his head and let forth a large bay that seemed to echo in the now moisture-laden air. I put my hands on my knees and tried to catch my breath but was jerked forward again. I tried to get some deep breaths while I trotted along behind.

He ran past a bush, halted, and came back to circle it. I followed him around the obstruction and saw Circe. She was sitting with her leash wrapped tightly around her wide neck. Her head was lowered to the tangled lead so she could get air. Her back legs were braced and she looked awkward and uncomfortable.

I quickly unhooked my pack, dug out my knife, and sliced the tangled lead. I couldn't take the time to undo the web of knots. She wasn't as excited about her rescue as I had expected. I was holding on to her harness for dear life with one hand, while I groped in the backpack for her extra lead. I shook it loose, hooked it to her harness, and released the catch of the severed one.

I breathed a gigantic sigh of relief, sat, and turned her head toward me. I sucked in air. Her face was swollen to almost comic proportions. Her right eye was shut. The right side of her muzzle looked as if air had been pumped under her skin.

"Ah, baby, you've been snake-bit," I crooned. I pulled out several packages of wipes and began cleaning her face. I wiped the area thoroughly, trying to get all the drool and possibly excess venom off her hair. She drooled bubbles, which meant she was upset. I kept wiping and crooning.

"Poor Circe. You couldn't dodge the mean old snake. It's okay, sweetheart. You feel bad now, but you'll get better soon."

Did I mention that bloodhounds revel when they

receive attention? They act like hypochondriacs
when someone sympathizes with them. She groaned
pitifully and tucked her head under my left arm
while I patted and cooed. Caesar stood close, smelled
her, and sensed she was hurt. He also wanted his
share of the loving I was dishing out and moved in
closer. The three of us were nestled together when
Mark Anthony, Wayne, and Donnie Ray arrived.
Wayne was carrying the backpack and Donnie Ray
had his camera with him. He had obviously run back
for it when I told them to wait five minutes before
advancing. I had forgotten, but not Donnie Ray. He
taped some close-ups of Circe's swollen head, and
she tried to nuzzle the camera.

"Take her back to the van, Wayne," I signed.
"Give her water, but don't feed her. If she wants to
stop, let her rest. The strike was below her eye. I
don't think it was near her throat, so we don't have
to worry about glands swelling. Put her in a cage
and watch her. If the snake had been poisonous, she
probably would be dead by now."

I took Mark Anthony's lead. I'd work both dogs.
Donnie Ray filmed Wayne and Circe as they left.

We were now after men. I changed my refrain to
the animals. "Where's your man? Get your man.
Find your man." I let them smell Carmichel's scent
sample. They put their heads down and took off.
There was plenty of human scent to trail. Once
again, I had underestimated the ability of my animals. Caesar had, indeed, taken me almost directly
to Circe. Whether or nor he would have succeeded
without Circe's bay was the puzzle. If she hadn't

called, he might have passed her by. I couldn't be sure.

"Donnie Ray, a small lecture before we continue. If I'm wrong and the bad guys are still roaming around out here, do *not* try to tape them. Keep out of sight. We'll just fade back into the woodwork, if possible."

"Gotcha."

I frowned.

"Yes'm," he amended.

Donnie Ray filmed more footage of me handling both dogs and then turned off the camera. It was now almost two o'clock. I started some mental arithmetic. There were thirty-three men to account for. Subtract Hank. Subtract Watson and Phillips, the governor's men. Subtract Fray, the GBI, Lyons, and the Gilsford County deputy; they were waiting back at the vehicles. Subtract Wayne. That left twenty-five I had to find and point in the right direction. I seriously doubted if any of the sixteen bad guys, more or less, were still here, but anything was possible today.

It took us until three-thirty to find them. Without a compass, a person will veer slightly to the right. There's a logical reason for this, but I had forgotten it. So, if a person travels long enough, he will circle. Carmichel and his troops had covered the same general area twice. Not the exact trail, but close enough to call it an oval. The dogs trailed them faithfully. There were enough scents for them and almost enough trail markings for me to do it alone.

Some woodsman had started carving the bark on the trees to blaze a trail and finally decided they weren't going straight. This was fine, but the cutter had forgotten an important point: You should always cut on the same side of the trail and not switch back and forth, picking out the nearest trees.

We walked up on the men while they were taking a break. The dogs were happy and went from man to man, expecting pats and praises. Only the deputies who had worked with me in the past reached out and gave them their reward. The others, afraid the dogs were vicious, shied back.

Carmichel rose and came forward. "Glad to see you. Been searching for us long?"

"Since two. Anyone hurt?" I questioned.

"Nope, just tired and hungry." He gave me a rueful grimace. "Sitting behind a desk, or the wheel of a unit, doesn't prepare you for a ten-mile hike. Most of us are out of shape."

"Did you see or hear anything?"

"Not a thing."

"We have less than two hours of daylight," I explained. "We have to get moving."

"Right." He straightened and stretched. "Which way?"

"Let's try south," I said with a grin. I turned and started off with the dogs leading the way.

I kept my attention on the compass. Every time we deviated from true south, I worked back till we reached the heading. In less than fifteen minutes, I cut into the trail. I motioned behind me

and everyone got down. I leaned back to Carmichel.

"James, pass the word back for Donnie Ray to
get up here."

He had moved back among the men to film some
of the guys again. He was probably working on his
new truck fund. Soon he was beside me.

We were in planted pines with medium ground
growth. The falling straw was the reason we could
navigate fairly easily. In some spots the straw was so
deep it retarded the growth of weeds and bushes.
These were the twisted trails we walked. A large old-
growth pine was near us. It had been spared to mark
a boundary.

"Think you can shinny up that tree a few feet and
take a look around?"

"Sure," he whispered. He laid his camera down
carefully and crawled off.

I watched his progress. The noise he made was
minimal, no more than a few squirrels would make
scampering and jumping from tree to tree if no
intruders were present. It was still overcast. I
expected rain before midnight.

He arrived back, breathing hard. "You're not
gonna believe this. I saw six men. Others could be
in the hut. You know what they're doing? Loading a
cart with packages. It's attached to a riding mower. I
thought you said they'd be gone!"

"Great balls of fire! You're putting me on! Three
of them know we're in here. They had Hank and
me. What's going on?"

Carmichel moved closer. I gave him the news.

"How should we handle it?" he asked, like I was an old hand at leading raids. I almost laughed but, with difficulty, kept a straight face.

"Your best bet would be to spread out a little, and all of you go charging in on signal, I guess. Donnie Ray and I will wait right here. Good luck."

I wanted him to know he was in charge. He nodded and crawled back to tell the men.

"I want to film it!" Donnie Ray protested.

"From here. You have to wait until we see if there's any shooting."

"Why didn't they leave? You said they had a truck," he said.

"Beats the hell out of me. The only thing that comes to mind are the three illegals. They must have scrammed without warning the others. But you said these guys are using a ridingmower. It isn't a mower, it's a small tractor. That's what they dumped Hank and me into when they hauled us to the truck. This is getting weird. One of the three had to bring it back to the camp, or someone had to go after it."

"Maybe it's two different groups," he suggested.

"Operating this close? No way. That tractor could be heard quite a ways, and it would mean they both had one. Not feasible."

Donnie Ray shrugged. We watched the men move past us and begin to spread out. Donnie Ray crawled off to get his camera, and I pulled the dogs closer by shortening their leads. They were sitting quietly. They hadn't been put on a new mantrailing scent, and as far as they knew we were exercising. I found a strong branch on a nearby bay tree, traced it down to the roots with my fingers, and tied them both, separately and securely. I dug out deer jerky and gave them several pieces.

Donnie Ray started to crawl forward. I hooked my hand beneath his belt and tightened my grip. He turned to protest, balancing the camera on his shoulder. I gave him a grin.

"Not without me, boychick, not without me."

# 27

## Great Balls of Fire
### *May 4, Saturday, 10 A.M.*

I was kicked back, feet propped on my desk, with the phone cradled on my left shoulder. Hank and I were discussing the events of the past week.

"How many will be sent back?" I asked.

"Out of the thirteen, nine were illegals, according to immigration. They'll be deported after sentencing."

"I wonder if the kind lady I spoke to at the camp was the wife of an illegal?"

"You asked me that Wednesday, and I haven't had a chance to get back to you. I checked the list. Only one couple had a fourteen-year-old daughter. They're legal. The husband was a foreman. He'll probably get ten years."

"Did they have any children besides the snotty teenager?"

"Wait a minute. I have the list of relatives right

here. Have to know who can visit the prisoners.
Yeah. A six-year-old son."

I was glad. Maybe Mama could do a better job
raising the son without her old man than they did
together with the girl.

"What else have you heard?" I asked lazily. My
world was settling down. The seminar had ended in
the early afternoon yesterday. All six trainers were
happy with their new housemates. They were a
good bunch. I'd missed Monday and part of
Tuesday. I had gone to the sheriff's office with
Donnie Ray. Both of us had filled out forms up the
ying-yang. I had spent the rest of the week getting
to know the trainers. I was certain the dogs would
have good homes.

"You're gonna love this," Hank said, sounding
happy. "Remember my second cousin I told you
about? Lives in Waycross and works at the courthouse?"

"Yep. Part of your web of informants. Your
extended family, which covers third and fourth
cousins twice removed and so forth," I answered
dryly.

"Hey, don't knock it. It works. We keep in
touch."

"I wasn't knocking. What you heard was envy.
All those relations. Family reunions. All those genes
mingled in several generations. It must be comforting to be part of it."

"You know how you too can have a family like
mine," he said, lowering and softening his voice.

"Don't start, Hank."

"Marry me, and all my relatives will become your relatives."

"I'd hang up, but I want to know what your cousin told you."

He chuckled. "I should let you stew, but I'll take pity and tell you. My cousin heard that John Fray got his ass chewed for all those wild accusations he spouted at Monday night's press conference. Best of all, he got a written reprimand placed in his permanent file. In the GBI, that's bad news."

"Damn, I was hoping he'd get transferred out."

"It could still happen," Hank suggested.

"Nah. He'll remain here and cause me more grief. I'm not that lucky."

"Well, you were lucky with Judge McAlbee," he ventured.

"That was a low blow, Hank. It wasn't my fault he got greedy and participated in illegal enterprises."

"I know that," he said softly, "I was referring to the blond-haired girl I saw you with at the funeral. Gilly, isn't it?"

"Hank, by now the whole town knows who Gilly is," I said impatiently. "What's your point?"

"All this was for her, wasn't it? I know there's a lot you're not telling me. Why did she come back to attend his funeral? She must hate him, knowing he killed her mother. What gives?"

"I called her Tuesday afternoon and told her Judge McAlbee had committed suicide after he heard the results of the raid. She's a good person. Her mother raised her well. She felt she should be there. I didn't agree, but I met her bus and went with her to the funeral yesterday at three. At nine P.M. last night, I put her back on a bus and she returned to her new family. End of story."

"I don't think so," he said. "I'll hear about it sooner or later. I always do."

"I'm hanging up," I told him.

"Bet I beat ya," he returned, and he did.

I rubbed my ear, walked over and flopped down in a side chair, and focused on the puzzle. It was almost finished. Jasmine had her head in a history book.

"I bet with pizza and beer tonight we could finish this puzzle."

Jasmine smiled. "If that's your polite way of asking if I have a date with Bradford, the answer is yes. We're going out to supper, then Porky's. Isn't Susan coming over?"

I sighed. "Nope, she's pouting. She called Wednesday after reading about McAlbee's suicide. I hemmed and hawed and hedged. She realized she wasn't going to hear an explanation of why I wanted clippings of the judge's hair, along with any juicy details. In retaliation she canceled last night. She was at the funeral. I invited her over tonight, but she said she was having supper with her parents. She's still pissed."

"Why don't you have supper with Bradford and me? We'd love to have you. Then we can go to Porky's. You haven't been dancing since—"

"Since I broke up with Jonathan," I said. "It's sweet of you to ask, but no way. I'm sure neither of you wants me tagging along tonight."

I wandered over to the kennel. Having nothing to do was a strange feeling. Last night I had worked on the AKC papers for the trainers while everyone else had gone somewhere and had fun. I had transferred ownership of the dogs to various law enforcement agencies. All my paperwork was neat and caught up, and I didn't have a sweep until two o'clock.

Wayne was mowing the training field. The smell of the newly cut grass and early roses from the trellis outside the front windows mingled with the smell of new leather, dogs, and the puppies' lunch. I began putting away the new collars and leads UPS had delivered earlier.

Donnie Ray lifted the basket containing twelve dozen eggs from the steaming cauldron and placed it in the deep sink full of cold water. The eggs would take care of today and tomorrow's feedings.

"Is the hamburger cooked?"

"All drained and in the pantry cooling," Donnie Ray answered. He was opening a gallon-size can of tomato juice.

"Need any help?" I offered.

"No, ma'am. Wayne should finish soon. He'll help with mixing. The vans are washed, and we're waxing them after lunch."

"Do you and Wayne have anything planned for tonight?"

"We're going to the drag races at Speedway."

"Oh." To me, there is nothing more boring in the universe than watching two racing machines line up and roar off for a quarter-mile race—over and over.

"Want to go with us?" Donnie Ray asked with a grin.

"Nope. But thank you for the invitation."

"Tomorrow, Wayne and I are making copies of the lab search tapes. I'm giving him half the money. Can we use your TV and VCR?"

"Sure. How many orders did you end up with?"

"Twenty-two. We're charging the sheriff's men twenty-five bucks. Fifty for the state attorney's men. Seventy-five for Agent Fray's GBI men."

"You won't do much business with the GBI, I bet."

Donnie Ray crowed. "Five checks for seventy-five smackers each are in the bank. Wayne suggested we wait until all the checks clear before we ship the tapes out. Agent Fray and the two men from the governor's office didn't order. Sheriff Cribbs didn't want one either."

"You're stinging the stingers. I'm teaching you bad habits. Why haven't I been invited to preview this best-selling epic?"

"Because I'm ashamed of it," he said, fluttering his hands dramatically. "It's not a training film. We didn't tape anything you could use to train others. You held on to me until all the action was over. I had to make all those lawmen reenact their captures individually. Lord, were they hams! I have over twenty Clint Eastwoods holding their piece on the lab guys. You won't believe this, but one actually said, 'Go on, make my day!' If you want to hoot and holler for thirty-five minutes, it's a scream."

"I'll take your word and pass, thank you very much."

"A wise decision," he said.

I stopped in the common room and picked up the lovely spring bouquet of assorted blossoms Bradford had brought to Jasmine Thursday night. We wouldn't be eating in here for a while. Miz Jansee was away for the next three weeks. Bradford had become a regular visitor. It was flowers, candy, or a silk scarf every night.

Back in the office, I placed the arrangement on the long rectory table by the window and stepped back to see if I had centered it.

"They're lovely, don't you think?" Jasmine murmured.

"Tonight, I hope he brings those little hunks of fudge with walnut slivers? They're delicious!"

"I told him not to bring any more candy. You've gained five pounds this month."

"I have not!" I retorted.

"Prove it."

I was saved by the bell. The phone rang. "Jo Beth? Glydia. Josh said he gave you the message that I was at my sister's in Atlanta. She had the baby Tuesday night. We brought her home Thursday. I got back here this morning and I'm baking cookies. Want me to send you some?"

"Jasmine is monitoring my caloric intake," I said gloomily.

"The reason I called, I'm not working today and tomorrow. Did Velma call you with Leroy's progress reports?"

"Yes. I really appreciate her doing that. I thanked her when she called, but will you thank her again for me?"

"She was glad to help. I have a question. Now that Judge McAlbee is pushing up daisies, do you still need a sample of his blood?"

"Now more than ever, but unless you know the undertaker and he saved some for you, it's too late. I'm just kidding. Aren't you?"

"Nope. You understood I couldn't leave a message for you with Josh. He knew nothing about your request. I couldn't call from my sister's either; the house was crammed with family my whole stay, and they all have big ears. Anyway, ICU was out of tongue depressors. I was in the emergency room borrowing some when they brought McAlbee in. The EMTs wasted a trip. They should've taken him directly to the funeral home. The judge must've flinched when he pulled back the hammer on that antique pistol he tried to eat. Tore off a good half of his face. Every one was running around doing their thing to save him, so I got into the act. I grabbed a syringe, drew twenty cc's of blood, and hustled out, like I was heading to the lab. He died about ten minutes later."

"Where is it now?" I was breathless. This wouldn't save Wade Bennett, Gilly's attorney, a lot of paperwork, but it would confirm my guess. It wasn't admissible evidence.

"It's in my vegetable crisper behind a cabbage. Better come get it before one of my brood uses it as a topping for ice cream—just kidding."

"We're both ghouls and I love you. I'll be over in a few minutes."

"How about that!" I exclaimed to Jasmine. "Glydia got a blood sample from the judge!"

"We haven't talked since Gilly's visit," Jasmine said. "Did you tell her your theory that he might be her father?"

"Gilly's so naive and sweet. Even after I told her on the phone that he'd left a note confessing to killing her mother, she cried for the bastard. Before the funeral, I told her he might be her father. She wept during the whole service. I know she's always longed for a father. I just wish I could've found her a better one."

"Now she'll know for sure before she presents a claim against his estate," Jasmine remarked. "You could be wrong, you know."

"*Moi?* Never! However, there's a small hitch in my grandiose plan to make her rich. She hasn't decided if she wants to contest the will. She's made me promise to give her time to make up her own mind. Do you know what she told me? 'If he was my daddy and didn't want me as a daughter, why should I want to claim him as my daddy now?'"

"Did you wise her up?"

"I told her everything I could think of, stopping just short of the birds and bees. Her new family will have to educate her on that. They are so protective. She's in good hands."

I went to dress. As I walked by Jasmine, she lowered her history book and said, "No cookies."

"How did you know Glydia said cookies? I didn't mention cookies."

"You only drool over fresh cookies. For all other forbidden sweets, you smack your lips."

"Nobody likes a smartass."

"It takes one to know one," she countered.

I wandered from room to room, trying to settle down. I took a book from the shelf and curled up on the couch in the office. Everyone had gone. Locked in my fortress, I was secure and lonely. I looked at my watch. It was only 7 P.M.

After reading fifteen pages, I checked the refrigerator. Nothing looked good. I didn't feel like fetching something from town or calling for something to be delivered. I'd have to unlock both gates and relock them. Too much trouble. I'd fix something later.

The phone rang. I stared at it. I really didn't feel like hearing drunken threats from Bubba if I happened to be on his mind at this hour. Usually, it's midnight or later.

I will not cower in my castle, I told myself. I stalked over to answer the persistent shrill before the message service came on.

"It's Jonathan. Please don't hang up until I say a few words. I swear I won't bug you. I've waited all this time to give you some space. Please hear me out."

"I'm listening," I said quietly.

"We're good together. Whatever risks I assume regarding Bubba is part of living, Jo Beth. No one is guaranteed a safe life with a happy ending. I need to see you. God, I've missed you! Say something."

"Oh, I was just thinking it's a shame we're so far

apart. I could use some company about now. I've missed you too."

"Well, I have a confession to make. I got hungry this morning, started out for breakfast, and just kept going. I'm at the Quick Change convenience store about three miles from your house. I'm still hungry. Can I bring something?"

"Make it pizza. It's easier to warm—later."

"Why can't we eat it while it's hot?" I heard the laughter in his voice.

"You've got to be kidding. Hurry." I gently replaced the receiver.

# Epilogue

Spring slides into summer so quickly in Georgia you barely have time to ponder the disappearance of pale green sprigs and cool mornings. Suddenly, hot days and warm nights are the norm, broken only by short respites brought on by thunderstorms and cooling breezes. One's pulse rate slows to lessen the blow from the heat. Longer days should mean shorter nights, but some of my nights seemed endless.

All the Hispanic lab workers were sent away. They were either deported or tucked into the slammer, except for the three who blindsided Hank and me. They were never found. Hank's advice was to forget them. They had probably slipped into another county and would be impossible to find. We both agreed our blunders were best left forgotten.

While Stace Conner sits in Hank's jail proclaiming his innocence to anyone who'll listen, and raves about the dogs making a mistake, his wife has been more practical. She has taken their kids out of school and left them with her sister in north Georgia. She has put their house up for sale. Even if Stace is found not guilty when he comes to trial, Aimee knows they have no future here in their hometown. Friends have melted away. The town has already judged him. Hank showed me the GBI lab report on Stace's clothing. They have several positive traces of Peter's clothing fibers. They also found the roll of duct tape in Stace's tackle box.

As I'm on the board of our local SPCA, I visit the pound often. A month after the lab raid, I went to check the animals and found two half-grown female hounds of unknown ancestry with humble demeanors and large appealing eyes. I bought their freedom from the long sleep for fifty bucks. Donnie Ray and I washed and groomed them and then loaded them, along with a hundred pounds of dog food, and went for a visit.

It was Sunday afternoon, and Pilter Phelps, the old man who helped us locate the illegal workers, was sitting on his front porch waiting for possible visitors. We went through the comfortable southern protocol of sitting awhile and conversing before I mentioned the dogs.

"Mr. Phelps, I come on an errand of mercy. Our local pound is trying to find foster homes for our dogs instead of killing them. We furnish dog food and free veterinary care, when needed. I wondered if you could help us out. We have two hounds nobody wants."

We strolled out and he looked them over, reaching inside the cage to fondle their ears.

"Wouldn't want to have them, get attached, and then lose them." He squinted and looked away.

"Oh, no, sir, Mr. Phelps. As long as you take care of them, they're yours, unless you change your mind about keeping them."

"Do I have to sign some papers?"

"Donnie Ray, fetch the foster document." I had come prepared. I had typed a one-paragraph agreement, with added lines for signatures, which Donnie Ray and I had already signed.

Phelps took out his glasses from his overall pocket and read it through.

"Big responsibility," he mentioned, as he prepared to sign it.

"Yes, sir, and we're much obliged."

When we left, he was kneeling in the driveway, running his hands over their velvet-smooth hides.

"God, you can lie like a rug!" Donnie Ray said with a grin.

"It's not lying, it's creative persuasion, and don't cuss."

Farley's mother was a tough nut to crack, but I worked on her, and now the young blind earwitness from the bank parking lot gets to visit on occasional Saturday afternoons. He always plays with the puppies awhile, but he spends most of his time with Bobby Lee. They go on long walks together. Farley returns once in a while with a few scratches, but his face is glowing and you feel it was worth every lump, to see them walking together. A small boy and a large bloodhound, bonded in mutual darkness.

Bubba was convicted of DWI and assaulting a

peace officer in a neighboring county. Ironically, he
was sent back to serve the balance of his last sentence, some eighteen months, just before Jonathan
grew tired of the long commute south. I had sensed
Jonathan's discontent and had pried the truth out of
Gilly: He was dating a widow with two small children. I did the right thing. I kissed him good-bye
and wished him well. Losing eighteen worry-free
months I could have spent with him bugged me, but
who can compete with a pretty widow and two tiny
tots?

Everyone in town was shocked that Judge
McAlbee gave up so easily and committed suicide
the day after the raid. Everyone but me. I admit I
had a hand in his decision. I called him Monday
night, told him about Clara Ainsley's letter to her
daughter, and said I had suggested to Gilly to start
proceedings to prove his paternity. He hung up
without speaking, but I knew he had gotten the message. I don't feel a bit guilty. McAlbee did the
crime, I just pointed out the consequences. He didn't
appear on Tuesday for his morning court session.
When his clerk called the judge and couldn't reach
him, he sent a bailiff to his house. He found him in
his study, the pistol by his side, with a brief note
admitting he had pushed Clara Ainsley down the
stairs, but he didn't mention Gilly. The final dis-
avowal of a lovely daughter.

Gilly took her time, but she finally decided to go
for the money. The DNA testing proved that
McAlbee, indeed, was her father. She's in for a
long protracted battle to contest the will. McAlbee

left it all to a self-serving southern private school that puts correct ancestry before God and teaching. Luckily, he didn't include a denial of any possible heirs who might come out of nowhere, and he hadn't stated a desire to disown them, should any appear. He left this out of his will because he didn't want anyone to think he would sully his lineage, and that omission is the one reason Gilly will eventually inherit. Poetic justice.

She recently came down to submit to yet another deposition for the school's lawyers. I invited her to spend the weekend with me. After supper when everyone had left, I went to the closet and fetched a large, flat wrapped package and put it in her hands.

"What's this?" Her eyes were wide.

"To help you to remember."

Gilly tore off the paper and gazed in awe at the face of her mother.

"It's Mama! How can this be? Where did you get it? There were no pictures left. The fire destroyed them. It's a picture of my mama!"

"A portrait," I corrected gently. "Gilly, do you remember a tall white-haired lady, very slim, who often came to dinner at Judge McAlbee's? She was a friend of the judge for a long time, up until about five years ago, when she stopped coming?"

"Yes'm," she answered after some thought. "She was a teacher. She asked Mama for a lot of her recipes. She loved Mama's cooking. I can't remember her name."

"Her name is Victoria Anderson, and she's the art instructor at the junior college. I went to see her. I was looking for a gifted student who could give me a sketch of your mother from the descriptions of a couple of people your mother knew. I had located a grocer and a druggist.

"Miz Victoria just smiled when I told her what I needed. She said she knew and liked your mother. She also said your mother was a nice person to chat with. She offered to try and capture her on canvas herself. I only remembered your mother from the one night I saw her, and that was years ago, but I think she painted a good likeness. Does it look like her to you?"

"Miz Jo Beth, it's perfect! How can I ever thank you? You gave my mother back to me!"

Sometimes you get lucky.

Bradford and Jasmine are lovers now. He stays over on Saturday nights and goes home Sunday afternoons. He proposed about two months ago. She said no. She's afraid to commit to a relationship. She confided in me that she would savor the arrangement as long as it lasted and wasn't expecting a happy ending. I try to tell her to forget her past and forgive herself, but who am I to be giving advice to the lovelorn? My track record is appalling.

On Mother's Day, Wayne and Donnie Ray threw a luncheon for Wayne's mother, Rosie. I was also invited, as was Rosie's fire-chief husband, Jasmine, the six trainers, Miz Jansee, Lena Mae, and Harvey, the vet. I was pleasantly surprised that he attended. It was a first.

The fare was delicious. It was takeout from Porky's: large slabs of barbecued ribs, French fries, cole slaw, hush puppies, and iced tea. The two hosts did all the heating and serving and the cleanup afterward. Before lunch, Wayne had given his mother a corsage of red rosebuds, and Donnie Ray shyly handed me one just like hers. I felt a lump in my throat. I'm the nearest thing to a mother he has. I thanked him warmly and embarrassed him by bestowing a huge hug.

After we finished eating, and before we left the table, Wayne and Donnie Ray appeared with a large tray of wrapped packages. We were instructed not to open ours until everyone had a gift in front of them. The women's had an oblong flat shape, and the men's were a flat square.

On command, we pulled off the ribbon and paper. Each of us had a handsome handmade wallet of genuine alligator skin. Laughing, we oohed and aahed over our presents, a souvenir of the visit the big monster had paid us. He had ended up as a pile of hand-stitched wallets. After admiring the detailed craftsmanship, I had a feeling that the new truck fund had suffered a reduction of its total proceeds. What tickled us pink was the fine italic scripted message stamped on the surface and repeated in black print every three inches: *Locally Grown in the Okefenokee.*

I went to Winn-Dixie this morning for groceries. As usual, I had put off shopping until there was nothing to eat. Then I stock up. I was lucky and found a parking space directly in front of the store. I was driving my black Ford Escort and trying to remember what I needed because, as usual, I hadn't prepared a list.

I watched a nice-looking family cross in front of me on their way to the store. They didn't notice me sitting there, greedily drinking in every detail of their appearance. The tall husband was redheaded with freckles and was in a wheelchair. The wife was walking in front. I scarcely glanced her way. I focused my attention on the man and his three red-haired daughters.

Jo Anne, the youngest, was sitting on her father's lap. She is three. Jannette, six, and June, nine, were pushing the wheelchair. I tried to engrave in my mind each smile and expression to remember on lonely nights when sleep eludes me. My forever friend Leroy and his daughters. I watched until they disappeared from view.

I returned home without any groceries and trained puppies for the rest of the day.

HERE IS AN EXCERPT FROM

# *BLIND BLOODHOUND JUSTICE*

## by Virginia Lanier

COMING SOON FROM HARPERCOLLINS*PUBLISHERS*

# 1995

## A COLD AND WINDY DAY

*January 3, Tuesday, 4:00 P.M.*

Hank Cribbs was sprawled on the couch with his shoes off, reading the *Dunston County Daily Times* and making an occasional comment. I was staring out the office window at the bleak view. Dull dormant grass almost blanketed with reddish-brown pine straw, a goodly amount of fallen pine cones, and wintering robins in equal proportions with clumps of gray Spanish moss scattered here and there by the wind. The sky was the color of slate. A brown and gray day which had gotten steadily colder since daybreak.

I was debating whether to brave the cold and help feed the animals, take a nap, or just sit there. I decided to sit. I turned my gaze on the Honorable Sheriff of Dunston County, Hank Cribbs, whose long lean frame was prone on my sofa. Being sheriff, he could dress as he pleased, but he always wore the full dress uniform, warm dark brown gabardine tailored to perfection. With black hair and dark hawklike eyes, he looked good against the contrasting background of the oatmeal-colored, rough-textured fabric of the couch. I jerked my eyes up to the area of his head, now hidden by the newspaper.

"Don't you have something to do?"

I sounded grumpy. Eyeing his bod was disconcerting. I wasn't about to start *that* again.

He lowered the paper.

"I don't see you bustling around taking care of business. Am I keeping you from some important chores?"

"I'm bored," I admitted.

"Bored? You with nothing to do? I'm amazed."

"I have plenty to do, I just don't feel like doing anything. The weather is depressing. Do you know the radio said the low would be eighteen degrees in the morning?"

"Which means a lot of frozen well pumps and busted water pipes tomorrow. Some people prepare for light freezes and think they can survive the hard freezes by ignoring them."

I didn't bother to agree with such an obvious statement. He watched me for a few moments, sat up straight, then neatly folded the paper and laid it aside.

"Say pretty please with sugar on it, and I'll tell you an interesting tale."

"If it's about who's doing who, and which partner caught them, I'm not interested."

"You *are* in a foul mood if you don't want to hear some juicy gossip. How about a double murder? Does that sound more attractive?"

"Here?" I scoffed.

"Yep."

"Recently?"

I felt a flicker of interest.

"Nope, it happened thirty years ago this month."

I groaned. "You've been reading old closed files, *again*. Don't you have enough to do with current cases? Maybe we only need a part-time sheriff if solving crime around here doesn't fill your days. I'll bring it up at the next county commissioners' meeting."

"I looked up the old file this morning, but only because I met the murderer for the first time yesterday afternoon."

He sat there looking smug.

"Aha!" I drawled in my best peach-dripping accent and smiled back at him, acknowledging that he had hooked me fair and square. I sat up straighter, turned my chair, and leaned my elbows on the desk. I was now all ears. "Is the story long and involved? Was it truly a double murder?" I sighed, and spoke before he had a chance to answer. "Wife and lover. Same ol' same ol', right?"

"Nope. Both were murdered, but he was only charged with second degree in the maid's death. They figured he shoved her when she tried to stop him. Hit her head on the concrete edge of the pool. Should have been felony manslaughter, but his lawyer didn't fight to get the charge reduced. It wouldn't have made any difference in his sentence, and he was probably sickened by the crime like everyone else. He didn't fight too hard, period. It

happened during the commission of a double kidnapping. That's federal. In my estimation Samuel
Debbs should have got the death penalty. He was
lucky to have received life without parole."

"So why is he walking around breathing free air?"

"Medical parole. When the parole board is sure
they're dying, they kick 'em loose. Heart condition.
He looks like death warmed over. I bet he doesn't
last a month."

"When you mentioned a maid, I smelled money.
Which old family around here had all these exciting
things happening thirty years ago and why haven't I
ever heard any mention of these crimes?"

"Well, you were two, and I was seven. All the
principals moved away soon after the trial and there
wasn't any extended family. With no one around
here to jog the memory, I guess everyone forgot."

"Let me guess. I bet the murderer swears he didn't
do it and wants you to reopen the case and restore
his good name before he kicks the bucket. Am I
right?"

"The case needs a lot of time to tell, and you're
only half right. He says he didn't do it, but didn't
act concerned about whether I believed him or not,
and he didn't mention that he wanted me to do anything about it. He was required to state his innocence, since he hasn't admitted his crime or given a
judge his statement of guilt. It's the reason he had to
report to my office within twenty-four hours of hitting town. His parole was conditional. He could
have received an unconditional if he had given them
the facts and owned up to his evil deeds."

"Are you going to do any work on it?"

"After thirty years?" He laughed. "No way. I just thought you might like to hear about it."

I held up a hand. I walked over and peered at the coffee left in the glass container. What was there had the consistency of sludge.

"I'll make a fresh pot."

I headed for the kitchen, and Bobby Lee sat up, stretched, and padded after me. In March, he'll turn two. He's a one-hundred-thirty-two-pound AKC-registered bloodhound. Twenty-nine inches to his shoulder, has a reddish-colored coat with a tiny bit of tan and white on his chest, and is an extremely handsome dog. He's also a champion mantrailer, my best canine friend, a permanent houseguest, and has been totally blind from birth.

Rudy, who was curled in a ball, raised his head to view our departure but was too lazy to get up and join us. He's a twenty-two-pound fat tomcat of indeterminate age who decided to move in a few years ago. His pelt is black as midnight and he has piercing bright green eyes. He's stubborn, spoiled, and tries to boss Bobby Lee and me around. When he doesn't get his way, he sulks. We let him get away with murder just to keep peace in the family.

In the kitchen I turned on the water and sat the Pyrex container beneath the stream. I tiptoed to the fridge, eased the door open, and stealthily slid two Chicken McNuggets from a Ziploc. Bobby Lee had kept perfect pace with me. I knew better, but it seemed he was able to sheath his toenails like Rudy. His passage was as soundless as mine. I had not bred a foolish bloodhound. He knew the treat would not materialize if Rudy appeared. He inhaled the McNuggets when I placed them under his nose. We crept back to the sink.

Bloodhounds are born hungry. They seem to crave food more often than other breeds. Now that Bobby Lee was a mature male, his weight had stabilized. He got plenty of exercise and wasn't overweight for his height and bone configuration. Rudy was. He had gained two pounds in the past year and was obese according to my vet, Harvey Gusman.

Bobby Lee and I entered the office. He went back to his place to the right of my desk chair to nap, and I made coffee. Hank was waiting patiently, hands loosely folded in his lap. I placed his coffee before him, took mine around the desk, and took a cautious sip.

Hank lit up, and I looked away from the enticing pattern of smoke curling upward toward the ceiling. I could smell the heady aroma from a distance of ten feet.

"The craving finally eased off some?"

"It's been three months, six days, five and a half hours," I answered, "but who's counting? And no, the craving hasn't eased off; I've just had a lot of practice trying to ignore it. No one who lives here smokes, which helps," I added pointedly.

"You want me to put it out?"

"Nope. Tell me about the murders."

I used up another chunk of my will power. I couldn't avoid smokers. It would prove that I still had something to fear.

"Do you remember that big hunk of white brick out on Baker's Mill Road, the one that has the tall white fence around it? It's been boarded up for years."

"The haunted house?" I blurted. "The one where the baby cries at night?"

Damn, I could feel the color flooding my face. Hank was emitting knee-slapping laughter and I felt six years old, about the same age when I was first told the house was haunted. A playmate had scared the bejesus out of me.

"Enough already," I said with a sheepish scowl. "You brought back a childish memory. Proceed."

"It used to be known as the Newton estate," he said, suddenly sounding somber. "The owner's name was forgotten when the older kids started rumors about it being haunted. Maybe adults started the tale to keep their kids from trashing the place, who knows? We've been called out on several occasions in the past ten years that I've worked on the force when teenagers on a toot have decided to investigate. The burglar alarm is wired into the sheriff's department. We make a lot of noise on the way out there and no one is around when we arrive. We've really had very little vandalism, so in theory the ghost stories work."

I felt a cold draft on my back and shivered. "Is that where the murders took place?"

"Yep. Jo Beth, tell me, do you believe in coincidence? Yesterday afternoon, I receive a mandatory visit from a convicted murderer who served thirty years of a life sentence for two murders that

occurred out there. This morning I received a phone
call from a New York law firm informing me that
the owner of the house is moving back next week.
Coincidence? I don't think so. I want you to check
it out for me. I want to know what's going on."

Hank gave me a winsome smile. "Are you willing?"

# DEATH IN BLOODHOUND RED

## by Virginia Lanier

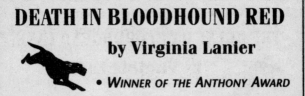

- *WINNER OF THE ANTHONY AWARD*

Jo Beth Sidden is a bloodhound trainer with a talent for search-and-rescue missions, and a bad habit of mouthing off to deputies who refuse to take orders from a woman. Then she's suspected of murder and finds herself treading a quagmire as thick and treacherous as the Okefenokee Swamp.

"Melding good old boy humor and action-packed adventure . . . Lanier gives readers a thorough insider's look at a unique occupation and a detailed view of Southern life. . . ."
—*PUBLISHERS WEEKLY*

"This first novel has more mysteries than fleas on a dog's back, and every one is neatly resolved. . . . Run, don't walk for your own copy of *Death in Bloodhound Red.*
—*MERITORIOUS MYSTERIES*

*DEATH IN BLOODHOUND RED*
ISBN: 0–06–101025-1
$6.50 U.S./$8.50 CAN.

HarperPaperbacks

# THE HOUSE ON BLOODHOUND LANE

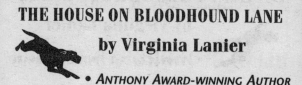

## by Virginia Lanier

- *ANTHONY AWARD-WINNING AUTHOR*

Jo Beth and her bloodhounds are running short of time. Somewhere deep beneath the earth in the woods of southeast Georgia, a man is buried. Alive. With the terrible knowledge of who put him in his premature grave.

"Absolutely smashing. . . . Sue Grafton meets Michael Malone in a dead-on voice that doesn't back off."

—MARGARET MARON

---

### THE HOUSE ON BLOODHOUND LANE

ISBN: 0–06–101086-3
$5.99 U.S./$7.99 CAN.

HarperPaperbacks

## Books by
# VIRGINIA LANIER

Published by HarperCollins*Publishers*

---

**DEATH IN BLOODHOUND RED**
ISBN: 0–06–101025-1          $6.50 U.S./$8.50 CAN.

**THE HOUSE ON BLOODHOUND LANE**
ISBN: 0-06-101086-3          $5.99 U.S./$7.99 CAN.

**BRACE OF BLOODHOUNDS**
ISBN: 0-06-101087-1          $6.50 U.S./$8.50 CAN.

**BLIND BLOODHOUND JUSTICE**
ISBN: 0–06–017547-8          $24.00 U.S./$35.00 CAN.

## *AVAILABLE*
## *AT BOOKSTORES EVERYWHERE*